Under Fire

BOOKS BY TEYLA BRANTON

Unbounded Series
The Change
The Cure
The Escape
The Reckoning
The Takeover

Unbounded Novellas
Ava's Revenge
Mortal Brother
Lethal Engagement
Set Ablaze

Imprints Series
First Touch (prequel)
Touch of Rain
On The Hunt
Upstaged
Under Fire
Blinded

Colony Six Series
Sketches

Other
Times Nine

UNDER THE NAME RACHEL BRANTON

Finding Home Series
Take Me Home
All That I Love
Then I Found You

Lily's House Series
House Without Lies
Tell Me No Lies
Your Eyes Don't Lie
Hearts Never Lie
Broken Lies
Cowboys Can't Lie

Noble Hearts
Royal Quest
Royal Dance

Picture Books
I Don't Want To Eat Bugs
I Don't Want to Have Hot Toes

Under Fire

TEYLA BRANTON

WHITE
STAR
PRESS

This is a work of fiction, and the views expressed herein are the sole responsibility of the author. Likewise, certain characters, places, and incidents are the product of the author's imagination, and any resemblance to actual persons, living or dead, or actual events or locales, is entirely coincidental.

Under Fire (Imprints Book 4)

Published by White Star Press
P.O. Box 353
American Fork, Utah 84003

Copyright © 2018 by Teyla Branton
Cover design copyright © 2018 by White Star Press
Originally published by the author under another name as *Line of Fire*.

Printed in the United States of America
ISBN: 978-1-939203-96-0
Year of first printing: 2018

For Liana

Acknowledgments

Appreciation goes to reader Mercedes Rose Herndon, who helped me with details about shamans and who pointed me in the right direction regarding the Marion County Sheriff's Office.

Thanks also to early readers Cátia and Gretchen, who helped me fine-tune the manuscript.

Chapter 1

eople don't usually feel strongly about countertops, so they don't contain many imprints, especially those at a gas station. I might experience a hint of someone's impatience or frustration—temporary, fleeting emotions that started to fade almost as soon as the customer moved on. That kind of imprint meant only minor discomfort. Nothing that would cause me to wear gloves or stare at the clerk in glazed horror.

That I was compelled to stop in the middle of my question to the clerk, one hand splayed on the counter as if glued to it, was my first clue that this counter was different.

Most people develop maybe ten percent of their brains. I happen to be one of the lucky few who developed a bit more. But I wasn't gifted in mathematics or music or something that people recognized as a boon to the world. No, I read imprints, emotions left behind on beloved personal objects or imprinted during events that evoked great emotion—love, hate, fear, terror. Unfortunately for me, most of these latter imprints are negative. Psychometry is the scientific name for my skill, and it's a questionable one at best, but it helped me find missing people and save lives.

"Autumn, you okay?" Shannon's voice came to me as if from far away. Strange when I could feel the pressure of his hand on my back. When imprints are strong, I live them as if the events happened to me and they become part of my memory. At the moment the Autumn he knew couldn't answer.

It was easy. Just take out the gun, point it at the clerk, and get what I'd come here for. And more. They'd had a lot of traffic that morning, and the cash drawer should be full. Do it now, during this lull. With the other employee out for an early lunch and the last customer driving away.

The solid feel of the gun in my hand was comforting. Racked and ready to fire. If that clerk hesitated, I'd shoot him. I'd do it anyway when I had what I wanted. Wipe that smug look off his face permanently.

Wait. A couple was coming into the store. I hadn't seen them drive up to the gas pump. They must not have seen the closed sign I'd placed out front to stave off potential traffic. Frustration and anger waved through me. An urge to shoot, to get what I needed.

No, better to wait. It wasn't just the money. I could never forget that.

It was odd watching Shannon and myself walk up to the glass doors, and it reasserted my sense of self as nothing else could. This was *not* my experience or my feelings but someone else's, a man, if I could tell by the thin, callused hands in the imprint. Sometimes hands were misleading.

"I forgot something," I/he told the clerk, voice rough with frustration. "I'll be right back." Heart pounding, I/he picked up the bag of chips he'd brought to the counter.

The scene vanished. Another imprint followed, weak and

faded by comparison. Vague frustration from two weeks earlier as a clerk stopped to answer a question from another customer in the middle of ringing up an order. I managed to lift my hand from the counter and it vanished.

"Autumn?" Shannon said again.

His hand was heavier on my back now, and I turned my head to meet his concerned gaze, the blue-green color of his eyes brighter and more intense than I'd ever seen them. Probably because of the light streaming in through the glass doors and windows behind me. The premature wrinkling around his eyes was also more pronounced. He wasn't tall for a man, which meant he was only a few inches taller than I was, but the graceful way he moved his compact body with no wasted effort always attracted women's gazes. He'd attracted me right from the beginning, even when he'd been so irritating I could barely stand him.

"Trouble," I mouthed. Because the man from the imprint was still in the store, and he was planning to rob it. Part of me wanted to run to the door and leave as he expected, but the other part knew our presence was the only thing preventing him from carrying out his plan. If we left, I didn't have any hope for the clerk making it through this day alive.

"Did you decide not to buy the drinks?" the clerk asked me. Kirt, according to his name tag. He was young, probably in his mid-twenties, a strong, handsome guy with dark hair that hung straight and a little shaggy over his ears. Would he hand over the money easily to the thief or would he try to be a hero? Given the emotions in the imprint, I didn't believe it would make a difference in the final outcome.

"Just a minute," I said. The antique rings on my fingers were exuding their usual comforting imprints, dulling the intensity of the counter experience. It was why I always wore them, to protect me against unexpected negative imprints.

"Sure. Let me know." Kirt shrugged and stepped back from the cash register, picking up a magazine lying open on the counter.

Shannon's hand left my back and inched toward the concealed weapon he always carried at his waist, even when he was off duty. As a consultant to the Portland police, I'd been through gun training and my concealed-carry permit was in my wallet, but I didn't usually carry. Today was no exception.

Shannon scanned the store, trying to pinpoint the danger. At least he'd learned enough about my talent to take me seriously. I didn't stop as I usually did to ponder how that tied in with his attraction for me—a feeling he'd fought since the minute we'd met. Or had until a few weeks ago.

Behind Shannon, I spotted the man as he pretended to study a row of cold cereal boxes. He was of average height and wore a tan coat that seemed a little large, a blue baseball cap pulled low on his forehead. A few light-colored locks escaped, curling tightly up over the base of the cap. His eyes met mine— and held.

Uh-oh. I'd never been good at masking emotions.

Something in his expression changed. Fire raged in his eyes. He went for his gun, his movements a blur.

"Down!" I yelled, pulling at Shannon, my left arm screaming at the strain. Though I'd removed the bandage from the fleshy part of my arm where I'd been shot several weeks ago, the muscles were still tender. A shot whirred over our heads.

Risking a glance, I saw the clerk had also dropped to the floor. Hopefully, the bullet hadn't found him first.

The man came toward us firing, his face grim with determination. Shannon rolled me behind him and went up on his knees, drawing his own gun, but the man ducked behind a shelf of toiletries. Shannon shoved something in my direction—his backup weapon, a compact 9 mil of a brand I didn't recognize. I froze with the weapon in my hand, steeling myself for a flood of gruesome imprints, but he'd used this gun solely for target practice, so the only thing I picked up were hints of frustration or satisfaction, depending on how well he'd shot at the range on any given day. Barely a distraction to me.

"Find a place to hide," Shannon said through gritted teeth. "Shoot him if he comes after you."

We'd had the gun argument before—my last gunshot wound had come from a gun he'd made me carry—but now wasn't the time to get into it again.

"Police!" Shannon shouted, edging around an aisle. "Put down your weapon and come out. Keep your hands where I can see them."

Another shot answered his demand. The clerk yelped, though he was behind the counter and presumably safe, except perhaps from ricochet. Shannon returned fire, and the glass case in the freezer section shattered. That caused the man to pause, and for a moment I hoped he'd run away. I mean, it was one thing to attack three civilians but quite another to face an armed police officer. Though the robber couldn't know it, Shannon was a crack shot and the best homicide detective in Portland, maybe in all of Oregon.

I heard a metallic clang, and black smoke oozed into the space around me. *Great, just great,* I thought. Apparently, this guy had come prepared. I crab-walked backward down the aisle, hoping to find a safe corner where I could pull out my phone to call for help. It was a long way to go, and my left arm burned.

Another shot and more splintering glass.

Shannon ducked behind a display of donuts. At least I think it was Shannon. Hard to tell with all the smoke.

A flurry of shots followed that had me cringing, wondering how they could even see to shoot in such thick smoke. One of the huge outside windows shattered, following closely by two more. Smoke billowed toward the openings.

Then I heard the slam of feet on the floor and saw a blur near the counter.

"Put down your gun," said a voice I recognized from the counter imprint. "Or I'll shoot him. I swear."

"Please," whined the clerk, his voice cracking. "Please don't hurt me."

Under the cover of smoke, the perp had somehow managed to get behind the counter. Though the smoke was now slowly clearing, I couldn't see where Shannon was, but I hoped he wouldn't give up his gun. I suspected the guy would shoot us all anyway. Though I couldn't read people as I could objects, I didn't need any unusual ability to feel the desperation leaking from him. He was angry and had something to prove, something I hadn't picked up in the imprint.

I'd crept far enough into the store that I was near a wall, huddled behind a display of canned foods. Behind me was a swinging door—an employee office or stockroom. I wondered if there might also be a back entrance so I could go for help.

I didn't think Shannon or the clerk could hold out that long.

The weight of the semiautomatic pistol felt heavy in my hands, though it was small compared to a full-sized weapon. If I were Paige Duncan, Shannon's partner, I'd rush the man from behind, jab the gun in his ribs, and demand surrender. Or I'd save the day by somehow shooting the perp without endangering the clerk. All while still looking as if I'd just come from a high society party. But I wasn't Paige. My weapons of choice were my hands and feet. My agility. I was a good shot on the range, better than good, but using those skills on a real person was quite another matter.

"Put down your gun," the robber repeated. "Now! Or I swear I'll shoot him through the head!"

"And then what?" Shannon asked. "Tell you what. You give up your gun now, and it will go a lot easier on you. No one has been hurt yet." From the sound of his voice, I guessed that Shannon was farther from me than I'd thought and much closer to the far end of the counter. Good. One distraction would be all he'd need to rush the gunman.

Yet even from my position, I saw the man's hand tighten on his weapon. The clerk moaned. "Say goodbye," the robber said, his voice gaining a lilt, as if in anticipation.

"There's no hurry," Shannon said. "Let's talk about this. What's your name?"

"What's my name? My name?" yelled the man, punctuating his words with spittle. "You don't care what my name is. This is all you understand." As he said the last words, he moved his gun and fired.

The bullet ripped through Kirt's right shoulder. He screamed in an agony I well remembered.

"Next one goes in his head."

"Okay," Shannon said. "I'll put it down."

"Kick it my way."

No, I thought, as I heard Shannon's Glock slide over the tiled floor.

It was now or never. Thrusting the 9 mil into my coat pocket, I grabbed a can of pork and beans. I hoped Shannon was as good as I thought he was or this might be the last thing I ever did. I rushed the counter, throwing the can as soon as I was close enough to hit my target. Sensing me, the man turned, his gun swinging in my direction.

I was already diving for cover, but that didn't mean I'd make it. The can caught him on the side of the head.

Using the distraction, Shannon hurtled over the counter, slamming into him. They disappeared from view. The clerk screamed again.

Jumping to my feet, I hurried around the counter, my hand once again gripping the weapon Shannon had given me. Terror at what I might see made my heart pound double time. It had taken Shannon and me months to admit there was something between us, and I desperately wanted time to explore exactly what that something was.

Neither of the men had a gun, but they were on the ground, slugging each other. The gunman had lost his cap. The clerk crouched nearby, agony on his face, his hand covering the wound in his arm. He would be no help.

I knew without checking that the gun I carried had a bullet in the chamber. I liked to have to rack a gun before I knew it could fire, but Shannon always carried his weapons ready.

Squeezing the trigger, I shot once, the bullet pounding into the floor by the perp. Both men froze. Shannon recovered first, slamming his fist in the other man's face before reaching for my gun.

"That was kind of close," he said mildly.

I relinquished the pistol. "I'm a good shot." I spoke as though my heart wasn't still having trouble finding a normal beat. Shannon wasn't dead. We were okay. I wanted to melt to the floor with relief.

Shannon smiled. "That you are." He forced the man to lie face down on the linoleum. "Get me something to tie his hands, okay? Then I'll call this in."

"You don't have handcuffs? I thought those were something you never left home without." I smirked because it kept me from doing something else, like weeping. Though I was only a lowly police consultant, dealing with men like this had become my job. I was still deciding if I was going to keep at it.

"They're in my glove compartment," Shannon said. "With the way trouble finds you, I really should have them in my pocket."

I lifted my hands. "Hey, I had nothing to do with this."

He spared me a smile that brought warmth to my face and pushed back my urge to run from the store. Moans from the clerk penetrated my brain. "I'll be right there," I told him, as I began rifling through the drawers and cupboards under the counter. Finding some twine that might have once held a stack of newspapers together, I threw it to Shannon before hurrying to the clerk.

I didn't think he was in danger of bleeding to death, but there was enough blood for concern. "Do you have a first-aid kit, uh, Kirt?" I asked, glancing at his name tag to make sure I'd remembered his name correctly.

"Through that door back there, by those cans. It's hanging on the right."

"I'll be right back."

I passed Shannon, who was barking into his phone, sounding annoyed. Though we were out of his jurisdiction, he'd work it out. He was good at law enforcement politics.

I found the kit and put on a pair of rubber gloves before using all the gauze on the clerk's wound, as well as a couple packages of car rags they had for sale in the store. I finished by wrapping his shoulder with the duct tape I'd discovered earlier in one of the drawers. "There," I said. "That will hold you until the paramedics arrive. Unfortunately, we don't have anything for the pain, except whatever you sell here. Sorry."

"Thank you," Kirt said. "If you two hadn't come in . . ."

"Maybe he just would have robbed the store and left." I didn't believe that, but there was no sense in giving him worse nightmares.

"I don't know. He seemed to have it out for me." He grimaced in pain. "I'm getting married in two weeks. I-I . . ." He stopped, and I patted his undamaged shoulder until his shaking subsided.

"Have you ever seen him before?" I asked.

Kirt shook his head. "He must have known this was our slow time. He must have watched and waited."

"Probably. The police will be here soon."

Customers arrived before the police did, hesitant at first when they saw the wounded clerk and the tied gunman but voicing enthusiasm once Shannon flashed his ID and they realized the danger was passed. Men and women alike gave me the once-over, and I knew they thought I was Shannon's partner. Probably a good thing I was wearing my black dress pants and red sweater instead of my normal jeans and T-shirt. More official looking.

"Stay outside!" Shannon ordered the crowd, but since much of the glass in the large windows was now missing, it didn't make much difference. I hoped the local authorities arrived soon so we'd have help maintaining order.

"Maybe he has something to do with that missing girl," said a woman with a pinched face, her head and shoulders leaning through the missing window next to the counter. "He looks the type."

"Shove it!" the perp said, punctuating his command by a slew of curses and threats. "You don't know anything about that girl!"

An admission of guilt? Maybe. If so, it would make what I came to do in Hayesville a lot easier.

"What do you know about Jenny Vandyke?" I asked.

He shot off more vicious words that included creative ways he would see me suffer. While the customers outside gaped at him in disbelief through the shattered windows, I tore off a piece of duct tape and plastered it roughly over his mouth. He glared at me, but I refused to react. My heartbeat was back to normal, and I liked it that way.

"He's just yanking your chain," said a broad, forty-something man with more muscles than most men half his age and less hair than most men twice his age. "My bet for the girl is on that old recluse who makes those tree sculptures. Didn't you hear the police were questioning him?"

I stiffened and glanced toward Shannon. He met my gaze, but his eyes didn't reveal his thoughts. That "old recluse" was the reason we were in Hayesville and the reason I wasn't in jeans. I'd told myself the dressing up was for Shannon, but he'd seen me enough times at my worst that even I had to admit my logic was thin.

"I don't think it was the old man," Kirt said. He was pale, but he hadn't moaned since I'd bandaged him. He might be afraid I'd try a second time. I didn't exactly have the gift of healing. "He comes in here sometimes. He's a nice guy. Quiet."

"He's a pervert, is what he is," the pinch-faced woman retorted. "The quiet ones are always the worst."

"Yeah, I bet he's guilty," said a young woman who had somehow come inside and now held a handful of candy bars. "My husband has a friend who works for dispatch at the sheriff's office. He told us they found one of the girl's boots on his property a couple days ago."

"That wasn't in the news," said a man with a thick head of graying hair.

The young woman shrugged. "Must be keeping it quiet for now."

"They ought to call for volunteers to search his land," the first man said. "I'd go." There was a ripple of agreement from several others.

I wanted to leave, more anxious than ever to get to our destination. The information about the boot bothered me more than I wanted to admit. Though I knew he'd done terrible things during his life, I'd been hoping the old artist was innocent of kidnapping Jenny Vandyke. But if he was responsible, I'd make sure he paid.

"Would you please wait outside?" I asked the woman with the candy bars in a tone that was far more polite than I was feeling. I thumbed at the clerk. "He really can't sell them to you right now."

"Oh, sure." Taking the candy bars with her, she sauntered toward the glass door that was remarkably unscathed.

We'd gathered nearly a dozen people by this time, including the other employee, who kept loudly voicing his desire to come inside the store so he could start cashing in on the interested bystanders. Apparently, this section of road outside Hayesville was more popular today than our gunman had anticipated. Or maybe the growing pile of cars outside convinced people to stop here instead of waiting to buy their gas in town. This was suddenly the happening place.

A murmur went through the crowd. "Sheriff's deputies are here. Ambulance, too."

Shannon took out his badge and waved the deputies over. In the light streaming through the broken windows, his sandy hair appeared lighter than usual, the ends curling as they always did when he needed a haircut.

"You're going to be fine," I told Kirt as the EMTs hurried over to us.

"Thank you." His gaze went to the gunman, his eyes narrowing. He said he hadn't seen the man before, but could he be wrong? He shrugged and turned to leave with the paramedics.

"Wait," I said. "Do you know the way to that artist's house? Cody Beckett, the old guy you said comes in here sometimes."

He nodded. "He lives even farther out of town than we are, in an unincorporated section of land. Just take the road behind the station. Keep going about a mile. Turn right and go another mile or so. Not sure how far. I've only been out there once since he finished the big scarecrow. But it's on that road. Just keep going until you see his sculptures. Can't miss 'em."

"You've seen his work?" He was the first person I'd talked to who'd actually seen Beckett's work in person, and I was curious as to what he thought.

He shrugged. "Everyone goes out there at one point or another. Great place to take a date after dinner. You know, artsy but private. If a guy's lucky, he might get a kiss or two. Last time I was out there, I proposed to my girl." He grinned. "Wasn't paying much attention to the sculptures then, if you know what I mean. Cody's work is out in his fields, and the road in front of it is public land for anyone to see, but nobody goes to his house. He keeps a shotgun handy."

I guess there wasn't much in the way of entertainment in Hayesville if going to see an old man's log sculptures was a favorite pastime of the local youth. I wondered if they all kept their distance or if the man used that shotgun to stave off vandalism.

"He's kind of a local celebrity," Kirt went on, "but shy about it, you know? The fact that he's been in prison, well, that just adds to the mystery." Kirt glanced over his shoulder. "Those people don't know him. They're looking for someone to blame. They're scared."

"And you're not?" That a fourteen-year-old had gone missing was huge news in this community.

"I think she just ran away. Kids do that."

"The police don't think so," I said.

Shannon had checked up on the case. Jenny Vandyke was fourteen but a young fourteen, tiny, slender, and blond. I'd seen her picture, and she was a beautiful child. Nothing in the girl's room was missing except her backpack, and she hadn't mentioned leaving to her friends. Two weeks ago, she'd simply never arrived at school. That was part of why I'd come to Hayesville to see Cody Beckett. I needed to know if he was guilty. "Do you know the girl's family?"

Kirt shrugged. "No. It's just a guess."

The paramedics led him off. I hoped they'd take him to the hospital before removing the makeshift bandage so the bleeding wouldn't start again, but he was in their hands now.

I walked over to the door where Shannon was standing with the sheriff's deputies, who'd finally managed to send away most of the gawking crowd. "This is Autumn Rain," Shannon said. "She's a consultant with us in Portland. Autumn, these are Detective Sergeant Greeley and Detective Levine. They're deputies with the Marion County sheriff's office. Hayesville and the unincorporated areas here don't have a police department, so the sheriff's office has jurisdiction. Detective Greeley is over their criminal investigations unit."

"Nice to meet you." Having left my gloves in Shannon's truck, I kept my hands in my coat pockets. I couldn't read people by touching them, but both detectives were wearing rings on their right hands, and I didn't want to peek into their lives.

"You too." Greeley pulled back his hand, the line between his eyes deepening. That was the way it often went—I offended people even when I was trying to be courteous. They had no idea how long it had taken me to learn *not* to offer my hand so that I wouldn't invade their privacy.

I was involved in a constant struggle to maintain my own identity. Where once I, the adopted child of hippie parents named Winter and Summer, used to be open and accepting of everyone, I was now reluctant to reach out to others for fear of coming in contact with objects that contained their innermost feelings. Some feelings should never be revealed, not even to those you love. Maybe especially not to those you love.

"I'll come in later to make a full statement," Shannon said. "Right now, we're on our way somewhere."

"First we need to call your precinct." Greeley pulled out a phone. "Just to check your story. Protocol, you understand." He was taller than Shannon by half a foot, several inches of it wavy brown hair. He had an impressive build and a face that brooked no nonsense. Maybe he was even a little mean.

Detective Levine was nearly the same height but slender with a pleasant face framed by short dark hair. His face was rounder, almost boyish, though he had to be nearing forty. He gave me a warm smile and a slight shake of his head that told me he didn't agree with his partner.

Shannon's jaw clenched as he bit back a retort. He pulled out a pad and jotted something on it. "Look, this is my phone number and where I'm staying for the weekend. You can contact me if you need to. I promise, I won't leave town." He turned his back on them. "Let's go," he growled in an undertone. "It's not as if I actually shot the man."

I didn't bother to hide my grin. "Wait, I never got my drinks." I found them on the counter where I'd left them. As I laid a few bills down for payment, Detective Greeley was talking into his phone, his small brown eyes on Shannon. Hopefully, he'd figure out Shannon was legit in the next few minutes or we might end up in jail ourselves.

Detective Levine nodded at us as we passed, the hint of his former smile still on his lips as he glanced at his companion over our heads. I grinned back. At least we might have one ally among the local authorities.

We left without further trouble, though the other gas station employee and the few remaining locals gave us odd stares as they noted the tension between us and Detective Greeley.

Outside, another car from the sheriff's office had pulled up, but the deputies who jumped out of it rushed past us without speaking. A breeze pushed cold air down my back, and I pulled my duffle coat tighter around me. The brown wool blend held up well to the rain, but it was damaged in the under part of the upper left sleeve where I'd been shot. I couldn't afford a new coat of the same quality, so I'd have to make do until the end-of-season sales. As it was only December, I had a bit of a wait. Fortunately, I was handy with a needle, and unless people had really good eyes, they probably didn't notice the repair.

Shannon's hand was once again on my back, the gentle pressure urging me forward. "You really know how to show a girl a good time," I drawled. "Not even noon and I already got to dodge bullets."

He laughed, the tension draining from his face. "I'm just glad I came with you today."

I was too. And I was glad my sister had kept her promise to stay home with her baby. Though she wanted to meet Cody Beckett as much as I did, I'd put them in enough danger in the past.

Cody Beckett. That's what this trip was all about—seeing if it was safe to open a dialogue with the man, even though he wouldn't likely welcome either of us.

Since this was a private case, not something authorized by his captain, we'd brought Shannon's truck instead of his unmarked white police Mustang. I still wasn't comfortable in the truck because it underscored the recent change in our relationship from reluctant associates to something more. Exactly what that more was I didn't know yet. Things had been much clearer when he hadn't believed in my abilities and had fought his unwelcome attraction to me. Back then I'd treated him in the same mocking, standoffish, annoying way he'd treated me. Now we had to decide where our feelings would take us.

The directions Kirt had given us were better than those on my phone's GPS, as was sometimes the case in remote areas, but with several odd turns in the path, I was glad Shannon was along to decipher them. Both my sister and I were directionally impaired.

Kirt was also right about the sculptures—they were hard to miss. We would have found them even without his help. Standing sentinel in the middle of a barren field of week-old snow, they were huge, some spiraling as tall as a two-story house. The first was a tall, thin scarecrow, his log legs looking unsteady. Next, a mammoth ear of corn, partially painted and looking as though it had exploded from the fat log from which it had been carved. Following these was a farmer, his head and hat carved from the bottom part of a tree, a few roots painted to resemble loose straw. These first three sculptures sported a weathered look, as though they'd endured the elements several years, but the aging only added to their appeal. Looking more recent was a half-finished boat bursting from yet another massive log. The artist's work in progress, I assumed.

Bales of straw, some in tall stacks, lay scattered among the sculptures like lesser entities. With no ladder in sight, I figured the artist must use the bales to reach the tops of his works. Somehow it was fitting that he used the straw, the effort of climbing adding to his unusual style. A stark loneliness clung to the sculptures as though a testament to their uniqueness. Almost, they seemed sentient, and I wondered how Cody Beckett had been able to part with any of his creations.

"Impressive," Shannon said, slowing the truck.

I nodded. "No wonder the locals come to ogle."

"He must charge a pretty penny when he sells them. Bet they take up to a year or more to complete."

Then we were past them. We drove through a thicket of leafless trees, where it looked as if the vegetation had tried to reclaim the narrow asphalt road but had been beaten back by the arrival of snowfall. We came upon our destination sudden-ly—a long gravel drive, layered with dirty, compacted snow, that led to the house I'd seen once in the newspaper and once in a drawing made by my sister. A house she'd never seen before. That was her talent, as potent and unpredictable as mine.

Shannon turned the truck down the drive. We hadn't yet reached the house when a grizzled old man came onto the porch dressed in worn jeans and a thick flannel shirt, a shotgun in his hands. Not exactly the welcome I might have hoped for. Of course, he didn't know I was coming or even who I was.

As Shannon brought the truck to a stop, I noted the white stubble on the old man's chin, the wrinkles around the eyes, and the too-long white hair that was uncombed. I was too far away to see the color of his eyes, but I knew that his right eye was hazel and his left blue.

Like my twin sister. Like me.

This was Cody Beckett, our father.

Chapter 2

C ody Beckett was my biological father, I should say, because my real parents had been Winter and Summer Rain, the hippie couple who'd sheltered my young birth mother and later adopted and raised me. Though they were both gone now, I felt lucky to have experienced such an unconventional upbringing. Being raised by Winter and Summer made up for the separation from my twin, Tawnia, who'd grown up states away with another adoptive family.

My feelings for Cody Beckett wavered between curiosity and disgust. Several weeks ago, I'd accepted that he might not be the monster I'd always believed him to be, but that didn't mean he was anyone worth knowing. We'd finally tracked him down, and when Tawnia learned he was a suspect in Jenny Vandyke's disappearance, she encouraged me to investigate. The unlikelihood of the two events—us finding him and the girl's disappearance—happening so close together didn't escape me. I didn't believe in coincidence. On some cosmic level I felt I was either meant to prove him innocent or help convict him and make sure he never hurt anyone in the way he'd hurt my young birth mother.

I was wearing a contact in my left eye that made it appear to be more hazel, like the right. Not an exact match but close enough to fool anyone who wasn't looking hard. The contacts belonged to my sister, who'd grown up trying to fit in, but since meeting me, she'd given up hiding her eyes and had been more than happy to give me her unused supply for this trip. I wasn't sure if she'd really done me a favor. I'd been taught to celebrate my differences and wearing the contact now seemed dishonest. Not to mention uncomfortable. But I didn't want this stranger suspecting who I was. Not yet.

Though gray clouds gathered overhead, I put my sunglasses on to further hide my eyes and climbed from the truck, checking to make sure my knit gloves were in my coat pocket in case I needed them. Snow crunched under my feet.

Shannon put himself slightly ahead of me as he reached for his badge. "I'm Detective Martin," he said. "We've just come to ask you a few questions."

"I'm through with questions," Cody Beckett growled. "I told the sheriff's deputies that. Either arrest me or leave me alone. If you ain't got a warrant, get out." He hefted the shotgun. "Or maybe I'll give you a reason to arrest me."

He was barefoot despite the cold, and I felt a curious, reluctant kinship with him. I hated Oregon winters because they forced even me, a die-hard flower child, to sometimes wear shoes, and though his shoeless state was probably due more to haste than to a desire to connect directly with the universe, it evoked a kinship I wanted to guard against.

I straightened my shoulders and pushed past Shannon before he could say anything threatening that might make the situation worse. He was irritating that way, if my experience with him was anything to go by.

"Unless you have something to do with Jenny Vandyke's disappearance," I said, "you might want to talk with us."

"And why's that?" He arched a bushy white brow. Up close, I could see that under the white stubble, the worn, leathery face had once been handsome and that if he cared to do so, he might clean up nicely. Maybe if he had to go in front of a jury, his attorney would convince him to do just that.

"Because we were sent by someone who wants to prove your innocence." Only a bit of a stretch. My sister did want to know the truth and she was hoping he wasn't involved, but that didn't mean she was invested in him emotionally. Not yet.

Cody blinked several times before words made it to his lips. "Why would anyone want to do that?"

"The person wants to remain anonymous for the time being, but that's why we're here." I shot Shannon a glance, warning him to keep quiet. We hadn't really discussed what would happen once we found Cody or how I'd tell him about our relationship—if I told him—but whatever happened would be my choice.

Cody rested his shotgun on the wood porch, barrel down, but his grip remained tight. "Let's see if I got this right. You're here to prove me innocent. Not to find the girl."

"We're here to prove whether or not you were involved," Shannon corrected. "We have not been assigned to look for Jenny, though if we uncovered information about her, we would certainly act on it. If you didn't have anything to do with her disappearance, you have nothing to lose by talking to us."

"And everything to gain, I suppose." His eyes ran over Shannon before sliding back to me. "So what do you two get out of this?"

"I do my job. I get paid." I was glad for the sunglasses that hid the lie.

In reality, I got to either confirm he was a lying, no-good creep or decide that maybe he deserved a measure of forgiveness. A measure only because I would never forgive him completely. Cody's eyes narrowed, reminding me of how Kirt had looked at the gunman back at the gas station. "You from around here? You look familiar."

My heart thumped heavily in my chest. "No, I'm not."

"How do I know you're actually on my side?" Cody rubbed his face with his free hand.

"We're only on your side if you didn't take Jenny," Shannon retorted.

Cody gave him an impatient scowl. "I get it, I get it. I didn't do it. I already said."

"Then you should talk to us." I shifted my weight, wiggling my confined toes in my leather boots. They were the most comfortable on the market, more like waterproof socks, according to the advertisement, and they'd been a gift from my twin, who was as practical as I was strange. Or so people who didn't know about her gift might believe.

"How do I know you ain't reporters or some such thing?"

Shannon took out his badge again. "As I said earlier, I'm a police detective from Portland. I'm not here officially but as a friend to Autumn. She's the one investigating your innocence or guilt."

Cody looked between us, still skeptical. "Can I see that badge?"

Shannon handed it over, and I knew the instant Cody touched it that he shared more than my mismatched eyes. Shannon recognized his glazed expression at the same time I did—probably from seeing me read imprints. He snatched it back.

"Well, it seems to be real," Cody said with a casualness that belied what had happened. He'd *read* the imprints on Shannon's badge, and because the badge was important to Shannon, there would have been plenty of imprints. In those few seconds Cody wouldn't have been able to read everything, but he'd seen enough to take stock of Shannon's character.

That this stranger shared my talent was both exhilarating and frightening. Exhilarating because he'd presumably lived his entire life with the ability and would know much more about it. Frightening because it verified beyond doubt that we were related. Questions threatened to burst from me, but with effort I held them back.

Not until I know for sure he isn't involved with the missing girl, I told myself.

"Okay," Cody said. "What do you want to know?"

I relaxed slightly. Of course, he could still be guilty and hoping to lead us astray or keep us away from any real information, but he didn't know I shared his gift, and imprints didn't lie. Actors could imprint on props during powerful scenes, but those fictional imprints still lacked the realism of actual imprints. My recent experience in solving the murder of an actress would help me tell the difference. Besides, Cody Beckett didn't know I could read imprints, so he wouldn't consider creating false ones.

Of course, there was always the off chance that he really was innocent and as outsiders we were the only ones he thought he might be able to convince. Whatever his motive, I needed to touch his things. Inside the house, preferably, though I would take what I could get. If I could read people, I'd simply touch him and be done with it.

Then again, an ability like that would kill any chance of romance. I already had too many of Shannon's secrets at my fingertips as it was.

"We'd like to see where they found the girl's boot," Shannon said.

"That's easy enough. Wait here. I need to get some shoes."

I was itching to take mine off, but if we had to walk more than thirty minutes in the snow, even my tough feet would be in danger of frostbite.

Before I could ask to use his bathroom so I could snoop, he'd reached inside the door and was pulling on some boots that looked as old as he was. They went well with his old jeans and flannel shirt.

"We can wait while you get a jacket," I said, pulling on the gloves I kept in my coat pocket, usually more to protect me from unwanted imprints than from the cold.

He shook his head. "My shirt's lined, and we'll be walking a good ways. A coat would make me too hot." He went down the porch stairs as he talked, pushing past us and heading toward the trees behind the house. Most of the trees had lost their leaves, but there were enough evergreens to make the woodland still seem green— or greenish gray with the encroaching overhead clouds.

I hoped they found Jenny before snow came again, which would make it even harder to follow any leads. If she was still out in the woods somewhere, it might already be too late.

We walked for a good ten minutes before Cody came to a stop beneath a particularly large pine tree. We'd covered a lot of ground, and I was sweating under my coat. Only my hands were cold, even inside my gloves.

"Here," Cody said, pointing under the tree, which was

littered with old pine needles. "They found it under there. Or a dog did."

"Is this still your property?" I asked.

Cody nodded. "I own a hundred acres. Bought it near twenty years ago when it was cheap. This here is the edge." He waved a hand behind me. "Through those trees there's a dirt road. Marks the end of my property and the beginning of a prune farmer's."

"They found nothing else?" Shannon squatted down to get a better look, and after removing and leaving my gloves and antique rings in my pockets, I did the same. I wondered what Cody would think when I began searching for imprints.

Only a little snow had penetrated under the haven made by the branches, and I could very well imagine the teen hiding there. But not for weeks. It was too cold.

No use in putting it off. I duck-walked under the branches and tried not to be obvious as I began searching. I didn't have to actually touch the ground or the tree because I'd learned to recognize a tingling in my hands when they were close to something that held a strong or recent imprint, but for Cody's benefit, I touched both the tree and the ground, turning over pine needles as though searching for what might lie beneath. My stealth was lost on Cody, who was now staring into the distance.

"They searched all my property," he said. "Didn't find any trace of the kid besides the boot."

"They're sure it's hers?" I envisioned an inexpensive pair bought at the local Walmart by half the girls in junior high.

"Her parents say it is. Bought them at a specialty store locally. Well, in Salem, that is."

"If it is her boot, she didn't just run away." I glanced at Shannon, who shrugged.

"Unless she met someone here and changed shoes, accidentally leaving a boot behind." Shannon stood up and scanned the area. "Is that likely, Mr. Beckett? That she'd come here to meet someone?"

"Well, she lives over there, through the woods." Cody pointed opposite the way we'd come.

West. Or at least I thought it was west. The problem with being directionally impaired is that sometimes all directions look the same.

"But it's a bit far," he added, "and this route isn't a short cut to anywhere. Doesn't seem likely."

My turn to shrug. "It's near a road, you said. Maybe she spent a night here hiding before meeting someone and taking off."

"Would have been mighty uncomfortable," Cody said, giving me a disgruntled look. "It's been really cold. I could work outside just an hour at a time. It only warms up a bit right before it snows. Like now." He squinted up at the sky. "Going to snow soon. Tomorrow at the latest. More likely sooner. Then the cold will really set in."

I had found absolutely nothing under the tree. If anyone had been here, the person hadn't cared enough about anything he or she touched to leave even a faint imprint. I sighed, coming out of the protective cover of the branches. The air felt colder away from the tree, and I'd be glad when we were moving again.

"That's all I got to show you," Cody said, scratching the back of his neck.

Shannon frowned. "You don't have any outbuildings on your property? Something remote that someone else might use?"

"A place I might hold the girl, you mean." Cody's scowl had returned.

"I'm sure the police would have already searched," I said.

"That's right, but you're welcome to look around if you want. I have a dirt bike you can use. The only buildings I have other than the house is a root cellar in back of the house and a shed near the field where I work. It's enclosed on only three sides, though, so it ain't ideal for kidnapping or for a runaway."

With that he turned abruptly and started back through the woods, as though he'd had his fill of us or perhaps of any company.

I looked at Shannon. "What do you think?"

"I want to look at the cellar."

I wasn't too keen on the idea. I'd had a bit of claustrophobia since I'd been locked in a root cellar during one of my earlier cases, but I knew Shannon would need my talent. "Okay."

Pulling back on my gloves, I plunged my freezing fingers into my coat pockets as we hurried to catch up with Cody. He was slightly taller than average, which meant taller than both Shannon and me, and apparently well accustomed to charging through the woods. The crisp snow passed steadily under his strides.

I was completely out of breath when we arrived at the house. Cody pointed to a tiny building that looked like an outhouse. "That's the cellar. I keep it locked. Sometimes the local kids come calling."

I bet. He was a perfect target for dares and other escapades. We waited as he dialed the combination on the rotary lock. His hands looked strong. Callused. Working hands. Not like I'd expected from an artist. But then he wasn't a typical artist.

He motioned us to precede him into the cellar, where a steep flight of stairs plunged into the earth. I hesitated. No way was I going down there with him holding that lock.

Cody followed the direction of my stare and gave a gruff laugh. "Here. You can take that with you. I'm going to the house. Just lock it when you're finished." He tossed me the lock, turned on his heel, and strode away.

I caught the lock in my gloved hands, slipping it into my pocket. I'd have to check it for imprints eventually, but I wanted to wait until I was sure Cody couldn't see.

Shannon watched me, a hint of a grin on his face. "I have my gun," he said, "if we need to break out."

"Good. Then you're not scared." Removing my gloves and sunglasses, I started down into the darkness, pleased to note Cody had left a flashlight on a hook inside. There wasn't a hand railing, but the wall lining the stairs was wood. I bet Cody had dug out and built this place himself. I went past the flashlight, leaving it for Shannon because of the imprints, though I'd have to check it later as well.

It was a long way down, definitely below the frost line. When I reached the bottom, I pulled off one glove and held the combination lock loosely in my other gloved palm so that if it held anything violent, I could drop it more easily. I touched it with one bare finger.

A feeling of satisfaction. Contentment. Of knowing I had food from my own garden preserved against winter. This vague imprint followed by an earlier, stronger, angry one.

Stupid kids. They have no right to break in here. Those were good potatoes they threw at the house.

The anger drained away as fast as it had come. I deserved what the kids had done. I deserved everything bad that ever happened to me. I had to make sure I never forgot that. It was part of my penance, and potatoes were just potatoes, after all.

More imprints came, all of them similar. Though few of the

imprints were strong, and Cody seemed to be divided between feelings of anger and guilt, there was nothing about a missing girl. I replaced the lock in my pocket.

"Nothing?" Shannon asked, following the movement. "Sometimes the kids break in and steal his vegetables. Nothing about Jenny Vandyke."

"He'd be stupid to have brought her here anyway. With his prison record and his oddities, they were bound to suspect him."

By oddities, he meant the artwork, I supposed. "He went to prison for attacking another man, not a child," I reminded him. A crime my biological grandmother claimed he hadn't been guilty of but to which he'd pleaded guilty in order to do penance for the secret crime he'd actually committed against my biological mother. If he'd gone to prison for that earlier act, the police would probably have him sitting in jail right now for Jenny's disappearance, proof or no proof.

Shannon offered me the flashlight, an apologetic grin on his face. Apologetic because he wanted me to read any imprints that might be on it and he'd seen how they could affect me. I wanted to remind him that he was here at my invitation, not the other way around, but he looked so appealing in the dim light that I decided not to make the point. I felt a sudden desire to step near him and feel his arms go around me.

Not now, I thought.

As I took the flashlight, Shannon drew out a pen-sized mini light on his key ring and began moving it over the bins of vegetables. That he kept running the light over the same area told me he was only pretending to pay attention to his search. He'd learned the hard way what might happen when I read certain kinds of imprints, and he still felt guilty for not protecting me from some strong ones. He worried for nothing—this time. Faint imprints came from the flashlight, but nothing strong or lasting. Nothing that stole my energy or made me lose sense of myself. I was glad. I shook my head.

The cellar was small, and there wasn't much to see. There were about a dozen bins and only one set of shelves about waist high, full of vegetables, some I recognized and a few I didn't. I removed my other glove and began running my hands near the shelves, the bins, the walls, and even the vegetables—all without the typical buzzing that alerted me to strong imprints. To make sure I wasn't missing even the faint ones, I touched everything. No luck.

Meanwhile, Shannon was tapping on the walls. I knew why. The last cellar I'd been in had a secret door to another room.

That was not the case here. I pushed aside a—a turnip?—and sighed. "Nothing."

He nodded. "Let's get out of here."

I beat him to the stairs. Above ground once again, I tried to dust off my hands without success. Gingerly, I replaced my sunglasses and started for the house.

"Where are you going?"

"To ask Cody if I can wash my hands."

"Won't he wonder why you got them so dirty?"

"He'll think it's because I want to search inside his house." He wouldn't be exactly right, but he'd be right in the sense that it was the excuse I'd been looking for. Shannon's comment, however, made me uneasy. What if Cody was actually dangerous?

It was more than a little pathetic that I already hoped he wasn't.

"Yeah?" Cody answered the door on my first knock.

I gave him back the lock to the cellar, belatedly remembering that he'd wanted us to put it back on the door. "I had a little, uh, accident. Can I wash my hands?"

His eyes narrowed as he peered at me, as though trying to see through my sunglasses. "You sure you're just not finding an excuse to look inside my house?"

The way he spoke made fear crawl up my spine. I scowled. "What if I am? It's not as if you have something to hide, right?"

"I, uh—" He broke off. "Whatever. Just don't touch anything."

I was hoping he said that as a matter of course, not because he suspected my talent. Maybe I should tell him about our relationship. Yet if he was involved in Jenny Vandyke's disappearance, I never wanted him to know about me and certainly not about Tawnia or her baby daughter.

I rolled my eyes, forgetting he couldn't see them behind my sunglasses. "I won't disturb anything."

He opened the door wider, and I followed him inside. Behind me, Shannon rushed to keep up. I wished he'd wait outside, but maybe he could distract Cody long enough for me to get some good readings.

The door opened onto a spacious living room with a large, modern, wide-screen TV sitting in front of a brown leather couch that had seen better days. This room adjoined a narrow kitchen where a small, round table took up most of the free space. A stainless steel sink sat below a curtainless window. Wisps of spider webs trailed over a painting of a mountain, the only decoration in the room. All the floors were hardwood.

Cody led me down a dark hall and pointed to a partially open door on the right side. He made a point of shutting the door opposite. *His bedroom,* I guessed from a glimpse of the double bed.

That seemed to be the extent of the house. It looked much wider from the outside, but I realized now that was because the ceilings were so low. Pushing my sunglasses on top of my head, I could see there was a lived-in quality about the entire place, from the scuffed floor in the hallway to the cracked light cover in the surprisingly large bathroom.

"Thanks," I told Cody, shutting the door.

I turned on the faucet, braced for imprints. Not finding any on the faucet handles, I washed my hands methodically, my eyes wandering over the room. Tub with shower, soap, and one bottle of shampoo, toilet with a toilet plunger tucked next to the wall, paper, the sink with a razor, extra blades, shaving cream, and a black comb. A towel hanging over the shower curtain rod. Everything was sparse and rather simple for the size of the bathroom. Just the basics. More what you'd expect from a bachelor with his first apartment than from an old codger who'd had years to accumulate belongings. Apparently Cody didn't hold onto much, or he didn't buy much. There wasn't even a cupboard to investigate, except the one under the sink, which was crammed with extra rolls of toilet paper and basic cleaning supplies.

I ran my hands over everything to be certain, wishing I was in the bedroom so I could find something he cared about more. Imprints were funny that way. Like countertops, no one cared much for their shampoo.

My hands drew near his razor on the edge of the sink, and I felt the familiar tingling in my hand. Wait a minute. I'd found something. I placed a finger on the razor.

Darkness fell over me. Darkness and a deep anger as I stared at the face of a man in the mirror. My face. Self-loathing. Regret. Dragging the razor over the stubble, wishing I could cut away as easily the black part of my soul.

The grim imprint ended, but another one exactly like it began. Was this proof of Cody's involvement with the missing girl? Certain killers might experience moments of agonizing regret, though that didn't cause them to turn themselves in or prevent an attack on their next victim when the pressure was too great. Not that Cody had to be a serial killer, exactly, or even a serial child abductor. But he could be. He might be responsible for far worse than what he'd done to my mother.

Regardless, this imprint proved Cody felt a guilt that weighed on him day and night, and it was my responsibility to figure out why.

Chapter 3

I was breathing heavily when I managed to open my hand and release the razor handle. It wasn't the kind of imprint that made me pass out, but it was close. What did it mean? Maybe I didn't want to know. I wanted to run outside and drive back to Portland, forgetting I'd ever tried to find my biological father. I felt dirty and weary.

That's the imprint, I reminded myself. Still, it had taken its toll, and I felt exhaustion creeping in. Using tissue, I picked up the razor from the sink basin and replaced it where it had been on the side. Then I washed my hands again, but the memory from the razor was mine for life, a memory I would need to deal with and bury in a mental corner with all the other terrible imprints I'd experienced.

Imprinted memories were like that. Once experienced, they were burned into my mind, and only the greatest amount of willpower redirected my thoughts elsewhere. It was one reason I didn't touch objects unnecessarily. I did it only to help someone else—in this case, my sister, who wanted to meet her biological father, and, of course, for the missing girl.

Okay, maybe I did it a little for myself too.

I slipped one finger into the pocket of my black dress pants, touching the drawing I always kept there—a rendition of the first photograph of me with my twin taken after we'd discovered each other last year. My sister had drawn it, each stroke imbued with her love. I soaked up the emotion, grateful for the steadying effect. Cody's self-hate faded, and I felt stronger, cleaner.

Thank you, Tawnia. I felt her, or at least a connection to her, though not nearly as strong as when we were together.

I pondered for a moment what would happen when Cody used his razor again. If I'd imprinted my horror at what I'd experienced, he'd feel it and know I'd been nosing around—and that I shared his talent. Fortunately, judging by the stubble on his face, I'd be long gone before he used the razor again.

Or maybe I'd decide to reveal my identity. Maybe.

I opened the door, expecting to see Cody waiting in the hall, his callused hands impatiently on his hips, but he was nowhere to be seen. I could hear voices coming from the living room. Shannon had done his job.

Without hesitating, I opened the door to the bedroom. Not exactly following guest etiquette, but I needed to know. Besides, there was more at stake here than my questionable parentage. A young girl was missing, and I might be able to find something here that the police hadn't.

The bedroom was as simple as the rest of the house, except for that wide-screen TV set in the living room. There was a big, plain dresser, a short bookshelf filled with thick nonfiction books, a wrought-iron lamp on a nightstand piled with more books. The double bed was covered with a beautiful hand-made quilt. It could use a good washing, but it was in excellent condition.

Forcing my gaze away from the quilt, I took several steps toward the nightstand. That would be where he'd store things that were important to him, or if not there, then maybe in the top drawer of the dresser or in the closet.

I touched the wrought-iron lamp first. I couldn't help myself. Being an antiques dealer, I recognized a beautiful piece when I saw it, and besides, imprints fairly jumped from the surface, they were so strong.

I loved this lamp, loved it because it belonged to my beautiful mother and her parents and grandparents before me. It meant continuity, family. A deep remorse that the family line would end with me. I'd failed everything in my life. The remorse left me with tears. With a deep yearning.

Other imprints followed, much less recent. Warmth of ownership. Nothing distinct, but pleasant and happy, like the imprints on my antique rings. I smiled. If I was at an estate sale, I would buy this heirloom despite the remorse because of the love imbued on its surface. Another owner would love it, replacing the remorse until it vanished and only the echo of love remained.

The lamp was obviously an heirloom, passed down from my ancestors. Being adopted, I hadn't really considered my lost heritage. My adoptive parents had been everything to me. It hadn't mattered that they had no extended family or that they hadn't collected things the way I did. But now I was assaulted with unexpected feelings. A new door had opened. I wanted the lamp to love and pass down to my children and grandchildren.

I forced my hand away, hoping I hadn't left an imprint that would tell Cody more than I wanted him to know, and began touching the books on the nightstand. Titles such as

Sculpture and Artistry, Carvings Come Alive, Build Your Own Solar Panels, and *Gardening Made Simple.* Cody was a practical man, it seemed. The imprints on the books were faded—curiosity, contentment, sleepiness.

One book was out of place: *The World's Worst Killers.* I placed a finger on the cover, worried about what I might experience.

Again the self-loathing, every bit as bitter as on the razor, but it was an older imprint, at least a year old, and it had faded a bit. Another imprint quickly followed. Laughter, giggling. A brief glimpse of Cody's front door. Nothing more. The last imprint, which would have made it the first left on the book, was too fleeting for me to decide who was laughing, but someone apparently thought this book funny enough to leave on Cody's front porch.

A prank.

I didn't know whether to pity the man or to fear him, but I rejected the urge to run. Shannon had my back, and if I couldn't trust him, I shouldn't be considering starting a relationship with him. Especially when it meant giving up Jake, my best friend and former boyfriend.

The top drawer held several pairs of reading glasses, four large bottles of nonprescription pills for pain, one half full, all of them outdated. A roll of toilet paper he was obviously using to blow his nose, as indicated by the handful of used tissue squares in the corner of the drawer. No significant imprints on the eyeglasses or bottles.

The bottom drawer was crammed with more books: *Fifty Delicious Meals in Fifteen Minutes, Do-It-Yourself Kitchen Tile, Caring for Your Trees, The American Gold Fraud, Politicians Aren't Really Working for You.* Again, no imprints of interest, though I did wonder at Cody's versatility. Had he really made the fifteen-minute meals? Was he active in politics? Did he subscribe to conspiracy theories?

The bed was next. Clothing and similar items usually didn't hold imprints well, perhaps because they were washed too often, losing minute bits of themselves in lint, or because they were mostly forgotten. But quilts, especially those used often, sometimes contained good imprints because people loved them so much. I had an afghan my mother had crocheted and which I snuggled in when I was really down and missing her. I used it sparingly, afraid my own imprints would take over, and I never, ever washed it.

Upon closer inspection, this quilt was particularly intricate. Each block had something different embroidered onto it—a cat, a house, a flower, a boy, a paintbrush, a window. On and on, nothing repeating. The needlework on these had been done by hand; no machine could have been so accurate and detailed.

Whoever did this was an artist, I thought. Eagerly I placed a finger on a strip of material that ran around the outer edge of the entire quilt like a frame.

Pain. Despair. She can't be dead. Please, God, no! Never to see her face. To feel her hand on my head or her arms around me. I would never get her out of that place.

I sank to the floor, trembling with agony—not mine, the boy's. The child Cody, I suspected. It felt like mine. Before I could recover, another imprint came from the quilt border.

The quilt was finished. It would warm and comfort him when I was long gone, each square representing something from our past. He would always know how much I loved him.

A woman's thoughts, I knew, from her memories of a baby at her breast nursing, playing in the garden, and opening her arms for her little boy to run into them.

I arose, eager for more. This was history. My history.

As I touched each square, I experienced a memory of the depicted event—a boy covered in paint, laughing at the beach, eating ice cream, crying over a dead bird, holding her hand.

The boy had to be Cody and the woman his mother. My grandmother. I wanted to experience all the squares, but the next imprint on an embroidered flower made me hesitate.

I was going to take you away from there. I told you I would that day, but it was already too late, wasn't it?

Not the woman's imprinted thought but Cody's, placed a decade later as he touched the quilt, much as I was doing now.

Then came the woman's earlier imprint, from the same square.

I looked up to see Cody standing in the doorway of a bedroom where metal bars blocked the windows, his face sober, flowers in his hand.

"I'm going to take you away from here, Mother," he said somberly.

"I know you will," I said. "I'm getting better every day."

But I wasn't. I wasn't at all. The visions were still coming, and the doctors told me every day that I was crazy, a danger to my teenage son. But I loved him. That was the only thing holding me together.

I withdrew my hand. Cody had left his feelings after his mother's imprint. Did he often touch a square, reliving their memories together? Did he touch a whole bunch in one sitting or did he limit himself to one at a time, fearing he would too often leave his own imprints, as it was natural he would on something he loved this much? Tears filled my eyes, though I didn't want to feel anything for this man who, in my view, had been the cause of my biological mother's death.

I forced my thoughts back to the task at hand. Nothing about Jenny Vandyke would be on these squares, or if there was, it would take too much time to find it. I needed to move on. I took a step toward the foot of the bed, thinking to check the closet.

The door behind me slammed open. "What in the devil's name are you doing in here?" Cody demanded.

I had been so involved in the imprints that I hadn't even heard footsteps in the hall. I turned to see Cody's reddened face glaring at me. Behind him Shannon frowned, apparently blaming me for taking so long.

"I, uh, got mixed up," I said unconvincingly. I'd always been a terrible liar. "Then I saw the quilt. It's so beautiful." I reached out but stopped short of touching it. I couldn't risk being mesmerized by an imprint, though I longed to know more of my grandmother.

"Get out!" Cody bellowed. Thick, ugly veins stood out on his neck. He lifted his hands as though to throttle me, and I could well imagine him kidnapping a child. Or hurting one.

Behind him Shannon tensed, his hand going to where I knew he kept his gun.

"I'm going already!" I said, lifting my hands in submission. "Lighten up, old man. One would think you had a body hiding in that closet."

His face grew more flushed. "Is that what you want to see? You want me to prove I don't have that poor little girl stashed in there? As if the police didn't already search this place stem to stern." He pushed roughly past me and dived for the closet door, yanking it open. "See for your—" He broke off as a man burst from the closet, staggering two steps before collapsing, face down, onto the hardwood floor. From all the blood, it was apparent that if we didn't do something soon, he wouldn't be around to answer any questions.

"But . . . I swear I . . . How did he . . . I-I-I didn't . . ." Cody stuttered.

"Help him!" This I directed at Shannon, who had drawn his gun. Already I was kneeling, rolling the man over. He was younger than I'd estimated at first glimpse, his clean-shaven features drawn by pain and blood loss. Maybe in his late twenties.

"I got a pulse," I said. Opening the man's jacket, I peered at him. At least two wounds, but there could be more. No imprint on the jacket.

"Some kind of knife." Shannon had reholstered his gun and was dialing a number on his phone. "We need an ambulance. There's a man here who's been stabbed. He needs immediate attention. I don't know the address, but it's on the north outskirts of Haysville. The artist's place. You'll have to track my phone's location or called the sheriff's office for the exact address." He paused. "No, I'm not the artist, and I'm hanging up now so I can try to stop the bleeding. No, I don't need you to talk me through it. Just hurry!"

Cody had disappeared but returned with the towel from the bathroom. I tried not to think about cleanliness as I held it against the wounds. Cody had left an imprint on the towel, strong enough to have stayed on the cloth, though already it was fading:

How did he get in my closet? They're never going to believe I had nothing to do with this. They'll never stop looking now.

The man moaned.

"Who did this to you?" Shannon asked. The man's eyelids

fluttered, but he didn't respond. Shannon's attention whipped to Cody. "What do you know about this?"

"No," I said for him. "You can see how surprised he was."

Cody gave me a gratified look while Shannon's eyes showed irritation. Good, that I understood and could fix. I met Shannon's gaze steadily until he nodded his understanding.

"Okay, do you know who he is, at least?" Shannon asked Cody.

Cody shook his head. "Looks familiar, but I swear I can't place him. I don't get out much."

"Well, you think about it and tell us if you remember anything."

"The police are going to arrest me." Cody's voice was gruff. "They'll think I did it."

Shannon frowned. "Maybe. Unless he wakes up and tells a different story. You two stay with him. Keep pressure on his wounds. I'm going to check the rest of the house and outside." He lifted one of the man's eyes and shook his head before drawing his gun and sprinting to the bedroom door.

Minutes ticked by slowly as we waited for the ambulance. I wished I could search the man for imprints, but I couldn't relinquish my pressure on the wounds, and with Cody being the prime suspect, it didn't seem prudent for him to touch the man.

"Maybe we should check him for a wallet," I suggested, as Shannon reappeared minutes later.

Shannon shook his head. They'll fingerprint everything. Better leave it."

The sheriff's deputies arrived then, seconds before the ambulance. Unfortunately for us, they were the same detectives who'd been at the gas station shooting. Maybe Cody wouldn't be the only one who ended up in jail.

Detective Sergeant Greeley gave the all-clear to the EMTs before letting them into the house. "We'll get his statement at the hospital if he wakes up," he said as they took the unconscious man away.

His gaze turned to us, his voice hard. "I suppose you're going to say you had nothing to do with this."

"Of course we didn't," Shannon said.

"What are you doing here, anyway?" Detective Levine sounded considerably more friendly.

I gave him a smile. "We're here to visit Mr. Beckett."

Greeley's small eyes glittered. "I see." He turned to Cody. "What happened here, Mr. Beckett?"

"He must have come in while we were in the woods." Cody lifted his chin against the accusation in Greeley's eyes. "I never saw him before."

"What were you doing in the woods?" Greeley pressed.

"Sightseeing," I said before Cody could respond. I really did not like the detective. The only thing he had going for him was his badge and a nice head of hair. "Look, Mr. Beckett has nothing to do with this. He was with us the whole time."

"The man's wounds could be several hours old," Shannon said.

There he went again, being a cop instead of my friend. I narrowed my eyes at him. "Mr. Beckett didn't have anything to do with it." The imprint on the towel had made that much clear to me.

"We'll determine that down at the station," Greeley said. "We'll want to question all of you, of course."

"Of course," Shannon said at the same time Cody growled,

"No way. I've been questioned enough. My only wrongdoing is leaving my doors open on my own property while I take a little walk."

He called our long trek in the woods a little walk?

"What's so funny?" Greeley asked me.

"Nothing." I wished I had Tawnia's poker face, but my twin had been given all the subterfuge talent in the family.

"You're all coming with us." Greeley motioned us to go ahead of him. His hand was near his gun.

"Thanks, but I'll drive," Shannon said. "Wouldn't want to have to come back out here for my truck."

"Right. How am I getting back if I don't drive myself?" Cody muttered. I'd seen an ancient-looking gold Honda out front when we'd arrived, and it must belong to him. I wondered what he did when he had a lot of snow, since he didn't seem to have a garage.

"We'll have someone drive you back." Levine placed a tentative hand on Cody's arm. "Or I'll drive you myself."

"If we don't arrest you," Greeley amended.

Great. Greeley had his suspect and wasn't going to look further. We'd better hope the victim regained consciousness. Not that I really cared where Cody ended up, but he shouldn't be charged with something he didn't do.

Grumbling under his breath, Cody preceded all of us from his house, stopping on the porch to make a show of locking the door. "Now I have to go and put this on the cellar," he said, holding up the combination lock. "Don't want any more trespassers."

Detective Greeley sighed but allowed Levine to accompany him around back. Shannon started for his truck, his hand on my arm.

"You can follow us in," Greeley said to us. "We're located in Salem."

Shannon nodded. "I know the address, and I have a GPS. We'll meet you there."

That seemed to satisfy Greeley.

In the truck, I said to Shannon, "You're taking this suspect thing a lot better than I thought you would."

"Ha." He put the truck in gear. "We're not suspects or we'd be going with them. He's called my precinct and knows who we are. He's just trying to remind us that this is his turf."

"Who cares whose turf it is as long as someone finds Jenny Vandyke? Do you think the stabbing is related?"

"I don't know. If Beckett's telling the truth, it's odd that the man chose his house at all. I mean, why there? Either Beckett knows more than he's letting on or something is going on nearby and that man was simply trying to hide until he could find help."

"You mean maybe he was being chased and since Cody wasn't home, he hid from whoever stabbed him."

"That's one explanation. I'm not saying it's the right one."

"You should have let me touch his wallet," I said.

Shannon's eyes left the road briefly. "Not with Cody there. Besides, you were kind of busy saving his life. We'll go see him later. The police should keep his things for evidence."

"I hope he doesn't die, especially for Cody's sake."

"Me too. He might know where Jenny Vandyke is—if the two events are connected."

I felt bad for not thinking of the girl first. I hadn't been called in on her case, but I was beginning to feel responsible for finding her.

We'd reached the paved road, and still the police car had not moved from the house. Probably awaiting the backup deputies speeding toward us. More people to look for evidence.

"You know what we really need," Shannon said casually.

I nodded, meeting his gaze. "For me to touch Jenny Vandyke's boot."

Chapter 4

Need and want are two very different things. That I needed to touch the boot to see if Jenny had left an imprint didn't necessarily mean I *wanted* to touch it. Imprints could be dangerous for me if they were powerful and I got stuck in a loop.

Imprints were sometimes unreliable because what I saw was always filtered through the experience and perception of the person leaving the imprint. I felt as that individual did at the time the imprint was left, and often he or she lacked knowledge that was key to solving the mystery. Without the ability to see through my own experience, I was limited.

Regardless, I still needed to read Jenny's boot. Reading imprints she might have left on something she was wearing at the time of her abduction or going through her room and personal belongings in search of imprints leading up to her disappearance could open up a world of possibilities that the police hadn't considered.

I'd found people who'd left of their own accord, people who had hidden pasts, people who'd been attacked because they followed their dreams, people who'd been held prisoner by others.

Not all of them did I find in time.

"You think the police will simply hand over the boot?" I asked. Detective Sergeant Greeley wouldn't, but thankfully he wasn't in charge of the entire sheriff's office.

Shannon shook his head. "Not without a bit of haggling. That's why we're going to see the parents first. Maybe if we have something to offer the deputies in exchange, they'll be less quick to cry interference and accept our help."

"Good idea," I said, though I doubted we had enough time in a single weekend to prove we'd be useful—especially to convince them of my ability. "If they uncover my relationship to Cody, we'll be dead in the water. They'll think my whole purpose is to clear his name."

"No way to find that out unless we tell them."

"Shouldn't you go above those detectives' heads and call the Marion County sheriff or whoever is in charge of the investigation and let him know you're interested in lending a hand?"

"Not until after we see the parents. If he's as backward as that man Greeley, we'll be shut down before we get anywhere."

We rode in silence for a few minutes, and then I put my hand on his arm. "Thanks for doing this. I know you have enough work at home."

"Of course I'd come," he said. "You have to know. One way or the other."

"I guess I do. Especially for Tawnia."

"No, for you."

I thought of the quilt and the antique lamp. Both should be mine and Tawnia's one day, complete with the memories they held. A longing for connection filled me. I'd always been attached to history, which was good given that I owned an antiques store, but this history belonged to me in a way nothing else could. Shannon was right. Not only did I want to know but I *needed* to know. Of Cody himself, I wasn't sure what to think. I didn't plan on having any kind of relationship with him, and yet he also held important memories.

The truck was slowing. "What are you doing?" I asked, as Shannon pulled over.

"Going to check the maps on my iPad to see if we can determine roughly where the Vandykes might live, given the general direction Cody gave us in the woods. There's not much out here. It's not even really a city. If we can get close enough, we'll be able to get the exact location from the neighbors." He paused for the space of two heartbeats. "But I also wanted to do this." He reached over and pulled me close, surprising me so I didn't have time to prepare myself for imprints before my hands hit the front of his shirt.

Fear. Worry. The overpowering urge to act, to save Autumn.

His emotions from the gas station had been strong enough to imprint on his shirt in the passion of the moment. I saw me as he did—brown hair cropped short, with dyed red highlights on top, slightly upturned nose, and my strange eyes. Perfect to him, though I knew they were set slightly too far apart for real beauty and their mismatched colors often turned people off. The imprint faded, and though I knew it would begin again, it wasn't uncomfortable enough to pull away. In fact, it was rather flattering.

His lips met mine, sending sparks that ignited fire in my veins. The world tilted as passion rolled through me. I had to admit that it had never felt like this with anyone else. Kissing

Shannon was like finding a new part of myself I hadn't known existed.

Then his lips left mine as he pulled me tighter. "You've got to learn to feel comfortable with a gun." His breath warmed my ear and made me want to kiss him again.

"I'm fine with a gun. I just don't want to shoot anyone."

He blew out a frustrated breath. "Not even someone who wants to shoot you?"

"Not even. Look, your gun got me shot the last time, and with my niece growing up, I have to be careful."

"You can raise kids with guns. I was raised with guns."

Goose bumps arose on my arms even inside my coat. We'd gone from talking about my niece to something far more important. I didn't know if I was ready. I'd been wanting a relationship, one I'd thought I'd found with my best friend, Jake, but my feelings for Shannon had trumped them, and I realized I'd only chosen Jake because it was easy. Because I trusted him. He knew me almost too well and accepted me exactly the way I was. He didn't ask too much. With Shannon, life would be a compromise. He would push me to be the best. Our relationship would require effort. I didn't really care how much work it took, and that scared me even more.

I kissed him again, slowly, and eased away.

He smiled. "I'm being a jerk, aren't I? About the guns."

"You're being you. You can't stop being a police officer."

"I guess I can't. Any more than you can stop being a flower child who hates shoes and refuses to use a microwave."

I laughed. "That's right."

"You know what?" His voice became suddenly grave.

"What?" I hoped he wasn't going to call it all off—us off—however nicely.

"I'd probably have starved by now if it weren't for my microwave."

I rolled my eyes. "You and half the world's population."

That easily we were back to normal, exchanging banter without the barbs it had contained during our early days together.

He reached under the seat and pulled out his iPad. "These emit radiation, you know. Just like that phone the department gave you."

"So does the sun." But that reminded me to turn off my location on the phone Shannon's department had gifted me. When it was on, not only could I find places I was looking for but Shannon and anyone in his precinct could find me. I hated feeling like someone was looking over my shoulder all the time.

"Ah, this might be it." Shannon pointed to the map on his iPad. "These houses are directly across the woods from Cody Beckett's unincorporated land. Seems a likely place for the house. Too bad I can't find an address listing for them."

"Maybe you can call your new buddy, Detective Greeley, and ask him for an address."

He laughed.

As Shannon drove to the location, I called Tawnia. My sister answered on the first ring, as though she'd been holding her phone and waiting for my call.

"Did you see him?" she asked.

"Hello to you too. Is the weather as gloomy there as it here? It's kind of cloudy. Looks like snow's coming."

"Autumn."

"Can you put Destiny on? I want to talk to her. Wait, never mind. The radiation from your phone probably isn't good for a baby." My niece, Destiny Emma Winn, was almost four months old, and I doted on her.

Shannon laughed out loud.

"Autumn Rain," Tawnia said, irritation beginning in her voice, "I'm going to strangle you. What's he like?"

My levity vanished. "He's like me. He reads imprints. And his eyes are like ours, just like we heard."

"What did he say when he saw you?"

"He told me to get off his property."

"What?"

"Well, I didn't tell him who I was, and I'm wearing one of those contacts you gave me, so he won't guess." Quickly I outlined the rest of the visit to Cody Beckett's, leaving out both the event at the gas station and the stabbed man. She'd only worry.

Tawnia made me repeat the bit about the quilt, and I knew she valued it as much as I did. Though she couldn't read imprints herself, she might be able to create a quilt with similar strong imprints like she had with the drawing she'd given me.

"So what's he like?" she asked.

"Just an old man. A little grumpy. He looks like he's been out in the sun a lot, and he's in good shape. Walks a lot. Apparently he owns a hundred acres here."

"What's his artwork like?"

As an artist herself, Tawnia would want to know that. "Big," I said. "He makes figures out of huge logs. Compelling but kind of strange. I took some pictures. I'll email them in a bit. But I warn you—they aren't like, well, normal art."

"Good."

"What?"

"I like the unusual."

If there was one thing my sister did *not* like it was the unusual. She was someone who planned and organized everything, including every cupboard in the kitchen she tried her best never to use.

"Speaking of unusual," I began.

"No, I haven't drawn any pictures. Not of a girl or of anything else."

Too bad. If she could draw a picture of Jenny Vandyke, maybe that would give us some clue where the girl was or who she might be with.

"Anyway," she went on, "I have a project due Monday. My group is pitching a huge company then. If we can get their advertising business, we'll all receive big bonuses. But Emma woke up with a bit of a fever today, and all I've been doing is holding her. She's miserable. If she's not better in the morning, I'm taking her to urgent care."

Immediately I was worried. Emma—I called her by her first name, Destiny—was the most important person in the world to me after my sister. "Look, you take plenty of those vitamins I gave you so she'll get them through your milk. And she's old enough for you to put a little vitamin C directly in your milk, if you express it."

"I'm having to anyway—to dump it. She's not eating very much."

"Well, keep trying."

We continued talking remedies all the way to what I hoped was the Vandykes' neighborhood, where Tawnia said suddenly, "What's he really like, Autumn?"

I was quiet a moment. "I don't know yet."

"Do you think he did it?"

Unfortunately, I had to answer. "He could have. I don't

have anything solid yet to go by, just a feeling that he's hiding something. Sorry."

"You don't need to be sorry. We knew the score going in. I just hoped . . . well, he was under the influence of drugs when we were conceived, and everyone seems to think he turned over a new leaf after that because he felt so terrible about what happened."

Everyone meaning Laina Drexler Walkling, our newly discovered biological grandmother on our mother's side. But she hadn't seen Cody in years, so she didn't really know anything about him now.

"Maybe he did change. We may turn up something else in our investigation that explains my feeling. We're going to see the girl's parents now." I waited for her usual spiel, warning me to be careful or begging me to let the police do their job, but she held true to her promise to trust me.

After my last case I'd decided to quit sleuthing altogether because I'd come close to losing both Tawnia and Destiny when my negligence had involved them in the case. Only her pleas, Shannon's understanding, and the suspicion against Cody Beckett had convinced me to try again. I still wasn't sure I would stay in the business. Problem was, I cared about people and I wanted to help them. It was the way I'd been raised.

Shannon was already outside the car questioning a woman who was walking her dog when I joined him. "You don't have the address?" the woman was saying. "If you're on the case, you should have it." She tugged on the leash to pull her collie back when he tried to sniff at my legs.

"I am a police detective, but I'm only helping my friend here. She's been engaged by an outside party to look into the matter."

"A private detective?" The woman stared at me with admiration, though it was hard to tell since she wore a heavy coat buttoned up over her chin and a knit hat pulled down over her ears and eyebrows. "It's about time. Those sheriff's deputies are getting nowhere on the case. Poor Gail is out of her mind with worry."

Shannon nodded in sympathy. "I imagine she is. So can you help us?"

"Oh, yes. The Vandykes live on the next street over. Second house from the end, across from the little neighborhood park. Huge flowerbeds, though they'll be covered in this crusty snow. You can't miss it."

I assumed she meant the Vandykes' house had huge flowerbeds, but she could have been talking about the park.

"Thank you," Shannon said.

We didn't speak as he drove to the house. Like all the others on the block, it was newly built, and also like all the other houses, earth tones were the color choice. But the Vandyke home was set back a little farther than the rest, and sure enough, there were sizable flowerbeds whose outlines were easily detectible under the snow. The sidewalks had been cleared, though I suspected not by the occupants. Who cared about snow when a child had gone missing?

We started up the walk, and I prepared myself for both rejection and acceptance. One would slam a door shut to our investigation, but the other would open me to the family's private grief. Both seemed equally poor outcomes.

My gloves and antique rings remained in my pocket, so I was ready to read imprints. I touched the doorknob before Shannon rang, but it held no feelings at all. I shook my head at him.

A woman in her early thirties opened the door. My age. She must have married early to have a fourteen-year-old daughter already. "May I help you?" she asked.

The fragile skin around her eyes was dark and swollen, and tiny red lines crisscrossed the whites of her eyes. This was a woman who wasn't getting any sleep and who had been worrying for too long. I'd planned to let Shannon do the talking so I could maintain an aloofness that would protect me during the reading, but who was I fooling? I was either in this or not, and now that I'd seen Jenny's mother, I knew I wanted to help her even more than I wanted to clear Cody.

"Are you Gail Vandyke?" I asked. At her nod, I continued, "My name is Autumn Rain. I've been hired to look into someone who has been connected to your daughter's disappearance. I can't tell you any more than that, but if you'd speak to us, maybe let us see Jenny's room, we might be able to help."

"For a price, I bet." Bitterness filled her voice, and I wondered how many investigators had contacted her and how many were crackpots who had an odd name like mine.

"No charge at all to you," I said.

Shannon pulled out his badge. "I'm a police detective with the Portland police. I'm helping Autumn, and we hope to be working with the local law enforcement on this. We've already been out to see Cody Beckett and have talked with several local deputies."

"Mr. Beckett didn't do this," Gail said, examining Shannon's badge. "He wouldn't hurt anyone."

Bile rose in my throat. Cody hadn't indicated that he knew the family; if he did, the possibility of his guilt increased. Most children are not abducted by people they don't know. "So you know Cody Beckett?"

"Oh, no. Not really. I'm involved in raising money for several local charities, and Mr. Beckett has always supported our causes. One of our board members commented to him once about his generosity, and he said he didn't have family and couldn't take it with him, so what was the point of putting it all in the bank?"

Cody a philanthropist? I had a hard time accepting that.

"He's never met Jenny?" Shannon asked.

She shook her head. "I've only met him twice myself when we went to his bank to collect his donations. He doesn't have a checkbook. He was very polite, not weird at all."

"What did you talk about?" I pressed.

"His art, mostly. I was asking questions. But we didn't talk about our families, if that's what you mean. Mr. Beckett rarely leaves his home. He won't even come to the appreciation dinners, and all his donations are anonymous. I know he's been in jail, but that was for attacking a man at a bar thirty years ago. I think the police are so hung up on him that they won't find any real leads."

I would have agreed, except I knew this connection to Jenny's mother made Cody more of a suspect than ever.

"Anyway, my husband talked to the mayor of Salem—he's a friend of ours—and he promised to urge the sheriff's office to look at all possibilities. We need to find out who was after my little girl and why." Gail's eyes widened. "The mayor didn't hire you, did he?"

I was about to deny any connection, but Shannon smiled. "I'm sorry. We can't divulge the name of our client, but I promise we will look at every angle. In fact, Autumn here has some abilities that we use quite often in Portland. She's an official consultant there."

Gail's eyes narrowed. "What kind of abilities?"

"I observe things," I said quickly. What was Shannon thinking? Most people ran away from me when they discovered what I claimed to be able to do. "I piece things together."

"Oh, well, come on in." Gail backed away from the door, inviting us into the entryway. "I'll answer your questions."

"Could I see her room while we talk?" To me the questions and answers were secondary. Obviously the sheriff's office had gotten nowhere with the information she'd given them, and I didn't pretend to be smarter than they were.

"It's upstairs, but let me call my husband first. He'll want to be here to meet you and to answer questions too."

Shannon and I exchanged a glance. Was she afraid to talk to us without her husband, or was she simply hoping he'd add something that would help us find Jenny? Shannon took out his phone, and I knew he was texting his partner in Portland so she could dig further into Kenyon Vandyke's background. Shannon had completed the usual checks on everyone involved in the disappearance before coming here, but Paige had a way of finding helpful facts that lurked under surface reports. If Gail was afraid to let us see Jenny's room without her husband, there might be something more to Mr. Vandyke's past.

As Gail spoke to her husband on the phone, I began work, walking into the adjoining sitting room to touch the knick-knacks on a nearby shelf, fingering a book, pretending to study or straighten several photographs.

"This is Jenny?" I asked, pointing to a large photograph on the wall of a young Gail with a baby in her arms.

New tears started in Gail's eyes, but she smiled as she joined me. "Yes. She was three months old."

"A beautiful baby. I have a niece who's not quite four months. She's twice that big already."

"Jenny was always petite."

Petite, unlike her mother. Some would call Gail pleasantly plump; most would have also called her striking. Though she didn't have her daughter's delicate build or her bright blue eyes, she did share the same beautiful long blond hair, and the features of her face were appealing.

Gail turned. "Come on. I'll show you her room. Kenyon will be here in a while."

I touched the frame of the photograph before following her back to the stairs in the entry way. I felt love. As huge and all encompassing as anything I'd ever experienced, though the imprint was obviously more than a decade old.

I adored my baby. I was so grateful for her and would do anything, sacrifice anything to raise and protect her. Yet I also felt an underlying current of worry.

How can I raise this child alone? The responsibility felt impossibly heavy.

I didn't care. Somehow I would manage. I'd give my life for her.

The imprint vanished, and nothing else followed. Was Gail having problems with her husband at the time of Jenny's birth or had she simply recognized that she would be the primary caregiver of that precious soul? That seemed to be a common feeling shared by new mothers. Tawnia often voiced feelings of inadequacy, and I had to remind her at least three times a week that she wasn't raising her baby alone, that she had her husband, Bret, and me to fill in any gaps.

There were more pictures going up the stairs, and since Gail's back was to us, I was able to touch all those within my reach. Nothing significant except on a picture of another baby—a boy this time. The same love, only now instead of inadequacy, there was confidence.

Gail had paused at the top of the stairs. "That's Kenyon Junior, our son. He's eight now. Our latest family picture is that one near the bottom of the stairs."

"It's a beautiful picture," I said. Unlike Jenny, the boy was chubby, and from the other photographs, I could see that he'd caught up to Jenny in height.

Gail gave me a tremulous smile and waited as I finished the climb. No more photograph touching for me. Shannon arched a brow, and I gave a quick shake of my head.

More photographs filled the upper hallway. "My husband likes to take photographs," Gail explained. "He even takes most of the family ones. He turns on the delay feature on his camera. See? This is one of us with our extended family. The older couple are my parents. Kenyon's parents have passed away, but these are his two siblings." She pointed to a couple near the edge.

"You don't have siblings?" Shannon asked, his eyes scanning all the photographs along the wall. I knew what he was looking for, but not one of the pictures was inappropriate. If Kenyon was abusive toward his daughter or had anything to do with her disappearance, there was no evidence of it here.

"I'm an only child."

"They're great photos," Shannon murmured.

Were they a comfort to her now, or a reminder that her daughter was missing?

Jenny's room was at the end of the hall. Decorated in pastel pinks, the spacious room obviously belonged to a little girl. A young girl. Even the posters on the walls were of cute animals and the occasional girl singer.

"You look surprised," Gail said to me.

I shrugged. "The fourteen-year-olds in my building aren't into pink or Disney pop stars."

"I know. Jenny has some friends like that, especially those who look older. But Jenny is a very young fourteen. She loves this room. We painted it together."

I nodded but wondered if Jenny really loved the room or if her mother only thought so. I'd had no secrets from Winter at fourteen, but we'd been inseparable after my mother died when I was only eleven.

I began to walk around while Shannon asked questions. "It doesn't look like she has a computer here. Do you have a family computer she uses?"

"Yes, the kids and I share one. Jenny uses it for school reports and Facebook. We have her password, and we approve all the friends she adds. The rule is that she must know them in person, and we have to meet them. The police took the computer. They still have it."

"Does she have email?"

"Yes, but she doesn't use it much. She has an iPod we got her for her birthday. She can text here in the house where we have wi-fi, so she uses that instead of email. She took it to school that day, or I'd let you see it."

"You mentioned she had Facebook. What about other social sites?"

"No, we blocked the other social networking sites. We didn't want to have to patrol more than one. All her friends use Facebook. They talk about school and family and their plans for the weekend. It's real innocent stuff. There's only one friend that I worry a little about, and we've been trying to have her over more. You know, influence her toward good."

"Does Jenny have a phone?"

"No. We decided that would wait until she was sixteen. Children spend way too much time on their phones. She borrows mine sometimes."

A picture of Jenny and two friends on a bookshelf drew my attention, and I let the conversation fade from my mind. Shannon would fill me in when we left. What was more important at the moment were the things Jenny might have felt but left unsaid.

I picked up the photograph, but it held only contentment and joy in friendship, with a tinge of envy toward one of the girls, who apparently had a new short skirt and leggings. The girl resembled Jenny's favorite singer.

Next to the picture was a bracelet with a large, heart-shaped charm and a key attached by a gold chain. A beautiful piece of costume jewelry, but besides contentment of ownership, Jenny hadn't felt strongly about it. The second imprint on the bracelet showed it had belonged to someone before Jenny—a woman named Cindy, who had been afraid of the man who'd given it to her. No apparent connection to Jenny, so it must have been purchased secondhand.

I let my hands trail over the rest of the items on the shelves, which was heavy on the knickknacks and sparse on the books. The dozen books she did have seemed to follow a princess theme—*Ella Enchanted, The Princess Academy, Cinderellis and the Glass Hill, The Land of Magic.* No vampires or werewolves here. Jenny loved these books, though, and the imprints told me she'd read them dozens of times.

Coming up with nothing but irrelevant imprints, I moved to the walk-in closet and from there to the daybed by the window, covered with dolls and stuffed animals. Finally, I reached the small vanity near the bed that sported a brush, lip glosses, a small figurine of a fairy with one broken wing, carefully glued, and drawers full of clips and elastic bands.

Once again I came up empty, except for the figurine, which held imprints from a month earlier.

A rush of disbelief and anger, followed almost immediately by quiet acceptance.

Silly boy thinks I don't know he did this, I thought, examining the glued wing. That's okay. I'm really too old for this fairy anyway, though Mom doesn't think so. I'll always love Kenken more than the statue, and I love it even more now.

This was followed by an imprint of Kenyon Junior playing in his sister's room uninvited.

I was holding the fairy carefully. Jenny loved it so much. With these wings it could fly. Wouldn't even need an airplane.

I threw it gently into the air, catching it. Horror spread through me when I missed.

Oh, no! Have to fix it. Don't want Jenny to get angry—and especially don't want her to cry.

The glue for my model airplane would work. There, good as new. You could hardly see the break.

I would still save up money and buy her a new fairy. I'm sorry, Jenny.

Earlier imprints testified of how much Jenny had loved the little statue when she was younger and how she'd told Kenyon never to touch it. I withdrew my finger, blinking away tears at how sweet it all was and how horrible that Jenny was now far away from her family, perhaps afraid and in danger. Maybe even dead.

"What is it?" Gail was standing beside me, though I hadn't heard her approach.

I met her gaze. "It's a beautiful little fairy."

"No," she said, shaking her head. "You've been touching everything. Downstairs, the pictures on the stairs. Everything in this room. What are you looking for? Are you some kind of psychic?"

I hated that label. "No," I said. "I can feel emotions on certain objects, and sometimes those scenes give me clues that help me find people."

"I see."

I could feel her skepticism, and I didn't blame her. Too bad I'd alienated her without finding anything of real value.

I waited for Shannon to confirm that the police in Portland used my talent, but before he spoke, Gail said, "What do you feel on that fairy?"

She wanted proof. Well, I could do that, though I didn't know if it would do any good. "Jenny loved this fairy and played with it all the time as a child."

"You could say that about any child's toy."

"Yeah, but Kenyon Junior—or Kenken, as Jenny thinks of him—came in here while she was gone. In the afternoon. He wanted to make the fairy fly, and he threw it in the air. He missed catching it, and a wing broke off. He fixed it with glue from his model airplane because he didn't want Jenny to be angry or cry. She was angry but only at first. She decided she loves Kenken more than she loves the fairy."

"Broken? What are you talking about?" Gail snatched up the figurine. "Oh, it is broken. But when—"

"A month ago. On a Friday." I saw dates of imprints in my mind as a calendar with a certain day or section highlighted. The more recent the imprint, the easier it was to pin it to a day and time.

"You must be making this up." Gail's gaze shifted between me and the figurine.

"She's not," said a voice from the doorway.

Startled, we all looked in that direction. I recognized Gail's husband from the photographs, though he was bigger and taller in person. Unlike Gail, his face held no beauty but there was kindness, and the gentle way his gaze rested on Gail told me he worshiped her.

"How do you know?" Gail asked.

Kenyon walked over and placed an arm around his wife. With the shifting of the light, I could see he'd spent time crying— probably as recently as on the way home.

"Kenken told me what he did. He asked if he could do extra chores to buy Jenny a new fairy."

Gail swayed against him. "Why didn't Jenny tell me? I knew how much it meant to her. I would have bought her a new one."

"She thinks she's too old for it now," I said. "She only keeps it because her brother broke it and cared enough to fix it all by himself."

Gail began to weep. "Oh, Jenny. Oh!" This last was drawn out in a keening wail. "I want this to be over. I want my baby back here in her room. Who would want to kidnap a sweet little girl?"

Kenyon's arms tightened around her. "We'll find her, sweetheart. We will!" I could hear a note of despair in his voice. Was it real or faked? I'd begun thinking maybe the father had something to do with her disappearance, but seeing him now, I was having second thoughts.

"Did you find anything here that will help?" Gail asked through her sobs.

I shook my head. "Not yet, but I haven't looked at everything."

"We heard they found her boot," Shannon said. "That is really our best bet. If they let us see it, Autumn might be able to identify who took her."

Kenyon's jaw hardened. "They'll let you see it. I'll talk to the mayor and make sure of that."

Gail's tears were falling more rapidly now, and she clung to her husband for support. Kenyon blinked back his own tears as he met Shannon's gaze. "I think she needs to lie down. If you'll wait a minute, I'll be back to answer any more questions you might have."

Shannon nodded, and we watched as Kenyon tenderly led his wife from the room, his bulk dwarfing her.

"He was not what I expected," I said.

"My thought exactly."

"So where does that leave us?"

"Without any suspect except Cody Beckett." I sighed. Back to square one.

"While you were doing your thing, Gail did wonder if there might be a request for a ransom. Apparently Kenyon came into some money a few years ago when his grandfather died. And he's more than just a friend to the mayor of Salem. They're actually related some generations back, the mayor's line being the more prominent."

"So he was the poor relative?"

"Before the money, apparently. Guess the grandfather was the intersection. Anyway, Kenyon works for the city as a manager over building roads. Not a bad job for someone who flunked out of engineering school."

"He seems very devoted to Gail." I scanned the room for

anything I might have missed. But despite what I'd said to Gail, there was little more to touch, except Jenny's shoes and maybe inside her closet. We'd come here, it seemed, only to put a nail in Cody's coffin.

"You really didn't find any useful imprints?" Shannon asked.

"Well, I get the sense that Jenny was a little frustrated that her mother didn't understand her wanting to grow up, but at the same time, Jenny really did love this room and she was very much a little girl. I didn't catch one imprint of her being hung up on a guy."

"That's unusual."

"I'm not saying she didn't have any secret crushes, but if she did, the feelings weren't strong enough to imprint here. Maybe if we checked her school locker, it'd be different, but if a boy is involved, I'd think something here would have imprinted as well."

"Unless some things have been removed."

"The report said that nothing here was missing, but I guess the parents could have missed some things. Maybe there are imprints on the computer."

Half-heartedly, I tested several more objects, but nothing important came to me. The closet also revealed nothing new.

"Let's go wait downstairs," Shannon said finally.

He was hoping I'd find something else to read, but Kenyon Vandyke met us in the hallway. "Sorry for taking so long."

"Can I use your bathroom?" It wasn't just a ploy. After the fifty-minute drive from Portland that morning and our two adventures, I really did need the break.

"Sure, there's one here, but the kids share it, so maybe you'd rather use the downstairs one."

"This will be fine." I'd never found good imprints in guest bathrooms.

Minutes later I joined the men in the entryway with no added information. I could scarcely ask Kenyon if I could check out his room and bathroom, which I wanted to do to rule him out completely.

"Look," Kenyon was saying, "I'll talk to the mayor. He'll see that you get a shot at the evidence. I see no reason why the sheriff's office shouldn't work with you. One more set of eyes."

"What about the FBI. Weren't they called in?" Shannon asked.

"Yes, and they came here, but they didn't find anything. I call them every day, and they're still following leads, but the local authorities care more. My wife has held fundraisers for them, and they know her."

"Mr. Vandyke," I said, "could I see your car keys?"

He blinked, his eyes blank. "Uh, sure. I guess." He reached into his pocket and passed them to me.

Car keys were a great imprint holder, as they were used so often, and especially keys owned by men, who were often more attached to their cars than most women. I was rewarded immediately with an imprint from less than an hour ago.

Worry. The need to hurry home to protect Gail. She was too fragile these days.

The imprint faded, followed by one several days ago.

I'll drive up and down all the streets again. Jenny had to be somewhere. Somehow I would find her and bring her back to Gail. Love spread through me at the thought of my wife and for Jenny.

This imprint was echoed by several similar ones spanning the entire two weeks Jenny had been missing. The last imprint on the keys was a much fainter one from earlier in the year when Kenyon had bought the new car.

Pride, excitement. Gail will go in the style she deserves.

Again I was enveloped with love for his wife. Swallowing with difficulty, I handed back the keys. "You've searched for her. For hours. Days."

Kenyon nodded. "Almost every day. Please, if you can do anything to find our girl."

"We'll do all we can." Shannon said.

I was glad he replied because I wasn't sure I could. The FBI and the sheriff's office had turned up nothing, not even enough evidence to arrest Cody, their prime suspect. Even if we found leads the others missed, we had probably come too late to save Jenny.

"Mr. Vandyke didn't do it," I told Shannon as we left the house. "No way. The imprints on the keys proved that."

"Good. One less suspect."

I didn't reply. "What is it?" Shannon asked. "You're glowering."

"We should have come sooner."

"There was that little thing about you recovering from a gunshot wound."

"Just a scratch."

Shannon grinned at our standard joke, but I was halfway serious. A flesh wound in my upper arm wouldn't normally have kept me away. No, the reason I hadn't come was that I didn't want to face Cody Beckett.

Shannon opened the passenger door to his truck so I could climb inside. "Look, Autumn, you are not responsible for solving every crime you hear about. You can't. You just do what you can. One after the other. It's hard to lose, hard when you can't make it in time, but it happens, as you already know. You can't dwell on the losses. You go on to the next case and pray it will turn out differently."

"Is that what you do?"

He nodded and shut the door.

I waited until he was seated beside me to ask, "What can we do that the FBI can't?"

He laughed, throwing back his head in genuine amusement.

"What?" I scowled.

"Since when did you ever trust anyone else to do a better job than you? I seem to remember pleading with you multiple times to let me do my job, only to have you beat me to it. Look, you've been here one day, and already you've eliminated the father as a suspect. That's more than the FBI and the deputies have been able to do in two weeks."

A smile tugged at my lips. "Okay, so get going already. That boot is waiting for me."

Chapter 5

ore than the boot was awaiting us at the Marion County sheriff's office in Salem. Not only were Detectives Greeley and Levine there but also the commander of the enforcement division himself.

An angry-looking Greeley led us directly to his superior's office. "Here they are. Finally."

"Thank you." With a nod, the commander dismissed Greeley, who gave us a hard stare before retreating.

"I'm Matt Huish," the commander said, coming around his large oak desk and extending his hand. He was about Shannon's height, though at least a decade older than Shannon's thirty-five. His brown hair had receded to the point where it was a thick half ring around the back of his head. He had a stern face, a solid build, and a stomach that showed perhaps a few too many good meals.

"I'm Detective Shannon Martin from the Portland Police Bureau," Shannon said, taking his hand. "This is Autumn Rain. She works as a consultant for my department."

"I know who you are," Commander Huish said. "My men tell me you're doing some investigating."

"For a private party," Shannon clarified. "But we will, of course, share any information we learn with you."

Since I'd put my gloves back on, I didn't mind shaking the commander's hand. Let him wonder why I kept them on. I hoped the subtle difference in the color of my eyes, despite the hazel contact, wasn't noticeable because I didn't want them contemplating my ulterior motives. All I wanted was the truth.

"Hello, Miss Rain." Commander Huish had brown eyes that reminded me of Kenyon Vandyke, though Huish's expression was one of business and tight control. Unlike Kenyon, he wouldn't willingly show us his softer side.

Huish released my hand as quickly as he'd offered it. "Information," he said, going back around his desk, letting the silence drag out.

Uh-oh, I thought. *He knows something.*

From the disgruntled expression on Shannon's face, I knew he'd reached the same conclusion. I normally celebrated when anyone put that look on Shannon's face, especially me, but I wasn't looking forward to what the commander would say now.

He had brown eyes. Why did I keep thinking about brown eyes?

"The interesting thing about information," Huish continued, his gaze on Shannon, "is that you find it everywhere. I, for instance, just had a nice chat with your police chief at the PPB."

"Oh? What did she have to say?" Without being asked, Shannon sat in one of the padded chairs in front of the desk, now appearing unconcerned. "She knew I was coming here to help Autumn with this case."

Huish indicated the other chair to me before seating himself behind the desk. "She didn't say much except that you're her best homicide detective and that you solve more cases than anyone else. Apparently, she'd trust you with her life."

Shannon's mouth curled in a half grin. "As I would her."

Huish smiled. "Even more interesting is what I learned about Miss Rain." The commander shifted his gaze to me, falling briefly to my gloved hands. "If what they say is true, maybe you *can* help us. The thing is, the Vandykes are relatives of the mayor here in Salem, and he wants this case solved by any means possible. In fact, I'd no sooner hung up with your chief when the mayor himself called and asked me to cooperate with you. I'm willing to do so, as long as you keep me in the loop and as long as this doesn't turn into a media fest."

Reading between the lines, this meant he knew about me and my so-called talent and was willing to suspend disbelief to please the mayor.

I could live with that. "Thank you," I said. "When can we see the evidence? The boot, in particular."

Huish's gaze dropped to a framed photograph near his computer monitor, his attention appearing to wander. A second later he was staring intently at me again, as though the lapse had never happened. "First," he said, "I'd like to know what, if anything, you've learned."

Shannon nodded at me, so I uncrossed my legs and began. "We know that Cody Beckett had nothing to do with the wounded man we found at his house. Or rather, he didn't stab the man, and he didn't know he was there. However, I can't verify whether he had dealings with the man before today. I asked Mr. Beckett if he knew him, and all he said was he seemed familiar."

"How do you know Beckett didn't stab the man and then stash him when you two appeared on his doorstep?"

I smiled, bracing myself. "From a towel. Usually soft goods don't have good imprints, except if you touch them during or directly after a traumatic event. Even then cloth simply doesn't retain imprints well." I was about to go on, as I tended to ramble when I'm nervous, but the amusement on Shannon's face stopped me.

"A towel." Huish's doubt was plain on his face. His gaze fell to the picture again, and I found myself curious to know who could bring that look of distraction to his stern face.

"We can't rule out Beckett for the kidnaping," Shannon added, "but we didn't find a single thing that confirms his involvement."

Except his self-loathing, feelings of guilt, and his prior connection with Mrs. Vandyke—not to mention the fury he'd shown upon discovering me in his bedroom. His heated reaction could simply be driven by the weight of suspicion, but there was always the possibility it might have root in Jenny's disappearance.

"There is something you should know," I said. "In case you don't already. Gail Vandyke has met Beckett at least twice during fundraising efforts. She says he didn't meet or know about her daughter, but she could be wrong."

Commander Huish steepled his hands on his desk. They were stubby hands, made for hard, no-nonsense work. "We are aware of this connection, which is why Mr. Beckett continues to be our main suspect. Unfortunately, he escaped while being brought in today for questioning."

Maybe that explained Greeley's foul mood. "What happened?" Shannon asked.

"Apparently he went to lock his cellar and then went around the back of it and into the woods before Detective Levine could stop him. We've got an arrest warrant out for him now."

My hands tightened on the arms of the chair. "Well, he didn't stab the man, but I do want to ask him more questions."

"We have a few questions for him ourselves." Huish's eyes drifted again to the photograph on his desk.

Shannon nodded. "Is he your only suspect?"

"We'll let you look at the file, but in a nutshell, yes, Cody Beckett is our main suspect. Mr. Vandyke is also a person of interest, but since we haven't found any solid evidence to support the idea, we haven't made that public."

"Kenyon Vandyke had nothing to do with the disappearance of his daughter." I couldn't help the frustration that crept into my voice.

Huish blinked. "What?"

"He's not responsible." Shannon leaned forward in his chair. "But that's all we know. We can't even clear the wife."

"It wasn't Gail." For the first time, irritation showed in Huish's voice, which I suppose was fair since I'd let my own frustration show. "I've known her for years. Or of her. Her life is her children and her charity work. The fact is, I don't even know for sure if Jenny was taken or if she took off by herself. While it doesn't seem Jenny would do something like this, there is no evidence of foul play, either."

"I doubt a child would plan to leave without taking something from her room," Shannon said.

Huish shrugged. "She could have met someone on the Internet who promised to take care of her. It's happened before."

"Maybe we could rule that out," Shannon said grimly, "if Autumn looked at the computer."

Huish sighed. "She could tell us about *that* computer, you mean. Assuming I believe this whole imprint thing. But what about Jenny's friends' computers or those at the school and the library?" Discouragement radiated from him, and for the first time I felt pity at the pressure he was under. He was caught between the mayor, the parents, and the public, and he had nothing to offer any of them.

"The boot might tell us more," I said. "It really would save us time if we could see the writeups of the interviews with her friends, and if you could call the school and clear us to look at her locker."

"We can do that." Huish opened a drawer and handed me a file from his desk. "This is a copy of all the information our department has gathered as well as everything the FBI has shared with us. You can take it with you, though I'll want it back."

He pushed the intercom button on his desk. "Stacy? Have Greeley bring in the evidence from the Vandyke case."

"Sure thing," came a crisp voice.

"Thank you."

Minutes ticked by as we sat in silence. Feeling hot in the stuffy room, I handed Shannon the police file and removed my gloves and coat, setting them over the back of my chair. Looked like we were going to be here awhile. Before I could retrieve the file from Shannon, his phone vibrated loud enough for all of us to hear.

He checked the caller ID. "If you'll excuse me. It's my partner."

Huish nodded as Shannon rose to his feet and took several steps to the other side of the small office. "So," Huish said to me as if we couldn't hear Shannon's every word, "how long have you been consulting with the police?"

"Just this year. It's been very . . . interesting."

"And dangerous, according to Detective Martin's chief."

"Sometimes." As he looked at the photograph again, I asked. "Your family?"

"Excuse me?"

"In the photograph."

"Oh, yes." He lifted it and turned it in my direction. "My wife and kids. It was taken about six months ago. My boys are in high school."

A laughing woman with long dark hair nestled against Huish's arms amidst a pile of fall leaves, a teenage boy on either side of them, one a few years older than the other. Huish was slightly thinner in the middle and quite handsome without the stern expression, though he had nowhere near his wife's beauty.

"You all look so happy."

He nodded. "It was a good day."

His fascination with the photo told me there was more he wasn't saying. Had his wife left him? Died? Well, it didn't have anything to do with my case.

What was taking Detective Sergeant Greeley so long? He was probably trying to show us who was boss, while every second that passed meant less chance we would find Jenny alive. I clenched my jaw.

"So were you able to ID the stabbing victim?" I asked Huish. "Is he from around here?"

"Unfortunately, not yet. He had no wallet or ID on him. We're running his fingerprints now. We can't rule out the fact that maybe he was Beckett's partner in Jenny's kidnaping. They may have had a falling out."

"Cody didn't stab him. I promise you, there's someone else involved."

Huish studied me, as though trying to see inside my head.

"Maybe," he said. "We'll know more once we process the evidence. Hopefully we'll find the weapon."

Greeley had still not appeared. This was beginning to go beyond ridiculous. He wouldn't be dragging his feet if *his* daughter were missing.

"Well, thanks, Paige," Shannon said across the room. "That might help. Sure, keep looking, if you have the time."

"Well?" I asked as he hung up.

"Nothing on Vandyke, but she did learn that this is Gail's second marriage."

Commander Huish folded his arms across his chest. "That's true. Gail was married before, right out of high school, but it turned out he was abusive, and she left him after only a few months. Got an annulment. We heard from the people we interviewed that no one was surprised when she later married Kenyon. Apparently, he always had a thing for her, even when they were in school."

"Wait a minute," I said. "How long had Gail's marriage been annulled before she married Vandyke?"

Huish opened a file on his desk. "Looks like about six months, but she'd left him long before. Takes months to annul a marriage. I'm not sure of the exact timeline, but they were living in Portland then. By the time the Vandykes moved back here, Jenny was already five or six years old."

All at once my fascination with brown eyes, coupled with the imprints on the picture in Gail's living room, made perfect sense. "Better get them down here," I said.

Huish's brow furrowed, his irritation back. He arose stiffly from his desk. "Why? We've asked them enough questions. They can't tell us anything else."

"They can tell us why they didn't feel it important to tell us Kenyon isn't Jenny's biological father."

"Why would you say that?" Huish asked, his voice becoming icy.

"Jenny has blue eyes, but both her parents and her brother have brown. Do you know the probability of two brown-eyed parents having a blue-eyed child?" Being curious about my own strange eyes, I'd researched eye color somewhat obsessively in my teens. "Brown eyes are dominant, and the odds aren't good."

Huish snorted. "It does happen, depending on what color the grandparents had. This isn't proof. I'm sure the Vandykes would have told us if there was any chance it might help find Jenny."

"That's not the only thing," I said. "There was an imprint on a photograph at the Vandyke home. Gail was worried about raising a baby alone. If Kenyon had been in her life then, there would have been some pictures with him and Gail and the baby. But those pictures don't start until somewhat later. Kenyon's rather obsessive about taking photos."

"Maybe he wasn't into photography then." Huish stopped short of rolling his eyes. "Look, I'm playing along with this whole imprint thing, but I'll tell you right now I think it's a bunch of baloney. I don't know what you pulled to get their cooperation in Portland, but you are definitely barking up the wrong tree here, and I won't have you upsetting people for attention. Maybe it's best if you two leave town."

Anger rushed through me. Shannon's jaw worked as he struggled for control, and it was only a question of which of us would blow first, though doing so would solve little.

Leaning forward, I grabbed the photograph of Huish's

family, determined to prove myself for Jenny's sake. The imprint came instantly from earlier today when Huish had held this picture in his own hands.

Wrenching sadness. Unending, all-consuming despair. When we'd taken this photograph we'd thought it was all behind us. Five years should have meant a cure, but a week later everything changed. After all we'd been through, the cancer was back and this time it wasn't responding to treatment. Janine had begun preparing to die. To leave me. I didn't know how I would go on without her. I couldn't even bring myself to tell the boys. Not that Mack would even care, with his head so full of drugs. If I didn't find a way to pay for a treatment program, he might be the one we lost first. But we had nothing left after the cancer treatments. I was losing everything I loved.

The photograph was pulled from my tightened grasp, and I could breathe again, could recognize that it wasn't me mourning Janine and Mack, but Commander Huish.

"Autumn?" Shannon bent to look into my eyes, the picture now in his hands. "You okay?"

I'd meant to find something to prove my ability to the commander or at least to alleviate his hostility, but using this kind of pain went against all my instincts. I slumped in my chair. If I hadn't already been sitting, I might have fallen.

"Why's she acting like this?" Huish demanded. "What's wrong?"

I lifted my gaze to meet his. "I'm sorry. I'm really sorry."

"Sorry about what? Make sense, would you, woman?"

I wasn't offended, not after what I'd seen. "I'm sorry about Janine. I'm sorry about the cancer coming back and that it hasn't responded to treatment. You need to tell the boys, though. They need as much time as possible to deal with losing their mother. And Mack, you have to do something about him now. Before it's too late."

The color seeped from Huish's face. "How did you . . . you couldn't know . . . we haven't told anyone. We've been going to Portland for her treatments."

I nodded. "Until last week, when you stopped."

"How could you . . . ?" Commander Huish looked around as though trying to find someone to blame. "Have you been snooping into my personal life?"

"No, it was this." Shannon set the photograph back on Huish's desk. "It was imprinted on the frame. Believe me, commander, we have no interest in your personal life unless it affects the case."

He was wrong. I cared. I was sorry for Janine, for Huish, and for their boys. It was all so senseless.

Huish reached for the photograph. "You're right," he said, his voice devoid of emotion. "My wife is dying, but no one except us and her doctors know yet. And her sister. When we took that photo, we hoped for good news, but she'd been having headaches. She suspected."

He sighed and punched the intercom. "Stacy, I need you to give the Vandykes a call. Tell them I need to see them right away." To me, he added, "We'll make sure to check out the first husband more thoroughly, but for now you can read what little we have on him in the file. I'm afraid it's not much more than I've already told you."

"Thank you," I said.

"You'd better be right about this."

I knew I was right, and that meant the suspect pool had widened. Besides, if Jenny's biological father was involved, she might still be alive.

A tap came on the door, and Huish, his rigid control reestablished, barked, "Come in!"

Greeley entered, an angry expression on his disagreeable face. "It's not there."

Huish's eyes narrowed. "What's not there?"

"The boot. It's missing from the evidence locker."

Huish stood. "No."

"Yes."

"Well, who took it?"

Greeley's face flushed. "Levine is tracking down the last person to sign it out, but we don't know yet. It might be with the feds."

"Find out," growled Huish. "I want it on my desk within the hour."

"Yes, commander." Greeley backed out the door, casting an accusing stare at us. In any other situation I might have laughed at his reaction, but the missing boot could mean the difference in whether or not we'd find Jenny.

"Oh, and Greeley," Huish said before the door closed, "any sign of Beckett?"

"Not yet. But we'll find him."

"We'd better." Huish's jaw worked.

"What about the computer?" I asked.

"I know the FBI did take that. I already sent someone to get it. They can ask about the boot when they get there." Greeley nodded at Huish and let the door close.

Shannon took out his card and passed it to the commander. "Here's my number. We'll wait to hear from you about the Vandykes. Meanwhile, we'll grab some lunch and go over this." He tapped the file tucked under his arm.

At Shannon's words, my stomach growled. We'd left

Portland in the morning, grabbing breakfast and eating it on the drive here, but that had been hours ago and I was starving. Problem was, I was particular about my food, and with all that was going on, taking time to find a decent organic restaurant couldn't be high on my list of priorities.

We were all the way to the door when Huish said, "I'd appreciate it if you wouldn't say anything about my wife's condition."

I inclined my head. "Of course not."

I walked in silence to Shannon's truck, contemplating our next move. I didn't know where Cody was, so talking to him was out, and with the evidence unavailable, Jenny's parents not yet here, and Jenny's file in our possession, there was nothing holding us to the sheriff's office for the time being.

I only hoped the missing boot didn't mean a bad cop or a leak in the department. If it did, we'd probably never find Jenny, and Cody would likely go to jail whether he was guilty or not.

Chapter 6

"Now what?" Shannon asked, opening his truck door for me.

"The hospital. If we're investigating Cody, we need to find out what that man was doing at his house. Since we're already here in Salem, we might as well stop by."

Shannon gave me a crooked grin. "I was hoping you'd say that."

"Oh? And I was hoping you'd insist on finding a good restaurant."

He laughed. "This isn't Portland with all its health weirdos."

"Are you calling me weird?"

He stepped away from the door, but instead of going around the truck, he reached in the back and brought out a small cooler from under a tarp. "Maybe I am, but I came prepared."

He set the cooler on my lap and shut the door. I opened it, almost weepy to see two whole wheat turkey clubs from Smokey's, the organic restaurant across from my antiques shop. No, not two but three sandwiches.

"Two for you," Shannon said with a grin. "But we'll have

to find a place for dinner later. Maybe Commander Huish can help us find something."

I'd nearly been shot, had read disturbing imprints, and suspected my biological father was hiding something serious, but suddenly the day was perfect. It always was with Smokey's.

"Thanks," I said.

Shannon shook his head. "It was for my own protection. I know what you're like when you're hungry."

"You're no picnic yourself." I busied myself with a sandwich, not wanting him to see how much I wanted to believe he knew me that well. But I wondered if his feelings for me would last, if maybe he'd grow tired of me stomping around barefooted most of the time and reading imprints. Did I care? I mean, women changed boyfriends all the time. Maybe I wasn't even ready to settle down. I'd thought I'd been ready with Jake, but my surprising feelings for Shannon had destroyed that notion. Maybe I was better at solving cases than maintaining a relationship.

Sighing internally, I opened Jenny's file with my free hand and began reading.

Shannon ate in silence while he drove, doing both with such finesse that I knew he'd done it many times.

"Listen to this," I said. "One of Jenny's friends says that Jenny was tired of her mom treating her like a baby. That's a motive for running away."

"Do any other friends corroborate the idea?"

"No. But she might have been closer to that girl."

Shannon shook his head. "We might have to talk to her."

I'd read half the file, eaten my first club, and made a good start into the second before we arrived at the hospital and entered their underground parking garage. I chugged down one of the drinks I'd bought at the gas station after the shooting and reluctantly tucked the remains of my second sandwich back into the cooler.

"He could still be in surgery," Shannon said before eating the last bite of his food.

I started for the elevator. "If he's awake, are they even going to let us talk to him?"

"Depends on how organized the sheriff's office is and what orders they've given to the hospital. My badge might be enough, but if we have trouble, we'll have to call Huish."

"Hey, it's you."

We looked to see Kirt, the clerk from the gas station, emerging from the elevator. He held hands with a pretty brown-haired woman, his right arm in a sling. Under his coat, I glimpsed a fresh change of clothes. His narrow face was relaxed, and the slightly unsteady way he walked told me he was under some heavy painkillers.

"These are the people who saved my life," Kirt said. To us he added, "This is Diana, my fiancée."

"Thank you so much," she gushed, her heart-shaped face coming alive. "I don't know what I'd do without Kirt. He's my whole life."

He smiled at her with a mildly patronizing expression, his profile stirring some memory in me I couldn't pinpoint. Probably something from when he'd been shot at the gas station.

"Aren't you supposed to be wheeled out of the hospital?" Shannon asked.

Kirt laughed. "Oh, I was treated in the emergency and released. Since we were here, we stopped in to visit Diana's friend who had a baby."

"Now I'm taking him right home to rest," Diana added.

"Good idea," I said.

"Well, thanks again." Kirt dipped his head to us.

Shannon nodded. "No problem." We stepped onto the elevator.

Inside the hospital, we learned our stabbing victim was out of surgery, and Shannon's badge was enough to get us in to see him, but the man still hadn't awakened.

"He might be in a coma," Lisa at the ICU desk told us. She was a grave woman with a narrow face and brown hair that was just beginning to go gray, and she spoke with the clipped tone of the very busy. "He really should be awake by now. All but one of the wounds were not severe and that one didn't take long to fix, but he'd lost a lot of blood before he got here. They gave him five pints of blood before and during surgery. We'll have to wait and see if he wakes at all. Poor thing. We don't even have a name for him."

"There was a lot of blood at Cody's place," I said in an undertone to Shannon, "but nowhere near that much. The attack definitely didn't happen there."

"The deputies will realize that soon, if they haven't already."

Down the hall, a bored-looking man in blue overalls was dragging a mop halfheartedly over the floor. He looked away when I met his gaze.

Raising his voice, Shannon spoke to the nurse. "What about his clothing? And any belongings? Do you have those?"

"The clothes were removed or cut off during surgery. The sheriff's office asked us to save them. I believe they're sending someone to pick up the bag." She leaned forward and said confidentially. "My coworker's cousin works for the sheriff's office, and he told her they're in an uproar there. So much going on.

They might have forgotten about it." Her brow furrowed. "Oh, wait. I bet that's why you're here—to get the clothes. The nurses were careful to touch them only while wearing gloves, so hopefully they'll lead you to his attacker. Come on, I'll show you where they are. We've locked them in a cupboard in his room." She glanced at a monitor. "Looks like a nurse is with him now. He's probably due to receive his next round of medication, but after we get his belongings, we can check to see if he's showing any signs of waking."

She motioned us to follow her down the hall that circled around the main desk. Rooms faced onto the hall, the walls and doors made of glass, with curtains for privacy. Our stabbing victim's room was only four doors down, just around the bend from the desk, and I wondered if that meant he was still critical. His curtains were pulled, obscuring our view.

The male nurse turned as we passed through the curtains, a needle in his hand. Lisa headed for the cupboard near the wall.

"Does he look close to waking?" she asked. "This officer needs to question him." She unlocked the cupboard door and removed a large, clear plastic bag.

"I don't believe so." The nurse had longish black hair and broad shoulders that barely fit inside his green scrubs. He turned back to the patient, but he fumbled as he neared the arm of the unconscious man. His syringe dropped to the floor and rolled under the bed.

"Why aren't you giving it to him in the IV?" Lisa asked.

The nurse shrugged. "Doctor's orders."

I didn't like the way the man wouldn't meet our gaze. "I'll get it." I dived under the bed and retrieved the syringe. I didn't make it to my feet before the imprint came.

Hurry, quick, give him the drug. He wouldn't be able to tell the police anything. Too bad it had to end this way. He'd been a good man but squeamish in the end. After all, money was money. It didn't matter if it was drugs or other cargo you had to move, if the price was right. He should have learned that by now. Had to do my job. Nice little bonus in it for me. Maybe when this was all over I'd take a vacation.

I staggered to my feet knowing the imprint was going to repeat, and I didn't want to experience again the disjointed reasoning of a man who was obviously a paid killer. No time to alert Shannon to pull his gun, but close combat was my department anyway. I could handle it.

"Here." I lifted the syringe, but instead of placing it into the nurse's outstretched hand, I plunged its needle deep into his arm. I didn't intend to push in the medication, but this at least would keep him from murdering the man in the bed.

"What are you—" Lisa began.

The intruder pulled out the needle and launched himself toward the bed. I kicked his leg to stop him, my blow landing on his knee. His next lunge was at me. I threw a jab and tried to spin out of the way, but he was faster than I'd anticipated for his bulk. He threw his arm around my neck, dragging my body to him, using me as a shield.

"Step away from her." Shannon had his gun out, pointing it at the man.

"I don't think so. She's my ticket out of here." The man glanced at the syringe that had fallen again, obviously weighing the odds of completing his mission. If he tried, I'd give him an elbow and kick his knee again. I trained several times a week with people a lot better at taekwondo than I was, and though he had the advantage of weight and reach, I was faster and strong for my size. I wouldn't make the mistake of underestimating him again.

His grip on my neck tightened for an instant as he arched his body, pulling something from under his shirt. The hard feel of a barrel against my back told me what it was.

"Give her that sack and move away from the door," he ordered. "Or I'll shoot."

Lisa looked at Shannon, who nodded calmly. With faltering steps, she came toward me, shoving the bag of bloodied clothes into my arms before skittering to the other side of the bed. Shannon edged slowly away from the door, his head moving back and forth slowly. I didn't know what he was trying to convey, but I knew if I left this room with the gunman, I probably wouldn't live to see Shannon or my sister again.

"Don't even think about shooting him," Shannon said as my captor's gaze went to the bed. "Or rather, go ahead. It will give me the perfect opening to shoot you."

"Put down your gun, or I'll kill her."

"No. If you do shoot her, you won't make it out of here alive."

I knew Shannon was making the best choice he could. If he put down his gun, the man in the bed was dead—and probably Lisa, Shannon, and me into the bargain. This man had come here with murder in mind, and unlike at the gas station where Shannon had put down his gun in the hope of negotiation, there would be none here, and I didn't have a gun to back him up. Neither was I free to throw something, as I had then. Still, it was odd hearing Shannon talk so calmly about the man shooting me.

With a grunt of frustration, the gunman started toward the door, dragging me with him, keeping his body lowered and behind mine. I wanted to struggle, but my training made me wait for the right opportunity. At least he was moving with difficulty, after my blow to his knee.

I went over and over it in my head. I had to hurt him enough that I could be free to drop to the ground, giving Shannon a clear shot. I didn't think the man would shoot me before he'd cleared the door and maybe the ICU altogether, but I could be wrong.

The opportunity came when he pulled me through the curtain and reached for the door.

Dropping the bag of clothes, I struck. Elbow to stomach, foot to knee.

"Ow!" He struggled to hold me, but I gained enough purchase to worm free. He brought up the gun. My stomach dropped. Thankfully my next kick landed on his arm, and though he maintained his hold on the gun, it was no longer in position to shoot me. By that time Shannon was through the curtain, ready to fire.

The gunman leapt for the door, clearing it as he let off a wild shot. Determined to keep hold of the evidence, I swooped up the bag of clothes and hurried after him, only to dive behind a cart in the hallway as another volley of shots followed. More shots than from just one gun, though behind me Shannon wasn't shooting. All around us people screamed and darted for cover.

I spied the man who'd been cleaning the floor running toward our perp, who hobbled on his hurt knee. He also carried a gun. They rounded the bend near the desk, the fake janitor supporting his friend. Shannon and I ran after them.

They fired off more shots at the entrance of the ICU, but by the time we'd reached the doors, they'd vanished.

"In there," said a security man sprawled on the floor, holding his hand over a wound on his leg, pain etched on his face. "The stairs."

We followed. Sure enough, we heard pounding on the steps, though they were already out of sight. We vaulted after them, taking multiple stairs at once, Shannon slightly ahead. We heard a scream below and a voice shouting for someone to hurry. Then everything fell quiet.

We reached the lowest floor and slammed through the door into the parking garage. A couple, an older man pushing a woman in a wheelchair, and a young mother with a baby on her hip gaped at us.

"Police," Shannon shouted. "Which way did they go?"

The young mother dragged her gaze from his gun. "That way." The elevator arrived and with a frightened glance at me, the young mother jumped inside, followed quickly by the others.

"Stay here," Shannon said to me. A good idea, one I actually would have agreed to if a gray van hadn't come careening from the opposite way our gunmen had gone, screeching to a stop not ten yards away.

"Move!" Shannon ordered, grabbing my hand and not giving me a choice.

As several men piled from the van, we ducked behind a row of cars, hunched over and still running. The bullets began flying, one ricocheting much too close to my head for comfort. Shannon fired over his shoulder, miraculously hitting one of the men.

More shots, this time from the other direction. My heart sank. The gunmen we'd followed from inside the hospital were coming back, obviously planning to meet up with their associates for a clean get away.

Shannon fired in their direction, and I was pleased to see

two shadows disappear behind some cars. If only we could keep them there until the police arrived. Someone must have called them by now. Shannon aimed more shots at the guys from the van, who'd now taken refuge behind more parked cars.

Why wasn't the van going forward to pick up the men we'd been chasing now that they'd made themselves known? I dared peek out from behind the Chrysler I was using for cover, only to be rewarded by several more shots from both directions.

Shannon pulled me down, slapping another magazine into his Glock. "Go that way and cut over," he said, motioning behind us. "I'll cover you and follow."

"They'll get away."

"They aren't even trying. We've seen their faces, and since it seems no one has bothered yet to call the police, maybe they've decided to eliminate a few witnesses."

I was about to protest before I remembered the gunman's willingness to shoot his own unconscious colleague. But risking capture this way meant something big was going on. Something more serious even than a missing young girl.

"Drugs," I said, remembering the imprint from the fake nurse's syringe. Moving drugs or other cargo at a price was all he cared about.

"Probably. Now go!"

They were shooting again. I heard a shout from somewhere else in the parking lot and a car door slamming. I hoped whoever it was stayed down. These guys didn't care who they hurt.

Shannon covered me as I scurried in the direction he'd indicated. Heart pounding, I made it to a row of cars. Now it was Shannon's turn, but there was no one to cover him. For once I wished I'd let Shannon give me a new gun. He let off a volley of shots as he ran toward me. I waited, holding my breath for him to suddenly arch and fall.

Where were the police? Or the sheriff's deputies? Where was that arrogant Greeley when you needed him?

Shannon made it, but already I could see the gunmen moving, too, angling toward us. We could run again, but there was no exit in that direction and eventually we'd be trapped.

"We need to draw them over. I don't have much ammunition left." Shannon handed me his backup pistol. "When they come looking for us, you'll have to shoot."

I took the gun.

"Come on. Before they get closer." Closer meaning more accurate. I'd been shooting with Shannon enough times to know that.

Tawnia would hate to see me now. I wondered if she was pacing her kitchen with a sick Destiny or if she'd taken the baby to a doctor.

Funny how the brain worked when you faced death.

We ran to the next row of cars, saving our bullets. The drug dealers didn't have such compunction. Their rounds dug into the cars around us, and idly I wondered how much damage they were causing. Another disconnect. I needed to focus.

"Maybe we should separate," I said, crouching close to a front bumper.

"I'm not leaving you." His stubbornness was showing again, but since my martial arts training wasn't helpful against gunfire, I had to admit this time it was in my favor.

"I shouldn't have read that imprint or at least not acted on it. Maybe whatever he had in that needle wouldn't have killed the guy right away."

"I bet it would have. He's on the verge of death as it is.

If you hadn't read that imprint, that guy would have gotten away with killing him, and at the moment he's our only lead."

"A lead who can't talk. But what does this have to do with Jenny?"

"I don't know." The bullets had stopped, and Shannon peeked out from our cover. "They're circling around. They'll be close enough to pick off in a moment."

His confidence was amazing. We were outnumbered and outgunned, and he was planning to pick them off one by one. And probably to capture at least one or two thugs relatively uninjured so he could question them. The idiot. No wonder I was so attracted to him.

The least I could do was help him. I was a better shot than I should be for the novice I was, as I seemed to have a natural talent at the target range, but my reluctance to hit a real person could hinder my ability now. I'd be much more comfortable punching them.

A flurry of shots slammed into the car we crouched behind. Uh-oh. They'd found us.

I wanted to tell Shannon I was sorry for delaying things between us. I'd known how he felt about me for a long time, but I'd clung to my relationship with Jake because he was safe and a known factor. Shannon irritated me, made me crazy, but he also made my world spin.

Now in all likelihood I was going to lose my chance with him because I'd dragged him into my past. If Cody Beckett were standing in front of me now, I'd strangle him myself.

More shots pierced the air, this time closer. A lump formed in my throat. Then tires squealed on the pavement. Doors slammed. We heard shouting.

Now what? I thought.

Chapter 7

The shouting grew louder, now coming from a bull-horn. "Police! Put down your weapons! I repeat, put down your weapons!"

Daring a peek, I saw at least two police cars. "Finally." I sagged to the ground.

"What? You were never happy to see me when I came rushing in to save you." Shannon eased next to me until our arms were touching.

"That's because I usually wasn't happy to see you. You were too annoying." I was lying. Those times I'd been very happy to see him, even if I'd never let it show.

We heard more shots and squealing tires. We climbed to our knees to see what was going on.

A huge ball of flame erupted where once there'd been a police car. The van crashed through it and skidded around the corner, heading toward the exit. Moments later we heard a similar explosion.

Shannon shook his head. "I don't believe it."

"What was that?"

"I don't know. Something with a lot of juice. They obviously came prepared to fight their way out. They had to know the police wouldn't expect it."

"This is big, then."

He nodded. "Really big."

Of course it was. I never seemed to do anything small these days. "I need to talk to Cody, find out if he's involved."

"I thought you said he wasn't."

"No, I said he didn't stab the man. He's guilty over something, and maybe it's not just about my birth mother. He's hiding something."

"The Salem police will handle this. We're here only to see if he's involved with Jenny."

I shook my head, dusting off my hands on my now dirty pants. At least they were black so maybe it wouldn't be too noticeable. "I need to know if he's involved in anything else. We follow any leads we find."

Shannon climbed to his feet, regarding me intently. "Okay," he conceded.

"Put down your weapons and put your hands up!" came a shout from a police officer heading our way.

It took us a full thirty seconds to realize he was talking to us. He had his gun drawn, and two more officers, using cars as cover, had their weapons trained on us as well.

Shannon bent over and put his gun on the ground. "I'm a police officer," he called. "I was chasing those guys."

"More like you were about to become their fish bait," the officer said. "You too, miss. Put it down."

I sighed and laid down the gun. Here we went again, from being the good guys to suspects.

"They're okay," came another voice from farther away. "They're with us." I looked up to see Detective Sergeant Greeley striding our way. He had his ID out to show the officers, though he was still wearing his sheriff's deputy uniform. "We're working a case together."

We were making progress if he was vouching for us with the local police instead of letting them cuff us just for the joy of watching us squirm. I smiled at him.

He didn't return the gesture, but his partner, Levine, did. It was a flirty, shy kind of smile that for some reason reminded me of Deputy Barney Fife in the black-and-white reruns of the *Andy Griffith Show*, though his face, for all its plainness, was more appealing.

"Do you want to tell us what's going on?" Greeley asked.

"We came to see the stabbing victim and found one of those guys trying to give him a drug," I said. "We didn't know they had backup down here."

"You think you can ID any of them?" Greeley's tone doubted that we had enough intelligence.

"Oh, yeah. At least two of them." I glanced at Shannon, who nodded.

"I hit one," Shannon added.

Greeley picked up the Glock, sniffing it. "With this?"

"Yeah."

"We'll have to confiscate it until the scene's been processed."

Shannon sighed. "I know."

Greeley sniffed the other gun. "This one hasn't been fired."

"That's hers," Shannon said, stretching the truth. "If you're taking mine, I'll need a loaner."

"Trouble does seem to follow you." Greeley handed me the gun.

I put it in my coat pocket. "You have a permit for a concealed weapon, I expect." Greeley sounded almost hopeful at the idea of arresting me.

"Of course."

He gave me a smile without any real warmth. "Good."

Levine looked at Greeley. "I'd better go make sure the victim is secure. Don't want them trying anything else."

"I have two of my men there already," said the police officer in charge.

Levine shrugged. "It's probably not necessary now."

"It is necessary," I said. "They tried to kill him so he wouldn't tell about the drugs. If it's that important, they'll probably try again."

All the men stared at me.

"Did you get that from ah—what did the commander call it—an imprint?" Greeley asked, his lip curling.

"Yes." I lifted my chin, daring him to challenge me. "From the needle they were going to inject him with."

"That's great!" Levine shifted from foot to foot, apparently having no idea it made him look like an excited little boy. "Did you get anything more?"

I shook my head.

"But couldn't you touch our John Doe?" Levine's brow creased. "You know, to see who stabbed him?"

"It doesn't work with people. Only with objects."

He looked disappointed. "Well, that's tough. But it's sure good to have your insight anyway. We'll have to follow up on it."

Did he just wink at me? I glanced at Shannon, whose face showed annoyance. Yep, Barney Fife, AKA Detective Levine, had winked at me. I would have laughed, but he was too nice. You didn't hurt the awkward, shy boy next door.

Levine leaned toward the lead police officer. "She's sort of a psychic."

"You'd better get going," Greeley told Levine pointedly. "Make sure you talk to hospital security. I'll go to the station with these two and see if they can identify the suspects."

"Okay, sergeant. I'll hurry back as soon as I have our John Doe secure."

"Make sure to bring back his clothes."

Levine snapped his fingers and pointed at Greeley. "Right. That's why we came." He strode away, swaggering slightly.

Greeley frowned as he watched his partner leave. As the detective sergeant over the criminal investigations unit, I wondered if he'd assigned himself Levine because no one else liked him. For my part, I'd rather deal with Levine's awkward eagerness than with the irritable Greeley.

"We'll need our own detectives to take their statements," the police officer told Greeley, motioning to us. "This happened in our city, not in your jurisdiction."

"Of course. Send them over. Oh, and we'd appreciate it if you'd keep officers outside our John Doe's room until I can send more deputies here. Tell them not to let anyone in the room with him except those cleared by hospital security. My partner will talk to your officers, but I'm sure they'd rather hear it from you."

He nodded. "Will do."

I barely paid attention, my thoughts now on the stabbing victim's clothes. Where had I dropped the bag? I remembered letting go of it in the room when I'd kicked free of the gunman and picking it up again, thinking I had to protect the evidence, but I didn't have it now.

"We'll meet you at your office," I told Greeley. I couldn't

leave the clothes behind, and I wasn't in the mood to listen to a tirade about losing evidence. Under fire, it could happen to anyone. Besides, I wanted a look at those clothes before I handed them over.

"It has to be now," Greeley said. "The commander has the Vandykes there. He wants to talk to you about them. He wants your input."

"We'll be there," Shannon said.

I started out in front of him, retracing our wild flight. Shannon jogged to keep up with me. "The truck's that way. I think." He jerked his head to the right.

By now I was so turned around I had no idea where the truck was parked, but it really made no difference. I had to find the bag. "I dropped something."

Shannon followed me without asking questions. Another thing I liked about the man. When we reached the cars where we'd first taken cover, I found the bag of clothes, the blood stains plainly visible through the clear plastic. No wonder the young mother had looked so frightened when she'd glanced at me.

"You managed to bring these?" Shannon picked up the bag.

"We'll turn them in, but first I need to see if there's an imprint."

He gave me a crooked smile. "Just don't leave fingerprints."

"I won't."

We made our way back to the truck, casting uneasy glances around to see if we were being watched. I told myself we weren't doing anything wrong with the clothes, but I wondered if we were breaking the chain of evidence and if that would prevent the man's attacker from being prosecuted. Yet Cody was on the run, and if he was somehow connected, I needed to know. There was a chance he was involved in something besides Jenny's abduction, and if I discovered what, it might give us a lead to her as well.

If we weren't already too late.

Miraculously, no bullets had hit Shannon's blue truck. It was some distance away from the shooting scene, but many of the cars around his hadn't been as lucky. That reminded me of the gun in my pocket. "Here, take this. Why did you tell them it was mine?"

He bent to replace it in his ankle holster, where he always kept his backup. "So they'd lend me a gun to replace my other one while we're here. With all that's been going on today, I don't want to be caught without a backup."

That I could understand. We'd come to start one investigation and had stumbled onto a completely different one.

Shannon opened my door before going around to his side. But he didn't start the engine. "Better do that now," he said, indicating the clothes. "That way we're close to the hospital in case anything happens." He smiled but the amusement didn't reach his eyes.

"I'll be okay."

Opening the drawstrings on the bag, I contemplated the clothing. What to touch first? Having been involved in a crime didn't mean for sure anything here would hold an imprint. Even people being stabbed didn't necessarily imprint emotions on their clothing. Now, if they'd been holding something in their hands at the time, or fingering something as they lay dying, they would most certainly imprint on the object.

I shivered, not appreciating the scenes in my head. Gingerly, I put my hand inside and hovered over the coat. Still no imprint, and I hadn't expected one since nothing had registered on it at Cody's house. Next, the man's dress pants. Those emitted the faintest tingle, so I touched them with the knuckle of my finger, avoiding the blood. Nothing but a weak impression of satisfaction at the fit. The imprint was so faint I might be imagining it.

The blue button-down dress shirt contained nothing. But already I could feel my fingers buzzing as they neared the white undershirt. Too bad I couldn't tell if the imprint would be bad or good. Not that it really mattered. I had to know.

Fear fell heavy on my shoulders. Had he stabbed me? Why didn't I feel pain? My hands groped at my shirt, coming away wet. Then pain rushed out at me. Oh, the pain! I shook with the onslaught.

Not my pain. But the imprint was so powerful the distinction made little difference as the imprint continued.

"Where?" the man screamed in my face. "Where? Tell me, or I'll gut you."

I'd known he was capable of violence. You had to be in this business. I was. The people I worked with were.

No, not me. It was John Doe who worked with those kinds of people. The part of me that was Autumn clung to that thought, trying to keep us separate. It was the only guard against the pain in my chest.

Oh, the pain.

"Where?" the man repeated. His knife came closer.

The Autumn me knew him, even without his baseball cap.

"It wasn't my fault!" I sobbed, my voice unrecognizable. "I swear I'm telling the truth. If they did it, they didn't tell me. I tried to talk them out of it."

"Not hard enough. Where can I find them?"

"They'll kill me," I moaned.

"So will I."

Even with the knife in his hand, my attacker was less frightening than they were. There was too much money involved, and money was all they lived for. "I can't."

The man screamed in frustration. "You will!" Pain shuddered through my body as he thrust the knife into me again. Intense pain. Blackness eating at my vision. I was falling. Falling. I never seemed to hit the ground.

"I will find out," the man grated, his face blurring in my vision. "I know about your cousin. Maybe he'll tell me what I want to know."

What had I done? Why had I ever gotten involved? I should have known so much money would have a price. Yet even if I got out of this alive, I didn't know if I would stop. Money was an addiction. I needed it as much as those pills I took to stay on top of things.

At last, the blackness came.

"Autumn?" Shannon was holding my hand, rubbing his thumb gently in my palm.

I took a breath, expecting agony in my chest, but the pain was gone. Not my pain. John Doe's. I could make the distinction better now that I was no longer in contact with the undershirt. With great effort, I forced open my eyes.

"You were jerking," Shannon said. "Then I think you blacked out for a second. Are you feeling okay now?"

I nodded. "But on the whole I think I'd rather be shot than knifed." Knifing was up close and personal. More frightening.

Shadow flared in Shannon's eyes. "I'm sorry you had to go through that."

I lowered my eyelashes so he couldn't see how terrifying the experience had been. "If it'd really been me, I think I could have gotten away." The right kick would have done a lot.

"Probably."

"Lot harder to escape a gun."

"So?" he prompted.

I wanted to hit him over the head, but he was right. We had to go on with the case. "I don't know who John Doe is, but I know who knifed him."

Chapter 8

There were no imprints on John Doe's shoes or socks. Shannon used the plastic gloves he seemed to carry in bulk to search all the pockets, but there were no personal items except a short shopping list—yogurt, juice, chocolate bars, a comb. No wallet or keys, and I wondered if his attacker had taken both.

We'd have to tell Commander Huish, and he was either going to be excited about the break in one of his cases or he was going to put me in jail for tampering with evidence. It was a chance I had to take.

Shannon started the engine. We found Greeley waiting for us at the entrance. Motioning impatiently for us to follow him, he jumped inside his patrol car and drove off.

"Not very trusting, is he?" I reached for Jenny's file, but before I could open it, my phone rang.

"Hi, sis," I said into it. "How's Destiny?"

"She seems to be feeling a bit better. She finally let me put her down for a nap. I was hoping to get my project finished—I mean, if I can't get this done at home, they'll start making me come in—but instead I drew something else. Something weird."

"What?" I hoped it wasn't a shoot-out in a hospital parking garage.

"A woman and a man sitting around a table with another man, a balding guy, and she's thinking of a woman in bed holding a baby. You know, it's like a cartoon thought bubble. Nothing like I usually draw. So I got to thinking it was probably the one clue you needed and if I didn't get it to you, you'd end up locked in a crate in the middle of the ocean somewhere, and Bret and I would lose our jobs trying to find you, and we'd have to sell the house and go live with my parents in Kansas, and Emma would miss you so much she'd end up in the hospital even sicker."

"Tawnia," I said. She sometimes went off on outlandish fantasies like this, though usually they were more humorous.

"I know. It's because I haven't slept. Anyway, I'm going to email it to your phone. I'll scan it in and send it so you'll get better detail. Maybe it has something to do with your case."

Her strange drawings usually did. "The bald man could be the commander here."

"He is wearing a uniform."

The description of her picture made perfect sense to me. The Vandykes were talking to Commander Huish, and Gail was thinking about having Jenny and how she raised her alone before Kenyon came into the picture. I didn't think it would help the case, but I was too grateful Tawnia hadn't drawn me dodging bullets or in that hospital room with a gun in my back to tell her I didn't need it.

"Thanks," I said. "And kiss the baby for me when she wakes."

I related the conversation to Shannon, who nodded thoughtfully. "Her drawings usually give us some clue, but the imprint on that picture at the Vandykes' was ahead of her on this."

"Hopefully, the Vandykes have come clean with the commander."

"Then what does he want us for?"

"Maybe he's found the boot." I ran my finger along the edge of Jenny's photograph in the file on my lap. The file told me nothing new except for the friend's comment about Jenny's frustration at being treated like a little kid. But had Jenny been frustrated enough to run away? Maybe her computer and her boot would tell me.

"What if they can't find the boot?"

Shannon took his eyes off the road, meeting mine briefly. "That would mean we have a dirty cop."

"My bet's on Greeley. He rubs me the wrong way."

Shannon laughed. "Me too, but I doubt he's dirty. He's too dedicated."

"Could be for show."

"Could be. But for putting up with Levine, he deserves a medal. Now that's one annoying guy."

I grinned. "Aw, I think he's kind of cute. Well, in an awkward, pitiful sort of way."

"You always did like the underdog."

"So what does that say about my liking you?" We both laughed.

"If there is a problem here," Shannon added, "it could be anyone. They have at least a dozen more officers. They're responsible for large sections of unincorporated territory."

We were coming up on the sheriff's office, so I flipped to

the last page in Jenny's file to reread the last few paragraphs. Nothing screamed out at me.

"Here," I said, placing the file next to him. "I just don't see anything that helps. Maybe you can find something I've missed."

"I doubt it, or they would have found her by now. I mainly wanted the file to see if there were any noticeable gaps."

"Like the gap about Jenny's biological father."

"Yeah. Like that."

He killed the engine and picked up the file. "Well, here we go again. Are you going to take in the clothes, or should I?"

"You do it." I didn't want to explain to Commander Huish how they came into my possession. I'd have enough on my hands defending my reasoning for touching them. Was it too much to hope that he'd be grateful for my information?

Inside, we were checked through security, and Detective Greeley led us to a large room where half a dozen officers sat at their desks. Commander Huish was inside his office at the far end, but when Greeley knocked, he hurriedly stood and met us outside, his eyes going briefly to my bare hands.

I understood as clearly as if he'd spoken: he didn't want me near any of his personal belongings. I couldn't blame him.

"Good. You're here," he said. "Come with me."

He hurried across the open desk area to stand outside a room with one-way glass. Inside, the Vandykes sat at a table, soft drinks in front of them. Kenyon had his arm around Gail, comforting her.

"They admit Kenyon isn't Jenny's father," Huish said, "but they don't see what it has to do with her going missing."

"They don't think the father might have taken her?" Shannon asked.

"Gail says that's impossible."

"Did she tell you who the father is?" I asked.

Huish blinked slowly. "I assumed it was her ex-husband."

"You said he was long out of the picture by the time the marriage was annulled, so maybe there's someone else." I studied the couple. Gail had recovered her composure and was sipping her soda, Kenyon eyeing her watchfully.

Huish shook his head. "Gail doesn't strike me as a woman who would have a child with a man she wasn't committed to." His gaze met mine. "Still, she does seem to be hiding something, and it could be the identity of Jenny's father. We talked about you, and they seem to have some measure of trust in you. I'd like you to talk to them."

"Maybe they left imprints on the soda cans," Shannon said.

I shrugged. "I can try. But she's only touched it once that I've seen, and she's calm now, so unless she really values the can or is really good at hiding her emotions, I doubt it will have an imprint."

Huish frowned at the couple through the glass. "Anything you can tell us would be helpful." He reached for the doorknob.

"Before we go in there, I need to give you this." Shannon reached under his coat where he'd stashed the bag of clothes. "These were dropped by the perp who stole them from the hospital when he tried to off your John Doe. We thought it best to bring them back here."

"Why didn't you tell me you had them?" Greeley growled, his mean little eyes glittering.

"Must have slipped my mind." Shannon gave him an empty smile.

Huish took the bag and motioned to a man at the nearest desk. "Collins, these belong to the stabbing victim from

Beckett's house. You and your partner see that they get to processing."

"Will do." The deputy jumped up, grabbed the bag, and strode from the room, followed by another man.

"Autumn discovered something interesting on one of the items," Shannon added a bit belatedly.

Huish stared at us, his eyes widening. "You opened the bag? You contaminated my evidence?"

"We didn't contaminate anything. Or at least not enough to matter. Autumn only briefly touched them with the tip of her knuckle. She discovered some very important information."

"What?" Greeley shot. "John Doe's identity?"

I shook my head. "No, but that man at the gas station this morning, the guy who shot the clerk? He's the one who stabbed your John Doe."

Huish blinked. "You're sure? The two crimes seem in no way related."

"I'm sure."

"Where did it happen?" Huish asked. "If we could find the original crime scene, we could gather more evidence. Maybe retrieve the knife."

"A house, I think. Maybe the victim's. I didn't recognize the place." Not saying much since I'd been here less than a day.

"Well, we have identified him," Huish told us. "Unlike our John Doe, his prints are in the system." He looked at Greeley, indicating for him to fill us in.

"Name's David Bremer," Greeley said, less disagreeably than normal. "He has a record of violence—robbery, domestic abuse, that sort of thing. Been in and out of prison."

"What about the gun he used at the gas station?" Shannon asked.

"Probably stolen. We're tracing it now. We're also comparing the gun to see if it was used in any other crimes in the county."

Detective Levine took that moment to appear, and he hurried across the room toward us, slightly out of breath when he arrived. "Did I miss anything?"

"You find Beckett yet?" Huish asked.

"Not yet. I was getting the clothes at the hospital, but they're not—"

"We got them." Greeley cut him off. "I'll explain later."

"You two better go have a chat with David Bremer," Huish said. "Tell him we have a witness who places him near the stabbing victim. See what he'll tell you." Huish turned back to us and stepped toward the door. "Come on, let's get this over with." He stopped, hand on the knob, and looked at me. "But don't you ever again touch evidence without my permission, or I'll throw you in jail myself."

So much for hoping he'd be grateful.

Feeling suddenly too warm, I slung my coat on a coat hanger near one of the desks before following Huish inside the room.

The Vandykes looked up anxiously. "Did you find any leads?" Kenyon asked, directing his question to me, not to the commander. I guess in their view he'd had his chance.

"Maybe," I said, sitting across from Gail. "First we need to ask you a few more questions."

They nodded. "Whatever we can do to help find Jenny," Kenyon said.

"To begin with, we need to know who her biological father is." I started to put my hands on the table but thought the better of it. The many perps who'd been interviewed here might have left powerful imprints behind, negative ones. Instead, I placed my hands in my lap.

Kenyon looked at Gail, waiting. Whatever secrets they had, he wasn't going to say anything without her permission. Gail stared down at the table, fingering her wedding ring, turning it around and around.

"I'm sure the commander's told you that most children are abducted by relatives or people they know," Shannon said into the silence. "Right now that makes your ex-husband the primary suspect. We should know if there is some reason we shouldn't bring him in for questioning. Because that's what the commander has to do. He's probably already sent someone to pick him up."

I glanced at Huish and knew it wasn't true, which irritated me. From the moment he suspected Kenyon wasn't the father, he should have acted.

"Eric's not the father," Gail blurted out. "Jenny was born at least a year after we separated."

Huish rubbed a hand over his receding hairline. "Could he have found out later about the baby and thought it might be his?"

Gail dragged in a breath of air, her eyes flying to her husband. "You don't think he would think something like that, do you?" Her fingers rubbed harder at her ring, as though trying to rub the idea away.

"He'd have to be a total idiot not to know how biology works," Kenyon said.

Gail's lip curled. "Or drunk."

"To imagine that Jenny is his—that's crazy. Isn't it?" Kenyon tore his gaze from Gail, directing his question to Shannon.

Huish answered. "I've seen worse, especially in control freaks with an alcohol problem. Any idea where Eric is now?"

"Portland, last I knew." Gail shifted uneasily in her chair.

"But that was at the time of the annulment. He could be anywhere."

"That's out of our county. I'll contact the FBI and the police there. We'll find him. Last name was Perridew, wasn't it?"

"Yes, Eric Perridew," Gail said. "At least he wouldn't hurt her. I mean, he'd be awful and controlling, but he'd also be trying to win her over."

Kenyon shook his head. "Jenny's smart. She would have found a way to call us by now if she was with him and had any kind of freedom. We've talked to the kids over and over about what to do if they were ever taken. She would play along and then run away the first chance she got."

Gail's tears began again.

"Your ex-husband could have changed a lot over the years," Huish said. "There's no telling what he's become."

That made Gail cry harder. Huish made a sympathetic noise in his throat as Kenyon pulled his wife into his arms.

"I'll go make those phone calls," Huish said. "Be right back."

I exchanged a glance with Shannon, who nodded at me. I took that to mean he'd come to the same conclusion I had: we had to dig deeper. With Huish out of the room, we had the perfect opportunity.

Stifling my pity for Gail, I opened my mouth. "That brings us back to the original question. Who is Jenny's biological father? Power-hungry drunks aside, he would still be my main suspect."

Gail gulped, the tears coming faster. "I don't know! I don't know who the father is." Then, as if realizing how that sounded, she added, "I mean, I didn't know him well. It was just a . . . a mistake. I . . ." She came to a slow stop and looked around at our faces, including Kenyon's.

"Gail," I said as gently as possible, "Jenny is missing, and she needs your help. Tell us what you haven't been telling Commander Huish."

"It's not important! He doesn't know. No one needs to know." She rubbed the ring on her finger.

I stood up and walked around the table, squatting beside her chair. Slowly, I reached for her hand, the one with the wedding ring, squeezing her fingers in comfort. "You know who he is, Gail, and it's a sure bet someone else does, too."

"No. It's irrelevant. I can't tell you who the father is."

"Gail, please," came Kenyon's agonized voice. "If it's someone important, they'll protect his identity." The way he said this told me the subject had been a sore one between them at least at one point in their marriage.

"No." Her voice was final. "He has nothing to do with it. It's just some pervert that took her. Someone probably related to drugs. That's what you should be focusing on. We need to find whoever it is so my daughter will be safe!"

I squeezed her fingers again, purposely allowing my finger to fall on her ring. The way she'd been rubbing it during this emotion-filled interview had to mean an imprint. It was a dirty trick, but Jenny's life was at stake and Gail was withholding information. I took a deep breath as the images came.

I can't tell them. No one can ever know. Jenny is mine. Mine!

A flashback to two women, one lying in a bed. "Take her," the sick woman said. *"Pretend she's yours. I can't ever let him know about her. She wouldn't be safe."*

"We'll raise her together," I promised. "We'll tell her when she's older."

The woman in the bed fell into a coughing fit. "I can never repay you for this."

"Who was there for me and helped me get away from Eric? Of course I'd do this for you. You're my best friend."

I looked down at the baby in my arms. I'd already been taking care of her for weeks while Cindy recuperated from the birth, and I loved her more than I'd loved anyone in my entire life.

The memory inside the imprint ended with a final thought: I won't let them know. I can't. Jenny's mine.

Another imprint began, but this one came from several months ago when Gail had an argument with Kenyon about whether her aging parents should come to live with them. Weak enough now that I could pull away.

I rocked back on my heels, breathing faster, trying to make sense of what I'd seen. The image reminded me of something. My brain sifted through my memories for the answer.

Finally I had it. Not one but two things: the gold heart bracelet on Jenny's shelf, which had first belonged to a woman named Cindy, and the drawing Tawnia had described to me over the phone.

"Autumn?" Shannon had come around the table.

I arose a bit unsteadily, drawing my phone from my pocket and pulling up my email.

"What is it?" Kenyon asked.

"Just a minute, please. I need to see something." Tawnia's was the sixth message. I clicked on the attachment link.

There it was, a drawing of the Vandykes being interviewed by Commander Huish. A thought bubble had Gail thinking of a woman in bed with a baby and her younger self standing nearby.

With the imprint I'd experienced, it was all clear to me now. Or some of it.

Gail was not Jenny's mother.

The idea blew me away. I understood now her reluctance to tell the truth. Gail didn't know the father of the child well because she hadn't shared any kind of a relationship with him.

My thoughts ran at high speed, struggling for focus. Okay, Gail was not Jenny's mother, but what I didn't know was what had happened to the woman who gave birth to Jenny, or why she wasn't in Jenny's life now as she and Gail had planned.

The Vandykes were watching me, Kenyon with hope, Gail strangled by fear.

The door opened, and Commander Huish reentered with Detective Greeley. The commander started to speak, but Shannon lifted a finger, asking him to wait. The Vandykes didn't appear to notice either Huish's return or Shannon's signal.

"Gail," I began, "you left an imprint on your ring. I know about Jenny. I know you didn't give birth to her."

Gail's face crumpled, while everyone else stared—at me, at her, at each other.

"I know Jenny is the daughter of your best friend, Cindy, and that you took Jenny at her request. What I don't know is where Cindy is now. Did something happen to her?"

I really hoped Gail hadn't been involved in her death, though I knew troubled women did terrible things.

Gail brought her hands to her face, sobbing. This time Kenyon didn't reach out to comfort her. "Tell them, honey," he said. I was glad his voice was still gentle, though it was apparent he was as confused as the rest of us.

Commander Huish walked over to Gail's side. "Take a moment to compose yourself, and then tell us what happened."

Gail nodded and took a shuddering breath. A few minutes later she could talk. "Cindy and I worked at a sewing factory when I was having problems with Eric. Because of her encouragement, I finally left Eric and filed for an annulment. I wasn't even nineteen. Cindy had her own problems. Her boyfriend was in jail when I met her, but he got out eventually, and almost every day she'd come to work with a black eye or with bruises on her arms and legs. We celebrated when he was sent to prison. She asked me to share her apartment, to help with rent, so I did. Then we found out she was pregnant with Jenny.

"Cindy had Jenny in our apartment with a midwife. Everything went fine, but Cindy got sick after. She had a cough. A terrible one. I took time off work and took care of her and Jenny. Then when Jenny was a few weeks old, Cindy got a letter from her boyfriend in prison. It scared her. She didn't want anything to do with him, but she said she'd have to do whatever he said or he'd hurt her. She didn't want him to know about Jenny, so she asked me to pretend Jenny was mine. She even got the midwife to change the names on the birth papers since we hadn't sent them in yet."

"Did Cindy see a doctor about the cough?" I asked.

Gail nodded. "At some free clinic. They sent her home, saying they'd contact her in a few days to let her know the results of the tests, but they were too late. She died. Jenny wasn't even two months old."

Huish walked around the table. "The boyfriend ever come looking for her?"

"He came once right after he got out, but I made sure he didn't see Jenny. I told him Cindy was contagious and to come back later. He was so angry, as if it was her fault she was sick, but he left." Gail closed her eyes, as if remembering brought her pain. "After Cindy died, I crashed at a coworker's until I could rent a room for Jenny and me. A month later, I ran into Kenyon. We started dating and fell in love."

"You should have told me." Kenyon's arm was back around his wife.

Gail leaned into him, twisting her neck to stare up into his eyes. "Oh, honey, I was barely twenty. I'd had a failed marriage, watched a good friend die, and unexpectedly become a mother. Jenny was my entire life by then. I loved her so much. I couldn't risk her being taken away. Cindy wanted me to raise her, and I'd promised her I would." Her voice grew hard. "Besides, her boyfriend had supposedly paid his debt to society, but I couldn't let Jenny grow up with him. What would a thug like him do with a baby, anyway? He'd been in and out of jail since he was barely a teen, and he was almost thirty then."

"Do you remember the boyfriend's name?" I asked.

"Cindy and his friends called him Geyser because of some stupid trick he did with a bottle of beer, but that wasn't his real name."

No leads there. "What about Cindy's family?"

"She had a mother, but she was homeless. Cindy tried to get her mother to live with her, even got her a job several times, hoping they could share rent, but her mother would always quit working and go back to living on the street again. I was the only person in Jenny's life able to take care of her."

I wondered if Gail had married Kenyon more for what he could do to keep her and Jenny together than for love, but in the end it seemed to have worked out. He was obviously gone on her, and she shared a real affection for him, too, or she wouldn't have continued the marriage and had another child with him.

With Gail's confession, our suspect pool had become wider. I knew I should be happy about that, but at some point I'd switched goals. Instead of trying to prove whether or not Cody had anything to do with Jenny's disappearance, my primary goal now was finding her. But more suspects meant more time it would take to discover who actually took her.

"Does Jenny know any of this?" I asked.

"I never told her about me," Gail said. "But she knows Kenyon's not her father."

"I insisted we be up front with her about that," Kenyon added. "I didn't want her to stumble on the information later and feel we kept it from her." His voice faltered when he saw the hurt on his wife's face. "I didn't mean . . ." He didn't finish.

Commander Huish pulled up a chair and sat down at the table, pulling a writing tablet from his pocket. "Okay, Gail, I'm going to need every name you can remember. From your coworkers to neighbors to the midwife who delivered Jenny, if you can remember her name. Whoever might have known you and Cindy then and who knew or might have suspected she was pregnant or that you weren't."

Gail furrowed her brow. "I don't understand. Geyser didn't even know she was expecting."

"Someone might have tipped him off," Huish said. "He could have come looking for her. If you tell us everything, we can start the search before the FBI gets here."

"The FBI?"

"They're sending someone to check out your story about your ex-husband, but believe me, they'll be far more interested in this."

Gail took a shuddering breath. "But what if after all this time I have to fight him for custody?"

"I think," Shannon said, "we need to worry about finding Jenny first. If this Geyser has as long a record as you say, custody won't be an issue."

"Okay," Gail said. "I'll try to remember everything."

Huish looked at us. "You can stay, if you want, but you may be interested in the guy my detectives just caught up with."

"Cody Beckett?" I guessed.

"Yes, and he's asking to see you."

Chapter 9

"If Jenny knew Kenyon wasn't her father," I said to Shannon as Detective Greeley led us to another interrogation room, "it's possible she went looking for her birth father. Physically or over the Internet."

"Maybe she assumed Mrs. Vandyke's ex was her dad and took a bus to Portland."

Greeley shook his head. "No one remembers selling her a ticket. Though that's not saying much."

"She would have had to come into Salem to get the bus," Shannon said.

"It would be a long walk." Greeley paused outside a door. "Maybe she had a lift into town."

"One of her friends then," Shannon said.

The boot might have told me if she'd left on her own, but they apparently hadn't found it yet.

"So," I said, "what did your prisoner have to say? The guy from the gas station, I mean. Not Cody Beckett."

Greeley gave me a flat smile that did nothing to soften the lines of his face. "David Bremer denies stabbing anyone."

"That's strange." I worked hard not to roll my eyes. "And

I thought he'd jump right up and volunteer the information. After all, he wasn't shy about trying to shoot us all at the gas station."

"I didn't say I believed him." Greeley's lips tightened. "He's lying, of course. But unless John Doe regains consciousness or Bremer left fingerprints on the victim, we can't prove it until we find the crime scene. Maybe not even then."

"Maybe he's working with those men at the hospital who also tried to kill John Doe." I frowned, even as I spoke. The two parties involved didn't seem to go together. Bremer had been wearing jeans and a baseball cap and was carrying a stolen gun, but the men who climbed from the van to shoot at us were wearing dress pants and sported ample firepower.

"I'd bet not," Shannon said. "You mentioned drugs in the imprint from that syringe. That could mean more players. A lot more."

I had to agree. "The stabbing, the drugs, and Jenny's disappearance have to be connected somehow. It can't be coincidence that it all happened now." We needed answers, and Cody Beckett might be able to give them to us. I set my jaw. "Okay," I told Greeley. "Let's go in."

Greeley opened the door and entered first. I had to wait for him to move to the other side of the room before I could see Cody Beckett seated at a table opposite Detective Levine, his long white hair looking more wild since the last time we'd seen him.

"Fancy meeting you here." I noticed his hands were in his pockets, as if afraid to touch anything. I knew exactly how he felt.

"Stinking communists," he muttered. "They think everyone is guilty."

"Well, you did disappear." Shannon slipped into one of the two empty seats next to Levine while I remained standing.

Cody lifted his grizzled chin. "I wasn't under arrest, was I? Maybe I didn't want to answer no questions."

"You're under arrest now," Levine pointed out.

"For what?"

"For avoiding arrest."

Cody spluttered a laugh. "You can't arrest me for avoiding arrest unless you have enough to arrest me in the first place. You can't prove I did anything!"

"We found a man stabbed nearly to death in your bedroom." Greeley walked closer to Cody, placing a hand on the table. "And a missing child's boot on your property."

Cody held his gaze. "I told you, I don't know how that man got there. Or the boot. I can't control when people trespass on my property. Any time you waste on me is less time you have to find out who was really after that girl."

Cody and Greeley glared at each other for a long minute. Cody didn't back down but neither did Greeley. I knew enough about them now to bet the two could sit there glaring all day.

"Well, they have the man who stabbed that guy in custody," I said into the heavy silence. "He's the guy who held up a gas station this morning outside Hayesville and shot the clerk. What's more, you are no longer the only suspect in Jenny's disappearance. That's got to be good news."

A brief shadow of relief passed over Cody's face. Or was that only my imagination? And what if he was relieved? It didn't mean he was getting away with anything.

Greeley's mean little eyes shifted to me, his lip curling. "Did you have to tell him that? How am I supposed to get anything out of him now?"

"Well, it's true, isn't it?" I shrugged. "I've never been good at hiding the truth. Now if you'd stop glaring at me, I'd like to ask Mr. Beckett a few questions."

Detective Levine gave a short laugh, which Greeley quelled with a mere look. Shannon winked at me, his lips twitching.

"He still has to answer for the boot," Greeley said.

"Then I hope you find it so we can see if he's involved in some way."

Cody blinked at me and then looked back to Greeley. "You lost evidence?" He shook his head. "That poor little girl." The sympathy in his voice appeared genuine, and I steeled myself against it.

"It's not lost," Greeley told him. "I have a call out to the FBI for it. They must have taken it with the computer."

I could tell from his tone it was more of a hope than a certainty, and I found I liked Greeley better when he was uncertain. Of course it could be an act. Maybe he'd purposely mislaid the evidence. He or someone else. For Jenny's sake, I hoped I was wrong.

"Look, Mr. Beckett," I said, "you thought the man at your house looked familiar. Have you remembered where you might have seen him?"

He shook his head. "Wasn't him. Just someone who looked like him. But I can't remember who." His face scrunched in thought. "Nah, just can't place him. It'll come to me, though. It always does. I have a good memory."

"Then can you tell me how many times you've met Mrs. Vandyke?" I asked.

"Not exactly. A few times. In passing, is all."

"You've never seen Jenny?"

He sighed. "Once. At my bank. She was outside waiting for her mom."

Did I give him credit for being honest or was the admission one more bit of proof against him? "How did you know she belonged to Mrs. Vandyke?"

"When Mrs. Vandyke left the bank, she took her hand. The girl pulled away, though. I remember thinking that besides the blond hair they didn't look much alike."

"You didn't talk to Jenny?"

"No reason to." He frowned. "Look, just because I saw the child doesn't mean I had anything to do with her going missing. You said you had a lead on the stabbing. Maybe it's connected. Shouldn't you be chasing that?"

My turn to sigh. "They're following up on it now." I was about to give up, but his expression had suddenly changed. "What?" I asked.

"I remember now. The man bleeding all over my room? I just put it together with what you said about that gas station. It was the one closest to my house, right? Well, he reminds me of the clerk there. The really young-looking one. They have the same build, the same lines of the face. If I didn't know better, I'd say they were brothers."

"What does that have to do with anything?" Levine said.

Thoughts racing, I remembered the feeling I'd experienced when I saw Kirt in the hospital parking garage. "Now that he's pointed it out, there is a resemblance."

"You think they're related?" Greeley asked.

"They wouldn't have to be," Shannon said. "Bremer would just have to think they were. Maybe he saw them together. He didn't get what he wanted from one so he went for the other."

"Or they could actually be related." I looked at Shannon pointedly, remembering the imprint on John Doe's undershirt. "Maybe cousins. What's Kirt's last name?"

"Henry," Greeley said. "Kirt Henry."

Shannon tapped the table with his fingers. "Maybe he can ID your John Doe."

"Seems like a long shot." Levine arose, sending his chair back with a loud screech. He gave us an apologetic shrug.

Cody came with us as we gravitated to the door. "Does this mean I can go? I got a deadline, you know. For my next sculpture."

"Not until the commander says so." Greeley paused at the door. "You might still be under arrest."

"You can't hold me if you aren't arresting me."

Greeley's expression hardened. "We can until tomorrow. So if you don't want to sleep in a cell tonight, sit down and let me go talk to the commander."

Cody stomped back to his seat, mumbling something about beady-eyed detectives and a nosy woman who wanted to know too much and how if he stayed in that cold room or in a cell with other detainees, he'd probably contract a rare disease and fall so sick that he wouldn't finish his project, which would then make it so he couldn't pay his bills, and the city would take his land because he'd default on the taxes, and he'd have to try to find a bed at the local shelter and probably end up dying in the street of exposure.

It sounded so much like a story my sister would make up to joke about a point that for a moment I couldn't move. It was a sense of family I wasn't prepared to experience with him. I'd known she shared his artistic talent, but this seemed more personal somehow.

"Autumn, you coming?" Shannon stood in the doorway. There was a question in his eyes that I recognized from when he wanted to know about the imprints I'd been reading. He would have noticed, though, that I hadn't touched anything in the room.

Having nothing to say, I nodded and swept past him out into the hall where the two detectives were talking.

"I still say it's him for the stabbing." Greeley glanced at the door Shannon was closing behind him.

"Agreed," said Levine. "I don't think this lead with the clerk is going to pan out. He was shot. He certainly would have said something if he knew the robber was after him."

"Beckett only came up with this because of what Miss Rain here said about the gas station."

I felt deflated at the idea. Greeley was right—I had brought up the station first.

"Or the clerk could be into something up to his neck," Shannon retorted. "Either way, it's too big a coincidence that Bremer stabbed John Doe before hitting the gas station. The clerk needs to be questioned."

Levine scratched the short hair on his head. "Remind me again—who says the gas station robber stabbed John Doe?"

"That was me." I smiled at him. "It was something I picked up from John Doe's clothing."

Smiling, Levine leaned toward me, a little too close for comfort. "I'd really like to hear more about how this works sometime. It's fascinating."

Greeley gave the ceiling a save-me-from-idiots look, which irritated me more than if he'd come right out and said he didn't believe.

"So are you going to pick up the clerk from the gas station

or not?" Shannon asked. "The commander said he'd help us. Ask him. I bet he'll tell you to pick him up."

Greeley sighed. "I guess it wouldn't hurt to have a chat with him."

"I'll take Schmidt and do it while you talk to the commander." Levine looked eager to please.

"He might be at his fiancée's," I said. When I saw Greeley's annoyed expression, I added, "But I guess you probably already have information about her in your report."

Levine didn't seem concerned at my interference. He snapped his fingers and pointed at me, walking backwards. "When this is all over, you and me, on the town. I know a place that makes great steaks." He winked—and then stumbled into the wall. Face reddening, he hurried away.

Greeley sighed but didn't comment on his partner's awkwardness. "Let's go see the commander. Let him know what Mr. Beckett has come up with." The way he said it was a challenge, but I wasn't afraid of Huish. I knew too much about his personal anguish.

Maybe I should touch something of Greeley's, so I could feel the same about him. But not before I ate some protein—a huge steak at the least, or maybe two chicken breasts. I'd read a lot of imprints already today, and even thinking about reading more was exhausting, especially if they were anything like the last one on John Doe's undershirt. Protein was as good as positive imprints to restore my strength.

"You know," Shannon said to me as we followed Greeley, "Hayesville would be the perfect place to set up a drug smuggling operation. Near enough all the conveniences offered by a city like Salem, but far enough away to slip under the radar.

We may have stumbled onto something really big. I hope their narc guys are as good as ours."

"I'm just interested in Jenny," I said.

Shannon's expression told me he didn't believe me.

"Okay, and Cody too." I didn't have time to say more because Commander Huish was coming our way.

"The FBI is here with the Vandykes' computer," he said. "They've finished with it and come up empty. It's cleared for you to see."

"I thought you sent someone for the computer," I said, "not that they were bringing it."

Huish gave me a smile that didn't reach his eyes. "Apparently, they're interested in what more you guys might discover."

"What about the boot?" Shannon asked. "They bring it too?"

"Actually, no." The commander's gaze shifted to Greeley. "How are we coming on that?"

"Still tracking it." Greeley shrugged one broad shoulder. "I'll check with Celia and see how it's going. But I wanted to let you know I sent Levine and Schmidt to pick up that clerk who was wounded this morning." He explained Cody's recognition of Bremer and the possibility that the attack at the gas station wasn't random. "It's a long shot, and it probably means nothing. We don't even have proof that Bremer was involved in the stabbing." This he spoke with a hard glance at me. "But I thought we'd cover all our bases."

Huish only nodded. "Good call. Maybe we'll catch a break. Meanwhile, we've located Mrs. Vandyke's former husband. The FBI has a warrant to search his house in Portland and are questioning him now, but none of his neighbors have noticed anything out of the ordinary. We're not counting him out, but at the outset it doesn't look as if he's involved. They're still checking to see if he has any other properties or a remote place where he might take a child."

"Wish I could interview him myself," Greeley said.

I was thinking the same thing, but that didn't mean I liked Greeley any more for it.

"It might come to that." Huish flashed the briefest of smiles. "For now let's concentrate on finding the child's real biological father. If he's back in prison, that changes everything. No way to kidnap a child if you're in prison. And him paying someone else to do the job seems unlikely."

Huish led the way to the room where the FBI agents were with the Vandykes. "Meet Liz Cross and Ben Morley," Huish said as they rose to meet us. "They're the FBI special agents investigating Jenny's disappearance."

"Two of the agents," Cross corrected. "We have more on the case." She was a beautiful blonde with ultrashort hair and a hawklike nose that was more striking than ugly.

Agent Morley could have been Greeley's twin, except for the face that was narrow compared to his muscled bulk. Both agents were in plain clothes, but the weapons at their waists were conspicuous.

Shannon offered his hand. "Detective Shannon Martin, Portland Police Bureau."

"You've already met Detective Sergeant Greeley," Huish added to the agents, indicating Greeley. "He's still running point on our end."

More handshaking, and then gazes shifted to me. "Autumn Rain," I said. I'd left my gloves in my coat pocket so I didn't offer my hand to anyone.

"She's the one who reads things." Gail Vandyke came to her feet.

Agent Cross smiled, looking predatory. "Psychometry. Yes, I've heard of it. You read people, too?"

"No."

"Then why didn't—oh, we're both wearing rings."

Exactly. I was saving what was left of my energy for the Vandykes' computer.

"We're glad you're here," Cross said. Apparently, she was the senior of the two agents, or at least the more communicative one. "We need every bit of help we can get, though already you've been a great help." Her eyes went briefly to the Vandykes.

Agent Morley added, "We weren't able to get anything special from the computer. Unfortunately some things were erased, and we weren't able to retrieve the information. We can't verify that Jenny was talking with someone over the Internet, but we can't rule it out completely either. Maybe you can do better."

Their acceptance of my ability instead of mistrust and suspicion was unexpected, especially from someone as confident and together as Agent Cross. The only other person to react that way had been Shannon's partner, Paige.

I stifled a grin. "Okay, I'll get to it." The Vandykes looked so hopeful I had to add, "Don't expect too much. There may be nothing to find."

Only when I sat down before the computer and closed my eyes in preparation did the weariness crash down on me. The imprints of today and those from all the months before came to the surface, mixing in with my own memories. I was too tired to force it all back into the little compartments in my brain.

It was hard enough keeping my own life straight, much less the events from other people's lives.

Shannon moved past the Vandykes to stand beside me, replacing his phone in his pocket. I hadn't heard him calling, so he must have been texting. I wondered if it involved a case he and Paige were working on back in Portland. He'd taken time off to come with me, but that didn't mean his cases could wait.

I was delaying again. Not good given how long Jenny had been gone.

This close to the computer, my skin was tingling. The keyboard contained imprints. Major ones. Odd because the half-dozen computers I'd read before retained only mild imprints—more often frustration than anything else.

Then again, Shannon had never asked me to read imprints from computers taken in pornography raids, for which I was infinitely grateful. At any rate, if these imprints were negative, I'd need the watch Shannon had unbuckled from his wrist. It had been his grandfather's, and the imprints on it had helped me recover on more than one occasion when I hadn't been able to reach Tawnia's drawing.

I set my hands on the keyboard.

Happiness. I loved my friends. They were wonderful! Chatting on Facebook was almost as good as being with them in person. Even if my mother didn't want me to grow up, they knew I was grown up already.

Not that Mom and Dad were terrible. They were great, as far as parents went. Love filled my heart at the thought of them. Big and deep and long-lasting love. They would do anything for me. Not like Mindy's parents, who barely cared if she came home at night. Sure, she had a lot of fun, but being at her house alone at night was sometimes uncomfortable. Then again, if her parents hadn't been absent so often, I wouldn't have been able to go over there to search adoption reunion sites.

My birth father. What was he like? I would meet him someday, if I could find him. Six false alarms, where the details of my birth didn't quite match up. Frustrating. But I'd added information to my profile, and maybe today I'd have new messages, which I'd check today at Mindy's. The thought made me want to burst out in song. Mindy would be occupied with her boyfriend watching the video, and she would never know. Not yet.

Too bad I couldn't look at the site now, but Dad checked the pages I visited, and I'd already deleted enough of my computer's history that he'd mentioned it. I didn't know how to tell him or Mom that I was curious. I didn't want to hurt them. I'd just have to wait until I got to Mindy's.

The imprint faded, leaving me reeling with the intensity of Jenny's emotions, though the imprint was already nearly six months old. The emotion was made more intense by the fact that I understood her longing only too well. I was infinitely glad I was seated.

Earlier imprints followed, most of them full of laughter and fun—Jenny had loved connecting with friends—but mixed in were a few instances of disappointment that had been alluded to in the first imprint.

He's not the one. Maybe he's dead. Maybe I'll never meet him.

There were also a few faint imprints from Gail and Kenken, but Jenny's imprints all started only eight months earlier, which was when I gathered her parents let her have Facebook.

I lifted my hands, my eyes refocusing on the room. The first person I saw was Gail Vandyke, her red-rimmed eyes staring. She wasn't going to like what I'd discovered. I was glad to feel Shannon's hand on my shoulder, steadying me.

"I take it there was something?" Agent Cross prompted.

"I call them imprints," I said. "There were several. Jenny was looking for her birth father on adoption reunion registries. She's had several disappointments, but on the last imprint, actually the first I experienced because I always see the latest one first, she was planning on going to her friend Mindy's house to check for messages on a new profile she'd filled out. She didn't do it on this computer because her father"—I looked at Mr. Vandyke—"always checked the sites she visited."

"When was that?" Shannon asked.

I closed my eyes to remember. "A month ago, on a Thursday, I believe."

"Mindy's parents just don't keep a good eye on the girls," Gail said. "That's why I always encourage Mindy to come to our house. But sometimes, you just can't . . ." She trailed off.

Something was off in her reaction, but I couldn't pinpoint what. Gail added, "Geyser didn't even know he had a child. What if Jenny found someone who was only posing as her father? He could be anyone."

I glanced at Agent Cross and saw she had come to the same conclusion. She finished a quiet exchange with her partner and pulled out her phone.

"Jenny wouldn't have been stupid enough to go with just anyone," Mr. Vandyke said. "She would have asked for proof."

Gail bit her lower lip. "Like what? What did she even know?"

"That a midwife delivered her, that it was in Portland, where you worked. Your name." Vandyke's words seem to soothe his wife.

"Well, she wouldn't be the first girl who was lured by a

pedophile," Agent Cross said. "But we'll hope she's with her birth father, as that is her best hope of remaining safe. We'll need to re-interview the friend and confiscate her computer. With any luck, we'll find out what sites Jenny visited and which people responded. Regardless of whether she found her birth father or not, whoever she's with has committed a felony. We'll find him and put him away."

The FBI agents and Detective Greeley excused themselves and left the room, leaving the Vandykes looking as though they didn't know whether to shout with hope or to scream in fear. I didn't know myself.

"We'll let you know the minute we hear anything," Huish said to the Vandykes. "For now, go home."

"What if they don't find anything on Mindy's computer?" Gail asked.

"They'll have their best experts on it before the end of the day." Huish opened the door for the Vandykes. "Don't worry. They'll find it. Meanwhile, I'll also assign a few detectives to contact the most prevalent reunion sites on the Internet to see if she's registered there. One way or another, we'll find out what happened."

"Thank you," Mr. Vandyke said. To me he added, "And thank you. If you hadn't come, we wouldn't have known any of this."

I refrained from pointing out that if his wife had told the truth from the beginning, the commander and the FBI might have gone in this direction all on their own. They might even have found Jenny by now. "You're welcome."

Huish walked the Vandykes to the exit while Shannon and I retrieved our coats.

"Is it just me," Shannon said in a low voice, "or did Gail Vandyke not seem very surprised to learn that her daughter was searching for her birth father?"

I turned to him, my jaw dropping slightly. "You're right. I knew something was off. But why would she hide that?"

"I can't think why." He shook his head. "I know she didn't tell us her husband wasn't Jenny's birth father because she didn't want her own secret to come out, but if she knew Jenny was searching the adoption sites, not telling the police sabotages the entire case."

"Must be shock," I said. "Unless she's covering up for something else."

"What?"

I didn't know. "Must be shock," I repeated.

Shannon sighed. "Well, I canceled our reservations at the hotel tonight. The FBI and the commander have the Internet leads covered, so it looks like Portland's where it's at for us. I'd like to talk to the neighbors at the apartment building where Jenny was born. We may be able to track down Jenny's birth mother and get a line on the birth father that way before the FBI gets a warrant for the information they need from those websites."

"Won't they be following that lead, too?" I pulled on my coat.

He grinned. "Yeah, but they can't read imprints. Besides, Portland's my city. If he's there, I'll find him. I've been texting Paige about the circumstances around Jenny's birth, and she's already looking into it. If we drive home now, she may have something by the time we get there. Maybe we can find Jenny tonight."

He had a point, though I still felt reluctant to leave. I wasn't satisfied that Cody wasn't involved somehow. He was hiding something.

Beside me, Shannon stilled. I looked around and saw a young detective leading Cody in the direction of the exit, his hands still plunged deeply into the pockets of his worn jeans.

"They letting you go?" I asked. It was more than I hoped for, seeing as the detectives had already made up their minds about him.

He paused. "Until they find a knife with my prints on it, I guess they can't really book me. And I can guarantee they ain't going to find that because I didn't do it."

Huish returned in time to hear Cody's comment. "You may be right about that, Mr. Beckett. I just got word that we've identified the John Doe at the hospital from his fingerprints. He's Weston Millard, the registered owner of the handgun Bremer used at the gas station. And we found Millard's car parked down the road from the station, where Bremer must have stashed it. So the two cases are definitely related. Hopefully for you, the evidence will show that, for reasons yet undetermined, Bremer attacked Millard with the knife and then stole his gun."

"Ha!" Cody said. "I told you I didn't do it."

I felt almost as if his comment was directed toward me. I pulled my coat tighter around me.

Cody's gaze shifted in my direction. "What are you hiding from, anyway?"

"What makes you think I'm hiding?"

His curious expression vanished, replaced by a shuttered look I'd seen many times on my sister's face, one I wished I could copy. Unfortunately, I knew my annoyance at his question was plain on my face, right along with my own curiosity about him, my anger at what he'd done to my birth mother, and whatever else was hidden in the mixture of emotions raging through my body.

"Your eyes never meet mine," he said. "Besides, I've been hiding myself long enough to recognize it." Without waiting for a response, he headed toward the exit, the young detective trailing him.

I watched him leave, once again remembering Jenny's emotions. If she had found her birth father, I hoped her experience was better than mine.

Chapter 10

Before he let us leave the sheriff's office, Greeley made us view head shots to see if we could identify our attackers at the hospital, but none of those we'd seen were in the pictures.

As we sped back to Portland with the aid of Shannon's portable police light, I pondered Jenny's curiosity about her birth father. I shared that with her, at least in my teen years, but I'd never considered trying to find him until last year after being reunited with my sister and discovering my ability. The ability was the real impetus. I'd felt I needed to know more about it. I still needed to know, and yet here I was heading back to Portland without ever having made myself known to Cody Beckett.

It's better this way, I thought. He could still be guilty, and if so, all I had done by going to Hayesville was to muddy the investigation with my discoveries about Jenny's birth parents.

Could it be a coincidence that Jenny had gone missing so soon after beginning the search for her birth father? I shivered, glad that I hadn't made the same mistake, glad I hadn't appeared on Cody's doorstep as a child, perhaps as they hauled him off to prison or after he came home in one of his drugged stupors.

No, not drugged. I'd been told he'd sworn off drugs after the night he'd hurt my mother, and from what I could tell, that might be true. But there was still the alcohol abuse and the fact that he'd moved to a remote area. Was it so he wouldn't hurt anyone again?

"Whose name is on the birth certificate as Jenny's father?" Shannon asked.

"Kenyon Vandyke." I tapped the police file. "But it's an amended one. Gail must have changed it later."

"The irony is that if Kenyon Vandyke hadn't insisted on telling his daughter the truth, she might still be safe at home."

"Or she might be dying of a rare disease and her birth father could save her life but doesn't because they don't want to tell her she's adopted," I countered. "Life throws curves. That doesn't mean you start lying." I'd known from the beginning that I was adopted, and Winter and Summer had told me all about my birth mother and how she'd stayed with them during her pregnancy. They hadn't known about Tawnia; only the doctor who had separated us at birth had known our mother had twins. Later, Winter had told me he'd go with me if I ever wanted to search for my birth father. Maybe that openness was why I never tried.

"I'd better call my sister," I said when Shannon didn't respond. "She'll want to know what's going on and how her picture tied into it." My stomach gave a loud growl, though it hadn't been that long since I'd finished my second sandwich.

Shannon laughed. "We need to think about dinner too."

"Uh, yeah." My appetite, always large, had grown even more since my ability blossomed.

Tawnia's husband, Bret, answered her phone. "She's taking a nap with the baby," he said. "She's had a tough day. Unless it's important, I'd rather not wake her."

"It can wait. Let her know I called."

"Wait. There is something here that might interest you. She has the kitchen table and her computer full of drawings for her deadline tomorrow, and I was looking through them as I always do—she's so amazing. But I found one that doesn't seem to belong."

"What is it?" I asked, pressing the phone harder to my ear.

"It's a group of children, all girls, I think. The strange thing is they're in a dark room with no furniture. Just carpet, and they're sleeping on the floor. Only a few have blankets. Does that tie in with anything you're working on?"

I didn't see how. "Not really, but she has a client who sells carpets."

"Well, this won't sell anything. It's gloomy."

"Is there anything that places the drawing in a location? Or do any of the faces look recognizable?"

"No, it's all very vague. Dark. The walls are plain. Window has something over it. She did it all in shades of gray. Just a quick sketch. That's why it's so odd."

"Well, it's probably nothing, but I'll keep it in mind." I thanked Bret and hung up the phone, wondering. Had Jenny connected with a child predator who had taken more than one child?

I voiced the idea to Shannon, but he shook his head. "It's unlikely. We haven't had any more reports of missing children in Oregon, or none that I'm aware of, so simultaneous victims would have to mean a larger scope. An organization, maybe. Multiple perps."

That was a relief, at least.

We reached the outskirts of Portland within thirty minutes, cutting significant time off the usual fifty minutes it took from Salem. Shannon flipped off the police light and pushed Paige's number on his phone. "Well," he asked, "what do you have?" He listened for several long seconds. "Okay. Thanks."

To me, he said, "She's sending an address to my phone. She's been talking to Gail Vandyke and the feds. Guess what? Gail's old apartment is near yours. Better yet, Smokey's is on the way. Why don't you call in an order? I know you have them on speed dial."

Smokey's was across from my antiques shop and Jake's herb store that used to belong to Winter and Summer and then me before I sold it to Jake. Thera Brinker, one of the employees we shared, would be closing up my store now. Fridays were my slowest days. Both she and Randa, Jake's sister, would be working full time tomorrow on my busiest day. Tawnia had promised to help before her baby became sick, but she'd probably have to stay home and work on her deadline now.

"I think I'll have the beef pot pie, two rolls, and a smoothie," I told Shannon. "You?"

"Pot pie sounds good. But I'd better have a sandwich instead so I can drive. Barbecue chicken. And a strawberry smoothie."

"Mmm, sounds good. I'll get my pie and a sandwich as well. For the road."

His upper lip quirked into a smile. "I thought it was all for the road."

"It is." It would cost more than I really could afford, but I needed to keep up my strength to read imprints. I couldn't skimp on a case this important.

For a long moment we were quiet. Early darkness had

stolen over the city, and I could feel the evening cold beating at the windows. Was Jenny somewhere in this city? Or was she back in Hayesville somewhere?

Shannon sat in the idling truck while I ran into Smokey's. I was leaving the takeout counter when I nearly ran into Jake coming into the restaurant. He looked good in snug khakis and the leather jacket that he wore even in the coldest weather when everyone else was reaching for ski parkas or full-length wools. His short locs were partially hidden by a rather handsome knit hat, and where most people looked peaked during the winter, thanks to his mother's African-American genes, his brown skin looked healthy and glowing.

"Hey," he said, furrowing his brow. "I thought you went to Salem. Or Hayesville or something."

"The leads brought us back here. We're on our way to question a few people."

He laughed. "But you were hungry."

"Yeah. You know how I am." I felt immediately guilty for saying it. Because Jake did know. He knew almost everything about me. If it hadn't been for meeting Shannon, we might be picking out cutlery together—or would if I didn't already own some.

"Well, let me know how it goes."

"I will. Wait, you dropped your keys." Without thinking, I bent to grab them.

As my fingers touched the metal, I was suddenly looking at myself turning from the counter.

Pain swelled in my heart until I wondered if I could hold it all in. I loved her so much. Enough to let her go.

I dropped the keys back on the floor, swallowing hard and trying not to show what I'd experienced. Why hadn't I put my gloves back on? I'd touched his keys before, and I knew he always imprinted on them.

"What?" he said.

"Nothing."

"You're such a bad liar."

Tears bit at my eyes. "Jake, I'm sorry."

"It's okay. Really. I'm dealing with it. No worries. We're cool."

No, we weren't. He was still there for me in every way I wanted, and I'd be there for him in every way but the one he wanted most. My heart ached. The thing I had worried about most when I'd chosen to pursue a relationship with Shannon was losing my friendship with Jake. Would we ever get past the awkwardness? Would we ever be friends the way we'd been before romance entered the scene?

I hoped so, because I loved Jake. He'd been there for me when Winter drowned, when I had no one else. He'd gotten me through the dark nights when I hadn't cared enough to eat, when I'd kept vigil on the banks of the Willamette for a week as rescuers combed the bottom for bodies. If he couldn't find happiness, I wasn't sure I could, either. Maybe if he could find love, I wouldn't feel so guilty trying to find it without him. He had an old girlfriend I knew still cared for him, but he hadn't contacted her after our breakup. Maybe it was time for me to make that call.

I hugged Jake, nearly tipping the contents of my takeout bag. "See you tomorrow or Monday."

"Call me if you need me, okay?" He grinned, drawing the attention of half the females at the tables around us. "I still have a little bit of investigating left in me."

"You hate it."

"I just hate you being in danger."

"I'm not this time. I promise." I felt I was telling the truth. It wasn't likely I'd be shot at again while looking for Jenny's father. Well, unless we actually found him.

Jake looked relieved, so I decided not to examine my thoughts too closely.

I smiled and backed toward the door. My last picture was of him squatting down to pick up his keys.

Shannon was studying his GPS when I climbed into the truck with the bag of takeout. "We'll make it to the first stop in five minutes. We won't be able to eat much."

"Watch me." I was a pro at fast eating. You learned to do that when you were sole owner and only full-time employee of a store.

As I took the first bite, my eyes wandered across the street where the lights were already out in Autumn's Antiques and The Herb Shoppe. I smiled, feeling a vague nostalgia for the time when that was all I'd known—before imprints.

I managed to eat half the steaming pie before we pulled up at the apartment building two blocks away from my own. These buildings were similar to those on my block—four to six stories high and built decades ago. The location wasn't as central, however, and the buildings not as well cared for. Even fourteen years ago, the rent would have been less, especially for one-room apartments such as Gail and Cindy had shared.

"Well, this is where Jenny was born," Shannon said, tucking the uneaten portion of his sandwich into his cooler with my extra one. "There should be at least one or two who remember the girls." It was late and dinner time but still early enough to catch those who planned to spend Friday night on the town, which was where I might be with Shannon if I hadn't decided to go to Hayesville and connect with dear old dad.

I sighed and climbed from the truck, my breath making puffs of white in the night air. I buttoned my coat and sent a thankful thought in the direction of my sister for the leather sock boots. Shannon smiled at my huddled figure and put an arm around me. "Maybe you should move to California."

"Maybe I will."

Shannon laughed. "No, you won't."

He was right. Oregon was my home, and the only way I'd ever consider moving was if Tawnia and Bret did. They were all the family I had left now.

I lifted my face and planted a kiss on his lips, one that warmed me better than any Californian beach. "Don't be too sure of yourself."

"I never am with you." His smile didn't falter, but I sensed seriousness behind his words. I remembered he'd once said that he never fully believed anyone. He'd been talking about suspects, but I knew it extended to his personal life, and all because of a woman he'd once dated who'd left the force to become a private detective and had been killed. I wasn't the only one bringing baggage into this relationship.

"What I mean," he added, "is that I know with your ability the next surprise is always just around the corner."

That much was true, for both of us. Maybe a good thing. Maybe not.

We made our way through the crunchy snow that was hardening further as night and colder temperatures settled in. Shannon's badge easily got us into the building, but no one we questioned seemed to know anything.

Finally, we reached the fifth floor and found a crumpled, ancient lady with white hair so thin we could see her pale scalp.

"I remember the girls," she said in a frail voice. "And the baby. A girl in pink. Lived right there, across the hall from me."

"Were they from around here? Did you know their families or relatives?"

She shook her head. "I didn't even know which was the mother, the short, scrawny one or the other one. Both were blond, you see, and the smaller one wore big clothes. All she had, poor thing. The bigger one always carried the baby. Five floors up and the elevator broken most of the time."

"Do you remember a man?" Shannon asked.

"There was a man staying at one time with the thin one, but I never really saw him. I only heard about it. He kept really late hours."

"Could you identify him to a sketch artist?" Shannon asked.

She frowned. "No. I couldn't even say what race he was."

"The baby was born in their apartment," I said. "Do you remember a midwife coming?"

She straightened, lifting her chin slightly—probably as much as she was capable of lifting it. "I don't recall any midwife. I never had occasion to use one. We always went to a doctor."

Shannon nodded. "But you know about the baby being born here?"

"No. That was at the time my daughter was having her own baby. I spent a few weeks in Washington with her."

"Does anyone else from that time still live in the building?" I asked.

"Only old Jim downstairs, but he has Alzheimer's and doesn't even know who I am these days."

Just our luck.

"I already told this to the FBI about an hour ago," the lady said, a touch of excitement entering her voice. "But I don't suppose you all share information. On TV the FBI and the police always fight over cases. Is that what's happening here?"

"No." Shannon's voice remained remarkably calm. "We're just helping them out. Sometimes people remember things later."

"Well, that's all I know." She sounded disappointed, as though she'd had more fun during our visit than she'd had all month and didn't want it to end.

"Do you know where any of the other people who lived in this building live now?" Shannon pressed.

"I don't socialize much. Sorry."

"Thank you for your time."

We'd already knocked on the other apartment and received no answer, so there was nothing else to do but head back down to the lobby and go out into the cold once again.

"Wait!" the old woman called as the elevator began to close.

Shannon stopped it with a hand. "You remember something?"

"Yeah, just now. Not sure why, but this young lady reminded me of something." She indicated me with a tiny jutting of her chin. "Anyway, a woman did visit here once after I returned from Washington, one with golden skin and a whole bunch of dark hair pinned up on her head. I studied English in college, and she looked Celtic to me—small nose, dark, oval eyes, but she was tall. I remember her mostly because she wore a lot of unusual jewelry. Really strange stuff. I asked Jim about it later, and he told me he'd talked to her in the lobby and that she was a shaman. You know about them, I suppose. They say they heal the body by healing the spirit, or some such nonsense. I guess the girls called her because the thin one kept coughing." She frowned. "Or did that come later?" She shook her head. "Anyway, she was here once that I knew about. She helped me bring my groceries up the stairs. She had marvelous endurance. I envied that."

Shaman beliefs were different from the hippie lifestyle I'd been raised in but not so far removed that I hadn't heard of them. When I was eight a shaman had stayed at our apartment for a week, sleeping on the couch. He'd claimed to go on spiritual journeys and talk to his ancestors. He was half Indian, though he'd assured me there were many types of shaman and offered to teach me their ways. It was probably the only time Summer had asked me to wait until I was older to learn something.

"She gave me a charm," the old woman continued. "Said it was for strength to keep climbing the stairs. I saw one like it in a store, and it cost over three hundred smackers. Anyway, I keep it in the change pocket of my purse, though they fixed the elevator the next year." Her eyes gleamed. "Maybe that's why I'm still so spry."

"May I see it?"

Grinning, the old woman shuffled slowly inside, leaving her door open, and returned long minutes later with her purse. She handed over a circlet of wood half the size of my palm. The only imprint was a faint one of looking out over the Willamette River and carving, slowly carving. Methodical strokes while singing a song that sounded like praise. The piece of wood held nothing except the well-wishes of a woman who liked to be helpful.

I gave a single shake of my head to Shannon. "Thank you." I returned the carving to the old lady. "Could this shaman also be a midwife?"

"Probably," the old woman agreed. "They're into healing."

"Thank you for your time."

"You have my card if you remember anything else." Shannon walked over and pushed the elevator button.

I waited until we were in motion before saying, "Well, we didn't learn anything here, except the midwife might also be a shaman. Maybe someone knows something more in one of the adjacent buildings."

"Maybe the shaman is the key," Shannon said. "If she was the midwife and Cindy convinced her to put Gail's name on the birth papers, they might have had some sort of prior relationship. She may not be from around here at all but someone from Cindy's past. She might even have known that Jenny's father wasn't a good man and that's why she agreed to help hide her birth from him."

"So maybe if we find the shaman or midwife, we find the birth father."

"Except there are a lot of shamans in Portland. I mean, if you count the lay ones without professional training."

I laughed. "This certainly is an interesting city. Did Paige find addresses from Cindy's background?"

He checked his phone. "No one seems to know where Cindy grew up or anything about her schooling years, but Paige asked for a courtesy update from the FBI, and they've tracked down her mother. She's still alive and in a government rest home. She's too far gone, though, to give them any information." Shannon gazed at the next building. "Not sure it's worth knocking on all those doors, though we'll do it if we can't think of anything else."

Disappointment reeled through me. We'd come so far only to slide to a screeching halt. If Cindy hadn't grown up in this area, and if the shaman or midwife was someone she'd known before, canvassing all the nearby apartments would be a waste of time.

"Agent Cross strikes me as a thorough woman." Shannon raked his hands through his hair. "I bet she's already having her associates talk to all these people."

"I think we should go see Cindy's mother. Even if she can't tell us anything, her stuff might be able to." I grimaced. "Well, provided she's kept something from that time." I *wanted* to find Jenny, for me every bit as much as for her. I didn't want this to end up like my first case with Shannon in which a ten-year-old girl had gone missing on her bicycle. I'd helped her family find closure, but they would never see Alice grow up.

"All right. Let's do it," he said as he started the engine. "You know what? I'm surprised Paige didn't meet us here."

"She's probably getting ready to go out. It is the weekend, you know." She'd been dating a doctor for a month now but hadn't as yet let Shannon know his identity for fear he'd scare him off with background checks and interrogations. "She actually has a life— unlike us."

He laughed. "Is there someplace you'd rather be?"

It was a mixed question, because I wanted to be with him but not necessarily tracking a possible kidnapper or trying to learn whether my biological father was a child predator. Instead of answering, I said lightly, "Be quiet and drive."

White flakes began falling, fulfilling Cody's prediction and ramping up my worry. If Jenny was hurt in a field or forest somewhere, the snow would further obscure any tracks.

"Aren't you going to eat your sandwich?" Shannon asked, munching on his as he dodged through the busy Friday night traffic.

"Maybe later." We were crossing one of the many bridges spanning the Willamette, and that always brought memories of losing Winter. But at least I had overcome most of my terror of crossing the water.

Shannon cast me a significant look and didn't say anything. I was glad. I didn't want sympathy. I wanted to focus on Jenny.

The rest home was at the edge of the commercial district. I peered through the windshield as we arrived. Snow was still falling, though the roads were clear, the flakes being ground into water beneath the many passing tires. The building was a squat, pallid place surrounded by gray snow, looking like something from the slug family wallowing in a freezing, muddy pond. Weak lights lined the walkway that already retained a fresh, dusty layer of snow.

Shannon checked his watch. "Seven-thirty. They'll have eaten dinner hours ago. Might already be asleep."

"They're old, not infants. Besides, this is important. We'll wake her up if we have to. Better have the badge ready."

We walked briskly up the path and into the building. A blond receptionist barely out of her teens looked up from a book as we entered.

"May I help you?" she called, as we shook snowflakes from our heads.

"Chemistry," she said with a grimace as she saw me glance at her book. "I should have taken physics instead."

I nodded sympathetically, while Shannon said, "We're here to see Maureen Quincy."

"Are you family?"

Shannon took out his badge. "I'm investigating the case of a missing child. We believe Mrs. Quincy may have information."

The girl's blue eyes gleamed. "Cool. You're the second ones

who wanted to see her today. Right after dinner, the FBI came. Is it because of that girl from Hayesville who's been on the news?"

We nodded.

"I'll call the orderly and have him show you to her room. I wish I could go myself, but I have to watch the desk." She frowned, the idea apparently making her depressed. She picked up the phone. "Anyway, I don't know what Maureen can tell you. She never leaves here, and she's never had any visitors except the FBI today. She did tell me once that she had a daughter who died."

"We're hoping she can direct us to someone she knew a long time ago," I said, taking pity on the girl's curiosity.

She grinned. "Maureen knew a lot of people. She lived on the street most of her life." She shivered and rubbed the sleeves of her green sweater. "Don't know how she did that on nights like this."

My wonder was how Maureen had raised a child on the streets.

The orderly was a short, wiry old man with bright green eyes and hair shaved to a half inch all over his head. "What's this about?" he asked, when Shannon flashed his badge. "Maureen's sleeping."

"We'll have to wake her," I said. "We're looking for a lost child."

"I see." The green eyes showed wariness. "You won't upset her, will you?"

What an odd thing to say. "Why do you ask?" I pressed. "Did the agent from the FBI upset her?"

"I wasn't on shift yet when they came today, but the last guy who came to visit asked questions about a baby, and she got upset. Cried for hours after he left."

Shannon stopped dead in the hallway. "When was this?"

"Some months ago." The orderly looked at the ceiling in thought. "It was in the summer, so maybe July. I brought him here and waited in the hall to make sure it was okay. I didn't like his eyes. He yelled at her, asking about a baby. She kept telling him her baby died. She was crying and screaming. It was awful. I made him leave."

I gave Shannon a meaningful glance. The man had to be Jenny's birth father. "What did he look like?"

"Thin like me, average height, blond hair that curled at the ends." He looked up at Shannon. "Lot like yours, only more blond. His eyes were light blue, washed out. Narrow face. Kind of shifty, if you ask me."

Shannon nodded. "Did he have any distinguishing marks or tattoos? Anything that made him stand out?"

"He was wearing a hoodie, so I could only see his face, but it didn't have any marks. He seemed to know Maureen well. She knew him, too, so she probably knew him from a long time ago. She doesn't even remember what she ate for dinner these days."

"If you sat down with a sketch artist, do you think you could help us draw a likeness?" Shannon brought out his phone.

The orderly shrugged. "I doubt it. It's been months. But I'm willing to try. Can't leave work, though, so it'll have to be after my shift."

"I can probably have someone come here." Shannon took down his information. "Did he or Mrs. Quincy say anything else?"

"Not that I heard, but I was down the hall for part of his visit. I wish I hadn't left her at all." His words were a pointed reminder about not upsetting the woman.

We continued to Maureen's room where the orderly knocked on the door. "Maureen?"

"Come in," came a groggy voice.

He opened the door, but the room inside was dark. "Sorry for disturbing you, but you have some visitors."

"Oh?" Her voice was suddenly wide awake, and we heard someone moving. "Well, send them in."

The orderly flipped on the light, revealing a scrawny woman dressed in pink flannel pajamas. She was sitting up in bed, her thin white hair awry.

"I'll be out in the hall, doing my rounds," the orderly told us. More likely, he'd be right outside the door, after what happened the last time. I was glad she had him for a defender.

A lifetime of living on the streets—of too little food and too much drink—had not been kind to Maureen. She was a curled, wizened creature with heavy wrinkles that made her look far older than the sixty-five years she could claim. Her deep-set eyes were the only thing that still seemed to work properly, rolling back and forth between me and Shannon. Their bright blue color reminded me of Jenny's baby picture.

She finally settled on me as being the least intimidating. "Do I know you?"

"No," I said.

Maureen looked relieved.

I walked closer to the bed. "We're looking for someone."

"Who?" The eyes now had a shuttered look. She pulled her knees to her chest and wrapped her arms around them.

Given the orderly's story, maybe I should start with something simple before asking directly about her daughter. "A shaman woman. She might also be a midwife. When you knew her, she would have had dark hair, olive skin, dark eyes.

Wore a lot of jewelry. I think she may have lived in your neighborhood."

She smiled, though it looked more like a grimace in her aged face. "You mean Divone. I knew her. She's a great healer. She liked my Cindy."

I was tempted to ask how well Divone knew Cindy and if Maureen knew she had a grandchild, but I'd rather have the midwife's address, and I didn't dare risk her breaking down now. "Do you know where she lived?"

"Down by the bridge. I had an apartment there once."

"Which bridge?" Shannon asked.

Maureen blinked at him, as though she'd forgotten he was in the room. "Do I know you?"

"No." To his credit, there was no trace of impatience in Shannon's voice.

"What were the apartments called?" I asked.

She shook her head. "You don't want to live there. They had cockroaches and rats. Lots of skunks around outside. If you asked for something to be fixed, it took forever. I had a leak once, and it took three years before they'd fixed it."

So at least for three years she—and maybe Cindy—had a roof over her head. "Did the shaman live there?"

She squinted at me. "Do I know you?"

"We're trying to find a missing girl," I said. "Is there anything else you can tell me about where the shaman lived?"

Her wrinkled lips pursed. "Baby," she whispered. A single tear ran down her cheek.

"Maureen, please focus." I leaned closer to her. "We need to find the midwife. This is about Cindy's baby, not yours."

She laid her head on her knees and rocked soundlessly, her eyes still open but unfocused.

"What about Cindy's boyfriend, the baby's father?" I asked. "Can you tell us his name?"

Maureen continued to rock. She was completely gone.

"I'm sorry," I whispered. Suddenly there was so much I wanted to know about her. Like why she'd chosen to be homeless instead of living with her daughter. Why she'd quit her jobs. -

"Autumn."

I turned to see Shannon standing beside a narrow five-drawer dresser. On top was a basket full of mismatched items. Maureen's treasures. Defeated, I walked over to him and went to work.

Strangely, these were the most enjoyable prints I'd experienced all day, excepting a few in the Vandyke house. Everything, from the small stuffed animal to the narrow-necked decorative green bottle, the piece of sea glass to the small Latin prayer book, showed me a life of simple joys. These objects weren't expensive, but Maureen had loved them with a simple heart of immaturity and single-minded innocence. I knew then that something had broken a long time ago inside Maureen, and the life she'd chosen was the way she dealt with that hurt. Day to day, not worrying about tomorrow, about possessions, and sadly, people. People who could hurt but also those who might have helped her heal.

I picked up a small, white cardboard box. Inside wrapped in tissue was a silver ring so tiny and thin that it couldn't have cost much and wasn't worth hanging onto outside any emotional value. I reached out a finger.

She'll wear this ring until it no longer fits, and then I'll hang it on a chain around her neck.

"See this, sweetie?" I showed it to the baby in my arms.

I sat in a hospital bed, the baby wrapped in a receiving blanket, arms bound tightly to her sides. She was so tiny I was afraid of hurting her accidentally.

"This is yours, my sweet baby. I bought it when you were still inside my tummy. We're going to live in a nice apartment the social worker found. We get to stay there all day together for six weeks. Then I'm going to work, and you will go play with some kids while I'm gone. It'll be great, except I'll miss you, and maybe you'll miss me, though probably not since you'll be having so much fun. Everyone says the woman is amazing. She watches all the children around here. It's close to the Hudson—that's the name of where we're staying—so I'll pick you up on the way home."

Fierce love grew inside my breast, almost but not quite breaking through that part of me hidden from all the world.

There was nothing more, so I let the ring drop. Compassion for Maureen and baby Cindy choked my voice so I couldn't speak.

Shannon offered me his watch, but I shook my head. I didn't want to obliterate the imprint. Someone needed to grieve for Maureen.

"I hope you found a good lead," Shannon said, "because there's nothing else here. No pictures, no journals. Nothing."

"When Cindy was born they lived at a place called Hudson. Cindy went to daycare nearby."

"That was more than thirty years ago, but I'll call Paige and see what she can dig up." He took out his phone. "Looks like I'll have to call the precinct instead. Paige texted to say she was leaving the office."

"Have them look at government-assisted housing."

Shannon nodded and called while I went back to the bed

with the little white box. I held it in front of Maureen's eyes for a few seconds before setting it on the bed next to her.

"You did right getting that apartment for Cindy," I said. "And whatever else happened in her life, she grew up and was able to take care of herself. The rest wasn't your fault. Sometimes people just get sick." I lowered my voice. "I'm doing everything I can to find Cindy's baby. If I do, I'll ask her adoptive parents to bring her here."

I knew I was promising a lot, but with Gail's dedication to charities and helping others, I couldn't believe she'd say no. Maureen wouldn't be around long. Her many years on the street had taken its toll, and more of her was in the next world than in this one.

There was a movement on the bed as Maureen unclasped her arms long enough to grab the box from the bed and shove it into my hands. "Please find her," she whispered. "We always knew he shouldn't have her."

So she knew about the baby. "What is his name?" I asked. But she was gone again, eyes staring at something I couldn't see.

I had the feeling that sane or insane, Maureen would not have given Jenny's birth father any information—if she had any to give.

I set the white box back on the dresser with her other treasures and joined Shannon at the door. The orderly walked us out—after first checking on Maureen.

By the time we'd tramped through the snow and were back inside the truck, Shannon had a call from the police station. "Thanks," he said. "Yes, send it to my phone."

Hanging up, he looked at me. "The Hudson was sort of a halfway house, where those in the apartments paid only part of the rent and utilities until they got back on their feet. The families had to have children or they couldn't qualify."

"Then let's go."

He frowned. "The hitch is that it was demolished ten years ago to make room for new waterfront condos."

Another dead end.

"There have to be some older buildings nearby," he added. "Looks like we'll be knocking doors after all." He started the truck, and I reached for my sandwich.

Ten minutes later, I was beginning to feel anxious as we neared our destination. If this was another dead end, we would be no closer to finding Jenny's father, and I wasn't sure what to try next.

"We could check the prisons for new releases," I told Shannon. "See if any inmate was called Geyser."

"He could have gotten out months ago. Or years. Maybe he just now ran into someone who knew Cindy and found out she'd been pregnant. Or maybe he found out years ago and only now decided he wanted to meet his daughter." He sighed. "There are so many variables. Anyway, the FBI is checking on former employees at the sewing factory. Anyone who knew them at the time might have told Geyser about the baby."

Finding those people so they could identify Geyser would take time. How many employees had come and gone? How many neighbors and friends?

"They might not even realize they told him anything," I said. "I mean, if it was in casual conversation, and they didn't know his identity—even Gail, who became her best friend, met him only once. They might not be able to identify him. Our best bet is to find someone who knew them from the past. Someone who knew Cindy when she and Geyser were together."

Shannon nodded, his face tight. "We're almost there."

I peered out into the darkness where the businesses were quickly giving way to apartments. The snow was light enough that the flakes reflected the light from the street lamps instead of further obscuring my view.

"Wait," I said suddenly. "Pull over."

"What is it?"

I could see the darkness of the river behind the apartments on the edge of the snowy road. I had never physically been on this road in my life, but the view of the river here was familiar.

I'd seen it today in the imprint on the wood talisman.

"I know where to go," I said. "I just hope our shaman is still there."

Chapter 11

We climbed from the truck, and I led Shannon to an apartment building. Whoever made the talisman the old woman had shown us had once lived here, in one of the apartments—on the right side of the building, because it was closer to the bridge in the distance. The apartment had a balcony out the back so the shaman could gaze onto the Willamette, and it had to be high enough to see the water over the boatyard nestled between the apartments and the water, but probably not as high as the top two floors.

Craning his neck, Shannon counted the stories, six in all. "So maybe the fourth."

"That's my bet. But maybe the third."

"With any luck, there will only be one back apartment on the right."

It could still be on the left, of course, depending on the perception of the shaman when she'd imprinted on the talisman.

I did up the buttons on my coat. "Whether or not she's still here is the question. It's been fourteen years. And there's always the chance there's another apartment near the river and a bridge that gives almost the same view."

The shaman also could have been visiting someone else when she imprinted on the talisman, but I wasn't going to dwell on that possibility. Instead, I would think about Cindy living in this area with her mother. Safe for at least those three years, or possibly longer.

I felt a stab of sympathy for Cindy, but there was nothing I could do for her now except to find Jenny and see her safely back to the people who loved her.

The old building had a door protecting its lobby, but the lock was broken. Inside, we found peeling paint, twenty-four old metal mailboxes set into the left wall, and outdated light fixtures. Even the marble stairs showed signs of wear—decades of use had worn off some of the rock. But the small lobby was clean, the lights were working, and several large and well-tended plants sat by the outside doors and to the side of the steps.

"Looks like the elevator works," I said.

We rode directly to the fourth floor, where we found four apartments, two in the front and two facing the river. Shannon motioned to the back apartment on the right side. "Want to do the honors?"

I pulled off my gloves and held my hand over the bell. Imprints tingled. I let my finger rest on it without pushing.

Hurry, please open. We needed help. Desperation. With no money or insurance, this was the only place I could think to go. Maybe the shaman would be able to help.

The imprint came from last week. I let my finger fall before another imprint began and smiled at Shannon. "She's here. Or was last Wednesday."

He rang the bell.

The woman answered almost immediately, as though she'd

been expecting us. She was a tall, hardy woman, with a small, round nose, full lips, a wide face, and brown eyes. She looked regal in a black dress topped by a large, flowing purple and black scarf. Her golden skin was unblemished and had few wrinkles, but her dark hair, swept high on her head, was woven liberally with gray.

"May I help you?"

"Are you Divone?"

She inclined her head. "Yes."

"We are looking for the midwife who delivered Cindy Quincy's baby fourteen years ago," I said.

Her eyes narrowed. "Why?"

"The baby's name is Jenny Vandyke, and she went missing two weeks ago. We believe her birth father may be involved."

"Ah." Divone looked first at me and then at Shannon. "Then you are with the police?"

"He's a detective," I said as Shannon fished out his badge. "I'm a consultant. We know you agreed to change the name on the birth papers fourteen years ago, and we know you did it to protect Jenny. That's not why we're here. We want to know anything you can tell us about the birth father."

She opened the door. "Please, come in."

The door opened into a narrow ten-foot hallway that led to a living room. The room held a sofa and two matching chairs, the backs of which held large draped shawls, similar to her scarf, though the colors were more earthy and muted. In front of the sofa sat a cherry coffee table with a glass top where incense burned in a tall crystal vase. A wide cherry buffet and hutch spanned one wall, the upper part all shelves with glass doors, the deeper bottom part containing drawers and cupboards with wooden doors. The buffet top was large enough to hold a variety of serving platters or even a small television. Instead the space was filled with quartz crystals large and small, some in clusters, others in cut crystal bowls.

More crystals glistened from the upper shelves. I recognized an amethyst cathedral geode, similar to one I'd picked up at an estate sale, though this one was three times the size. Braids of grass filled one of the shelves, and below that was a shelf of wooden talismans like the one she'd given the woman at Cindy's old apartment. Several baskets next to the cabinet held bundles of what looked like different kinds of sage. Behind the sofa sat a table layered with another flowing cloth, this one a calming blue, and beyond the table, curtains covered the glass doors leading to the balcony.

Shannon gave me a look that told me he thought the contents of the room and its occupant strange. I was with him on that, but the feeling was calming and peaceful, and I was glad to be here.

"Please have a seat." Divone indicated the sofa before removing a cut crystal bowl filled with colorful crystals from a shelf and placing it on the coffee table near the burning incense.

"You did know Cindy, didn't you?" I asked. "Even before the birth."

She pulled a large feather from a drawer and sat in a chair opposite us, leaning forward to fan the incense. A gentle smoke rose around the room. She set the feather down. "I knew Cindy very well. I tended her every day from the time she was six weeks old until she was twelve and her mother went back on the streets." She pointed to a framed photograph among the many that filled the entire wall behind her. "That's her there, right in the middle of my five children and four others I watched at the time. She'd just turned twelve."

"What happened to her after that?"

"She stayed with friends, or sometimes she'd come back here for a few weeks. There were three foster homes. Sometimes in the summer she stayed with her mom. It wasn't a bad life. Wherever she was, she knew she always had a home here."

The tightness I'd felt in my chest since leaving the nursing home eased. "I'm glad to know that."

"Her child has been happy?" Divone asked.

I nodded. "She has two parents who love her very much."

"I knew she would." Divone smiled and fanned the incense again. "I burned the sage and cleansed the room. I prayed to the Almighty to help the child come. Afterwards we gave her a name." She picked up the bowl of crystals. "These are birth stones, red calcite, moss agate, jade, peridot, moonstone, opal, among others. Some of these were the same ones we had at Jenny's birth. They soothe and give strength to the mother."

Shannon was holding back a smirk, but I'd felt imprints do exactly what she was describing. I didn't know if the stones themselves had any curative qualities, but I believed in positive thinking and emotions. Jake sold a lot of crystals in his herb store, and though I'd never used them, his customers usually returned to buy more.

"The birth went well?" I prompted.

"Jenny was breech, and it was hard, but she came okay. In the hospital, Cindy would have been given a C-section, but breech births are possible if you know how and if the placenta is strong. Cindy did hemorrhage afterward, and that was a bit of a scare, but I managed to stop the bleeding."

"When did Cindy get sick?"

A slight frown passed over her face. "I'm not sure. I went to see her the week after the birth, and she was healing well. She was determined to give her baby everything she didn't have, even if that meant giving her up or watching her grow from the sidelines."

"But she didn't have even that." Like my own young birth mother who'd died in childbirth.

"I don't know why she didn't call me for help when she got sick like she did. Maybe I would have been able to help if she'd called me early enough." Divone offered a brief smile. "At least I would have gotten her to the doctor in time."

She took up the feather and fanned the incense once more. "I can say that I believe Cindy was needed elsewhere, and Cindy's friend— Gail, wasn't it?—she attached to that baby from the moment I put her in her arms. It was she who held and calmed her while I attended to Cindy, as though fate knew what they would mean to each other."

"If you knew Cindy, did you know her boyfriend?"

"Oh, I knew him." Her voice indicated disapproval. "Or at least I'd seen him with Cindy a few times. He was smart. Really intelligent. He knew so much about everything. But he was also a mean and vicious man. One of the times I saw them, Cindy had a black eye, and another time when I touched her arm, she winced. I didn't need her to tell me who did that." She paused, her face pained. "He drank, but he didn't need the drink to be mean. He let all his intelligence go to waste. He was into fraud, and Cindy suspected he'd taken part in several murders, but she didn't know how to get away from him. The last time I saw her before the birth she was relieved he'd gone to prison. That was before she knew she was expecting."

"Do you know his name?" Shannon's phone must have vibrated because he took it from his pocket as he asked the question.

"Geyser, I think. I never caught a last name." She sighed. "Sorry, I wish I could be of more help."

"Did he come to see you recently?" I asked as Shannon pushed a button on his phone. "Maybe searching for information about his daughter?"

"I haven't seen him." Divone's brow gathered. "You think he took her?"

"We don't know. Jenny was searching for her biological father online. If he ran into someone who'd known Cindy while she was expecting, that might have been enough for him to track her down. Especially if he thought Gail might have raised her. If Jenny put the name of her mother and her place and date of birth online, it wouldn't be hard for him to connect the dots."

Shannon showed me a sketch on his phone before passing it to Divone. "This is a preliminary sketch our artist made from a description an orderly gave at the home where Cindy's mother is now. Does this look like Geyser?"

Divone studied the photo. "It's been fourteen years, you understand, and I only spent a couple hours with the guy all together, but this doesn't ring any bells. I mean, all the features are right, but it's not him. Sorry."

Shannon sighed. "It happens sometimes. The orderly only saw him briefly."

"He could have changed a lot in fourteen years," Divone said. "Prison can do that to a man."

She sounded like someone who spoke from personal experience and I was curious. On any other day, I would have loved to keep her talking.

"Would you mind working with a sketch artist?" Shannon asked.

"Of course not." Divone glanced at the phone once more before handing it back. "But my description would be the same as this, except he was younger, of course. Don't know that you'll get anything different from me."

She stood and walked to the cabinet. "I do seem to remember that we took pictures one time. It was the first time I met him and the first time I'd seen her in three years. It was the only really good visit we had because after that I'd realized what he was. Maybe he's in one of the pictures."

Divone removed a photo box from a drawer, found a tab, and began thumbing through two inches of photographs. I caught glimpses of women who resembled her, giggling toddlers on their laps. Probably her own daughters.

"Here they are." Divone's flipping slowed, and her lips pursed. "Oh, there's only one with him. It's not good."

In fact, it was the back of his head and a partial side of his face, and he was wearing a baseball cap, so it really didn't help. His height was average and though he was on the slender side, that didn't set him apart from millions of other men.

Great.

"We'll keep this if you don't mind," Shannon said. "Maybe the FBI can do some enhancing."

"Sure."

"Wait." My heart started thumping in my ears as a thought occurred to me. "Do you still have the camera?"

Divone nodded. "Oh, yes. Even in this digital age, I like the old-fashioned kind of photos. Most people I know don't ever get around to printing their digital ones. Why do you ask?"

Because even if she didn't have the photos, if the day had been so good for Divone, there might be an imprint waiting for me. "Can I see it?"

My tone must have been urgent because she stopped asking questions, walked to the middle of the cabinet, and opened a cupboard.

"Here it is." She handed it to me.

Imprints assailed me. Happy, vague ones but strong enough to make me smile. Not enough to take over, to blot out who I really was. Divone enjoyed taking pictures of those she loved. Her grandchildren, especially. Occasionally, a stronger imprint emerged when Divone was worried or when someone else wielded the camera, but for the most part, the imprints were easygoing and pleasant. I sat back on the couch, willing to wait. Ten years, eleven, twelve. A blur of faces as the years passed, the imprints more faded.

I almost missed it when a happy face, two happy faces, came in a blur like all the others. But this one had pale blond hair and a face that looked like Jenny's. It had to be Cindy. I focused more tightly on the imprint, willing it to be enough, though nothing I could do would change what was there.

I wasn't experiencing voices now, the later imprints having mostly taken over this long after the event. Only the faces. Closer. Look at him. But Divone was looking at Cindy, who seemed happy.

No, look at him, I thought.

Then Divone did look at him, and I saw him. Young, very thin. Blond hair that curled at the ends. Narrow face.

One I'd seen before.

I must have gasped because the camera was yanked from my hands. I blinked, for a moment not seeing the room I was in but still focused on the faint images in the imprint.

"Autumn?"

Shannon's face came into view, and I gave him a weary grin. "I know who he is."

"What?"

"I know him. He's in Salem." I searched my brain for his name. "It's Bremer. David Bremer, the gunman from the gas station. The one who stabbed the man we found at Cody's." Jenny's biological father had been in the custody of the Marion County sheriff's office all along.

Shannon and Divone stared at me, Shannon with a look of triumph and Divone with one of confusion.

"We'll need to call the commander and Agent Cross," Shannon said.

A rush of self-doubt assailed me. What if I was wrong? No. David Bremer's being Jenny's father would explain at least to some point the apparent coincidence of people pulling guns on us twice in one day.

"This means those men at the hospital," I said. "It's all related." Shannon nodded grimly. "Probably, though what drug dealers have to do with Jenny's disappearance, I can't imagine."

"The key is Bremer. We have to question him." I turned to Divone. "Thank you so much for your time. You've been a lot of help."

"I don't know how . . . I'm not sure what—" She shook her head. "It doesn't matter. As long as you find that little girl." She opened yet another drawer and pulled out a scarf with wide stripes of purple, mauve, and green. "I paint the colors onto white silk," she said. "These colors are soothing. Take this with you on your journey. Maybe it will help."

"Thank you." I accepted the cloth without protest, mostly to save time but partly because it was so beautiful.

As my fingers touched the silk, an imprint came to me of her painting the cloth, exuding calmness, comfort, and love in much the way my sister did when she was drawing. I met her eyes, this shaman midwife who had spent her life helping others and making things for them.

"It's beautiful," I murmured."

I wondered if I should try to fold it further and put it in my pocket, but she took it from me, shook it and draped it over my neck. "It is to be used," she said, smiling. "Come on, I'll show you out."

I followed her, tucking the ends of the scarf inside my coat. It didn't match my red sweater, but there was no one to see, and the calm that pervaded my body was worth it.

"You drive. I'll call," Shannon said as we left the building. Strangely, it was darker than I remembered in the street. What had happened to the street lamps? Sure enough, those around the building were out, though I could see others glowing down the road. A lone car drove past us through half an inch of snow, disappearing around a bend.

"Watch out!"

Shannon's warning came too late. Rough hands grabbed me.

Chapter 12

Instinctively, I lashed out, my fist connecting with something big. I followed up with another punch and a roundhouse. Next to me, I could hear Shannon locked in his own battle. More snow fell to join the soft blanket already on the ground.

My assailant jabbed at me, a blow that grazed my jaw as I ducked. I launched another round of punches, landing two with a satisfying crunch. His next jab hit me in the face with enough force to knock me to the snowy ground. He laughed and reached for me, but he was overconfident and slipped on the snow. I helped his descent by kicking his legs out from under him. He fell with a moist thud. He was significantly larger than I was, though, and no matter how much faster I was, he was trained enough that I knew this was a fight I wasn't going to win. Fleeing was the wisest option.

Springing to my feet, I dared a look at Shannon. He'd felled one man, who was struggling to his feet, and now fought with a third who was twice his size. Just as Shannon punched, I kicked the back of the man's legs and he collapsed. Shannon punched him again, and he lay still.

The first two men were back on their feet. Shannon tried to go for his gun, but they lunged at us too quickly. So much for getting out of there. I sidestepped my opponent, took several steps away as if I were going to run, and then turned and leapt at him, foot out, using my momentum to increase the power of my kick. The move was good, even though I was hindered by the weight of my coat. He took it in the stomach, grunting, but he lashed out as he tumbled back, catching me in the thigh with a painful blow.

Ignoring the pain, I slammed my fist into his jaw. It was a perfect move, or it would have been if I'd been taller. As it was, his head barely jerked back with the force. He growled, slamming his fist into my stomach once, twice, and again. I twisted away, feeling sick and weak.

No time for that, I told myself. I kicked out blindly, and this had more effect than my planned moves. He screamed as I found his knee.

Fueled by hope, I threw another punch at his face as he hunched over, hoping to land it with enough force to knock him out or at least make him dizzy. This time luck wasn't on my side. He recovered easily, his right fist connecting with my left shoulder and his left slamming into my mouth. Warm blood dribbled down my chin.

I knew I should run, but I was in too much pain. Though he hadn't hit my healing gunshot wound, jabbing the shoulder on the same side was bad enough. A cry escaped through my gritted teeth, an involuntary reaction that would direct him to punch the same area again.

His fist rose, and I lifted my right arm to block, hoping he wouldn't break it.

A movement behind him. Shannon, who had managed to

free himself enough to draw his gun. A glint of metal came down on my attacker's head. He fell and this time didn't get up.

"Behind you!" I shouted at Shannon.

He whipped his gun around, but the other man also had a gun now too. Whatever their initial plans had been about subduing us, they apparently weren't above resorting to shooting us if necessary.

The two men stood, guns pointing at the other. "Put it down," Shannon said.

The man didn't reply.

"Who are you?" Shannon demanded. "Who are you working for?"

Again the man gave him no response.

Shannon raised his gun an inch. "Look, assaulting a police officer is a serious offense. It'd go easier on you when we get to the precinct if you'd put it down now and come voluntarily."

That's when I noticed vehicle lights coming toward us down the street. Maybe someone had heard the fight and would call the police.

The man laughed. "You ain't going nowhere, except with us."

I could see now that the vehicle was a black van—and it was heading our way fast. The driver slammed on its brakes as it reached us.

This did not look good.

Shannon lunged, bringing his gun hand down on the wrist of the other man, who'd also glanced at the van. His gun thumped into the snow.

"Run!" Shannon shouted.

We ran. Loud cracks split the air around us. I heard a bullet rip into the base of a tree not a foot away. Shannon let off his own volley of bullets, but without cover we didn't dare to stop for him to aim. We were near his truck now, and I heard him use the keyless entry before pushing the keys into my hand. "You drive."

I started the engine, while he let off a few cover shots. Surely someone would call the police now. Of course, our attackers would come to the same conclusion and be more anxious to accomplish whatever they'd set out to do. Namely, taking care of us.

I slammed my foot down on the gas pedal, and we were in motion. Shannon fired another shot out his still open door just before I swerved around the corner and the van temporarily vanished from sight.

In seconds, they were in my rearview mirror again. Shannon was calling for backup. I pushed harder on the gas, wondering if I might slide from the snowy road. But my next turn took me into a street where the busier traffic had kept the snow from sticking. The traffic was safer for us, maybe, but I worried about someone else getting hurt.

They were still behind us.

I swerved into oncoming traffic to pass the slowpoke in front of us, swerving back in time to avoid a collision. Half a block, I turned up another street that held more moving cars. I had no idea where we were or where I was going. I only hoped my next turn didn't lead to a dead end.

Sirens. Relief shuddered through me as I heard them. Police lights reflected down the street behind and in front of us. The van took an abrupt turn, disappearing from my mirror. Shannon reported the information into his phone, and the police cars put on speed, following the direction taken by the van.

"No plates," Shannon said grimly. "Hope they get it."

"Should we stop and wait?" I asked, passing the car in front of us. It felt good, putting more space between us and the van.

"Our guys can handle it. If they catch them, we'll come back to ID them. But for now, let's get to Salem. I'll call the commander and the FBI on the way." He let several heartbeats pass by before adding with a grin. "You can slow down now."

"I'll drive however I want," I retorted. "This is an emergency, remember?"

"Ha. You always drive like this. That's why I gave you the keys. I knew we'd get away with you behind the wheel."

"Very funny." I pulled onto what I hoped was the right freeway, pushing harder on the gas pedal.

Shannon said nothing, but he reached over me and put on my seatbelt and then his own.

"How do I turn on the police light?" I said.

"I'll do it." He retrieved the equipment from the floor, opened the window, and placed the magnetic light on top of the truck. The siren cleared the cars in front of us like magic.

Five minutes out of town, the snow stopped, but I could tell the storm had been here earlier by the fresh layer of white on either side of the black strip of road.

Shannon answered his phone. "Did you get them?" A long pause. "Well, keep a lookout, though I doubt they'll stick around. He hung up and said heavily, "They didn't get them."

"Who do you think they were?"

"Well, we know the drugs and the shooting and Jenny's disappearance are all related, so apparently someone thinks we're nosing around too much." He sighed. "They've been following us. Probably all day." He didn't sound surprised.

"You knew? Why didn't you tell me?"

"I didn't want to worry you—and because I thought I might be wrong. It was a blue sedan at first, but I kept an eye on them, and I doubled back several times, and they disappeared. Must have had another car waiting. They're good."

To have fooled Shannon they had to be, but there was more he wasn't telling me. I could see it in the crease of his brow.

"What else?" I asked.

Shannon shook his head. "You okay?"

I was too exhausted to demand that he answer. "Just a scratch."

Shannon grinned. "That good, huh?"

Nodding, I grabbed at the tissue he offered and dabbed my lip, which was still oozing blood. My right cheek felt hot and fiery, and my left thigh and ribs ached, though I didn't think anything was broken. I pondered what I would tell Jake and my sister the next day, if we were back in Portland by then.

An ugly bruise was forming on Shannon's jaw, and I bet he was in as much discomfort as I was. He reached out and turned on the heater. Good thing since my black pants were wet with melting snow, and I was freezing.

"Guess I'll call Commander Huish and Agent Cross," Shannon said.

For the next fifteen minutes, he was talking on the phone, reporting Bremer's identity. I noticed that though he told Cross and Huish we'd found the information by tracking down the midwife, he didn't mention that the identification I'd made of Bremer had come from an imprint. Though both the commander and Agent Cross seemed to accept what I did, I knew full well my ability didn't translate well in conversation or on paper.

Strangely, I recognized Bremer more from the imprint on

the stabbing victim's shirt than from the brief incident with him at the gas station. I also remembered the pain of the knife entering my chest, so maybe that was why his face was clearer in that memory, the one that wasn't really mine.

I swallowed hard.

"We're almost there," Shannon was saying into his phone. "But, look, there was an incident in Portland at the midwife's house. We were attacked by men just like at the hospital, except this time they were aiming for us, not to protect their men. I'd bet it's the same group. No. The midwife will be fine. I sent officers there to make sure."

I lifted my hand to the scarf, and calmness soothed my worry and the fear I'd experienced during the attack—fear that I could still feel radiating from my sweater, where I must have created an imprint. Not a strong one, though. I hadn't been focusing on it, and I hadn't really believed I was going to die. With a few washes and time, it would fade.

I hoped the attack meant we were getting closer to solving the case and finding Jenny, but Bremer remained the key. We had to find out what he knew. I pushed harder on the gas.

When we arrived back in Salem, I was pleased that we'd beaten the FBI agents to the Sherriff's office, though not by much. I was still hanging up my now-damp coat when Agents Cross and Morley entered the station.

"We found Jenny's accounts at several adoption reunion sites and confirmed that she did talk to someone claiming to be her father," Cross said without preamble. She slid out of her wool coat and hung it next to mine. Her eyes wandered over my split lip and the bruise I knew was forming on my cheek, but she didn't comment.

"Did this guy talk about her birth mother?" I folded Divone's scarf and slipped it into my coat pocket on top of my gloves. I was glad no fear was imprinted on the cloth.

Cross grimaced. "Yes. Worse, he told Jenny that Gail stole her and maybe did something to Cindy. I think that's why Jenny didn't go to her parents about what she'd found. Maybe she wanted to determine the truth for herself."

"She should have known how dangerous it was." I sat on the edge of the desk next to the coatrack.

"Oh, she didn't plan on going with him anywhere." Cross nodded at Morley, who thumbed through a sheaf of papers in his hands. He found a paper and passed it to Cross, who in turn handed it to me. I took it gingerly, relieved when there were no imprints.

Cross continued, "Bremer, who goes only by the name David on the site, tried to convince her to visit him in Portland, but she refused. Said she'd only meet him at a local restaurant."

I reviewed the conversation on the sheet. "It also mentions phone calls that she made from a pay phone. Maybe the plan changed."

Commander Huish shook his head. "We have someone looking at the phone she used at the school. The only incoming calls we can't identify are dated prior to this communication."

"So he took her," I said. "And if Bremer is still here, that means Jenny should be nearby too."

"That's the part that doesn't jibe." Agent Cross collected the paper from my hands. "Why kidnap someone and hang around for two weeks afterward? If he wanted to keep his daughter, I'd expect him to leave town and hide in another state. Or if he wanted a ransom, he would have given the Vandykes a call by now. But he's not doing any of that. He's stabbing people and holding up gas stations. Why?"

She had a point. "He doesn't have her," I said. "Either she ran away from him or—" I broke off as a worse thought occurred.

"Or he did something to her," Shannon finished.

"I think it's high time we ask Bremer himself." Huish looked over at Detective Greeley.

"He's ready," Greeley said. "In interrogation four."

"I'll go in," Agent Cross said. "I'd like Ms. Rain there as well. Maybe she can pick up something from him." She leveled a gaze at me. "But let me ask the questions."

No one objected, so I agreed, though I wasn't excited about seeing the foul-mouthed man again. It wasn't as if I could pick up anything from the air, and how close would I get to touching something he'd imprinted on? At the same time, I was curious, and that was enough motive.

"I'd like to go in, too," Greeley said.

Cross nodded, and minutes later the three of us entered the interrogation room. Greeley was wearing an earpiece, and I knew that if Shannon, Huish, or Morley had questions for Bremer, they would ask through him.

"Did you ever find the boot?" I asked Greeley in a whisper as we went through the door.

"Not yet."

"Well, it probably doesn't matter now that we know who Bremer is."

He nodded but with a reluctance that bothered me. He was hiding something. Had he misplaced or tampered with the evidence? I usually liked most everyone, but this man annoyed me to no end, and I almost wanted to believe he was dirty.

I wondered how I'd fare against him in a fight on a dark street. I shook off the notion. The detective was several heads taller than me and hard as a rock—and I wasn't talking only about his thick head.

"Is something funny?" Greeley asked tightly.

I was tempted to make a joke about his losing the evidence but decided not to antagonize him. We were supposed to be on the same team. "Not at all."

Agent Cross was already at the table, seating herself across from Bremer, who was no longer wearing his baseball cap. Thin frame, narrow face, washed-out blue eyes, blond hair curled slightly up at the ends. He looked exactly like the orderly at the retirement home had described but nothing like the drawing his description had prompted from the sketch artist. The lines of his face were harder, with more angles, and intelligence gleamed in those pale eyes.

We joined Cross, Greeley standing next to the table while I took the other chair next to her, careful to keep my hands from touching the table.

"I'm Special Agent Liz Cross from the FBI," Cross began, pressing a button on a small recorder. "I'll be recording our interview today. You know Detective Greeley, and I believe you've met Autumn Rain. She's a consultant with the Portland police."

Bremer didn't acknowledge Greeley, but his eyes flicked to mine with obvious recognition. Since I had effectively caught him by throwing the pork 'n beans and nearly shooting him with Shannon's gun, I expected him to be angry at seeing me. Instead, he turned flirty.

"Oh, yeah, I remember her. I never forget a pretty face. Though it looks like you need a new boyfriend, honey, if that cut on your lip is from him."

No one replied, though I could imagine Shannon bristling behind the one-way glass.

"To what do I owe the privilege of this visit from the FBI and the psychic?" Bremer continued.

Greeley furrowed his brow. "What do you mean? How do you know about that?"

"Everyone in lockup is talking about her—deputies and inmates both."

"Forget that," Cross cut in, holding Bremer with her stare. "We're here to talk to you about Jenny Vandyke. Where is she, Mr. Bremer?"

Chapter 13

Bremer gave Cross a charming smile that showed me a hint of why Cindy might have fallen for him so long ago. "You sure you work for the FBI? Because I think you should be a model. Little too tall for my taste, but you're a beautiful woman." His eyes moved back to me. "You're more my type, though. I like the red in your hair. Feisty. Dyed, I bet. But the brown underneath makes a nice combination. Unusual but not crass or cheap."

"My height has nothing to do with this," Cross said coolly. "Nor does Ms. Rain's hair. Please pay attention, Mr. Bremer."

"Where's the fun in that?" He pushed back his chair and lifted his feet onto the table. "Anyway, I don't know anything about a missing girl." He wasn't looking at either of us as he said it but someplace between. "You have me for what I did at the gas station, but I didn't stab anyone, and I didn't take no girl."

"I will find out," I said quoting him from the imprint on the undershirt we'd taken from the hospital. "I know about your cousin. Maybe he'll tell me what I want to know." He already thought I was psychic, and maybe that could work in my favor.

Bremer froze, but in the next second he shook his head. "Are you having a vision, dear? Because that really doesn't work for me. Totally unattractive."

Cross didn't ask the question, so I did. "What did you mean by cousin, Mr. Bremer? Who is he?"

"I have no idea what you are talking about."

"So you didn't say those words?" Agent Cross put her hand near the recorder. "I remind you that we're recording."

"And I have the right to be silent," Bremer said. "Maybe I need a lawyer."

"You can call one, or we can appoint one for you." Cross's voice was controlled, but I sensed icy fury beneath. I hoped it was directed at Bremer or her own ineptness at questioning, and not at me for disobeying her gag order. "Are you asking for one?"

Bremer smiled lazily. "No. But I know I don't have to answer if I don't want to."

"Well, let me tell you what we already have," Cross said. "Because of your prior convictions, we have your DNA, and we'll be comparing that with Jenny's. Also, we're tracing your conversation with her on the adoption reunion site. We know you talked to her over the phone and maybe even met with her before she went missing. With your presence here and your past record for fraud, drug running, and domestic violence, that will be plenty to convict you. Why don't you make it easy on yourself and tell us where she is?"

In an instant Bremer's boyish charm vanished. He leaned forward and said viciously, "They stole her from me. Stole her!

She's mine. They deserve to rot for what they did, and I will make them pay!"

We held our breath as Cross asked again. "Where is she, Mr. Bremer?"

His rage lessened marginally. "I. Don't. Know."

"What do you mean you don't know?" Greeley shot at him when Agent Cross remained silent. "Do you deny talking to her? Coming to see her? We know she didn't plan to leave with you. What were your intentions?"

"I did see her, and it made me even more determined to get her back."

"What makes you think you'd be any kind of a father?" Greeley sneered. It was the question on my own tongue, but I'd managed to hold it back.

"I take care of my own," Bremer said. "Are you saying a man doesn't have the right to know he has a child?"

"That's not for us to decide," Cross said. "Where is Jenny?"

"I told you. I don't know."

Cross stood, placing her hands on the table and leaning toward him. "Did you do something to her? Did you hurt her? Was it an accident? Or did she make you angry?"

Bremer rubbed his hands over his face. "I tell you, I don't know anything. I met with her, yes, at a restaurant. She wouldn't come with me. If she had, she'd be safe right now."

"Then who took her?" Greeley nearly yelled. "Why should we believe you?"

"It must have been those parents of hers," Bremer said. "They must have found out what I was planning." The difference in his tone was notable, but I didn't know what it meant.

"You're lying," Cross said. "What happened? If someone else has Jenny, the more you delay, the more you put her in danger. Is that how you prove you're capable of being a good father?"

Bremer jumped to his feet and mimicked Cross's stance, hands on the table, his face inches from hers. "I don't know anything. I want a lawyer. Now. You need to stop questioning me and get out there and find my daughter. If you can't hack it, you should quit. You could always turn to modeling."

Cross's jaw clenched and unclenched, but she kept her calm. "We'll get you an attorney, Mr. Bremer. Maybe he can talk some sense into you because we'll be adding attempted murder and kidnapping to your charges. When we do find your daughter, even if she's okay, you'll be in prison too long even to see her, much less have a relationship with her."

Bremer sat down and folded his arms across his chest, his jaw jutting out.

"Fine. If that's how you want it." Cross went toward the door. Greeley and I followed.

"Let me question him," Greeley said to Huish when we were in the hall. "I'll get it out of him."

Huish sighed. "He's asked for an attorney. There's nothing more we can do."

"He might be telling the truth about not knowing where she is," Cross said. "But he's still hiding something."

"He admitted to contacting Jenny and meeting with her," Shannon said. "If he knows where she is and won't tell us, there's only one reason for that."

"He's protecting himself," Greeley said.

"Exactly. But from what? We have to assume it's the drug connection."

Greeley's nostrils flared. "Some father he is."

"Whoever's in charge sent someone to kill Weston Millard

at the hospital," Shannon added. "He must have information about them they're afraid he'll spill."

Huish looked at Greeley. "We need to see if he's conscious yet."

"I'd like any information you have on him," Cross said. "We can work at it from our end."

I walked down the hall, my mind moving faster than my feet.

The drugs, Jenny, Millard, Bremer, and the men who jumped us—there was a connection, something I wasn't seeing.

Cody Beckett, my long-lost father? I sure hoped not, but why had Millard gone to his house? Maybe he'd been heading somewhere else nearby. Somewhere like the gas station.

"What about the gas station attendant?" I asked.

Everyone turned to me. Greeley, already halfway down the hall, turned and paused.

"He's not at his house, his fiancée's, or at work," Huish said. "Levine's still searching for him."

"He have family?" Shannon asked.

Greeley shook his head. "Not here."

"Don't you think that's odd?" I pressed. "He was shot, Bremer had it out for him, and now he's suddenly missing."

"Are you thinking maybe Bremer has a partner who went after him?" Agent Morley asked.

"Possibly." I shrugged. "But what I meant was that in the imprint on Millard's shirt, Bremer mentioned a cousin. And earlier Cody Beckett and I were talking about how we both think Millard looks like the gas station attendant. Maybe Millard was heading there for help and ended up at Cody's instead."

"Cody's place is at least a mile away from the gas station, maybe two," Greeley pointed out.

"Right," I said, "so it should be easy to find where the stabbing took place, if Millard was on foot. There's not much out there, and he couldn't have walked far."

"My best detectives are on it," Greeley said. "They'll find something."

"How long have Weston Millard and Kirt Henry been in the area?" Shannon leaned against the wall. The bruise on his face was darkening, looking worse than it had in the truck.

Greeley shook his head. "Millard hasn't been here long from what we've been able to tell. Maybe a few months. Kirt Henry has worked at that gas station for a couple of years, I think he told me this morning. Part time. I figured he was in college or something."

"We need to find him." Huish pulled his phone from his pocket and glanced at it, scowling when he read the message. Whatever it was, he didn't share.

Greeley started back down the hall. "I'll call the hospital about Millard and check with Levine to see what he's come up with. Could be he's found Kirt by now."

"Where does Kirt live?" I asked Huish as Greeley disappeared.

"We don't have a warrant."

Huish's reluctance frustrated me. "Well, it's not a crime for me to walk up and knock on the door, is it?"

"How about we just get a warrant?" Cross said. "He's missing, he was shot earlier, and he could be in danger, right? That's enough."

Irritation tinged Huish's face. "We don't need to search his place, we need to find the man."

"We might find a lead at his place." Cross's gaze was challenging.

"Okay. But it's probably a waste of time." Huish glanced at his phone, his expression distracted.

I wondered if something was happening at home.

The adrenaline I'd been running on since the attack outside the midwife's building was all but gone. My cheek hurt, my ribs ached, and I could feel a lump as big as half a grapefruit forming on my thigh. I was also hungry again.

Worse, I was still no closer to finding Jenny or discovering Cody's secrets.

I let the conversation roll over my head for a few minutes until Greeley reappeared in the hallway.

"Millard's taken a turn for the worse. Our guys at the hospital haven't seen anyone suspicious, but the doctors suspect some kind of poison. They found a patch on his leg. Wasn't there earlier when they took him into surgery."

So the drug cartel had tried again, this time with a more subtle method.

"Will he survive?" Huish asked.

"They don't know yet. I've doubled the guard. Two in the room at all times. We do have good news, however. We've located the boot."

I straightened my shoulders, my aches seeming to fade.

Everyone stared at me.

"You ready to look at it?" Cross asked.

"Absolutely." It was time for answers.

"Where was it?" Huish asked.

"Down in one of the evidence lockers. Someone must have misfiled it after the FBI finished their examination."

Misfiled. Shannon and I exchanged a look, which told me he was as skeptical as I was. But that would mean someone had deliberately sabotaged the investigation, and I couldn't imagine anyone I'd met here so far wishing Jenny ill. Maybe it really had been misfiled.

Huish sighed. "What about Levine? Has he found any leads?" His tone implied that he didn't expect much from Levine.

"No," Greeley told him, "but the other guys found a rental house they believe Weston Millard might have been using. There's blood on the doorknob. I sent Levine out there to help search it."

"Great." Huish looked at me and motioned down the hall. "Shall we get to the boot?"

"What about the warrant?" Agent Morley asked.

Huish stopped in mid step. "Will you fill in Detective Sergeant Greeley on the particulars of the warrant so he can get it started? We'll meet you in evidence."

Greeley didn't look happy about having to work directly with the FBI special agent, or maybe he wanted to see me read the boot. Whatever his problem, he didn't question his commander.

The rest of us followed Huish to a storage room where a broad African American woman stood at a window inside, holding a box big enough for several pairs of boots. Huish signed for the box. "Thanks, Jeraldine."

"No problem. I told them several times to look there when they called me to see if I knew where it was. Everyone in evidence must be blind. It was the first thing I found when I came in to work tonight."

"We're glad you're on top of things." Huish led us away to a table opposite the window. "No one should be coming or going too much tonight. I think we can look at this here."

It was all I could do not to rip the box from him in my

eagerness to solve the mystery of who'd taken Jenny, but at the same time I was fighting the urge to run. If she'd been assaulted while wearing the boots, or even murdered, any imprints I found might be horrifying. I sat down in the solitary chair at the table in case I passed out. Less chance of falling and cracking open my skull.

Huish brought out the boot and set it on the table. Light brown suede, unblemished except for a dirt smear above one heel. There was nothing else in the box, and I realized how little the commander and the FBI had to go on. No wonder they hadn't found her, and no wonder they hadn't protested more at my involvement. They were desperate.

Huish stood on my left and Shannon on my right. Agent Cross edged around Shannon and positioned herself almost across from me. I reached out a hand, and tingles shot into my flesh, signaling a strong imprint. I let one finger drop onto the boot.

These were perfect, not at all like the hateful black Mary Janes. I hated the horrible things. Maybe if I said it enough, Mom would get the hint. So what if the Mary Janes were part of my school uniform? It was unfair to make me choose those when I wanted these boots instead. They felt so soft. I wouldn't even have to break them in like the black pair or the other tan ones I already had. And these were much nicer than the gray ones she'd bought for me last week.

"Issy, take them off now. That isn't what we came here for."

My dumpy old mother couldn't possibly remember what it was like to be thirteen. If I didn't get these boots, I'd never be happy. Couldn't she understand that?

"I want these boots."

"*Not today. We need the Mary Janes. We really can't afford both right now. These are expensive.*"

"*I hate the Mary Janes. They're awful.*"

"*Take the boots off now, or I won't let you go to Jacob's party tomorrow.*"

I blinked as the imprint ended. Strange how logical the thoughts had been when I was experiencing the imprint, but as my own awareness reasserted itself, it was hard to believe such a selfish child existed. I was happy her mother hadn't bought her the boots.

"Well?" Shannon asked.

I looked up at him. "This isn't Jenny's boot."

Chapter 14

"What?" Greeley barked from the doorway. He'd apparently passed off the warrant to another detective before rejoining us, along with Agent Morley. His face had grown pale. "Her parents identified it."

"There's only one imprint," I said, "and it's not hers."

"Is it possible Jenny didn't leave an imprint?" asked Agent Cross.

"I'm sorry." I stood, hating the feeling of everyone staring down at me. "I didn't make myself clear." Sometimes it was hard to remember what I'd told people and what I'd experienced. "The imprint here was from a girl who wanted the boots quite badly, but her mother wouldn't buy them. It happened *yesterday*."

Cross knew as well as I did that Jenny's boot had been found and examined days ago.

"You can't tell who bought it?" Shannon asked.

I shook my head. "Either they didn't leave an imprint or they wore gloves when they purchased them." Nothing that would have been noticed this time of year. "If the young girl who tried them on yesterday hadn't left an imprint, I wouldn't be able to tell it isn't Jenny's boot. I would have simply thought she hadn't imprinted on it and that when she'd left it in the woods, she hadn't been under any stress."

"We'll get the parents in." Huish's mouth had a grim set to it. "See if they made a mistake."

I understood that he couldn't take my word for it, but I knew someone not only replaced the boot but had done it because of me. The FBI and the sheriff's office had finished with the boot, so someone had replaced it after I'd shown up in case I'd read something incriminating. But who? And what were they trying to hide?

"If she's right, commander," Cross said, "you have a problem here."

"A problem I'm going to take care of." But Huish's voice and expression had lost power. I wondered if that was because he was afraid of what his investigation would reveal or because he'd rather be home with his sick wife.

"Greeley, I want you to get out to that house with Levine," Huish said. "I want you supervising."

Will he really supervise, or will he destroy evidence? I wondered. But countering my dislike of the man was Huish's trust and Shannon's comment about his dedication.

"Yes, commander. I'll let you know the second we find anything." Greeley's voice was harsh and determined.

"I'd like to come along," Cross said. "This is now related to the kidnapping."

"It's my case," Greeley retorted.

Cross met his gaze steadily. "Not entirely." Did Cross not trust him either, or was she only reminding him that she ultimately had jurisdiction? Perhaps she simply cared about finding Jenny.

At a hard look from Huish, Greeley nodded. "You can follow me."

Huish's gaze transferred to me. "I suppose you'll be wanting to go along. You'll have to promise not to touch anything until our guys collect the evidence we need."

Shannon snorted. "You don't know how many times I've had to tell her that."

Traitor, I thought. "Actually, I'm more interested in the gas station clerk's house," I said aloud. "I already know who stabbed Millard and that Millard is involved in drugs. But I doubt Jenny is at that house or we would have heard from Levine by now. If Kirt's related to Millard, he can tell us more, or if he's not involved, he might be able to direct us to those Millard was working with."

"The warrant is going to take some time," Greeley said, "but both addresses are in Hayesville, so you might as well come along." He said it grudgingly, as though hoping I'd turn him down.

"I bet Millard knows something about the kidnapping," Shannon said. "Could be why Bremer was mad enough to stab him."

I gave Greeley my best smile. "Thank you for the invitation, detective. We accept."

"You can ride with us," Agent Cross said. Her offer gave me more credibility, so I agreed.

"So," I asked Shannon in an undertone as we followed Cross and Morley out into the cold, "do you think one of the sheriff's deputies is dirty?" I blinked my left eye, trying to make it feel more comfortable with Tawnia's contact. Ever since we'd returned to Salem, the eye had been bothering me.

He shook his head. "More likely someone paid one of the

clerks to get to the boot." He hesitated. "You're sure, though? About it not being Jenny's?"

I scowled. "Don't tell me we're back to that again." Back to him not quite believing. Or was he accusing me of lying? No, he knew I didn't lie. And yet now that the idea had come into my mind, I had to admit there had been times when I didn't tell him everything in an imprint, especially one of his own.

"It's a disappointment, that's all. An imprint on the boot could have told us a lot."

I let out a steadying breath and thought about removing the bothersome contact in my eye. It was dark enough that no one would probably notice. Then again, the detectives and FBI agents were trained in observation. The contact had to stay.

Fifteen minutes later we pulled up at a small house a mile southeast of Cody's place, built at the edge of his property, in fact. My stomach growled to remind me it was hungry again, but thankfully no one seemed to hear.

Detective Levine was waiting out front for us on the snow-covered drive when we arrived. He grinned almost shyly at me before looking away. "The houses to the south of here are closer than Beckett's. It doesn't make sense that he would go through the woods unless Beckett's involved."

"Unless he was trying to get to the gas station," Shannon said.

Levine shrugged. "Awful long way to go. Three miles at least, I'd say, from here to the gas station."

"Where is the Vandykes' house in relation to here?" I tried to peer through the darkness, but nothing except fields and trees met my view.

"Directly west of here," said Cross, motioning behind me. "About a mile."

I wondered if the FBI listed good directional skills as a job requirement. If so, that cut me out.

"Any trace of Jenny Vandyke inside?" Greeley asked Levine.

"Not at first glance. But they're fingerprinting, so maybe we'll find something." Levine paused before adding, "This is all unincorporated land out here. Nothing really to see."

Inside there wasn't much to see either—besides the blood in the kitchen and hallway. I recognized the place from Millard's imprint, but he hadn't given much attention to the sparseness. All the basics were present in the old two-bedroom house— beds, dressers, table, couches, but everything had a sense of age and belonging. The only odd thing was that in one of the bedrooms, the single bed had been pushed on its side and leaned up against the wall.

"The furniture came with the house, didn't it?" I asked Levine in the kitchen after my rushed tour.

He nodded. "Rented furnished. The old couple who lived here died a few years back, and their son's been renting it out to people looking for solitude. Said he's had a few writers and a painter. Millard's been here at least a couple months."

"Did Millard tell the owner why he was here?" Shannon had donned rubber gloves like everyone else, except me, and was going through a kitchen drawer.

"Nope. He got the impression that Millard was a little shifty, though. He wasn't all that surprised to hear from us."

Agent Morley rolled his eyes. "And he still rented it out?" He shook his head. "What people will do for a little money."

I drifted away. The kitchen looked rarely used, and if I was to have any luck, I'd have to check the bedroom and bathroom. The detectives, however, had beaten me to the rooms, bagging anything of interest. Fingerprint dust was everywhere. I took that as permission to begin combing for imprints.

I learned a lot about the older couple who had lived here. They had loved, laughed, fought, prayed, and raised their four sons within these walls, starting as lovers and becoming best friends. They died within weeks of each other—she first and he following shortly from a broken heart, at least according to their son, who'd left an imprint on the bedpost as he watched his father pass peacefully into his final sleep.

I couldn't help wondering what it would have been like to be raised in such a traditional family. My adoptive parents had been far from ordinary, I'd lost Summer, my adoptive mother, to breast cancer as a child, and I'd never known my grand-parents. Only recently had I met my one surviving biological grandmother.

Why weren't there any imprints from Millard? I could find absolutely no imprint saying he'd ever been in the house.

I went back to the kitchen and touched Shannon's shoulder. He turned. "You find something?"

"I don't think Millard ever actually stayed here."

"Well, there is the blood. Isn't this the right place?"

"Oh, he was stabbed here, but he didn't leave imprints. I bet you anything it was simply a storage place for whatever illegal activity he's up to. Drugs, probably."

Shannon nodded. "That would explain why there's nothing in the fridge but a six-pack of beer and some takeout growing so much mold it's probably almost sentient."

Agent Cross looked up from where she was examining the largest blood stain. "We'd better test for drugs. But if they were here, someone's moved them."

Levine gave a disgusted sigh. "They would have had to do it almost as soon as he was stabbed. We didn't find a cell phone on him, so he didn't call anyone. How did they know?"

"The same way they knew he was at the hospital." I scanned the room to see if there was anything I'd missed. "We're lucky they didn't torch the place."

"Maybe we just beat them here." Levine swaggered a bit, pushing out his chest awkwardly. "At least we have proof that this is where our vic was stabbed."

Greeley entered the room, his nose red with cold, a bloody knife dangling between two gloved fingers. "Look what I found in the bushes out front. I think we have our weapon." His eyes grazed mine, as if in challenge.

I wanted nothing more than to ignore him—I certainly didn't want a direct line into the mind of an attacker—but too much was at stake. "If there's an imprint on it, we might learn why Bremer stabbed him."

Greeley shook his head. "Got to get it to forensics first. Sorry." He didn't look sorry at all. Mocking was the better word.

"Just fingerprint it here and let her touch the handle," Shannon said.

"Look, I don't know how you do things in Portland, but we follow protocol here." Greeley's mean eyes glinted. "That means careful investigation in a lab. I don't want to mess up any conviction because we tampered with evidence."

Shannon looked at Cross, but she shrugged. "It shouldn't take long to clear the knife."

Before Shannon could respond, Greeley took out his phone and read a text. "Good news," he announced. "We have a warrant to search the gas station attendant's place. One of our detectives will meet us there with it. Levine, you're with me. We'll leave the rest of the guys to finish up here."

"I'm coming," I said.

Cross stepped forward. "I'll come too."

"Okay, follow us." Greeley turned to a short detective whose name I hadn't learned. "I want a report the minute you know if the place tests positive for drugs. Test the spare bedroom first."

"Will do, sergeant," came the reply.

Less enthusiastically, Greeley added, "Please forward everything to the FBI, and let them examine anything they want." He nodded at Cross and hurried to his squad car.

Less than ten minutes later we pulled up at the gas station attendant's place, a small, new house in a block of new structures. The place was utterly dark inside, but street lamps illuminated the road and front lawns. Somewhere a dog barked.

"This used to be older housing," Levine informed us as Cross and Morley went with Greeley to talk to the detective who'd brought the warrant. "They razed them all and built new. It has really revitalized the place." His voice lowered. "Did, uh, anything happen at the precinct while I was gone? Greeley's acting irritable. Well, a little more irritable than usual, I mean. I know he's taking the heat for not finding Jenny, but he's done everything anyone could do."

"You think he's acting strange?" I asked.

"Just a little. That's why I wondered if something happened."

"Nothing I'm sure you haven't heard about," Shannon said. "Must be that whole boot thing."

Levine shook his head. "Poor Jenny. If this Kirt Henry character turns out to be involved, I'm never going to forgive myself. I can't believe I let him go this morning. Of all the stupid things. We should have searched deeper." Even in the relatively dim light of the street lamps, I could see he was becoming flushed.

"It's the biological father I'm upset with," I said. "He's not telling us everything."

Levine opened his mouth to speak, but Greeley motioned us over, and we hurried to join the others.

"You two wait out here," Greeley told me and Shannon. "We need to clear the house first. Agent Cross, will you and your partner take the back? My detectives and I will go in the front. We'll knock first, of course, so give us a minute."

"Sure." Cross and Morley headed around the back, pulling out their guns. They wore FBI bulletproof vests they'd taken from the trunk of their car.

"We'll come get you when it's all clear," Levine told us.

The detectives went up the three cement steps to the door. As predicted, no one answered, so they forced open the door and went inside, guns drawn. Shannon and I entertained ourselves by freezing in the snow on the front lawn.

"Clear," someone shouted. "Clear," echoed another.

I imagined them going room to room. I hoped they didn't find Kirt lying dead. The more I thought about that, the more I worried that the men who'd tried to kill Millard at the hospital had beaten us here. After all, someone had switched the boot, and that same someone could have reported our interest in Kirt. I felt a moment of sorrow for him and his too-friendly fiancée.

The sound of splintering glass broke the silence. Shannon and I looked at each other for a second before sprinting around to the side of the house, only to see a dark, masked figure hurl itself over the neighbor's wooden fence.

Feet pounded through the house on the chase, and Agent Morley emerged through the window, but the suspect had too much of a head start. They'd never catch him. Running to the six-foot fence, I pulled myself over, aware of Shannon doing the same. We were halfway across the neighbor's yard when the dark figure jumped the next fence. The suspect was larger than I'd first thought—a man by the way he moved—and he ran with a slight limp. We were gaining on him.

I hurtled over the second fence and landed with a crunch in a snowy bush. All my bruises hollered in protest, but I was on my feet in the next instant, running after the man. I could hear Shannon behind me. The intruder didn't seem to have a gun, or maybe he simply didn't want to risk stopping to use it.

He was heading to the back fence, slowing now as though running out of breath. He heaved himself over. I pushed faster, hitting the fence and swinging myself up with comparative ease. Either the man I was chasing was out of shape or he'd hurt himself going out the window. Even so, I'd only gone partway across the next yard when I heard a car engine roar to life.

No! I ran faster, my heart pounding and my lungs on fire. I reached the street to see a car speed away from the curb, its lights out.

"No," I moaned.

Shannon, reaching me, echoed my dismay. "Great," he panted. Morley arrived over the fence next, followed by Greeley.

"You get a plate?" Greeley barked.

"Naw." I shook my head. "No lights."

"Color? Make?"

I shook my head. "Light colored. Tan, or white, or yellow. Not dark. Car. Not a truck or Jeep or anything like that. Hatchback." Like a million other cars on the road.

"You sure it wasn't a gold Honda?" Greeley asked. "Like the one Cody Beckett drives. He's in on this somehow."

"I couldn't tell." Yet now that he'd mentioned it, I wondered if I'd seen the car before and if the masked figure could have been the old man. My old man. He'd seemed to be in good enough shape.

We trudged back to Kirt's house, the fences seeming much higher this time around. One neighbor challenged us from his back door, and Morley went to show him an ID.

At the house, Cross and Levine were waiting inside. "You think it was the clerk?" Levine asked.

Greeley shook his head. "Not with that bullet hole in his shoulder."

"Oh, right." Levine grimaced. "I hope whoever it was didn't have time to remove evidence."

"He wasn't carrying anything that I could see," I said.

"Let's get this done." Cross looked at me. "He was wearing gloves, so we won't find any prints, and nothing looks disturbed. That means it's not really a crime scene in the typical sense. We won't be calling in forensics. Not yet anyway. Touch anything you want. We'll look for evidence of where the clerk might have gone."

Greeley opened his mouth to protest but shut it again. "Fine. But keep the disturbance to a minimum, and let us know if you discover anything important. I'll be in the kitchen." I began in the bedroom where the man had burst through the broken window. I went there first, examining the splintered glass.

"Window's probably stuck," Shannon said from behind me. While he tested his theory, I let my fingers run over the frame. No imprints. He really had been wearing gloves.

"If it hadn't been stuck," Shannon added, "he might have

slipped out without us knowing. We weren't expecting anyone to be here."

"Fat lot of good it did us." I kept thinking of how the car sped away. "If that car had been half a block farther, I would have had him."

Shannon faced me. "Yeah, you would have. Despite the fact that you went over that second fence like an anchor. I've never quite seen that technique before."

I gave him a smile that bordered on a sneer. "Beats yours."

He laughed. "I guess so." Then he was reaching for me, kissing me. I could smell the cold on him, feel the warmth rushing through my body. My heart jumped into a faster rhythm. Everything around me vanished, my concern for Jenny, my hunger, my worry over Cody Beckett. Even Jake's kiss had never had such a profound effect, or at least I didn't remember a time when it did. That didn't make me feel any less guilty for walking away.

"Okay," I said, coming up for air. "I need to work."

Shannon grinned. "If you insist."

Imprints abounded here, though everything was fairly new. Kirt was excited about his life, about his upcoming marriage into a wealthy family, concerned about making ends meet at his job. He'd dropped out of college two years earlier to save money. He seemed to be everything he represented, but the lack of knickknacks and personal items in his nightstand and walk-in closet bothered me. The living room and the bathroom showed more of the same. Kirt's possessions could have belonged to anyone, and none of it inspired deep emotion. I wondered if he'd left more personal items at his girlfriend's. Was she planning to move here after the wedding, or would he be moving to her place? I couldn't say.

Leaving the bedroom, we found Agent Morley in a small office looking through Kirt's laptop. "Nothing incriminating here," he said. "Doesn't even have a password."

Levine turned from a bookshelf he was searching. "What do you bet he comes home tomorrow from visiting an old friend and tries to sue us for doing the right thing?" He laughed, but no one else found the comment amusing. He was like a little boy standing outside the circle of older kids who endured his company only because their parents forced them to.

I felt bad for his awkwardness, so I smiled politely before resuming my search. Levine lit up like a child given a cookie. Shannon rolled his eyes and hid a grin.

I was standing close enough to Morley that it was natural to hold my hand over the laptop to feel the buzz of imprints. Both he and Levine went quiet when I let my hand touch the keys.

All the money I needed. The good life. It felt good to no longer have to endure Diana's parents' condescension. My own business.

I blinked as the imprint faded. Odd that this imprint contrasted so strongly with the others I'd found. The imprint on his laptop was six months old, which meant more recent than the concerned ones in his bedroom.

"How many hours does Kirt work at the gas station?" I asked. "Didn't someone say part time?"

Levine shrugged while everyone else looked thoughtful. "I think Detective Greeley said part time when we were discussing the warrant," Morley offered.

"Then how can he afford this house? It might be small, but it's new. The monthly payment probably exceeds what he earns."

"Maybe his fiancée's parents helped." Levine said. "We haven't looked into his finances yet. Hasn't been time."

I shook my head. "I get the feeling her parents don't like him. Can't imagine they'd encourage the relationship by helping."

"Something's fishy," Shannon agreed. "Unless his fiancée is paying for some of it."

Agent Cross came into the office, jingling a set of keys in her gloved hands. "There is no car outside, but I found a set of keys inside a vase in the living room. Who leaves home without their keys? Maybe they're not his, though. They don't open the door to the house."

"The girlfriend's?" Morley said.

Shannon nodded. "Or work."

"Or a friend's, his last apartment, his parents' house, wherever that might be." Levine sighed. "Not much we can tell from those."

I reached for them.

A door opened in the middle of the night, casting a dim slice of light onto the ground. Flashlights swinging. Unloading a truck. Thrill of possible discovery. Confidence.

Just brief flashes of the scene and emotions, not a solid imprint. I held onto the keys, hoping for more. An earlier imprint followed.

I passed a hotel, my feet hurrying along the walk. I was excited about the big payoff coming soon.

Finally reaching my destination: a house, U-shaped with an odd circular drive leading through the carport at one end of the U.

I strode up to the double front doors, framed by thick columns, and entered an empty foyer. In a room to the left several men lounged on brown leather couches.

"Be ready tonight," I told them.

It felt good telling them what to do. They were my men now.

I became aware of Shannon's hand on my back. I set the keys slowly on the table. "There is a brief imprint that seems to be from the gas station. They were unloading supplies. Before that he went to a house with a weird circular driveway. The house was odd, too. Kind of U-shaped. Does that sound familiar?"

I watched as each agent or detective replied in the negative. "He was giving orders to some men," I added.

"You recognize anyone?" Levine asked, his face hopeful.

"Not sure I would even if I'd seen them before. It's all really vague. I'm not even positive Kirt is the one who imprinted on the keys."

"Probably something related to a job," Greeley said. "Maybe he's exactly what he seems."

I had to admit that was sounding more and more likely. Kirt had started a business, but I had no proof it was anything illegal. We'd reached another dead end. No Kirt, no evidence, no confession from Bremer, Millard was still unconscious at the hospital, and we'd found no sign of Jenny.

"We'll have to assume he's missing against his will," Greeley said, "and is in danger—probably from whoever Bremer is mixed up with. Maybe they thought Bremer's visit to the gas station meant the clerk knew something."

I said a silent apology to Kirt for my suspicions of him, though after the odd imprint with the men on the leather couches, it was only a half apology. Jake would laugh and say I simply didn't want to be wrong.

I became aware of Shannon watching me with his incredible eyes that did something to my pulse every time I saw them. He didn't know I was thinking about Jake, but I felt guilty, though there was nothing wrong with my thoughts. Jake and I had been friends a lot longer than I'd known Shannon Martin.

Romance-wise, the choice between them had become easy, but I was far more reluctant to give up the friendship.

When we left the house a half hour later in Agent Cross's sedan, my clothes had mostly dried from my tumble in the snow, but I was irritable and famished. I wanted nothing more than to rip the uncomfortable contact from my eye, eat three steaks, and collapse on the nearest bed possible.

Instead, we followed the others into the commander's office for more updates. Special Agents Cross and Morley had already checked in with their agency, and they had nothing new to offer us.

It was looking more and more as if we should all grab some sleep.

Huish jumped up from his seat. "Good. You're back," he said. "I have news, but let's get you all something hot to drink first." He urged us into the main room filled with the deputies' desks.

I suspected he cared less for our welfare and more for the need to keep his secrets from me and my strange ability. I didn't blame him.

Yet the boot had gone missing under his watch, so maybe someone should be watching him.

I declined the coffee and slumped into a chair, wishing he'd offered me a good cup of herbal tea instead, but I was too exhausted to remove my coat, much less to find energy to go on a tea-seeking mission. I put my arm on a desk and used it to pillow my head.

"Bremer wants a deal," Huish announced when everyone was settled. "His attorney has been with him this past hour and a half, and she's asked to talk to us. Maybe this time we'll get a handle on what happened to Jenny."

Chapter 15

The news of a possible confession revived me enough that I found energy to wriggle from my coat and hang it up. I noticed a new tear near the pocket from when I'd fallen over the fence, but the scarf inside was safe. I rubbed my left eye, wondering if eye drops would help the irritation.

"We'll have to get someone from legal here," Cross said.

Huish shook his head. "Let's wait and see what he has to offer. Enough time to get them involved if we agree."

I sank back into my seat that numerous perps had shared over many years. This time I'd kept my gloves on, and the rest of my skin was well covered. I'd had it with imprints for the time being. I felt drained and wrung out and hung up to dry. In fact, I was having trouble focusing on what Huish was saying.

"The Vandykes say the boot is definitely not their daughter's." Huish stifled a yawn like the one I didn't bother to hide. "Not the same one we found on Beckett's land. It's the same size, same style, but the scuff mark is different. Gail tried to get it clean, so she knows. Jenny's was more horseshoe shaped."

"It was locked up in evidence," Levine said. "Doesn't make sense."

"Could they just be saying that now because they know Ms. Rain said it wasn't their daughter's?" Greeley asked.

"I'd say the same thing, except I didn't mention Ms. Rain or my reason for asking them to reexamine the boot."

Huish's words shut them all up. I would have enjoyed the win more if I hadn't been so exhausted. I let my eyes shut as Greeley and Huish briefly discussed internal affairs and a lockdown of evidence.

The next thing I knew, someone grabbed my hands and cupped them around something so warm I could feel it through my knit gloves. I opened my eyes and saw Shannon grinning at me.

"Lemon," he said. "I raided their fridge for the rind. Had to use the microwave to heat it up. Sorry. Probably not very good."

It wasn't, but the thought went as far as the hot water to warm me. The cashews he'd also raided, full of fat and protein, helped further. Even my eye was feeling better by the time Bremer's state-appointed attorney entered the big room.

"This is Gretta Hansen," Huish said, standing from a chair behind one of the desks. "What do you have for us, Gretta?"

"First, I want you all to understand that I represent Mr. Bremer." She was a small woman with short brown hair and a heart-shaped face. A bit on the stocky side. Nondescript, except for her shortness. Though her expression was bland, her fists clenched and unclenched at her side as though expecting a fight. "I came in to talk to him tonight instead of in the morning because the commander believes he is withholding important information regarding Jenny Vandyke. I've counseled him to seek a deal, not to help you with the case but because it's in his best interest."

"We understand that," Greeley said with a flat tone. "You always put your client first, even if they're first-rate scumbags."

Gretta Hansen shot him a withering look before continuing. "If my client tells you what he knows about Jenny, he wants immunity."

Cross snorted. "Immunity from robbery, assault with a deadly weapon, attempted murder? That's a little much, don't you think?"

"He's willing to stand trial for those things, *if* they even make it to trial. What he wants is immunity from anything else that may be uncovered in the course of the kidnapping investigation."

"What are we talking here?" Huish said, shaking his head. "If he's done something to the girl, we can't give him immunity for telling us where he hid the body."

Hansen pursed her lips. "Okay, I can tell you this. He didn't have anything to do with Jenny's kidnapping, but he knows who did take her—and he has proof. But his dealings with these men aren't legal, and that's what he wants immunity from."

"Let me guess," Shannon said. "Drugs."

The attorney showed no expression. "I can't say unless we have a deal, but I'm telling you I think you should consider it."

Cross looked at Huish, who nodded slowly. "Okay, I think we can get him immunity from that," Cross said, "but only if we recover Jenny."

"Deal. But you'll have to hurry. He believes they may be planning to take her out of the country."

"Let's call the prosecutor," Huish said.

Sometime later, Commander Huish led the way to interrogation, while I found myself stumbling down the hall behind everyone except Greeley, who walked beside me, not appearing tired in the least. The detective's eyes met mine and did a slight double take. "Your eyes," he said. "They're different."

"Just the light," I muttered, looking away. Greeley slowed. "What are you hiding?"

"Me?" I snapped my head around to glare at him. "You're the one who lost evidence. You and your team, here. Meanwhile, I've made more progress than you have in two weeks, so don't talk to me about hiding. Someone in this department obviously doesn't want us to find Jenny. You're over the detectives in the criminal investigations unit, and that makes it your fault. Yours and Commander Huish's."

"Evidence isn't under my control," he snarled.

I shrugged and walked on. Okay, I shouldn't have alienated him, but he was like that annoying piece of gum I once stepped on. The sidewalk had been hot, and it'd taken several scrubbings with peanut butter to get it all out from between my toes.

This time Cross, Huish, Greeley, and Bremer's attorney went into the interrogation room while the rest of us watched from outside.

"We accept your deal," Cross said. "Information about Jenny in exchange for immunity from anything we uncover about you during the investigation. Provided it helps us find her. This will not affect other charges already pending or in place."

"I need it in writing," Bremer muttered, his former charm no longer in evidence.

"We have approved it with the prosecutor's office, and the

paperwork is pending," Agent Cross said. "I've been authorized to give you what you ask."

Bremer glanced at the recorder on the table and then at his attorney, who nodded. "Okay, look," he said, staring at the table. "I was dealing in Portland and hooked up with this group. They're based in Washington but have guys in every city along the West Coast. I worked for them a few months, but I quit and went my own way. I did a stint in prison after that, and when I got out they started hassling me. Didn't like that I wasn't going to work for them anymore. I had enough support—firepower—from my new associates that they didn't dare do anything to me in Portland, but they got to me any way." He stopped and heaved a sigh. "They found out I came down here for Jenny and sent guys to follow me. I saw two of 'em outside the restaurant where I met her. I recognized one of them, and I pushed her hard to come with me because I couldn't protect her where she was, but she got scared and told me she didn't want to see me again. Later, I saw two other guys at her school and outside her home. I argued with them, trying to get them to leave her alone, but they threatened me."

"You think these men took her?" Cross asked.

"I know they did. They left me a note saying she was payment for what I owed." He looked up at Agent Cross for the first time. "It's at the hotel where I'm staying. I don't know how they found me there, but they did. They had the manager deliver it."

Huish placed both hands on the table. "You say you recognized one of the men outside the restaurant? Who was it?"

"Millard, the guy I stabbed, and that clerk from the gas station. I knew Millard from Portland before I went to prison the last time. In fact, he was still in Portland up until a few months ago, or maybe it's been a year. Anyway, he was the one they sent to contact me about paying them when I got out of prison. I'd heard he had a cousin, and the guy with him outside the restaurant looked enough like Millard that I figured they were related. Later I followed them to the gas station and then out to some house Millard had rented. I don't know what the cousin is doing here—he isn't anyone I knew from Portland— but he's got to be involved, and that's why I went back to the gas station. I was going to see what he knew. Then the cop and that psychic came along and ruined everything."

That meant the clerk *was* involved. Everyone in the hallway exchanged meaningful glances. Shannon gestured to the microphone in Levine's hands. "Ask him what he did to make the drug guys so upset."

Levine repeated the question into the microphone. Inside the room, Greeley nodded slightly. "What did you do to them? You can't tell me they came after you because you decided not to work for them. They'd just kill you, if that was the case. What did you do? Or what do you have on them?"

Bremer didn't answer. Hansen leaned over and whispered in his ear. He gave a sharp nod and met Greeley's eyes. "Okay, I intercepted one of their payments. A quarter million. When you think about it, I actually did them a favor because it was part of a police sting. I got away at first, but the police caught up to me and sent me to prison."

"Don't tell me," Cross said, her voice dripping disgust. "You still have the money."

Bremer waited a few seconds before replying. "Well, they think I do."

Greeley slammed his fist on the table. "Why didn't you just give it to them? Do you think your daughter's life is worth that money? Do you think any little girl's life is worth any amount of money?"

"I tried!" Bremer shouted, his color deepening. "Don't you think I tried? But they want double, or they say they'll get more from her on the black market."

"What?" Cross asked.

Bremer's nostrils twitched as if he smelled something nasty. "They don't just traffic drugs. They also deal in girls and sometimes boys, mostly homeless or runaways. Kids no one is looking for. I don't even know how long they've been doing it. I was only into the drug side of things when I worked for them. I stabbed that man because I wanted to find her before it was too late."

Silence filled the room beyond the glass. I could see denial on every face, but we all knew he was telling the truth. I tried to tell myself this was good news for Jenny, that it meant she was still alive, but it was difficult thinking about the terror she must be experiencing.

"That explains why they tried to kill Millard at the hospital," Shannon said, turning his back to the one-way glass. He spoke quietly, though no one inside the room could hear what we said in the hallway. "They couldn't risk his talking about the drugs or the girls. Especially the girls. This entire city would be up in arms if they knew."

I swallowed hard, thinking of my sister's drawing of the girls sleeping on a carpet. It could all be related to child sex trafficking.

"The men who tried to kill Millard could have taken the gas station clerk." Agent Morley dragged his own eyes from the scene in the room, where Cross was once more questioning Bremer. "Or ordered him to lie low."

Shannon nodded. "Even if he's involved with them, like Bremer thinks he is. They'd want to make sure he doesn't tell us what he knows."

"He's got to be involved," I said. "And I think we just found out how he bought his house."

Shannon's gaze shifted back to me. "We have to find that U-shaped house from the imprint, the one you saw on the keys." He paced the width of the hall, his brow drawn in thought.

"You think they have some girls there?" Levine asked.

"Or the drugs." Shannon grimaced. Once again, he looked at me. "Do you remember if the men on those leather couches in the imprint looked like businessmen or thugs?"

"They looked like the type of men who'd stage a shoot-out in the garage of a hospital." I sighed, feeling frustrated. "How can we find that house? No one recognized my description of it, and by the time we drive around the entire city, they could be long gone."

Shannon stopped pacing. "Let's talk to Huish and Cross when they finish talking to Bremer. Discuss our options."

Morley held up a hand. "Wait. This might be interesting. He's talking about how he looked for Jenny."

We all focused on the room beyond the glass. "So you have no idea where Jenny might be now?" Cross asked Bremer. "None at all?"

"I thought she was here in Salem or maybe in Hayesville, but she could be anywhere by now. I've tried to stall them, saying I'll get the money, but I could never raise that much. I'm a small-time operator. If I give you names of the people I know in Portland, maybe you can find their connections here. But it has nothing to do with me. They had already opened shop in Salem—just like in other cities." He hesitated before adding heavily, "It was just stupid bad luck that one of my old buddies happened to be with me when I learned Cindy had a baby. He must have ratted me out to them."

Greeley's next question formed a knot in my stomach. "What about Cody Beckett? Is he involved?"

"Maybe if you showed me a picture."

"So you don't know the name?"

"Nope. Never heard of him. Is he connected to Millard somehow? That's not the name of that clerk at the gas station, is it?"

"No, it's not. Cody Beckett's a local artist."

My attention was drawn away from the room as Shannon returned to his pacing in the hallway. "Where'd Levine go with that microphone?" he asked. "I need to tell them something."

"He went to get a photo of Cody," Morley said.

I sagged against the wall. They all thought Cody was guilty, even now when a drug ring was clearly involved. Maybe they were right. After all, he'd been involved with drugs in the past.

Had it been his car I'd seen careening away from the clerk's house?

Shannon strode back and tapped on the door to the interrogation room. When Huish opened it, he said in a low voice, "I can call vice in Portland and verify any names he passes along, in case they aren't in your database."

"Thanks," Huish said. "That'll save us red tape."

"We'll get our guys on the line, too," said Morley, pulling out his phone. "Cover all the bases."

I knew that sometimes communication and information sharing didn't go as smoothly as it should between different law enforcement groups and was relieved that Shannon and Morley could cut through the bureaucracy. We needed to find

Jenny sooner rather than later—as well as the other girls, if there were any.

"I'm only giving you two names to begin with," Bremer was saying as Huish turned back into the room. "I'll give you more once I have a signed deal."

Greeley fumed and Cross looked upset, but Huish nodded. "We'll get it for you."

Shannon gave me a weary smile. "Looks like this is going to take a while," he said. "Why don't you go find some place to sack out? I'll wake you if anything interesting happens. Looks like most everyone's gone home for the night except the deputies who are directly working this case or those out on patrol. You should be able to find some quiet corner."

His idea was good, seeing as it was nearing ten o'clock already and we hadn't stopped all day. Except instead of resting, I wanted to be alone to go over the case in my mind, to see if we'd missed anything. I was also famished. Maybe I would look around the station break room to find something to eat. Better yet, I seemed to remember a restaurant not too far away. Probably not organic, but they would at least have something high in protein.

Leaving Shannon and Morley, I went to the ladies' room to freshen up. My short hair miraculously looked halfway decent, though nowhere near Agent Cross's perfection. I used a little water to tame down one side that had dried a bit funny after one of my falls in the snow.

I was opening the door when I heard a subdued voice in the hallway on the other side. "I'll get your money, but I need more time. I know he's done wrong, but I'll fix it. Please. You know I'm good for it. We're swimming in medical bills. You just need to give me a bit more time."

I stood still, the dull thud of my heart suddenly loud as I recognized Commander Huish's voice. Who was the "he" who'd committed a wrong that the commander felt he had to fix? Had to be his son, the one on drugs. Must be an embarrassment for the leader of the Marion County Sheriff's Enforcement Division to have a son who was hooked on drugs.

"Fine. You'll have it," Commander Huish growled. "Don't call me again tonight. I'm still at work."

Silence. I peeked out and saw the commander staring at the ground, facing away from me, his fists clenched.

Detective Greeley appeared farther down the hall, so I pulled back inside but stayed close to the door to see what else I might discover.

"Good. Just the man I want to talk to," Huish said. "What's with sending that stuff from that clerk's house to the lab without consulting me? I told you I wanted to be involved."

"That's my call. Always has been. Am I running the investigations unit or not?"

"I'm your supervisor." Huish's voice was cold.

"I know that. But you have to admit you haven't been on your game lately. Is something up with you?" There was heat in Greeley's voice, contrasting directly with the ice in his commander's.

I inched back farther, gently shutting the bathroom door. No way did I want to be involved in that conversation or let either one know I'd heard. But it was interesting that Huish and Greeley weren't as tight as they seemed. Did each suspect the other?

I was beginning to wonder about both of them. Huish hadn't immediately sent for Gail's ex-husband after learning about

Jenny's questionable paternity, not until Shannon mentioned it, and he also hadn't cared much for obtaining the warrant to search Kirt's place. Then there was the strange phone call I'd just overheard.

On the other hand, the disagreeable Greeley had sent his inept partner looking for Kirt, as though he hadn't really wanted to find him at all. He hadn't let me near the bloody knife at Millard's, either, when it would have been easy to find a tiny space free of fingerprints for me to touch.

Had one of them exchanged the boot?

Or were Jenny's parents lying? They had a measure of prestige in the area, and Gail had done favors for a lot of people in the course of her charity work. Maybe someone from the sheriff's station owed her enough to lose the boot until she could exchange it. Gail had lied before, or at least concealed the truth, and maybe the boot imprints would have shown that her relationship with Jenny wasn't all that it appeared.

What about Cody? My mind always came back to him and what he might be hiding behind that gruff nature. Tawnia would be devastated if he was involved. Maybe I would be too.

I reached for the bathroom door again, this time humming loudly and pasting a fake smile on my face. No one was in the hallway, though, so I let the smile go and went to find my coat, checking to make sure my wallet and phone were in one of the pockets. My handbag was in Shannon's truck, but I wouldn't need that.

Huish appeared in the big room. "Going somewhere?"

"Just leaving for a bit. I need a break—and to get some food."

"Good idea. But before you go, could you draw a quick

sketch of that house you were telling us you saw in that imprint at the clerk's? I'd like to show it to Bremer and also run it through our database. Hopefully, it's in there somewhere."

"Uh, sure. But I'm not that great at drawing."

"I've called in our sketch artist, but he was at his kid's play. He'll probably be here when you get back, but I want to get a head start on this."

I had on my gloves, so I reached for a pen on one of the desks and began drawing on a paper Huish gave me. When I finished, it was awkward but recognizable, at least to me.

"I'm going to get this to the police, too. Maybe one of their patrol officers will recognize the place. It's kind of distinctive."

Just when I'd begun to suspect him, he went all professional on me.

Huish took the paper. "Have the deputy at the door walk you out. Make sure there's no one there. We still don't know what those guys wanted from you and Detective Martin in Portland."

"Okay." I turned on my heel.

"Oh, and Jonathan's just down the street. Only a minute's walk, and they're open 'til midnight on Fridays. They might have a free table or two this late, or you can get takeout. They make an awesome steak." His smile looked genuine, and I wondered how he could hide his inner turmoil so well. "Tell them you're with the sheriff's department and they'll hurry the order. We're good tippers. I'll tell the guard to watch for you when you come back so you can get in."

"Thanks."

At the outside door, the guard and I looked around to make sure no figures lurked in the darkness. Not that I expected anyone to jump me in front of the sheriff's office in downtown

Salem. Many people lined the sidewalks in both directions, most of them wedding guests coming from the nearby Grand Theatre.

"I'll keep a watch on you just in case," the guard said, staying by the door.

The freezing air pierced my lungs, feeling much colder than I remembered from an hour earlier. This didn't stop the bride from walking into the snowy street in her wedding dress, her shoulders bare. I was glad for her sake when her groom placed his jacket over her shoulders and helped her into a waiting taxi.

Staying alert, I'd barely reached the front sidewalk, skirting a pile of snow someone had shoveled off the walk, when I heard a car door slam followed by a shout.

I whirled, fearing a van and men with guns or at the least an angry Greeley demanding to know where I was going. Instead, it was Cody Beckett, hurrying away from his gold Honda.

"Wait!" he shouted.

A chill crept across my shoulders that had nothing to do with the cold.

Chapter 16

I contemplated running down the street or hurrying back inside the sheriff's office, but he was one man and an old one at that. However good the condition he might be in, I felt confident I could defend myself. Plus I had a weapon he couldn't possibly match: the knowledge of our relationship.

I paused, waiting for him to reach me. He moved rather more stiffly than he had on our lengthy jaunt in his woods, and I had to wonder why. He wore his customary jeans but had added a gray knit cap and a black ski parka. I couldn't be sure because of the darkness, but the parka looked snagged all the way down one side of his chest.

"Thanks for stopping," he said rather grudgingly.

"Do you need to talk to me?" I scanned the well-lit area. Still no sign of anyone suspicious. Besides Cody, of course.

"I've been out here for a half hour debating what I should do," Cody said.

"What do you mean?"

"I got some information, but I'm not sure I want to tell

them." He tilted his head toward the station. "I don't think they'd even believe."

"But I might?"

"They said you were psychic."

I nearly laughed. I was as psychic as he was. In fact, any talent I had came from him, though he didn't know it.

"I'm not psychic, but I'll listen. Do you mind if we walk while we talk? I'm really hungry." I also knew the longer we stood here, the more likely the guard would alert the detectives and then whatever information Cody had might be lost to his fear of them.

He blinked. "Well, sure. I'm feeling a bit peckish myself." We'd gone a few steps when he asked, "What happened to your face?"

"Someone didn't like me snooping around."

"I'm not surprised. You shouldn't be out here alone."

A lump grew in my throat, but I told myself it had nothing to do with his concern. "Well, with that wedding just finishing, I'm hardly alone," I said.

"Look," he went on, as though our exchange had not taken place. "I don't want this to come from me. I wouldn't even come forward at all if it wasn't for that little girl."

"Why is she your concern?"

He stared down at the sidewalk, hunching in on himself. Several seconds of silence passed as we walked. "I promised myself I'd never stand by and see a child hurt, that's all. Don't make a big deal out of it. I ain't going to start attending community events or run for office or anything. Like I said, I don't want this to come from me. You said you were here to see if I was involved, well, I am now, but not in the way you might think. My only sin is trying to prove myself innocent. That's why this information can't come from me. They won't believe how I found it. They'll think I'm involved."

"But you aren't?" I eyed the vehicles parked along the road, making sure there was no one waiting behind them to pounce on us. Ridiculous, probably, but after what had happened in Portland, I wanted to be careful.

"Not with drugs or with whoever wanted that girl." Hunching over more, Cody rubbed his right leg, not missing a stride.

"You okay?" I asked, slowing my steps.

"Yeah. It's nothing."

I stayed at the slower pace. The station was comfortably behind us now, so I didn't think the guard would report him— if he was even still watching. The glowing lights of Jonathan's beckoned ahead, and my stomach twisted in anticipation.

"Let's talk inside," I said.

The place was nearly full, but a large group and several couples left as we arrived, so we were seated as soon as the tables were reset. Our booth was at the end of a row, deep inside the restaurant. Cody glanced around nervously as he sat, as if preparing to bolt. The waiter looked him over twice, and I noticed that Cody's black parka was not only snagged but also old and dirty. His jeans were torn, and with the stubble on his cheeks and his wild white hair, he looked nothing like a man who donated to charities and owned a house on a hundred acres.

I ordered a ten-ounce New York steak, and another to go for Shannon. I flinched a bit at the price, but I needed to recover my strength. Cody ordered his own steak, and I wondered if I'd end up paying for his and if I had enough money in my checking account. When the waiter understood that the extra steak and I were heading to the sheriff's station after our meal, he offered to bump our order in front of the others. Before he left, he gave Cody another once-over, and I wondered if he thought I was meeting with a homeless informant.

"So what did you find?" I prompted Cody when the waiter had finally left.

Cody didn't meet my gaze but scanned the restaurant, as though checking to see if we were being overheard. "I did some investigating on my own," he said finally, "and I found out something. How is probably better left unsaid, but I—" He met my stare, looked away and then back again, peering at me intently, whatever he'd been intending to say apparently forgotten. "Your eyes." His voice was strangled.

"What about them?" With the lamp light at our table, I could see the different colors of his eyes, but with Tawnia's contact in place, he shouldn't be able to detect the remaining color variation in mine.

"You have heterochromia. Like me."

I blinked. "You can't possibly—" But I knew what had happened. I'd rubbed my eye so much, I must have dislodged the contact. Greeley's comment should have alerted me, and it would have if I hadn't been so beat. Now I had to convince Cody it was a coincidence.

"Who are you, really?" he grated. "And why are you here? It isn't to find out if I'm guilty, is it?"

"Look, just because I have the same condition you do, doesn't mean—"

"You also look like her. Not her hair or the eyes, but the shape of your face. I'm an artist. I'm good with faces. You look like her, and that's why you seem familiar. Who are you?" His eyes dug into mine. "Tell me the truth."

I sighed. "Okay. But I really did come to see if you're innocent. Or guilty."

"But no one hired you."

For the time being I would leave Tawnia out of it. He didn't need to know there were two of us or that he had a grandchild. "I came because Laina Drexler told me about you. Or Laina Walkling now. She's my biological grandmother."

"Laina." The single word held a mountain of regret.

"And I guess you've figured out that her daughter Kendall was my mother," I added.

He grunted as though the revelation brought his pain to a level he couldn't hold in.

"I want to know about my past," I continued, keeping my eyes locked on his. "Part of that is finding out if you had anything to do with Jenny. I consult with the Portland police, and from what I'd read about the case you were their only suspect. If you didn't do it, I felt that wasn't fair to you or Jenny." I waited a second before adding, "I wanted to know the truth for myself."

"I don't want you here," Cody growled. "I don't owe you anything."

"This isn't about you!" Anger overrode my other emotions, even the nameless ones I didn't admit to. "I deserve to know what type of man my biological father is."

His lips twisted in an ugly sneer. "That man is dead. Long dead, and good riddance! Better you turn around right now and go back wherever you came from. I don't have anything for you."

"You have information. Whatever relationship there is or

isn't between us, I'm not leaving until we find Jenny Vandyke. So either you tell me what you know or I'll tell the commander that you're like me and you have information."

"Like you?"

I nodded, holding up my gloved hands. "It started last year after Winter—" I looked down at the table, swallowing hard before I contained my emotion enough to continue. "After my adoptive father drowned in the Willamette. I'd always been sensitive to things, but that's when it really started." When Winter died but also when I'd found Tawnia. Something horrible, something wonderful. Both traumatic. "Now this . . . ability . . . is how I help the police."

"They believe you?" He rubbed a hand over his unshaven face.

"Not at first, and still not all of them, but I get results. I find people. The bottom line is all they care about."

He chewed on his lower lip in the same way that I often found myself doing. I watched him weighing his options: to run or to go ahead with the information. To talk to me or to lock me out. His privacy versus the trouble of dealing with me. Was there any curiosity in him? Did he want to know what had happened to me during all these years?

My interest in him, of course, went far beyond the case. I wanted to know about his talent, about his mother and why she'd been in a sanitarium. I was afraid to say any of this now—afraid he'd turn me away. I'd experienced his guilt and self-loathing in the imprints at his house. If they had nothing to do with Jenny, it was possibly related to my mother. Perhaps he was not as disconnected as he wanted me to believe.

I tapped the tabletop. "Now what's so important that you waited for me outside the sheriff's office?"

His nostrils flared, and he gave a sharp nod. "Okay, fine. I went to that kid's house, the gas station clerk. I knew he was related to that stabbed man, and I wanted to find something to clear my name."

"Wait a minute." A sinking feeling grew in my stomach. "You went to Kirt's house? Don't tell me that was you we were chasing."

One side of his face twitched. "Almost got me too. I hurt my leg going out that window so fast. Ruined my good coat."

I leaned forward as far as I could over the table, talking fast and low. "Do you realize what they're going to do to you once they realize you were inside that house?"

He leaned over the table as well, both hands spread between us. "They ain't going to—unless you tell them." His expression changed. "Wait a minute. You didn't find anything from me inside the house, did you? Maybe you already told them I was there."

"By anything, I guess you mean imprints. I call them imprints, because the scenes and emotions seem to be imprinted on the objects. But no, I didn't find anything from you. Whatever you touched there, you must have remained calm enough."

"I didn't leave no fingerprints, either. But I would have been even more careful it I'd known you were—" He broke off. "Anyway, I had to clear my name."

"What you did is become more of a suspect. I'm going to have to tell them." A part of me wondered if I'd known it all along. The way he'd moved, the car that had seemed familiar. Perhaps I'd already been protecting him.

"Maybe they won't care once they know what I found."

"Go on."

"There was this, uh, imprint on some keys I found."

"The one of the U-shaped house or the back door of the gas station?"

He blinked. "Oh, you found them. Well, both were suspicious, don't you think? Anyway, I—"

"Here we go, all nice and hot."

We looked up to see the waiter poised by the table, our meals on a circular tray in his hand.

"That was fast," I said, sitting up straight so he had room to place my food in front of me.

"Well, if you're working this late with the sheriff's office, you probably need to get back, so I commandeered another order. Don't worry. With the lineup of steaks we have, it will only mean they wait an extra minute or so." He lowered his voice. "It's about that little girl, isn't it?"

I nodded. A real sheriff's deputy would have told him that information was confidential, but I was only a consultant. They didn't pay me enough to avoid questions. Actually, I wasn't being paid anything this time.

"Poor little girl. I hope you find her."

I glanced at his name tag. "Thanks, Sheldon. We appreciate the quick service."

"Your other order should be ready by the time you finish your meal."

He obviously didn't know how fast I could eat, but I repeated my thanks, making a mental note to give him a nice tip. I hoped my checking account had enough funds.

Cody ignored the waiter, cutting huge slices of steak and forking them to his mouth with a steady rhythm. I stared, fascinated, imagining myself telling Tawnia that I'd finally discovered the source of our huge appetites.

I pulled off my gloves and gingerly tested my fork. Just because Cody hadn't run into a nasty imprint on his utensils, didn't mean mine were imprint free.

Satisfied, I shrugged off my coat before digging into my own steak. Cody left his coat on. "So," I prompted. There had to be more to his story.

"Didn't anyone teach you not to talk with your mouth full, girl?" He pushed in two more pieces of meat. I wondered if in all his efforts to avoid the deputies he'd missed lunch and dinner.

I rolled my eyes. "What was so interesting on the keys, the house or the—"

"The house. It's here in Salem, and I know where. Used to be a mortuary. It's plenty big to hide drugs, and apart enough from other places that even if there were odd noises, no one would hear."

That meant a girl could scream to no avail. Or multiple girls. "I'm betting that's where that clerk's run to," Cody said. "And those men in the imprint? I've seen them before, outside the middle school." The magnitude of what Cody said came to me slowly. I'd had doubts about ever identifying the house, but Cody knew the place and had recognized the men in the imprint. He might even be able to identify them from mug shots.

But what had Cody been doing outside the elementary school?

"Okay, you tell me the address, and I'll get it to the detectives."

I sliced off a large piece of steak and put it in my mouth, knowing getting this information back to the police station was more important than my food and that the second he gave it to me, I'd have to leave.

"You won't mention me, will you?" Cody asked before bolting down another slice of meat.

I sighed. "Not right now, but eventually they'll have to know. The detective I work with isn't going to let it go. He'll want to know how I figured it out." In the old days, I could have told Shannon to take a flying leap but not now. Romance had its drawbacks.

He swallowed the food in his mouth. "You're sweet on him, ain't you?"

"What's the address?"

He scratched the stubble on his face. "The thing is, I don't know the address. I know where it's at, that's all."

"So how am I going to keep you out of it if you have to come along?"

His eyes glinted. "Tell them I recognized the house from your description."

That might work for the others. Maybe even for Shannon, if I decided to keep him out of it.

I drew out my phone and pressed Shannon's number. "Look," I said when he picked up. "I know where the house is, the one I saw. Or at least I know how to find it. I'll explain when I get to the station, but the thing is, Cody Beckett has to come along for the ride."

"What? How'd he get into this?"

"He's the one who knows where it is."

"How?"

"It's a long story," I said. "Well, actually it's not all that long, but I'd rather tell you in person. We're only a minute away. We'll be right there."

"You're not here?" Worry crept into his voice.

"I'm at a restaurant, just down the street. They have great steaks. Don't worry. I'm fine."

His laugh sounded forced. "I should have known."

"Don't be so snide, or I'll eat the one I planned to bring back for you."

"You're giving up one for me? Wow, that's got to say something." All at once that something stretched between us, taut and warm and wonderful. "I'll see you in a bit." I tried to swallow the sudden lump in my throat.

"See you. Be careful."

There he went, destroying the moment by reminding me that he was president of the Autumn Needs to Be More Careful Club, but since we'd been jumped that day and shot at several different times, I decided not to take offense.

"I will. But honestly, I'm a minute away, and the street is full of people."

I was smiling when I hung up. I took another bite and then motioned to the waiter, who hurried over immediately. "We have to go now," I said, not masking my urgency.

"You want to take your food with you?" His words faltered as he saw that we'd both eaten most of our steaks and that Cody was doing a great job with his rice and vegetables. I hadn't touched mine; carbs didn't go nearly as far to restoring my strength after imprints.

"No, thanks," I said, pulling out my wallet.

Cody coughed and pulled a small wad of cash from the pocket of his parka and peeled off some bills. "This should cover it," he told the waiter. "Keep the change."

The waiter's eyes widened. "Thanks, sir."

"I can pay for mine," I protested.

"It's paid for." Cody waved the waiter away and rose stiffly to his feet. "If it bothers you, think of it as payment for trying to clear me." He started toward the door of the restaurant with obvious difficulty, his leg apparently having grown stiffer during the inactivity. I wondered if he should see a doctor.

I hurried after him, pulling on my coat. "I don't want payment."

He stopped and stared at me. "Then why are you here? You want something, all right. It's just not money." He didn't wait for a reply but turned and limped along the aisle.

He was right. I did want something. I wanted his quilt. I wanted his memories. I wanted to hear his side of what happened the night Tawnia and I were conceived.

"Miss!" The waiter hurried toward me, carrying a carton that he placed in my hands.

"Thank you." Hard to believe I'd forgotten food. If he found out, Shannon would never let me live this down.

I reached Cody as he opened the restaurant door and held it so I could precede him outside. "Thanks," I said automatically.

He grunted in reply.

We covered several yards in silence. The streets didn't have as many pedestrians as when we'd entered the restaurant, though we hadn't been there long. Even many of the cars parked along the street had cleared away. It was cold enough that I wished I'd worn an extra pair of socks. Maybe two. I considered stopping to pull on my gloves, but the heat of the carton in my hands would have to suffice.

I pondered what I should say to Cody, but I didn't know exactly what I wanted from him. I'd have to let it all play out. Right now I needed to focus on the case. If only Cody could move faster.

"Is your leg—" I began when two men stepped out from

behind a white van, the first one grabbing Cody before I could scream a warning. His fist plunged into Cody's stomach. Without so much as a grunt, Cody was swinging back. Cody matched him in height, but his attacker was less than half his age.

I mentally kicked myself for being so hung up on what I was feeling about Cody that I hadn't anticipated the danger of the parked van. If I'd been paying attention, I would have made us cross to the other side where attackers couldn't hide, or waited until we had company from the restaurant. Instead I'd put us both at risk.

The other man lunged for me. I dodged his blow and followed with two jabs and a roundhouse kick. He was shorter than the other man but lean and tough. More than enough match for me in training.

His next punch left an opening. Deflecting the hit, I stepped behind his back and threw my arm around his neck, squeezing tight. I could hold tighter until he fainted, or I could pull him backwards to the restaurant and yell for someone to call the police.

"Let him go," said the man.

My eyes went to Cody and his attacker. For a moment, I thought Cody had stopped struggling because he'd set me up, but the metal barrel of a gun glinted in the light of the street lamp.

"Let him go or your friend dies. And maybe a few others."

I looked around, seeing that two couples had emerged from the restaurant and stood some distance away, staring in our direction uncertainly. One woman pulled out her phone.

No choice. I hadn't come to see Cody only to be the cause of his death. Or that of innocent bystanders. I released the man, who quickly distanced himself from me.

"Nothing to see," he called to the couples. "Just a demonstration."

He opened the side door to the van. I could see two rows of seats running the length of the back under each of the side windows, leaving the middle free. "Get in, dear."

I climbed inside, followed by Cody and the man with the gun. The last thing I saw before he shut the door was the white food carton from the restaurant, its contents strewn over the dirty snow at the edge of the sidewalk.

Chapter 17

he men didn't cover our eyes as we drove through
the city, and that failure hinted that maybe they
didn't plan to keep us alive long enough for us to
give away their destination. Not that I'd ever be able to retrace
our route anyway.

"You should have run," Cody muttered. "Don't the police
teach anything to their consultants? I'm old. I've lived a long
time. You should have left me."

I narrowed my eyes at him and said nothing. What I should
have done, besides keeping better watch, was to have mentioned
to Shannon that the house from the imprint was an old mortuary.
At least that would have narrowed down the search for Jenny.
Maybe for Kirt too, if that was where he had gone.

Across from us, amusement was plain on our gunman's
face. At this close distance I noted that he was huskier than I'd
first glimpsed, but his fleshy face told me it was more the bulk
of an athlete turned couch potato than muscles built from a
daily workout.

He had brown hair, dark eyes, and an oblong face. I felt I'd seen him before, though I knew neither he nor his companion had been among those who'd jumped us in Portland. Perhaps they'd been among the shooters at the hospital.

Cody was staring at him too. "The keys," he said under his breath.

Right. This man had been one of the men on the leather couches in Kirt's imprint. The man who was now driving the van, the one I'd nearly strangled, hadn't been among them.

"No talking," the driver called. "Dale, keep 'em quiet."

"Don't know why. They're not going anywhere."

"You know the rules. Now shut them up." He held up his own gun complete with a silencer. "Don't think I can't use this just because I'm driving."

He was smarter than I'd given him credit because I had been thinking of working with Cody to get the gun away from Dale. Two guns decreased our odds exponentially.

"Why are you doing this?" I asked.

"Because apparently you're psychic." Dale pointed to Cody. "He was just in the way."

The driver turned a brief glare at him. "We just follow orders. Now shut up."

I exchanged a look with Cody. If I'd been taken because of my ability to read imprints, that meant someone involved in the case, someone who believed in imprints, thought I might have information that would incriminate them.

But who?

Given her lack of surprise at her daughter's search for her birth father, Gail Vandyke might have something more to hide, yet I felt her love and concern for her daughter was real. She'd been protecting Jenny all her life. As for Kenyon

Vandyke, the imprints on his keys seemed real enough, so if the Vandykes had let anything spill about me, it had probably been unintentional.

Both Agents Cross and Morley believed in what I could do, but neither seemed to have it out for me. Besides, despite her occasional ineptness at questioning, Cross seemed dedicated to her job. However, she had mentioned in her car earlier that Morley was a new partner. How much did she really know about him?

Levine seemed too quiet and friendly to want harm to come to me, though wasn't it always the quiet ones who led secret lives? Maybe his Barney Fife demeanor was a cover, though how anyone could fake that kind of awkwardness was beyond me. He also hadn't been able to find Kirt for questioning, though maybe none of the sheriff's deputies could have.

Then there was Greeley. He had gone behind Huish's back while submitting evidence. Had he first tampered with it? Or had he submitted evidence that way because he suspected Huish of wrongdoing? He hadn't known where I was going, but he could have asked Huish or the guard. Any of them could have.

Commander Huish had known I was heading to Jonathan's. His wife was dying, his son was on drugs, and the resulting money problems might be a strong motive for betrayal. Maybe he'd received money for turning me over. The most damaging evidence could be his slowness to obtain a search warrant for Kirt's house where I'd found the imprint of the old mortuary. Had he wanted me to draw the place so he could find it or to discover how much I really knew? I felt sick, thinking the commander could be involved. If it was him, how far would he go to protect his secret? This was far larger than one young girl going missing. Huge amounts of money were involved, and people would go to great lengths to protect their profits.

It could be any of them or none at all. Even if I discovered who, I was in no position now to warn Shannon or anyone else.

How long would it take Shannon to realize I was gone? How long before he questioned people at the restaurant and discovered his steak in the snow?

Our captors hadn't taken my phone yet or searched me. I closed my eyes, thinking hard. If they left me alone, I could make a call, but it was unlikely that would happen, and I couldn't call without looking at the screen, so no chance of dialing and letting Shannon hear what was going on.

Thanks to my preoccupation with being spied on, he couldn't follow me by my phone's GPS, either, though maybe in time they could track me through the phone by more complicated methods. If Huish was involved, I didn't want to bet on that happening.

In other words, we were on our own. Or my own, rather. Cody slumped beside me looking discouraged and beaten. I wondered how severely his leg was hurting and if he was losing blood. It wasn't showing through his jeans.

"Where are we going?" I asked.

"Shut up!" barked the driver.

Dale scowled. "It doesn't matter. You won't be there long."

I looked at Cody, but he avoided my gaze. Disappointment filled me. I don't know what I expected from him. A last-moment apology for what he did to my mother? Sorrow that because of her pregnancy, she'd met an early death? Whatever, I wasn't getting it. I'd known for over a year that I'd never hear any kind of apology or see my birth father pay for his sins, and I thought I'd come to terms with it. I guess I'd been fooling myself.

Even so, I didn't want Cody to suffer at the hands of these men, regardless of the cosmic justice they might mete out.

Think, I told myself.

The uneasy feeling in my stomach increased when we eventually pulled up at a U-shaped house I recognized all too well—the columns framing the double front doors, the circular drive. The old mortuary.

Again I mentally berated myself for not telling Shannon more about the place.

The mortuary sat on a large triangular piece of land that bordered streets on the front and back. On the remaining side were businesses—all dark. In fact, with the exception of two lone street lamps, the whole area was dark. We could expect no help from the neighbors. A car passed, but it was the first I'd seen in a long time.

The van drove to the far end of the circular drive, which passed a side door before exiting the property. Probably where they used to load the hearses. I hoped it wasn't a statement of our life expectancy that we entered there now.

The driver kept his gun on Cody, while the larger man, Dale, stayed with me as we walked toward a ramp. "So are you really psychic?" he asked in an undertone.

If I ever caught up to whoever started that rumor, they were going to regret it.

Wait. Maybe I could put it to good use. "Of course I am," I said. "And this isn't going to end well for you. The only way out I see for you is to call the sheriff's office and tell them where we are."

His step faltered almost imperceptibly. "Yeah, right. You're a fake."

No help from him. Unless . . .

I had to time this exactly right and choose my spot carefully. Stumbling, I reached out for his hand, aiming for the gold watch just visible beneath his wool coat. Rapid images assailed me.

She was screaming. A quick pull of the trigger silenced the awful cries. I picked up the body and tossed it over the deck of the boat.

My stomach curled with horror. But that was only the beginning.

I was beating someone who lay on the ground, the victim's bloody face unrecognizable as male or female. Power spilled through me . . .

The scene was quickly replaced by an earlier imprint.

Remorse as I stared at the child's face. How did I get myself into this?

I walked to the briefcase sitting on the table, opening it. So much cash. More than I ever expected to have in my lifetime. Snapping the case shut, I picked it up, turned, and left the room without looking at the child again.

The heinous images faded, followed by another scene.

Pride flooded me as I stared down at the watch in my hands. This gift meant I was one of the elite. Maybe in time I'd have my own crew and earn enough money for a thousand gold watches and vacations on sun-kissed beaches. All the things I'd had to do to get here meant nothing. All the things I knew I would have yet to do.

Then the first imprint began again.

Dale shook me off him, and I fell to my knees, gagging. *What have I done?* I thought. *No. Not me. Him.* I was grateful the watch was relatively new and attached to Dale instead of in my hands, or I might have become stuck in that terror-filled loop.

"Get up," Dale growled, pointing his gun at me.

"You've hurt so many people," I said, realizing I was lucky he hadn't shot me already. "Are their lives really worth a thousand gold watches and a beach vacation?"

Dale's eyes widened. "Stay away." He took a step back, motioning me forward, up the ramp where Cody and the driver waited.

Disgust swept through me. "You'll never see that beach unless you leave here now and call the police." I didn't know any such thing, but he didn't know that, and I couldn't resist. It was less than he deserved.

"I said shut up!" a voice shouted. Pain echoed through me as the driver sprinted down the ramp and jabbed his gun into my left shoulder, reverberating through the newly healed wound in my upper arm. He half dragged me up the ramp.

Almost I wished I'd kept my mouth shut. Almost. Because the driver's presence meant Cody was momentarily unguarded.

Run, I screamed at him silently.

Too late. Another man had appeared in the doorway, the gun in his left hand pointing at Cody, his right arm in a sling.

Kirt Henry, the gas station attendant. My stomach dropped. "Get inside." His voice held no compromise.

We were led down a wide hallway where Kirt pocketed his gun to unlock a door. The way he fumbled told me he was normally right-handed. "Sorry for the digs, but it's all we could arrange at such short notice."

"Kirt, please," I said. "It's not too late. Think of your fiancée. Does she know about all this?"

He barked a laugh. "She believes exactly what I want her to believe. I'm her whole world, remember?"

He shoved me up against the wall with his good arm and

began checking the pockets of my coat and then my black pants. He threw my phone at the driver. "Open this and take out the battery. Just in case."

Nodding, the driver dismantled my phone and handed it back to Kirt, who tucked it in his pocket.

Dale had been checking Cody at the same time, coming up with a handful of rusty nails and his wad of cash. Cody looked ready to burst.

"I have nothing to do with this," I said to Kirt. "And neither does Cody. I saved your life!"

Kirt's gaze shifted to Cody and back to me. "Look, I appreciate what you did, but that's the way it goes. I'm not going to prison."

"Is that why you ordered them to kill your cousin?"

Kirt's eyes narrowed. "He knew the risks when we entered this business. We both knew the risks."

There was a hesitation in the way he answered that told me more than he'd intended. "You didn't order it, did you?" I guessed. "You only identified him when you were at the hospital for your shoulder, and whoever is really in charge ordered the hit. You didn't expect that, did you? You're nothing but an underling."

Kirt's nostrils flared. "I'm the one who schedules the drops. I'm the one who supplies the locations. This is my operation now."

"Your cousin was heading to the gas station for help, but all you did was sign his death warrant."

"He messed up. I should have shot him myself." Kirt nodded at Dale, who twisted the knob on the door Kirt had unlocked earlier. Kirt grabbed my shoulder, pushing me forward.

I struggled against him. "They'll cut you a deal, if you give up whoever's working with you in the sheriff's office."

Kirt stopped pushing.

Ah, I thought. He hadn't expected me to know about that. Instead of answering, he tightened his grip and gave me another shove. I tripped forward into the dark room, falling over something and sprawling onto the carpet.

Dale began tugging off my sock boots. "What are you—"

"So you don't run away," Kirt said.

For most people he'd be right, especially in the snow, but I felt only relief as I wiggled my freed toes. I could count on two hands the days I'd worn shoes the entire year.

The door shut behind us, and I heard the unmistakable click of the lock.

Cody snorted somewhere above me in the dark. "Don't you know when to shut up? Thought you were going to get yourself killed."

"What would you care? I'm nothing to you. You've made that very clear."

"He might have shot me too."

"You know what? You're nothing but the dregs of humanity, the leftover stuff that's too bitter and gross to do anything with but toss in the trash." It wasn't something Winter or Summer would have ever said, but I couldn't help myself.

"Just so you don't expect anything from me."

"Believe me, I gave that up a long time ago. From the moment I found out what you did to my mother."

On her fifteenth birthday, when he and my grandmother had been drugged out of their minds. He'd assaulted Kendall in her own room. Tawnia and I were the result.

Silence. Heavy silence. Then rustling from across the room and more movement nearby.

I squinted, willing my eyes to adjust to the darkness. "Who's there?" Hope arose inside me. Funny how hope works, appearing when you least expect it. "Jenny? Is that you?"

"There's no Jenny here," came a young, feminine voice. "Who are you?"

"You're a prisoner like us, right?" said another girl.

"I guess so. For now. We've been trying to find Jenny Vandyke. She's missing."

A tiny flame flickered to life across the room, revealing a girl who couldn't be older than twelve. "We're all missing," she said. "Can you help us?"

Gradually, I could make out two others standing next to the girl, and more spread out across the small room. One girl lay close to me, still half asleep, though it must have been her I'd stumbled over.

I counted at least twenty girls, arrayed in various articles of clothing. Not one wore shoes. Most of the girls huddled together in small groups in the cold room, some sharing a blanket. Several of the youngest looked as though they'd been roused from their beds only moments ago and taken from their families.

I met Cody's eyes, and though I couldn't see him well, I felt the same shock radiating from him.

"We'll help all of you," I said.

I would. Providing I could stay alive myself.

Chapter 18

The girls were from all over the country and all different ethnicities, mostly runaways and foster children, but two had been taken from different malls in the East. The girl with the light said her parents were dead and that her uncle had sold her. They didn't know where they were going, but I knew it wasn't anywhere good.

"What's wrong with her?" I asked, pointing to a prone figure near the boarded window. As the dim light washed over the teen, I could see the lank hair and the sweat on her face, though the room was decidedly cold. Someone had thrown a blanket over her.

"Drugs," Cody said without emotion.

"They give them to us if we get hysterical." The girl who answered sounded tough and streetwise, though her face put her near fourteen. "But she was already on them. A couple of us are." Her gaze landed on three girls huddled together under a blanket against the right wall.

"They'll all be drugged up before long," Cody said in an undertone. "Easier to control them."

Sniffling drew my attention to a younger girl under a

blanket with another child who slept the deathlike sleep of someone drugged. The weeping girl couldn't have been more than ten, and her tears made my chest tight.

I scooted over to her, removing the shaman's colorful scarf from my coat pocket and draping it around her. "Don't cry, honey. We'll get out of here."

A small hand closed over mine. "Promise?"

"I'll do everything I can. But if you get a chance to run, do it." I raised my voice several decibels. "That goes for all of you. If you ever have a chance—run."

"They'll shoot us," someone said.

Cody cleared his throat. "They can't shoot all of you."

Not exactly a comfort. No wonder they hadn't tried. None of them could know the horrors awaiting them that would make dying by gunshot seem easy by comparison.

"So how we getting out?" asked the tough girl.

The little girl with the light moved closer. "I heard them say something about moving us tonight. Wasn't supposed to be until a few more days."

"Then we'd better do something now," I said. "What is that you have, a lighter?"

She held it up for me to see. "Picked it up a few nights ago when one of them dropped it."

Could we set fire to the place? Would that help us escape or would the smoke kill us first? Probably the latter.

"Well?" asked the tough girl. My eyes had adjusted enough for me to see her hair was blue and her nose pierced.

"I don't know yet. Let me think."

Cody sat down a foot away from me. I expected him to tell me to give it up, but he said, "If we could take out a guard, we might be able to get a gun."

"You know how to shoot?" I asked. He nodded.

I thought a moment more. "How do we lure only one here? They take your shoes, too?"

"Yeah."

So no trying to use them on the boarded window.

"What about the bathroom?" I asked. "There's not one in here, is there?"

"Nope." The tough girl fingered her nose piercing. "They take us one at a time."

The girl with the light grimaced. "They stand in the hallway and won't let us close the door. It's embarrassing. We try not to go often."

"Just one man takes you?" I asked. She nodded.

"I could take one man," I said to Cody.

"Probably. But they know that after what happened outside the restaurant. They'll be prepared."

"Maybe."

"Let's think on it a bit more."

I nodded, but inside I was beginning to feel desperate. The darkness in the small room and the presence of so many was beginning to weigh heavily on me. It reminded me of other times in the dark when I'd been fighting for my life.

I had to do something.

The opening door made my choice for me. Kirt was framed by the light behind him, gun in hand. "Get your blankets and anything else you have. We're leaving in five minutes."

A tremor of fear rippled through the girls and in my own heart.

It was now or never. I stood and took a few steps toward the door. "I need to use the bathroom."

"You got to be kidding." Kirt shook his head.

"I just ate dinner at a restaurant. I drank a ton of water. Ask him." I thumbed at Cody.

"She's a regular camel," he said with a grunt.

"Come on. What's it gonna hurt?" What would I do if he said no?

Sighing, Kirt motioned to someone who came into view: Dale.

"Take her to the bathroom. Keep your gun on her and don't hesitate to shoot." To me, he added. "Don't try anything, Ms. Rain."

"Yeah, yeah." I waved his voice away, faking a confidence I didn't feel as I moved into the hallway. Another guard was there, a big brute of a man with black hair and bronzed skin, his handgun at the ready. I wondered if he knew any martial arts.

Kirt shut and locked the door to the room. "Tiny, make sure Harrison's got the van ready," he said to the big man. "I have a phone call to make, and then we'll get started with the girls."

I decided Harrison was our driver from earlier, the man I'd bested. "Twenty girls and all of you in that van?" I said. "Don't you think that's impossible?"

"I'm not interested in anyone's comfort." Kirt turned his back on me. "Take her to the van when she's finished."

Dale opened his mouth to speak but apparently thought the better of it. He waited until Kirt was out of earshot to say to Tiny, "I might be a while, if you get my drift."

Tiny boomed a laugh and let his gaze run over my body. "Take your sweet time."

"That way," Dale directed me, smirking with anticipation.

The bathroom was down the hall, around a corner, and

past a large room that had probably once housed coffins. Inside the room, I caught a glimpse of several overturned crates and packing materials littering the floor. They'd apparently finished moving their drugs. After they loaded the girls, they would likely leave for good.

"Give any thought to my suggestion about calling the police?" I said as we stopped outside the bathroom, sugar in my voice.

"You already got me in trouble with that nonsense, so shut your trap and keep it shut—unless you want a love tap from this." Dale tipped the pistol in a quick motion, indicating his willingness to follow through on the threat.

"I think I'll pass."

"Well, get your business finished then."

I shrugged off my coat, letting it slip to the floor in the hall. It would be a hindrance in any real fight. My pants were dried, but dirt stained the black material in patches all over, and there was a tear by the hem. I wished I'd worn jeans.

Stepping into the bathroom, I started to close the door.

Dale put his foot against it. "Leave it open. I won't watch." His grin told me otherwise.

"If you think I'm going to be cowed like those poor little girls, you're wrong." I folded my arms and calculated my distance from the door carefully. Use what is available, my martial arts instructor always said.

"Oh, yeah?" Dale's voice turned ugly. "We'll see about that. Because you and I are about to have a little fun." He lunged toward me.

Perfect. I slammed the door into him. A loud *thunk* answered my efforts as the door rammed his shoulder and head. Hard but not hard enough.

"You little—" he gritted.

I shoved the door into him again with all my strength, and then a third time, catching his arm. The gun fell to the floor. Whipping open the door, I punched hard, following with a jump kick to his stomach. As he curled forward, I brought my fist down on the back of his head, raising my knee to hit his face at the same time.

"That's for that poor girl crying under the blanket," I whispered as he collapsed, unconscious.

I reached to take his gun, but imprints tingled on it, so I leaned over him to get my gloves from the pocket of my coat before picking it up. The gun was a Colt with a silencer, and one of the .45 hollow points would take down just about anything on two legs—as long as I could bring myself to fire it. I took a few more precious seconds to work off his holster and clip it onto the right side of my pants. It was meant for concealed carry, which placed the gun inside my waistband, its bulk making my loose pants comfortably snug.

Shannon would say the comfort was a sign that I should always carry. If I got out of this alive, I wasn't going to tell him.

My heart thundered in my chest and pounded in my ears. No one had come running yet, but I wouldn't have much time. Grabbing Dale's hands, I dragged him past my coat and down the hall into the bigger room, hiding him behind a crate. He was even heavier than I expected. Sifting through the garbage on the floor, I found lengths of thick, rough, packing twine long enough to tie his hands and feet and strong enough to cut flesh before it would ever break. On his ankle I found a holster with a smaller gun, and I took it off and put it around my own ankle. It felt heavy and awkward, so I ripped it off again, took out the magazine containing the bullets, and slipped it into my pocket.

The gun I tossed into an empty crate. Better to stick with what I knew than to make myself clumsy with the extra weight.

Still unsatisfied, I tied another longer piece around his wrists. "Enough, already," I could imagine Shannon saying mockingly. "Godzilla couldn't break out of that."

I put a few extra lengths of twine in my front pocket. Better to plan for success.

From Dale's pocket I pulled a cell phone, but it was protected by a password. Even the emergency call option was unavailable.

I tossed it on top of him. What now?

I considered my choices. The safest thing to do would be to escape and call the police from a different location, but they were loading the girls now, and by the time the police arrived, they could be long gone.

I couldn't leave them.

Or Cody, though he hadn't given me any reason to care about his well-being.

So I was staying.

Two men that I knew of were still inside the mortuary, and at least one was getting the van ready. If the driver was alone, he'd be the best place to start.

The window in the room was the kind that lifted upward, and for a moment I feared it had been painted shut, but it opened easily under my hand. Pushing out the screen took a bit more effort, but soon I was climbing down into an overgrown bush covered in snow.

My callused feet noted the chill, but it wasn't that uncomfortable, not yet. On the other hand, the rest of me was freezing. I'd left my coat in the hallway, and it was too late to go back for it now.

I climbed out of the bush and sprinted around the back of the house, pausing at the corner where I could see the van parked near the ramp where I'd entered earlier.

Kirt, the driver Harrison, and Tiny were talking at the top of the ramp.

"I don't like it," Harrison was saying. "There's only four of us. We should take two vans with four guards each. There's too many girls."

"We don't have a choice," Kirt said. "The others aren't finished with the shipment. We'll shoot one of the girls if we have to."

"He won't like that," Harrison said.

Kirt's voice grew cold. "I'm in charge here."

"Sure." There was a bit of mockery in Harrison's voice that told me Kirt wasn't what he himself believed. The imprint on Kirt's keys indicated that he was relatively new to the operation, and I knew he answered to someone, but I had no idea who. Possibly some bigwig from out of town.

Then there was the informant from the sheriff's office. How involved was that person? Had he—or she—fooled everyone for years or only recently been sucked in?

Well, I'd wait until Kirt and Tiny went inside and then jump Harrison. I'd bested him once before, and I had surprise on my side now. Maybe I could drive away with Cody and the girls before Kirt and Tiny noticed.

Harrison walked down the ramp, pausing at the bottom. "What about the woman and the old man?"

"We'll bring her along," Kirt said. "She's valuable if she really can do what they say. She might even come around and work for us voluntarily. But we've no use for the old man. Once we have the girls loaded, we'll get rid of him."

I chewed on my bottom lip. Get rid of him? That messed up my plan big time. Even if I could take Harrison's place driving the van, I couldn't let them shoot Cody.

Harrison stalked over to the van and yanked open the sliding door. "Bring them, then."

I waited until Kirt and Tiny left. How long would it take them to get the girls? Since there were so many, they'd probably make the effort to tie their hands, but either way, they wouldn't waste a lot of time. They had to know that regardless of who their inside person was at the sheriff's office, before long those who were actually doing their jobs would catch up with them.

Like Shannon.

Unless they'd taken care of him too. He could have walked into a trap like I had—and he'd be just as useless to them as Cody.

The thought made my stomach cramp. I told myself that I'd feel the same way no matter who was working with me, but that wasn't the truth. I cared about Shannon a lot.

The driver drew out a cigarette and started lighting it. The perfect opportunity because I could see both hands. I pulled the gun from my holster and stepped out from the house. Harrison did a double take and dropped both his cigarette and his lighter.

"Keep your hands where I can see them," I ordered, hoping he couldn't tell how much I was shaking.

Harrison scowled. "You're making a mistake."

"No, you made the mistake. And now you're the one who needs to be quiet." I had no idea how I was going to tie him up without putting down the gun, and I wasn't sure I could shoot him. So all he had to do was rush me or pull out his own gun and I'd be the one fighting for my life.

"Even if you shoot me, they'll get you," he said. "All I have to do is call out."

"You'll still be dead. I'm a great shot."

When he didn't respond, I tossed him a length of twine. "Tie this around your wrist. Tie another knot. Pull it tight. Good. Now lie down inside the van on your stomach. Put your arms behind you."

He lay down in the open middle space between the two long seats running under the darkened windows. I jumped inside and put my knee on his back before tucking the gun into its holster. Though I felt clumsy wearing my gloves, it was ridiculously easy to finish tying his hands and feet, but I had to search in the dark van for a cloth to tie around his mouth. Instead, I found a roll of duct tape in a box under one of the seats. I suspected it had been used for just such a purpose before, probably with some of the girls. I also found more twine, a few short squares of cloth, and a liquid in a bottle that I'd bet was some kind of drug.

I had to hurry. Time was not on my side, which Harrison must have realized because he wasn't trying to resist. Or maybe he was afraid of me. Searching him, I found another useless phone, keys to the van, a knife, and two more guns, one a .45 like the one I carried. I relieved the pistols of their magazines before tossing them and the knife into the bushes along the back of the house.

The magazines and keys went into my pocket. After another rapid internal debate about what to do next, I started up the ramp near the van.

Almost immediately I heard voices. The back entry was large enough to accommodate several coffins, but the door from the hall was the regular size, so there was enough room in the entry for me to hide by pressing myself against the wall close to the hall door, though I felt exposed because of the bright lights.

Show time.

"Straight ahead," Kirt was saying. "Outside, down the ramp, and into the van. If any of you makes a move, Tiny here will have some fun with his gun."

The girls filed past me on quiet bare feet, all tied together in a row. A few were supported by their neighbors. In this bright light they looked young, forlorn, and near tears. One glanced in my direction, and I put my finger to my lips. She looked away quickly. More glances from others and a slight straightening of their shoulders when they saw me and my gun.

I hadn't even realized I'd taken it in my hand again.

I felt sick. How could I overcome two men without endangering the girls or myself? I searched for anything to tip the balance in my favor.

"I got it from here," Tiny said before reaching the hall door. "They ain't going nowhere with those ropes. And like you said, I can always shoot a few." He laughed at the terrified glances the girls cast at him. "Why don't you go back and do the old man so we can get out of here?"

"I thought, well . . . you'll probably need my help."

"Harrison will help. Besides, you got only one arm." A note of mockery entered Tiny's voice. "Unless you're not up to doing him. Dale is probably finished teaching that woman a lesson in the bathroom by now, so he can shoot the old man for you."

"Shut up." Kirt's voice was a growl. "You get them in. If anything goes wrong, it's your hide I'm taking it out on."

There was promise in Kirt's voice, and I knew Tiny didn't have much of a future under his command. Tiny didn't seem worried, which reminded me I didn't know who was really in charge. Maybe whoever it was had been grooming Kirt and his cousin to run the operation in this part of Oregon. Perhaps Tiny and Harrison and Dale were on loan until Kirt could arrange his own loyal thugs.

If he didn't get these guys so angry they killed him first.

I had no time to relish Kirt's footsteps going back down the hall. They only meant Cody was closer to death, and I needed to act fast to save him. Besides Tiny was coming into view, his gun held casually at waist height.

I squeezed tighter against the wall, lifting my gun. "Drop it!" I said in a low voice.

He froze. For a moment, I thought he was going to turn his gun on me, but his grip eased and he held it out between two fingers. The tough girl with blue hair lunged at it, toppling the two girls tied to her, but managing to secure the weapon.

"Down on your knees, scum!" she grated, pointing it at him. As he obliged, several of the girls started crying.

"Take this gun instead," I told the girl, "and hold it on him." I was fairly sure his gun was racked to fire, but I had to make sure, and I knew my gun was ready. His was another silenced .45, a match to the one I'd already stolen. I checked to make sure the chamber was loaded before slipping it into my holster.

She traded me and I whipped out my string and began tying his hands behind his back, threading the twine also around both ankles. "Hold still and she won't shoot you," I said, more to the girl than to him.

Searching him, I found his second gun and another useless phone.

"He has a knife, too," the tough girl said, stepping closer, the gun aimed at his forehead. "He used it for this rope when he tied us together."

"I'll find it. Don't shoot him unless he tries something."

"I hope he tries something," she said, her voice unnaturally high. "Then it'll be me having fun with his gun."

Nothing a little counseling couldn't resolve, I hoped.

I found the knife and cut her loose. "Free the others," I said, taking the gun and giving her the knife. She let the pistol go with relief, and I added its magazine as well as his other one to the growing collection in my pocket. Any more, and I might need a belt to hold up my pants despite the bulk of the holster at my waistband.

To Tiny, I said, "Down on your stomach! These girls are going to tie you up a bit more with some of your own rope and some duct tape that's in the van. Then they'll go out and wait for me there. Oh, and girls, there's another guy in the van. I'll help get him out when I come back so there'll be more room. Hurry, now! As fast as you can!" The girls who'd already been cut free sprang into action.

"Wait," I told the tough girl, handing her the set of keys I'd taken from Harrison. "If you see anyone that's not me or the old man come outside, you girls take off in that van and go somewhere with a lot of people where you can call the police. Got it?" If something happened to me, I wanted them to have a chance at getting away.

Her face hardened. "Got it."

If everything went like I planned, I'd get them away from here before any more criminals made an appearance. Then I'd find a phone to call Shannon.

First, I had to save Cody.

If I wasn't already too late.

Chapter 19

$\mathcal{I}$ sprinted down the hall on my bare feet, not bothering to muffle my steps. Maybe the noise would prevent Kirt from shooting Cody. He might think Dale or Tiny needed his help.

My entire body was tense as I waited for a shot that wouldn't come because surely he used a silencer like his goons. Even in this deserted area there had to be someone to report a gunshot to the police, and though Kirt was young and stupid, he obviously had some experience.

He was also cold-blooded, as his involvement with these girls proved beyond any doubt.

"Dale, is that you?" Kirt's voice, coming from the room where they'd kept the girls. I paused outside the door, waiting to hear more. "Get that woman to the van and get back here. We have some unfinished business. We'll need to dispose of the body."

"I ain't no body," Cody growled.

"You will be, old man. It's not like I want to do this—I actually kind of like you. But business is business. Before we get down to it, though, I want you to tell me where you stashed the girl."

I edged to the door, daring a peek inside. Good. Kirt's back was to me. I could only see a slice of Cody's arm. Kirt wouldn't be too much of a challenge to best with his wounded right arm.

"What girl? What are you talking about?" Cody asked.

"Jenny Vandyke. I saw you out in front of that restaurant just like we were, scoping her out. So where is she?"

"I didn't see you, and I don't have her. I don't even know what you're talking about." Was it just me or did Cody not seem surprised at the accusation?

"I think you do. Believe me, this is something you shouldn't mess with because it means a lot to the guys I report to. You don't want to get in their way."

"I didn't kidnap anyone, and even if I had, what makes you think I'd hand her over?"

"You will if you value your life."

Cody snorted. "You said you was going to kill me. You think I'd give up a little girl just so you can shoot me? I ain't stupid." *Like you,* Cody's tone insinuated. "So yeah, I have her, and I ain't telling where. There. Now you can't shoot me."

"I'll do it any way, old man. I'll find her without you." Venom laced Kirt's voice.

Cody might think he'd found a way out of getting shot, but he'd antagonized Kirt so much that the hothead wasn't seeing reason.

I took a step forward, raising my hand with the pistol.

An arm snaked around my neck at the same time a big hand closed over mine. "I'll take that back," said a voice I recognized as Dale's.

Great. So much for supposedly using enough twine. I hoped I'd done better with the guy in the van.

Dale marched me into the room.

Kirt looked up, annoyed, his gun still trained on Cody. "I told you to take her to the van with the others." His eyes narrowed. "What happened to your face?"

I turned to see that Dale's face did look bad, especially his nose, which was obviously broken.

Dale's arm tightened around my neck, forcing me to look forward. "She got away for a bit. I don't know what she might have done. Maybe she called the cops. Or them sheriff's deputies."

"That's exactly what I did," I choked out.

"Relax," Kirt said to Dale. "The sheriffs and the cops are covered. Don't choke her to death. Not yet." Kirt smirked at me as Dale's grip lessened. "Think you're real smart, don't you, Ms. Rain? Well, since you're here, you might as well watch how we do things. This old man is holding out on us and he thinks that might save his sorry self, but what he doesn't know is that we are searching his property right now, including the rentals we discovered he owns."

"The cops already searched everything," Cody said.

"Maybe not. Maybe they don't know yet about the properties you bought under that new corporation you formed. Maybe someone discovered that little tidbit but didn't think it necessary to tell the deputies yet. Make no mistake, we'll find that girl. We don't need you." He glanced at his gun, smaller than Dale's, a 9 mil maybe. Still able to kill.

I wasn't going to stand by and watch him shoot my own flesh and blood, no matter that Cody had never been and never would be any kind of a father to me. Maybe their greed for my talent would be enough to keep me from getting shot.

Maybe.

I whirled from Dale's loosened grip and sent a blow to his

face that likely broke more bones. He howled but had the presence of mind to bring up his gun, angling it toward me.

Unless Kirt ordered him to stop in the next second, I was going to die.

Cody lunged for Dale's arm, and a silenced shot whirred from the .45, slamming into the wall behind me.

I lashed out, chopping my hand down on Dale's and following closely with a kick to his ribs. Not to be outdone, Cody threw a punch and then another, and Dale fell to the floor.

I looked around for Kirt, but he already lay unconscious.

"He was distracted," Cody said with a shrug. "I hit him on his shoulder where he was shot. That boy is a wimp. Knew it the first time I laid eyes on him."

He ripped Dale's shirt and wrapped it around the butt of Dale's .45 before grabbing it. I was surprised after almost getting killed that Cody had the presence of mind to protect himself from the imprints. Half the time I still made that mistake. Maybe by the time I was in my sixties, I'd remember every time.

"Come on, now." Cody hurried to the door. "We got to get the rest of his guys so we can free those girls."

"I took care of that. The girls are waiting for us in the van." I hoped.

He tucked the gun into his coat pocket. "We'd better hurry. I heard him say he had a crew coming to torch the place. We'd better not be here when they arrive."

I searched Kirt's body, finding my phone and battery and taking his gun. We hurried down the hall to the back entry where we found Tiny tied so well that whoever found him would have a hard time freeing him. The girls had also plastered tape over his mouth, but his eyes stared at us murderously. Next to him lay a more complacent Harrison, with additional ties on his hands and feet. They'd done quite well without me, these runaways.

Cody was limping. "It's not much further," I said. He scowled at me and pushed ahead.

As we started down the back ramp, several of the girls jumped out of the van. "We found some clothes and our shoes," said the girl who had the lighter. "Yours are in the van. Saved 'em for you."

"We should call the police," another girl said.

"Gotta get away from here first," Cody mumbled. "More bad guys on the way."

I started around the van. "He's right. Get in. We'll call as soon as we're away from here."

I worried, though, about calling the police or the sheriff's office. Kirt had said they were no problem, and what that meant for us was that I didn't know who to trust. I'd have to call Shannon and talk it over with him. Maybe he'd have an idea that would keep us all safe.

Cody took shotgun, while I climbed into the driver's seat, where the tough girl had been waiting with the engine on and ready to go. She moved over to crouch in the space between the two front seats. I glanced back at the other girls who sat shoulder to shoulder on the seats and floor, packed in like eggs that might break at any rough turn. Eagerness and hope gleamed in their faces.

I pushed on the gas and peeled away. How far did we need to go before we would be safe? It was late, and not many people were on the road. The white van felt like a neon sign screaming "We're here! Come and get us!"

"We need to dump this van," I said, skidding around a corner.

"What about the police?" asked the tough girl, who wore a short-sleeved shirt that matched her blue hair. She rubbed her arms for warmth, which made me wish I'd retrieved my coat for her before we'd left the mortuary. Her face, illuminated by the bright moonlight, was young and animated. "Did you get a phone?"

"Right." I should have let her or Cody drive while I called, but Cody was obviously in pain and she wasn't old enough. Besides, I'd had experience in exactly one car chase, which made me the expert here.

I put in the battery and turned on my phone, flipping over to the screen that had the icon of Shannon's face. I chose the telephone option and held it to my ear.

Three rings. Four. Then a brief pause and more ringing. "Hello?" said a voice.

It wasn't Shannon. "Who's this?" I asked.

"Commander Huish. Is this Ms. Rain? Where are you?"

Fear rippled through me. "Why do you have Shannon's phone?"

"I don't. He went to look for you. Said he had an idea about something. He forwarded his calls to me in case he didn't pick up."

Maybe. Or maybe Commander Huish was the man working with the criminals. If he'd sold out, he would have plenty of money to pay his wife's bills and get his son into rehab. I couldn't trust him. There was too much at stake.

My location was still off, but even now they could be tracking me by using cell phone towers, both the good guys and the bad ones. "How do I know you're not working with Kirt and his goons?" I asked.

"What are you talking about?"

"Cody Beckett and I were kidnapped by Kirt Henry and taken to that U-shaped house I told you about. An old mortuary." The house that Huish had been so interested in. "Unfortunately for them, we escaped."

"Where are you now?"

I made a quick decision. "I can't tell you. Not until I know what side you're on."

"I'm on yours, of course. Now where are you? We have to get you safe. You can trust me."

"Someone replaced evidence right under your nose. Your detectives have failed to find any clue to Jenny's whereabouts in two weeks. You knew I was going to Jonathan's, where I was jumped. How do I know you didn't send those thugs after me? How do I know you don't have Shannon tied up somewhere?"

Silence on the phone and then, "You're right. There has been some questionable stuff going on, but I'm not involved. I swear to you, Ms. Rain. I only want to find Jenny and get the men responsible behind bars."

It sounded like the truth. I couldn't imagine Shannon forwarding his calls to the commander, unless he was sure Huish was clean, so either Huish was telling the truth or Huish had somehow relieved Shannon of his phone. How could I be sure?

"Please, trust me, Ms. Rain. Where are you?"

"Where's Detective Martin?" I countered.

"I don't know. I'm waiting for an update. Come in and we'll find him together."

I clicked my phone off.

Cody looked at me, one brow raised. "Commander Huish," I said. "But I don't know if he can be trusted." There was a plea in my voice, though I wasn't sure he heard it. I hated myself for it, for expecting leadership from a man who had done my mother so much harm.

Cody's jaw jutted forward. "The hospital," he said. "The girls should go anyway. The doctors will wrap them in so much protocol that it'll be impossible for anyone to get to them. Plus we should call the media. That should do it."

"They may have my friend, Detective Martin."

Cody grimaced. "They might kill him if it hits the news. Cut their losses."

"That's what I was thinking."

The tough girl had been following our conversation, her face swinging first to me and then to Cody. "What about his phone?" she asked. "Isn't there anyone you trust who can track it?"

I blinked at her, nearly steering off the road. Shannon always kept his GPS locator on, and while I didn't know how to track it, I knew someone back in Portland who could.

I turned back on my phone and called Shannon's partner, who picked up on the first ring. "Paige, I don't have time to explain, but Shannon might be in trouble. We've been separated and he's not picking up when I call. I need to track his phone to find him. In case it's related to those guys who jumped us in Portland earlier."

"What about the police there?" Her voice was calm despite the alarm I knew she must feel at the news.

"I don't know who to trust. Someone in the sheriff's office is working for the other side."

Paige didn't question further. "You're calling me on the department phone Shannon gave you, right?"

It wasn't a silly question when it was so easy to switch out sim cards. "Yes."

"Good, I'll text you instructions on how to track his location. You'll need to turn on your GPS to do it, and put in a password."

"I can do that."

"Hopefully, he's just run out of battery or dropped his phone. But Autumn," her voice became deadly soft, "you have to understand. If someone's working from the inside, while your phone is on they might be able to track you too."

"I know. I have to try."

"Meanwhile, I'll get ready to come down there," she said. "Call me the minute you know anything."

"I will." I disconnected the phone and handed it to the tough girl. "Take out the battery, please."

"Where're we heading?" she asked.

I took my eyes from the road to glance at her. "The hospital."

As soon as the girls were safe, I'd turn back on my phone and find Shannon.

"Cody," I added, "you have to give me directions. I have no idea where we are."

Chapter 20

The drop-off at the Salem hospital went more smoothly than the last visit I'd made to the place. After I explained to the woman at the information desk about the girls, two hospital administrators, three doctors, and six nurses appeared and began caring for them right there in the lobby. I heard one administrator on the phone with the police.

My nerves were taut with worry as I scanned the crowd, looking for possible trouble. I had left Kirt's gun in the van because my sweater didn't hide it adequately and I hadn't wanted to draw attention to myself. It seemed to be the right call.

I edged to the outskirts of the commotion, thinking about Kirt's cousin and wondering if the stabbed man was still unconscious. "When the police and detectives from the sheriff's office arrive, you need to tell them to question the cousin if he's awake," I said to Cody, when he hung up the pay phone where he'd been calling a news station. "They can't all be on the take. Maybe he'll regain consciousness long enough to give the police the whereabouts to any other location where they might have Shannon."

Cody grabbed my arm and hurried me toward the entrance. "Don't look now, but there's a deputy. Must have been one of the men assigned to watch that guy you're talking about."

He was right. I had to get away before more deputies showed up and detained me.

I headed toward the van, which I'd left on the street this time. The outside air was so cold, it hurt to breathe, and once again I longed for my coat.

As I walked, I turned on my phone and found the GPS icon. "Here goes," I told Cody, who was shuffling alongside me as fast as his hurt leg allowed. "Let's see." I clicked on the link Paige had sent and put in the password. "There. He's coming up."

The icon of Shannon's face popped up, as well as my own. Paige was also on the list, her location in Portland. I enlarged the map around Shannon's icon.

"Do you recognize this place?" I held the phone out for Cody to see. "It was updated fifteen minutes ago, which means Shannon's phone was there then."

Cody studied the map. "It's just outside Hayesville. Unincorporated land like mine."

So, not the sheriff's office. Had Huish been telling the truth? No, I couldn't jump to that conclusion. For all I knew, Huish had also been at that location when I'd called. At least it wasn't the sheriff's office, which would have been nearly impossible for me to break into, much less break Shannon out of.

As we reached the van, I pushed the option to ping Shannon for a check-in, but there was no answering change in his location.

Sighing, I dragged the driver's door open, wishing I had some other form of transportation, though the idea of using their own vehicle to find Shannon was deliciously ironic.

I was surprised when Cody climbed into the passenger seat. "What are you doing?"

"Going along for the ride."

"You don't have to come with me. This doesn't concern you."

"I know."

"And you should get that leg fixed."

"It's fine. If I stay, the cops will only keep me up all night with questions, especially if they find me with those girls. They still think I have Jenny Vandyke."

"And do you?"

He gave me a flat stare. "The sooner you get going, the sooner we'll be able to find your boyfriend."

I hit the gas. I suspected he was using me to get away, but it wasn't as if I could throw him out of the van. Besides, he had a gun, and he seemed to have as low an opinion of the drug runners as I did. He might be of some help.

If he didn't shoot me first to prevent me from telling the police what Kirt had said about Jenny and Cody's other properties.

We followed Shannon's icon for five more minutes until it abruptly winked out. "What does that mean?" Cody asked.

"His GPS locator was turned off, I think. Or maybe the phone has been shut off. Or broken. I'm not really sure."

"I don't know much about those things, but you'd better turn yours off, just in case someone can still track you."

Mistrust threatened to immobilize me. Maybe Cody did have Jenny, and maybe he wanted to make me disappear too. I swallowed hard. No, I needed to trust someone. He hadn't given me any promises, so maybe that made him the best person to trust.

I held the button on my phone that would shut it down completely. Then I removed the battery. Better safe than sorry.

"You still remember where it was?" I asked.

"Sure. No problem."

Obviously, I hadn't inherited my directional impairedness from him.

For ten more minutes I drove in a silence broken only by Cody's gruff directions. Then he said, "Maybe you should just go back to Portland. Talk to the police there. Let them find your detective."

I shook my head. "It might be too late."

"Turn left here," was his only reply. I obliged, driving onto what must have been a dirt road, given the snow-covered ruts. We were lucky the snow and mud had frozen enough that the tires didn't sink.

A short while later, we parked the van behind a couple of trees, which wouldn't hide anything during the day but was adequate for now. I took Kirt's gun and the holster from the glove compartment and shoved them into my waistband. On foot we followed another dirt road about half the width, its surface completely hidden by tire-packed snow. I was grateful the girls had found my boots and wondered if my coat was part of a bonfire at the mortuary by now.

I didn't like the coat anyway, I thought. Bad karma and all with that bullet hole.

Cody's coat was missing, too, though he'd had it when he'd joined the girls in the van. His limping was worse, but he didn't look cold in the large flannel shirt he wore. Probably he was used to working outside in this weather. I realized I knew next to nothing about this man who was biologically my father.

"You still have a gun?" I asked. Last I'd seen, he'd put it in his coat pocket.

He patted his stomach covered by his untucked shirt. "Yup. Had to make my belt tighter, but it's staying put."

We tromped along in silence until we spied a group of three buildings in a large clearing. "I've seen these buildings before," Cody said. "Used to belong to some farmer. Been deserted a long time now."

"Not anymore." Half a dozen cars and another van parked outside the middle building, which seemed to be more of a storage shed than a house or barn. Maybe it had once held tractors and other equipment. The foremost building was a tiny house, whose roof was missing. The largest structure on the far side looked like a barn and had humongous tarps spread over the roof. Something was being protected there.

"Another drug house?" I asked. "Why didn't they take the girls here? Looks bigger."

Cody grunted. "Too run down, maybe? There'll be no heat or running water. Can't have the girls freezing to death. Besides, it's not the sort of place they can bring customers."

I bet they'd moved their drugs to this place when the sheriff's deputies scared them out of Millard's rental house and after I'd seen the imprint of the mortuary.

"They're lucky all the roofs haven't caved in," Cody added. "Probably bought the land with the idea of expansion. Practically hidden from the road. Speaking of which, we should probably stick to the trees. That moon is far too bright now that the clouds are gone."

That meant walking through the newly fallen snow, which only slightly cushioned our steps from the crunchy, older snow beneath. "What Kirt said about you and Jenny Vandyke," I said into the silence.

Cody stopped walking and faced me. "What about it?"

"Did you take her? I mean, if Kirt's guys didn't. They seem to think it was you."

His eyes narrowed but didn't quite reach mine. "I did not kidnap anyone."

"Then why do I get the feeling you know more than you're saying?"

He turned his back on me. "Just focus on what's at hand. Better be quiet now. They probably have guards."

Anger smoldered in my chest, but he was right. I had to find Shannon, and then I'd deal with Cody.

A man stepped out of the trees. "Hold it right there."

My heart sank. I'd been stupid, stupid, and more stupid. What made me think I could approach a drug ring's hideaway without proper backup? At the very least I should have crawled through the trees so I wouldn't be seen.

The man was big, and he looked remotely familiar, probably from the hospital shooting but possibly from the imprint on Kirt's keys. He wore a bulky parka, boots, and a wool hat, which hinted that he'd been out in the cold a long time or planned to be. In one hand he held a gun and in the other, a two-way radio.

"Boss," he said, bringing the radio to his face, "I found two intruders. Don't look like police."

A surge of static. "Shoot them."

"Will do. But just so you know, the woman might be the one who was with that police detective."

"Bring them here then. If they resist, do what you have to do."

I strained to recognize the voice through the static, but the connection was too poor.

The thug put the radio into his pocket. He stepped close to me, and with a quick motion, grabbed Kirt's gun from my hip. He tossed it far into the darkness.

"You heard him," he said, motioning with his gun. "Get walking."

If we went with him, we probably wouldn't make it to another day. I wished I'd talked to my sister once again and cuddled my baby niece longer the last time I'd held her. I wished I'd kissed Shannon harder and more often and found out where our relationship was heading. I wished I'd said I was sorry to Jake. Sorry for not loving him the way he thought he loved me.

"I'm not going anywhere," Cody said, his voice turning cantankerous. So, he'd come to the same conclusion I had. I felt more than saw his muscles bunching under his flannel shirt. This time, at least, there were no innocent bystanders as there had been at the restaurant.

"It's all the same to me," the thug said with a flat grin. "In fact, I'd just as soon shoot you both here."

That's what I was afraid of.

I moved before Cody did. One swift kick to the thug's right hand. It was supposed to send the gun flying into the snow so Cody and I could jump him, but my muscles were cold and my blow didn't carry much force.

The man laughed as he brought the gun around to point at me again. "I'm not some lightweight like those guys you got away from in Portland. You broke my brother's arm, you know? And now you're gonna pay. Because unlike my boss, I don't much care for the idea of having a weirdo like you working for us." He grinned. "Say goodbye."

Cody jumped in front of me, lunging at the man. He jerked as a bullet caught him in the chest.

I gasped as Cody continued his forward movement, slamming into the man hard and toppling both of them to the ground. The thug jumped up, still in possession of his gun, but Cody had pulled out the .45 he'd taken from Dale. He fired a warning shot before our attacker could bring up his weapon.

"Drop it." Cody's voice was deadly.

The man dropped his gun, and I picked it up from the snow before rushing to Cody's side. "You hit?" It was a stupid question since I'd seen him take the bullet.

He grunted, his free hand clutching against his chest. The gun in his hand wavered. "Imprint," he muttered. "I'm not wearing gloves."

Whatever imprints were on the gun, they obviously weren't pretty. Taking advantage of our distraction, the thug lunged not toward us but away, disappearing into the trees.

"I should have shot him," Cody mumbled, dropping the pistol.

"You should have waited for a better opportunity," I countered.

"That was the best opportunity we'd ever have. We've already been really lucky, but that luck has finally reached an end." He gave a deep, shuddering breath. "If you know what's good for you, you'll get yourself back to that van and get out of here before our friend comes back with the cavalry."

"I thought the cavalry were the good guys."

"Not always."

Given my suspicions of the sheriff's deputies, I had to agree. Sometimes the so-called cavalry was on the wrong side of the law.

"Go on. Get out of here." Cody jerked his head in the direction we'd come.

"I'm not leaving you." I leaned over and grabbed his arm.

"Get out of here! I ain't nothing to you."

"Look," I growled, "I didn't come to Hayesville just for a missing girl. I came here too because you have information about my past. Information about my ability, about your mother, and about probably a hundred other things I don't know enough about yet to ask. I'm not leaving you—and don't you dare die on me!"

His brow furrowed. "So you lied."

"It's not as if I'm the only liar in the family." He knew something about Jenny Vandyke—I was sure of it. One way or the other, I had to find out what. With great effort, I heaved him to his feet.

"I'll never make it back to the van. You really should leave me here."

We hadn't heard anything from the thug and his buddies yet, though they were bound to come looking for us. I couldn't protect Cody here. Or hide him behind a tree. If his wound didn't kill him, the exposure would. The only option was to move somewhere.

I looked around, panic growing in my chest. Wait. The little house with no roof was close, just through the trees. If we could get there before we were discovered, maybe I'd have the chance to call for help.

I explained the plan to Cody as I shoved Dale's .45 into my holster and our attacker's smaller 9 mil into my left pocket on top of some magazines. It was an awkward fit, but I hoped it would stay put.

I pushed, pulled, and otherwise forced Cody onward. I worried about the tracks we were leaving in the snow, until I realized there were many others crisscrossing the area we hobbled through.

Were some of these tracks Shannon's? I hadn't much time to think about him in the past few minutes, but now my worry returned.

We struggled on. How could the little house be so far away? It seemed we hadn't made any progress toward it. Cody was heavy and growing heavier by the moment. The 9 mil fell out of my pocket, and I scooped it out of the snow and shoved it back into my pocket, feeling a seam inside partially give way.

We stumbled to a stop beneath a tree, and Cody slumped down, his head lolling against the trunk. Blood spotted the snow where we crouched. If I didn't get us moving, Cody was going to die right here in the snow, and I'd never learn what he knew about my talent or about his mother. I'd never learn if he was sorry.

In a swift motion, I pulled my red sweater over my head. I was wearing a fitted black tank top underneath, like the kind I normally wore in the summer. I caught my breath at the cold.

"What are you doing?" Cody demanded. "You need to get out of here. You see that, right? I can't go on."

"What I need is to stop this bleeding. Now hold this tight. There don't seem to be any imprints of consequence on it. Well, a little fear, but that won't kill you." He grunted in pain as I pressed the folded sweater over the wound and put his hands on top. I needed more, but it was all I had.

I pulled out my phone, removing my gloves to replace the

battery. Shannon's icon still hadn't updated. Feeling nauseated at the worried imprints I'd left on it earlier, I called Shannon's partner.

"Autumn?" Paige asked. "What's happening. Did you find Shannon?"

"Not yet. But I know for sure he's in trouble now, and I need help. Can you come?"

"I'm actually already on my way. But it looks like I'm still about forty minutes from your current location. I have another officer with me."

"Well, Cody Beckett's been shot. We're out here in the snow in the middle of nowhere, and it's not looking good. He needs an ambulance, but I don't want anyone else shot. And I don't dare call the sheriff's office. This is their jurisdiction."

"What about those FBI agents you're working with?"

They were the lowest on my list of suspects, worth the risk of contacting now with Cody so close to dying. "I don't exactly have them on speed dial."

"I'll do it. Meanwhile, try to stop the bleeding and find some cover," she said. "And keep him as warm as possible. I'll get someone there as soon as I can."

"There's a little house ahead. With a caved-in roof. We'll try there. Look, take down my location because I'm turning off my phone as soon as I hang up."

"Already did. Get to that house and sit tight." Paige sounded calm, the way she always reacted to serious situations, but inside, I knew she was dying of frustration that she was too far away to help me herself. "Don't do anything stupid," she added. "I'll be there soon."

"I might do something stupid," I told her. "I have to find Shannon."

"Oh, Autumn. I'm so sorry."

Sorry that I was falling for Shannon? That she encouraged it? That I made a lousy partner since I'd failed to cover his back?

"I'm hanging up now." Clicking off, I wiped tears away, turning my head from Cody. I could feel his eyes on me, and I was glad he didn't speak. I'd give myself a moment more to rest, and then I was going to make him move again.

"My ability started after they took my mother away," Cody said so softly I almost didn't hear. His voice grew stronger. "She was young. I wasn't even ten."

Another traumatic event, like the ones that had precipitated my ability.

"She went to a sanitarium?"

"They said she was crazy, that she was a danger to herself and to me."

"Why?"

"You were in my room. I bet you touched her quilt—don't you know?"

"I know she loved you, that she felt guilty for leaving you."

He shifted his position, drawing in a breath laced with pain. "That's not what I mean. Some of the things she put into the quilt, things in my life, she wasn't there to witness. I don't know how she did it."

To me it made perfect sense. His mother, our grandmother, had the same ability as Tawnia, only she'd been a woman alone in a world that was more interested in locking up what it didn't understand than with learning why.

"She saw things," Cody continued. "Or rather when she drew things, she said they'd come true. She drew all sorts of things—community events, bank robberies, even murders.

Of people she'd never met. She'd show them to me in the paper, and they always matched her drawings. One time she drew a family whose boat capsized, drowning all of them but a teenage daughter. She called the police while it was happening, hoping to save them, and for a while they suspected she'd done something to cause it. When she tried to explain, well"—he paused, his voice growing thin—"they took me away and sent her to that place. Said it was to fix her, but she was never right after that. She was very fragile. My whole goal in life was to survive the foster homes and grow old enough to get her out of there."

"But she died."

He nodded. "She died. From there on, it was downhill for me. I never found myself."

"You have now. What about your land, your art, your donations to the community?"

"It's all pretend. A make-believe life." He swallowed hard. "The truth is that every day I relive what I did to your mother." His eyes shut, whether in pain or in memory, I didn't know. "She'd imprinted all the emotions she'd felt on a stuffed animal, and once I touched it, I knew what I'd done. I couldn't remember a thing for myself, but I knew it all. I knew how despicable I was." He paused before adding, his voice lowering. "I should have been the one to die, not her."

Finally the admission of guilt I'd waited for, and yet it wasn't as satisfying as I expected. It was desperate and more than a little sad. I remembered the utter self-loathing on the imprints at his house. Once I might have been gratified to see his suffering, but now I only pitied him.

"Maybe you've paid enough," I said when I could finally

speak. "Maybe it's time to let that go, to forgive yourself and go on."

He shook his head. "There's no forgiveness for me. Not in this life. Not until I hear it from her. I deserve to suffer. In that one instant, I hurt so many." He bowed his head in defeat.

Several heartbeats passed in utter silence. What could I say to him? But I knew. The anger that had been building inside me this past year was gone. Anger that had only been hurting myself.

I took a deep breath. "I forgive you."

His head lifted, his strange eyes locking onto mine. "Why?"

"Because I don't think you intended to hurt her."

"I didn't protect her, either. I didn't know where I was or what I was doing because of the drugs. That was my choice."

"That's something you have to live with, but it doesn't mean you deserve death or to suffer forever."

Tears wet his grizzled face, reflected by the moonlight. "Please go," he said, his voice like gravel. "I don't want to be the reason you die too."

"You came here because of me. That makes all this my fault."

Before he could answer, I jumped to my feet, shivering because of inactivity. If I got out of this, I'd need a host of herbs and herbal teas from Jake's store to stave off pneumonia.

I kicked snow over the blood and adjusted the gun in my pocket. We faltered on, my toes so cold in my leather sock boots that I no longer felt them.

Sudden shouts in the trees urged us onward, though it was impossible to tell how close the voices were because of the large area and the muffling snow.

Cody stumbled, and we fell.

We weren't going to make it. Cody had been right all along. He was big and though I was strong, I wasn't strong enough. He was failing fast.

A rustle in the trees caught me by surprise. No time to reach for a gun or to hide.

Detective Levine stepped from the trees.

Chapter 21

"Ms. Rain, what happened? What are you doing here?" Levine's voice held concern.

He didn't draw his weapon, so maybe he was on my side. I sagged with relief. "Cody was shot. I'm trying to get him to that house."

In three steps, Levine was next to me. "Don't worry. I'll help." He touched my bare arm. "Gosh, you're like an ice cube. Here, take my jacket." He shrugged it off and slipped it over my shoulders.

I stiffened, half expecting an imprint, but there was nothing. "What?" Levine asked, gazing at me sharply. "Oh, is there one of those—uh, imprints? I didn't even think."

"No. I just have to be careful."

"Whew." He brushed a hand playfully over his forehead. "Because for a moment, I thought my jacket was telling stories about how much I like you."

I allowed myself a grin and reached for Cody.

"I'll carry him." He bent over and hefted the old man. "Okay, lead on."

We went much faster now, though Levine staggered at times under Cody's weight. "I can help," I said.

Levine shook his head. "I got it."

Too tired to protest, I decided to let him prove whatever he needed to. The 9 mil started slipping down my leg through the growing hole in my left pocket, so I took the opportunity to transfer it to a pocket of my borrowed jacket. Then I moved the magazines and my phone to the jacket as well.

Another distant shout urged us to hurry the last few feet to the little house. Like the roof, the door was missing, and I wondered how much shelter it could offer, but inside I discovered that part of the roof in the kitchen was still intact.

"Put him by that old stove," I said. "That looks like the most protected place." Too bad I couldn't start a fire.

Leaving Levine with Cody, I waded through the snow, dead leaves, and garbage looking for something I could use to tie up Cody's wound and maybe get him warm. Ancient furniture scattered around the place, destroyed by age, weather, and animals. At the foot of a broken bedstead, I found a battered old chest that despite its ruined outside had kept its treasure of bedding mostly intact. The chest was old enough and sturdy enough that with a little clean up, I could probably sell it in my antiques store for a few hundred bucks.

I took off my gloves and checked everything for imprints before carrying the bedding to Cody. In his weakened condition, a strong negative imprint could do serious damage.

"I can do this myself," Cody said as I used my teeth to start a tear in a sheet, its antiquity playing in my favor since I didn't have scissors. "You two get going."

Levine shook his head. "Hold still, Mr. Beckett. That's a nasty wound. What happened?"

"Gunshot," I said. "We ran into one of the drug dealers." I put a folded sheet on the wound under my now-soaked sweater and carefully threaded the torn sheet around Cody's back and over his chest. "How'd you find us anyway?" My suspicions were returning, though we wouldn't have made it to the house without him.

"I wasn't actually looking for you. I came here because your friend Detective Martin called and told me he was here and had found a lead."

"He told you? What about Commander Huish and your partner?"

"Just me. He specifically said not to tell them." He hesitated before rushing on. "To tell the truth, I've been a little worried about what's been going on at the sheriff's office. Evidence has never been tampered with before." He scratched his cheek, looking and sounding every bit like a boy I'd gone to kindergarten with.

"Huish has a son on drugs, you know," I told him. "And his wife's cancer is back. Tonight I heard him speaking to someone on the phone about giving him more time to pay something."

Levine's mouth gaped. "You don't think he's responsible for the missing evidence, do you?"

"Maybe. I won't know for sure until I talk to Shannon. There has to be a reason he came here." I'd finished wrapping Cody with the strips of the first torn sheet and began ripping another.

"How'd you get here anyway?" Levine asked.

"I followed Shannon's phone's GPS signal. But then it stopped. Have you seen him yet?"

Levine shook his head. "No." He paused and then added with a grin, "He'd be completely annoyed to find me here alone with his girl."

"Not when he hears how you helped us." I started wrapping another sheet strip around Cody.

"Stop," he protested. "I'm not a mummy."

"You might be one soon if I don't get you warm," I retorted, but I was pleased that his voice seemed stronger now.

"So Huish and Greeley don't know you're here?" Levine asked.

Caution made me say, "I'm not sure." I shook out two more sheets, a quilt, and a white crocheted bedspread I'd found in the chest and spread them over Cody.

Levine helped with the bedspread. "I hope they don't guess that you might be on to them. Not until we find out what's going on here."

Satisfied that Cody was as comfortable as I could make him, I arose. "So what now?" I was glad to have Levine's company, even if I'd rather have Shannon's. "I'm starting to think it's weird that the thug who shot Cody hasn't come after us yet."

"Maybe he and his buddies are busy with Shannon."

I frowned, growing more anxious by the moment to find Shannon. "Do you have Agent Cross's number?"

"I have the computer in the squad car. We can get the number there."

"Let's go, then."

"Maybe you should stay here," Levine said, half apologetically. "I don't want you to get hurt."

"Yeah, you should stay," Cody echoed.

"What? You were so hot to have me leave before. I'm going." I would make sure Levine called an ambulance. "Anyway, I'll be back. Just stay under those blankets."

I didn't look back at him as I left. If something happened,

I didn't want the picture of him lying alone, huddled under ancient bedding, to be the last memory I had of him.

Levine went outside ahead of me, but I stopped at the doorway and retraced my steps.

"Miss me already?" Cody said, opening one eye. His forehead glistened, and I hoped that wasn't a bad sign.

"Something like that." I pulled off one of my gloves and with difficulty worked it onto his larger hand before taking the .45 from my holster and giving it to him. "Just in case," I whispered as it vanished beneath the covers.

"You still have that gun from the guy who shot me?" he whispered.

I nodded, patting the side of Levine's jacket. "It's a 9 mil. Easier for me to handle."

"Keep it close. Don't trust anyone."

As I stole from the little house, that was the memory I carried with me—Cody giving me advice.

I half expected to be shot at as I left the house, but there was no cracking of bullets or whizzing of a silenced gun. What I found instead surprised me more. Several yards away, Levine and Commander Huish were facing each other, pistols drawn.

"Put it down," Huish was saying. "You're caught. You can't get away with it now. I don't want to shoot you."

"You put it down," Levine said. "How many you got here with you, huh? I don't see your pet Greeley."

My borrowed gun was in my hand before I realized it. Both men looked at me.

"He's behind all of this," Huish barked. "Get back. He'll shoot you."

Levine shook his head. "Don't believe him, Ms. Rain. You said it yourself that he needs money."

"How did you get here?" Huish demanded. "Tell her that. Better yet, I'll tell you. Detective Martin followed him here and then sent me directions when he was sure."

Levine shook his head. "No, Martin called me. If he called you, where are all the other deputies?"

"I wanted to check it out first. Detective Martin wasn't sure." They both sounded convincing, and I didn't know which one to believe. "Put down your guns, and we'll talk about this," I said. My right hand with the pistol wavered slightly, but I didn't dare support it with my bare left hand.

"I'm not sure I can do that," Levine said. "He might shoot me." He sounded scared and more than a little surprised.

"That's right," Huish answered. "I'll have to shoot him because there's no way he'll put down his gun. He doesn't want to go to prison. Don't buy his little innocent boy act. He's been playing us for months."

"You got it all wrong." Levine lowered his gun, tossing it gently into the snow. "There. But keep your gun on him, Ms. Rain, because I can't believe he won't shoot."

My eyes went to Huish, who lowered his gun. "I'm going to cuff him, now. Don't shoot."

"Don't let him cuff me." Levine looked toward me, almost pleading.

"You should have told me you were coming here," Huish said to me, ignoring Levine. "If Shannon hadn't told me where he was, this loser might have hurt you."

"So why didn't Shannon call me himself?"

"He tried several times, but no one picked up. That was before you called me, though, so maybe you didn't have your phone." Huish had taken out his cuffs and was nearing Levine.

Had there been messages I hadn't seen? "Stop," I told

Huish. "Don't move." I pointed my gun at him. "Drop your gun on the ground. That's it."

Levine edged toward me. "Good job. Now give me your gun. I'll cuff him and call for backup."

"Don't listen to him," Huish said, a desperate note entering his voice. "He's the leak! I have proof that he replaced the boot—probably because there was something on the real one that identified him. Then Detective Martin saw him leaving the office tonight when he was supposed to be tracing something for me. Leaving with confidential files, I might add. Martin followed him here, found the drugs, and called me. I think Levine's also been working with the Salem police, pretending to be involved in an underground investigation so he can float under their radar. He's in charge of this whole mess with the drugs."

I looked at Levine, who shook his head. "That's the way it happened, but he's the one who replaced the boot and stole the files."

"I'm going to kill you!" growled Huish.

"See?" Levine took another step toward me. "He's even more angry because you saved those girls. You've got to believe me."

"What are you even talking about? What girls?" Huish asked.

My world made an abrupt turn, leaving me feeling momentarily disoriented. Huish didn't know I'd been taken prisoner with the girls, but somehow Levine did.

Levine was within arm's reach, close enough that if I aimed the gun toward him, he'd see and react before I could finish.

"Take it," I said, smiling at Levine.

As he reached for the gun, I made a fist of my left hand

and hit him in the face. I wasn't as strong with my left hand as with my right, and since being shot in that arm I was even weaker, but I put in hours of practice with it every week, and I intended to make that count. My blow hit him hard enough that he staggered back. I pointed the gun at him.

"Autumn, what are you doing?" Levine's voice was wounded.

"Commander, pick up your gun and give me some help." I spoke too late because the commander was already halfway to my side.

"Autumn," Levine moaned. "Why?"

"You knew I took the girls. I didn't tell anyone, so the only way you knew it is if you had someone from the mortuary reporting to you."

Levine's face turned ugly and his hurt little boy act vanished. "You'll pay for this, I swear. Both of you."

"One more minute and he would have had us both disarmed without a shot fired," Huish said, bringing Levine's arms behind his back. "No telling what he would have done then."

That explained why Levine hadn't shot the commander immediately. In the role he was playing for me, he would have had to at least try to convince the commander to give up. If he'd shot too soon, he wouldn't have been able to disarm me nearly as easily as he almost had. Of course, the whole charade wouldn't have been necessary if his men were here. I hoped they weren't off chasing Shannon somewhere.

"Where's Shannon?" I demanded of Levine. My hand holding the gun shook.

"Easy." Commander Huish pried my fingers from the 9 mil and pocketed the weapon.

I brought my fists up instead. "Where is he!"

"Dead," Levine spat.

I felt as if he'd punched me in the stomach. Shannon and I had run out of time. My brain refused to process the idea.

"Don't believe him," Huish said. "Shannon called me after he'd had a run-in with these guys. He'd been shot, but he was still alive and free. I told him you'd escaped but were refusing to tell me where you were."

"Why did his GPS stop working?"

Huish made a face. "I believe he said something about not wanting you to track him here. He was a little busy staying ahead of those guys, or I'd bet he'd have tried to call you himself after he talked to me."

Shannon had probably checked my icon and seen that I'd turned on my GPS and was heading his way. "Then he's still alive," I said.

"He was before I found him again," Levine taunted.

"Shut up." Huish waved his gun. "You're just stalling. Forget it, Levine. Your thugs aren't coming. Why do you think they left you to deal with Ms. Rain here alone?"

Levine shrugged. "If either of you think you'll make it out of here alive, you're sorely mistaken." He grinned at me, as if everything had been a big joke. "Up until now I've played Mr. Nice Guy, but there's too much at stake here to have my operation compromised."

"We'll see about that," Huish said.

Levine dipped his head as if in a signal, his smile deadly. "Look around you."

Men stepped out from the trees, some I knew—Kirt, Dale, and Tiny. Only Harrison, the driver of the van I'd stolen, seemed to be absent from those who'd been at the mortuary.

I wondered if that was because he'd finally wised up, or if he was simply occupied elsewhere. With the newcomers was the man who'd shot Cody and another man I didn't recognize.

All of them had guns. We were surrounded.

"Looks like you didn't find the mortuary before they escaped," I said to Huish as he dropped his weapons into the snow.

"Remind me to dock someone's pay," he muttered.

Still wearing his sling, Kirt holstered his weapon and sauntered over to stand in front of me. His left fist lashed out, catching me in the stomach. I curled forward, gagging.

"That's for the girls," Kirt said.

"You forget I also saved your wasted life," I retorted, bringing up my hands.

Kirt made a fist again, his lip lifting in a sneer. "Bring it," he taunted.

I grinned. This would be almost too easy. Like Cody, I wasn't above hitting his wounded shoulder, and I knew from experience how much pain Kirt was going to be in.

"That's enough," Levine said, his voice calm.

Kirt stepped back, dropping his fists. "Yes, sir."

Sir? He'd called Levine sir? Ridiculous. Even with the change in Levine's demeanor, he didn't command that kind of respect. Except, I guessed, from these men.

"Besides," Levine added, "what happened at the mortuary is ultimately your fault, Kirt. You were in charge. You owe me." He sounded as though he was speaking about the weather, the casualness lined with something hard that made a shiver crawl across my shoulders.

"I'll make it up to you," Kirt promised. "I'll make my outfit the best you've ever seen."

"Good. We need to move out. The trucks are ready to go, but we're down a few men, so between the trucks and the cars, we'll all need to drive. I don't think the commander here notified anyone, but I don't want to take chances. In fact, I'll call the sheriff's office myself and make sure no one has been alerted."

"What about them?" Kirt tilted his head toward Huish and me.

"Tiny and I'll hold them until the others come back from disposing of that detective." Here Levine's eyes met mine, and I saw nothing that resembled the friendly, awkward man I'd seen earlier today. "Once we're sure that's cleared up, we'll take care of the commander and move out. Ms. Rain, however, is coming with us. Her unique ability will be useful in our future deals." His eyes bore into Kirt. "That means hands off unless I say otherwise."

So, I was still useful, which didn't make me feel any better. Because of me, Levine might learn of an intended double cross. Or know in advance how much a buyer was willing to pay. There were hundreds of different scenarios in which he could use my talent, none of which allowed me any kind of life. I'd met a mobster once who'd wanted to permanently take advantage of my skills, and though I'd escaped that fate, I still owed the guy one reading of an imprint. I often couldn't sleep at night worrying about it. Working for Levine would be even worse.

I was tempted to make a break into the woods, to fight until I couldn't move any more. Two things stopped me. Shannon was somewhere out there, and Cody was still in that little house. If I was going to get free, it had to be in one piece so I'd be able to help them.

"Move!" Levine barked. His men jumped into motion,

sprinting across the snowy clearing like wild rabbits, leaving the commander and me with Levine and Tiny. Unfortunately, Tiny had cuffed Huish with his own cuffs and was taking great pleasure in making sure my hands had little circulation with a length of rope I knew he'd rather be wrapping around my neck. At least my hands were in front of me.

How long had it been since I'd called Paige? Not long enough, I feared. She'd still have to find the right dirt road, which wouldn't be easy, even with my GPS location. The best I could hope for was that Levine would leave Cody here and that she'd find him in time.

Levine marched us across the clearing to the middle building where the cars were parked. Beyond that, in the largest building, I could see lights peeking from under the tarps and a semi emerging from the huge doors. I didn't believe it would make it down the snow-packed road, but they'd apparently driven it in.

Levine followed my gaze. "Wasn't quite ready to act as a storage facility, but the tarps worked in a pinch. But thanks to you and your detective friend, we may now have to find a new place." He spoke mildly, but there was controlled anger under the words, and I knew he intended to make me pay for the loss.

I didn't intend to stick around that long.

"I don't blame you, really," Levine added. "You were just doing your job. I knew it was only a matter of time until you found something with an imprint that pointed at me."

"So you decided to kidnap me."

His smile made my skin crawl. "Better working for me than against me. I tried to prevent you from finding certain imprints, but we saw how well that worked at Kirt's."

"You warned him, didn't you?" spat Huish. "And I bet you cleaned out his place before we got there."

"His and Millard's, though Millard didn't actually live there. I've been diverting information away from the sheriff's office for a very long time."

No wonder Huish and Greeley hadn't made progress in Jenny's investigation. Huish looked furious enough to attack Levine despite his cuffed hands.

"Calm down, commander," Levine said. "I'm the one with the gun."

The semi had reached our location, Kirt at the wheel despite his wounded arm. "Hey, boss," he called, rolling down the window. "I forgot to tell you. I found a lead on the girl. It was in the information you discovered from the sheriff's office last week—the old artist's new properties."

Levine nodded. "Find her. But only once the truck is safe."

My head whipped to Levine. "Do you mean Jenny Vandyke? If you know where she is, you have to let her go! She's just a little girl."

Levine regarded me, amusement flickering in his expression.

"She's not just a little girl. She's payback. She's retribution. She's insurance against a future double cross. And she'll also fetch a fine price on the market."

"You're sick," I said.

He shrugged. "I'm also very, very rich." He gave me a warm smile. "Who knows? You may become accustomed to the life."

I let the disgust in my eyes say it all.

"If you don't have Jenny, why exchange the boot?" Huish asked.

Levine grinned. "Interesting question. I handled the boot,

and I was worried I'd left something for Ms. Rain to pick up. But I also didn't want you finding the child before we did."

"You're scum!" growled Huish.

Levine laughed. The change in him was amazing. From shy boy next door to confident drug runner. Killer.

While we'd been talking, Dale had attached a vehicle to the back of the semi. His face, illuminated by the moonlight and the rear lights on the semi, looked ghoulish. They should have taken him to a doctor after the damage I'd done to him. When he finished, he got into another vehicle and drove away. We watched the semi follow his path across the snow, scraping its sides against the trees as it headed to the adjoining road.

Two men gone, which left Levine, Tiny, and the other two who'd been sent to the far building. I tested my bonds. Too strong. I wasn't going anywhere.

"Inside." Levine waved his gun toward the middle building.

I could do nothing but precede him to the door and, when he opened it, go inside.

Chapter 22

This building was almost warm compared to the outside, despite the concrete floor. A wood stove burned in the middle of the room, its black exhaust pipe snaking up through the ceiling. After the bright moonlight in the clearing, the place was dark, though I could make out boxes of supplies and bedding. Someone had been staying here, had maybe hoped to stay a long time. Would they really give it up now? Unless they captured Shannon, there was still a chance they'd have to. It wasn't a complete win for our side, but it was something.

"Wait." Levine ordered. "Search them."

Tiny felt the pockets of my borrowed jacket and grinned at me as he emptied first my phone and then the half dozen full magazines. "So that's where they went," he said.

"They made a nice collection." I lifted my chin.

"Sure they did." He spun me around, slamming my face against the door and began patting me further, obviously enjoying himself.

An imprint came through the skin of my cheek. Immediately

I knew who'd left it. I knew who'd looked out the small opening at eye level in the door only minutes ago.

Shannon was alive! It was the only thought of my own I could manage as the strong feelings in the imprint overtook me.

Relief at seeing Autumn unharmed. She was tied, looking more angry than scared. That's my girl, I/Shannon thought. Was Levine going to put her in the truck? I'd follow it if he did. Maybe the back doors were open, or the doors to the car that thug was hooking to the back. Calculating the steps to the semi. How long would I have to be in the open? They had guns, which unlike mine, were loaded.

But no, the truck moved on, and Levine was coming this way with Autumn.

Need to hide. Agony surged through my thigh as I pushed off the door.

The imprint ended, and Tiny pulled me away from the door, though not before I saw a second semi stopping outside. No one emerged from the cab to hook up a vehicle to the back as Dale had with the first truck. Whether that was good or bad, I couldn't know.

Shannon was here, and I knew he'd act before Levine killed the commander and drove me off to wherever he was heading.

I had to be ready to move when Shannon did. Hopefully soon, before Kirt found Jenny. I tried not to dwell on that too much because somehow it involved Cody.

"Levine, think what you're doing," Huish urged, as Levine turned on a light that looked like a lantern but operated on batteries.

Levine straightened. "What I'm doing is a favor for you, commander. Think of it this way. You won't have to see your wife die or your son overdose. You won't care at all about them where I'm sending you. I might even give your son a job. What do you think of that?"

"I'll kill you!" Huish lunged, but Levine punched him in the face, and he staggered back, knocking over a stack of supplies as he fell.

As if on cue, the outside door reopened. Detective Greeley loomed in the doorway, looking odd with his wavy hair matted to his head.

Huish grinned at Levine from the floor. "You really think I'm stupid enough to have come alone? Where do you think the rest of your guys went? We've been picking them off one by one."

As Greeley edged further into the room, Huish's grin faltered. "Where are the others?" he asked Greeley.

Greeley shook his head. A sinking feeling began in my stomach. Was Greeley in on it too?

The detective moved further into the room, and now we could see that his hands were behind his back and he was bleeding from a wound in his shoulder. The man who'd shot Cody was behind him, holding a gun to Greeley's neck.

"This deputy and his buddy tried to stop our truck," Greeley's captor said. "But don't worry. They learned their lesson the hard way."

Levine began chuckling. "I was beginning to think you'd failed me." His barbed tone made it clear that failing him would have been fatal.

"You stinking bit of slime!" Greeley snarled at Levine. "I suspected you were involved, but I still can't believe you're actually working with these scum."

So that was what Greeley had been hiding, the suspicion that his friend and partner wasn't all he seemed to be.

Levine barely spared him a glance. "No hard feelings, partner. Don't take it personally."

"Your thugs just killed Greg out there!" Greeley bellowed. "How's that for personal?"

"Maybe it will help to know that I'm not really Billy Levine. I just took his place when he was transferred here."

"That means you've been lying to us for two years!" Greeley's voice rose an octave. "When I get my hands on you, you'll wish you were dead."

"Gag him." Levine ordered before turning to some files and shoving them into a box. "I'll need these but we'll torch the rest. We won't be able to use this place anyway, not until we're sure how much the sheriff's deputies know. The insurance will pay us more than it would cost to upgrade the buildings anyway, and the fire will do us the added benefit of disposing of the commander."

I tried to catch Huish's eye, but he was glaring at Levine as Tiny hauled him to his feet and tied a dirty rag over his mouth. I squinted into the darkness, looking for Shannon. Where was he? Had I imagined the imprint?

No. He was here, and I knew he wouldn't leave.

The imprint told me he had no bullets in his gun. By gun I didn't know if that meant the backup he normally carried or the weapon he'd said he was going to borrow from the sheriff's office to replace the Glock they'd confiscated after the shooting at the hospital. Either way, I knew he'd have a 9 mil, because that's what he liked best. A few of the magazines I'd confiscated were 9 mil, and I didn't know if any might fit his gun, but it was worth a try. Maybe I could lean over the box where Tiny had set them and pick out those that looked to be the right size.

I stumbled forward, bumping into the box and sending the magazines skittering to the floor. I groaned. So much for that plan.

Levine stopped shoving papers into his box and turned to me. "Tiny, maybe we should give Ms. Rain something to relax her. I've got exactly the thing in one of these boxes." He smiled at me. "Can't guarantee you won't have a headache when you wake up, but that can't be helped. Ah, here it is." He glanced over at Huish. "Would you like some too? Ha! Sorry, commander. I'm kidding. It's too expensive to waste on a dead man."

Tiny grinned and lumbered toward me with a needle.

That was when Shannon rose from the shadows behind Levine. He'd tied a cloth around the top of his thigh, and drying red stains covered the front of his jeans. It looked like an awful lot of blood. Remembering the pain from the imprint, I wondered how he was still on his feet.

Before Shannon could strike, Levine turned his gun toward him, warned perhaps by a sound or some innate sense of self-preservation. I dodged Tiny and his gun, bringing up my tied hands and swinging them into Levine's shoulder. Not exactly something taught in my martial arts class but good enough to send his bullet wide.

Shannon leapt past me toward Tiny, his empty pistol in his fist to increase the weight of his punch. Behind me, I could hear Greeley also struggling with his captor.

I hit Levine again as he recovered his balance, this time succeeding in freeing his gun from his fingers. Sidestepping a punch to my face, I kicked out, surprising him, but his left fist caught me in my stomach where Kirt had struck earlier.

Fighting the urge to vomit, I swung my arms again, following with a straight kick between his legs. Not as effective as, say, keys to the eyes, but his abrupt intake of air told me I had his attention.

Behind me Shannon and Tiny were knocking over boxes. I heard a groan I was sure came from Shannon. If he'd lost a lot of blood, he might not be able to hold his own against Tiny.

I paid for my inattention as Levine, his eyes gleaming with fury, landed a punch to my left shoulder, sending pain reverberating down my arm. He followed with another strike to my face, but I was back in the game and blocked it with my tied arms, taking the blow primarily on my right. It'd leave a telling bruise.

Levine was a little taller than average height for a man, and though he was thin, he had a good thirty pounds on me. He also had a long reach and was in good physical condition. By contrast, my hands were tied, my arm and thigh ached, and I was exhausted. The only advantage I had was desperation.

Levine laughed. "Give it up. There's no way you can win."

I faked a blow to his head with my tied hands, missing him on purpose and allowing my momentum to give me the height I needed to swing my left leg high enough to slam my foot into his head. I was off by a few inches, catching him in the jaw instead, but it had the same effect.

He stumbled back, stunned, but recovered quickly, launching himself at me as I let fly another kick. A kick I immediately knew was going to fall short.

Huish, his hands still cuffed, rammed into Levine, knocking him forward against my foot. Pain shot through my toes and up my leg. Levine went down, crashing into a crate and landing hard. It shattered under his weight, and household items spilled over the floor. A toaster smacked him on the forehead. Commander Huish also fell, his head cracking against the concrete.

I jumped into the mess, pouncing on Levine's stomach and swinging my bound fists at his face. *That's for Cody,* I thought. *And that's for those poor little girls.*

Levine bucked and turned, throwing me off him. I slammed into a crate. I might have been able to recover without my hands tied, but before I could regain my balance, Levine's hand snaked around my neck as he dragged me to my feet. I saw the glint of a blade.

"Stop!" Levine shouted. "Stop, or I'll kill her."

I turned to see Shannon rising from Tiny's still form. Greeley hadn't fared as well, and his captor now swept up his gun from the floor and pointed it at him. Shannon's face, illuminated by the lantern, was furious. He took a step toward where Levine held me.

"Easy," Levine warned, sounding calm and in control, as if everything had gone according to plan. "Don't do something you'll regret. Or Ms. Rain will get hurt. I know how much you care about her."

But we had to do something. If we didn't act, Levine would torch the place and use the fire to kill Commander Huish and Greeley—and likely Shannon as well. Even if I could knock Levine into the stack of crates behind us, his remaining thug would have time to shoot the commander and Greeley. Maybe even Shannon.

They were all as good as dead whatever I did. We were all dead. The certainty made me sick. I twisted my head to see Levine staring at me, his face sharp and vicious, as though he knew exactly what I was thinking.

Huish seemed to be unconscious, but Greeley had to

understand the stakes and would be ready to act. I knew them
well enough to know that neither wanted to see Levine get
away regardless of the personal cost.

"Get on the floor!" Levine barked at Shannon. "I swear I'll
shoot her. Her gift might be useful, but I've done quite well
without it." He smiled at Shannon. "It's your choice."

Shannon took a step forward, and I felt Levine's knife press
into my neck. Glaring, Shannon slowly went down on the knee
of his good leg.

"Not so fast," yelled a gruff voice.

I blinked as a man emerged partially from behind the crates
beside us. His black-gloved hand shoved the barrel of a .45 into
Levine's head.

Cody. Though I could see him from my position, Greeley's
captor shouldn't have a clear enough view to get off any shots
without risking his leader.

"Move so much as an inch," Cody growled, "and you'll be
strumming harps. Or shoveling coal, rather. I can shoot faster
than you can use that knife. Tell your boy over there to put
down his gun."

When no one moved, Cody added, "I'll admit I'm a lousy
shot, but even I can't miss at this range."

The pressure of the knife against my neck eased. "Do what
he says!" Levine yelled, his eyes bulging. Ha. He wasn't so
calm now.

Shannon lunged toward Levine, grabbing Levine's hand
and ripping both him and the knife away from me. He
punched hard at Levine's face, dropping him to the ground.
In two quick steps, he snatched up one of the fallen guns and
pointed it at Levine's chest.

"Don't move," he grated.

One part of my mind registered Greeley taking charge of his assailant and Cody sagging to the ground with a satisfied sigh. But most of my attention was still on Shannon. His face was grim, the rugged lines harder than I'd ever seen them. His hand on the gun looked pale, as though he clenched the weapon too tightly.

He was close to pulling that trigger. Too close. I knew if he did, it wouldn't be for the drug trafficking, or even for the girls, but for what Levine had put me through.

"Move, please," I said to Levine with a smirk. "So he can shoot you. Of course, if we killed you we wouldn't be able to find out more about those partners you've mentioned."

"Like I'd tell you anything," he spat. But he didn't move, and his eyes didn't leave Shannon's gun. His face had lost every bit of color. I knew he couldn't tell whether or not Shannon would pull the trigger. Neither could I.

"Oh, I think you will." Shannon's eyes flicked to me and his grip relaxed slightly. "Anything to save yourself."

The tight knot in my stomach was gradually untying. Shannon was in control now. He wouldn't shoot.

"I think I'd still rather you move," I said to Levine. "How about it?"

Levine glared but didn't answer.

Shannon pulled out a knife with his free hand and began sawing at my bonds. His jaw tightened at the red indentations around my wrists, distinct even in the light of the lantern, but his grip on his gun didn't change.

"What about you?" I asked, "How's your leg?"

"Just a scratch Next time don't come after me. I had it under control."

"Yeah, I can see that." I rolled my eyes. "How did you

know Levine was involved, anyway? Commander Huish told me about the files he stole, but that didn't mean he was behind all this."

"I heard him talking on the phone after you called me from the restaurant. He mentioned you and Cody, but I was the only one who knew Cody was with you. After you went missing, I saw him take the files, and it all clicked." He glanced at Levine. "Hear that, Barney Fife? It was your big mouth that tipped me off." To me he added, "Better check on Cody while I cuff this jerk. The commander looks like he needs help too."

I knelt next to Cody. He was still wrapped in the sheet strips, but blood seeped through the white cloth, and his skin looked gray. "Are you okay?"

"Fine," he muttered. "I heard what happened outside the house, and I'd be hanged before I let that fellow get away with it. This place once had a chicken coop attached, so I snuck around and came inside from there."

From the ripped sleeves of his flannel shirt and the ugly-looking swelling on his forehead, I gathered it hadn't been as easy as he made it sound.

"Good thing you left me the gun," he added, tucking it inside his bandages.

I wanted to hug him, but the pain etched on his face warded me off. Besides, there was still the matter of Jenny Vandyke. Which reminded me of the time ever ticking onward. I had to tell Shannon what I'd learned.

"I'll be back in a minute." I limped over to where the commander still lay after hitting into Levine. Lying too still, I thought. But he had a pulse, and after I used Levine's keys to unlock the handcuffs, he began coming to.

"Thanks for helping me," I said, as I untied his dirty gag.

I'd done something terrible to my foot because of his help, but without it I wouldn't have been able to keep Levine from his gun, which had contributed to our success.

Huish spat onto the floor before saying in a soft undertone, "This is my fault. I should have been more aware."

I felt sorry for him, but things hadn't been right in his unit for a long time, and he was ultimately responsible.

"I should have taken a leave," he added. "I should be with Janine. But it's . . ."

"Hard." Hard watching someone you love die. Like I had with Summer the year she battled breast cancer. I'd been only eleven at the time. It had been far worse mourning Winter.

Huish nodded, and I thought the deep line in his brow softened with my understanding. Maybe it wasn't forgiveness he craved.

Shannon had finished cuffing Levine and started gathering up the magazines I'd scattered, looking at them carefully one by one. "I noticed you've taken up a new hobby," he said.

I shrugged. "They're shiny."

"Yeah, but totally wrong for my gun." He removed the bullets from one of the magazines, filling his empty one before slapping it into his gun and racking it.

Levine groaned. "You didn't have bullets?"

I laughed. I hadn't realized Shannon had picked up his own empty gun. There was some cosmic irony in that.

"You're lucky I didn't. Now don't move, not even to stand up, or I *will* shoot you." Shannon looked at Huish. "You should probably use those cuffs on the unconscious guy over there, just in case." He motioned to Tiny's sprawled figure.

"I'll do that." Huish straightened his shoulders and rattled the cuffs in his hands. "I'll call Cross. We'll need to round up any of the men you and Greeley left breathing. They'll freeze to death out there, and I'd rather they stand trial." He was looking more like his usual confident self.

"Shannon's partner is sending the FBI," I told him. "They should be here soon."

Shannon flashed me a crooked smile that warmed me to my hurt toes. "Then if you've got this, commander, we need to get Cody to the hospital. He's been shot." He took a step and winced.

Huish's eyes dipped to Shannon's leg. "Looks like you'd better go with him. Thanks for your help, detective." He strode in Tiny's direction.

"Except we still have a problem." I didn't want to tell Shannon about it, but I didn't see how I could go after Jenny alone.

"Big problem if none of the guys you took out is Kirt," came Cody's gruff voice. He was on his feet again, looking determined.

Shannon moved stiffly to Cody's side, placing a supporting arm around him. "You need to sit back down until I get a car for us. We'll call an ambulance, but we'll meet them part way. We're pretty far out."

"I need to know about that Kirt fellow," Cody insisted.

"He got away," I said. To Shannon, I added, "That's what I was going to tell you. Levine gave Kirt information about Cody's new properties, and as soon as he takes care of the semi he drove out of here, he's going after Jenny." I refocused on Cody. "Please, you have to tell me where she is."

Beside me Shannon stiffened. "He knows where she is?"

Cody nodded. "I'll take you there."

The sick feeling once again knotted my stomach. Cody had known where Jenny was all along.

Chapter 23

I tried not to show emotion at Cody's admission. I'd come to Hayesville to find out if my birth father had any connection to the girl's disappearance, and now I knew.

"Is she still alive?" I asked.

Cody scowled. "Of course she's alive."

"Why did you take her?"

He closed his eyes for a moment before opening them. "Look, let's just get there before Kirt does."

"You tell us where," Shannon said. "You need to get to a hospital."

"And after that, prison." Huish reappeared beside us, apparently having kept tabs on our conversation. "Give us the address, old man."

Cody shook his head. "It's a new place. Not on any GPS. You won't make it in time if he's already found the right location. I have thirteen properties I bought under my new company, but there's no telling how many he's already checked out." He grimaced. "I don't even know the exact address without my files. I just know how to get there." He folded his arms, trying to look tough, but only succeeded in looking closer to passing out.

Thirteen properties? Just how successful was his art?

Shannon met my eyes, and I nodded. "Commander, I'll take full responsibility for him," Shannon said. "It's not like he's going anywhere with that wound, and if we wait for backup, we might miss the opportunity to get there before Kirt does."

"You both should be in a hospital," Huish retorted.

"Do you want to save Jenny or not? Because if they take her, you'll never find her, and you're the one who will have to explain that to Mrs. Vandyke." Cody started toward the door in a shuffling gate that looked painful.

Huish didn't think long. "I'll call you after our backup arrives," he told Shannon. "Let me know where you are, and I'll coordinate with the FBI and local law enforcement to meet you there."

"Will do." Shannon caught up to Cody, taking one of his arms. At this point, I didn't know which one was holding up the other. I sprinted to Cody's other side.

We appropriated one of Levine's cars because of its proximity to the house, a sleek, black sedan. Cody collapsed in the back seat, looking considerably worse by the moment. I told myself I shouldn't care, not after he'd taken Jenny, but somehow I still did—and not only because I wanted to know about my heritage. He'd saved us. He was a hero, and yet he'd known where Jenny was all this time. The two things didn't make sense. I couldn't even dwell on why he'd taken Jenny or how much he might have hurt her.

"Head west toward Keizer," Cody said from the backseat where he was sprawled. "Yeah, turn here and go straight until I say to turn."

Police lights and sirens drew our attention. Three cars and an ambulance passed us, driving fast, and a double row of cars ahead blocked our way.

"Looks like Paige came through," Shannon said from the passenger side of the front seat.

Even after seeing Shannon's badge, the FBI agents wouldn't let us pass until they called Special Agent Cross and received permission.

After passing the blockade, I drove in silence for several minutes until Cody said, "It's not what you think."

I shook my head. "You knew all this time." Whatever he said couldn't possibly make it better.

Words tumbled from his lips. "It was my idea, but I was only helping Mrs. Vandyke. She knew her daughter had been searching for her birth father and about his visit. She was scared."

I remembered Gail's lack of surprise when we told her Jenny had been searching for her birth father. Not only had she known, but apparently she'd acted to protect her daughter.

Cody shifted his position carefully. "At first she just asked me to follow Jenny after school for a few weeks, make sure she got home okay. But the child met up with her birth father— that convict—at a restaurant, and two other men seemed to be following her every day to and from school. I never saw Kirt outside the restaurant like he claimed, but I saw Jenny's birth father arguing with the men following the girl. They talked about money and drugs before threatening him, and I knew Jenny was caught in the middle of something really bad. When I told her mother, she said she knew exactly what kind of man Jenny's father was, what kind of men he ran with, and asked me what to do. I told her if it was me, I'd hide Jenny, that I'd do anything to make sure none of those men got to her. She asked me to help, so I did."

My anger seeped away, leaving me defenseless and weary. "Mrs. Vandyke knew?"

"Yeah."

I remembered her assertion that Cody had done nothing wrong, how she'd defended a man she supposedly barely knew from her charity work. Now I understood her motivation.

"She should have come clean to the detectives." Shannon glanced over his shoulder and then back to the road.

"She was scared. She wanted the police to find who was stalking her girl but at the same time she didn't want to tell her secrets." Cody paused before adding, "Some secrets should never be told."

His words were so close to how I felt about certain imprints that I knew he'd also experienced private moments from others that he wished had remained secret.

"You're saying Mrs. Vandyke hoped the deputies would catch Jenny's birth father without their knowing his motive?" Shannon asked, shaking his head. "Reminds me of how Bremer wouldn't tell us he was her biological father just to save his own hide."

"Well, he's scum and he wouldn't since he was involved with drug running. Anyway, if Mrs. Vandyke had told the detectives the truth, Jenny would probably be far away with that Levine character—or whoever he is." Cody grimaced at a bump in the road.

I supposed Gail's behavior made sense in a twisted way. "So, instead, Jenny's *only* facing being kidnapped by a very angry, wounded man who has something to prove." I didn't keep the acid from my voice.

Cody shrugged and then winced at the effort. "Anyway,

I guess Mrs. Vandyke thought that if Bremer did claim to be Jenny's father, the investigation would still prove he wasn't fit, so he couldn't fight her for custody."

"Well, with the stabbing and what happened at the gas station, that part's taken care of." Shannon's voice was dry. "I don't think there's much chance of anyone giving him custody any time soon. But there could be charges for Mrs. Vandyke. Falsely reporting a kidnapping."

"That was Mr. Vandyke," Cody said. "He loves that kid. His wife should have told him, but she was too afraid."

"You mean too afraid to tell him Jenny wasn't her daughter." I wanted to shut my eyes and go to sleep for a million years.

Cody nodded. "I didn't exactly know all that in the beginning, but I figured it out soon enough."

"From imprints," I said.

Cody's eyes went to the back of Shannon's head before nodding again.

Shannon glanced at me. "He knows about you?" Who I was to Cody, he meant.

"He saw my eyes."

"Besides," Cody went on, "like I said, we had no doubt about those men's intentions. We both thought the detectives would work harder if Jenny was already missing."

I couldn't speak to that, but Shannon's jaw tightened, and I knew he didn't agree. "Why one of your properties?" I asked. "Weren't you worried about being a suspect?"

Cody shook his head. "We didn't think I'd ever be connected. But once they knew about my record, no one wanted to look further."

"Could have been Levine who pushed them to look at you," Shannon said.

"Yeah," I said. "Or maybe it was finding the boot."

Cody grimaced, his face looking skeletal in the dark car. "Jenny must have dropped it before she met up with her mother that morning. They pretended she was going to school so it'd look real. I was supposed to make a distraction for the men following her and then meet them. But Gail got stuck in a conversation with her neighbor and was late, so I made Jenny wait under that tree because it started snowing. Must have been then that she lost the boot. She had her backpack full and was carrying a bunch of other stuff."

If I'd touched the real boot, I might have learned all this. By exchanging it to protect himself, Levine had actually helped Gail Vandyke keep her biggest secret.

I had ten more minutes to contemplate the shift in facts and how I now felt about Cody. Even as I reported our heading to Commander Huish, I was thinking about telling my sister and how happy she'd be.

Or would be if Cody was telling the truth. I wanted to believe him. Finally, we pulled into a subdivision where only two houses had been completed. Construction supplies and machinery lined the entire block.

Cody pointed. "It's that one at the end. The one with the porch light." Shannon cut his headlights and drove down the street. "No cars. That's a good sign."

"Unless he's already been here," Cody said grimly.

A thought occurred to me. "She's not here alone, is she?"

"No. Mrs. Vandyke has a friend there. An old lady. Probably eighty-five or more."

"Not exactly great protection." Shannon eased the car to a stop.

"There was no reason for anyone to ever look here." Cody

reached for the door but let his hand drop. "You guys go ahead. I think I'm going to hold up this seat for a bit."

"You still have that gun?" Shannon asked. Cody's only response was a weak nod.

I went with Shannon up the walk. "We have to call an ambulance," I said.

"Agreed. Let's just make sure Jenny's still here."

"How do we get in?"

"We knock."

"At two in the morning?"

He grinned. "She's a teenager away from her parents for the first time. If she's there, she'll be up."

The house was a small, brown, modern home, perfect for a young couple with maybe one or two children. The door had a pane of glass that showed us the small entry way. On the porch, we could hear the TV blaring even at this late hour. Shannon stood behind me as I knocked. Wearing Levine's deputy jacket, at least I looked official—and my leg wasn't covered in blood.

I didn't stop holding my breath until I saw a thin, hunched lady with white hair shuffling toward the door. "Who is it?" she called through the glass, looking frightened.

"Police," Shannon said. "We've been sent by Cody Beckett and Mrs. Vandyke. We believe Jenny's in danger. Is everything okay?"

She nodded. "Fine. We're just watching TV. Before I let you in, let me see your badge."

Shannon held his badge against the glass. Satisfied, she opened the door and led us across the entryway into a living room where Jenny lay on the couch, her eyes glued to some late-night TV program. She looked about twelve and her long blond hair framed her delicate face like an unruly cloud. She gazed at us curiously. "Time to go home?"

I nodded.

She grinned. "Good, because even though Mom comes to see me, I miss my dad and my brother. Should I get my stuff?"

"We'll come back tomorrow for it. Right now, we have to leave." I didn't want to be here if Kirt showed up.

Shannon punched on his phone as we walked to the door. "Agent Cross? Detective Martin here. I take it Huish has filled you in? Good. We have Jenny. Yes, she's fine. We're taking her to the station, but I was wondering if you were up to a little stakeout to see if that clerk shows up. Commander Huish has his hands full at the moment, and I'm not sure who has local jurisdiction. Oh, good." Shannon lowered the phone. "She's already almost here. We'll let her wait for Kirt while we take Cody to the hospital."

My hand was on the front doorknob, but a movement in front of the house alerted me. Something wasn't quite right. "Wait, don't hang up," I said. I flipped off the lights and peered out. A van had pulled up next to our borrowed sedan. Shannon joined me as I counted five dark figures.

All of them carried assault rifles.

"Uh, change of plans," Shannon told Agent Cross, pulling out his gun. "We have at least five armed visitors who just arrived in a black van. I've only got ten rounds left. How far away did you say you were? Hurry! I'm going to barricade us in."

The old woman and Jenny stared at us. "What's going on?" Jenny asked, her voice high and thin.

I was still staring outside, willing none of the black figures to look in the backseat of the sedan.

Shannon dragged me away. "Is there any place without a window?" he asked, his voice remarkably calm.

"L-1-1-1-aundry r-r-r-oom," stuttered the woman, her eyes fixed on his leg and the red stains.

"Show the way. Go!"

We hurried through the kitchen to a little room, where Shannon holstered his gun and handed me the phone before locking the door and heaving the washer in front of it. Then he pulled out the dryer enough for people to squeeze behind it.

"Everyone, get down behind the dryer," he ordered, drawing his gun again.

"Agent Cross?" I said into the phone as Jenny and the old woman hurried to obey.

"We're on the street now. I see the van."

I sighed with relief. "There's a black sedan out there too. We have a guy there," I told her. "He's been shot. He's with us."

"Cody Beckett?"

"Please keep him safe."

"We'll do our best." The line went dead.

"Don't worry," I said to Jenny, who was in the old woman's lap now so that I had space to hunker down next to them. "The FBI is outside. This is only a precaution to keep you both safe."

"Then you're really the good guys?" Jenny asked, her voice quavering.

I forced a smile. "Yeah, we are."

Shannon met my gaze briefly before turning back toward the door. Fresh blood seeped through the makeshift bandage on his leg. I wanted to reach out to him, but we had to stay alert.

The shooting began.

We ducked instinctively as a bullet ripped through the top

of the laundry room door, followed by three more. Additional shots echoed throughout the house. Shannon's back was against the washer as he crouched behind it, his gun lifted partially over the side. Ten rounds. Would it be enough?

Two more shots smashed through the door, sending splinters flying. The bullets embedded in the cupboards above us. Jenny screamed and began sobbing into the old woman's arms.

Something rammed into the door, splintering it further. Shannon rose and fired twice rapidly, and for a blessed second there was nothing. Then a man's voice said, "Come out, and I won't shoot. We just want the girl."

Shannon's answer was another shot. The man grunted in pain and let off a continuous spray of bullets. They'd be through the door soon, and the washer wouldn't hold up to this kind of assault for much longer.

Shannon must have come to the same decision because he rapidly fired the rest of his bullets through the gaping holes in the door. *Boom-boom-boom-boom-boom-boom-boom!* The dry click told us when he was out.

But at least the spray of bullets had ended. We stared at each other, wondering if Shannon had killed our attacker, or if he'd only stopped to reload.

And where was Cross?

Shouts and more gunfire came to us but from farther away now. Shannon heaved a breath and threw me a reassuring smile. "I think we're going to be okay."

Seconds later, the faraway shooting ended, and we heard a voice outside the door. "Hey, Martin, you in there? Don't shoot. I'm assuming you're responsible for these two stiffs out here? Wait, no, one's still breathing."

We moved the washer and opened the door to find Cross

standing there, grinning, her short blond hair undisturbed. One of her agents was taking guns from the fallen men. Neither of them was Kirt.

"We got the other three, and with the way they're already jabbering," she said, "we'll be recovering the semi they got away with." She looked us up and down as we squeezed around the washer to join her. "I don't know which of you looks worse. Good thing we have a couple ambulances on the way."

Shannon smiled, but when he took a step, his leg gave out. I stepped close, helping him lie down on the carpet. "I'm okay," he said, his head in my lap, "but I think I'll wait right here for the EMTs."

"You do that." Cross holstered her gun. "Once when I was shot, I had to walk a mile for help. Hardest thing I ever did."

"What about Cody Beckett?" I asked.

Her smile faded. "Doesn't look good, but I'll tell the EMTs to take him first." She motioned to Jenny and the old woman. "Come on. We have agents ready to take you to the sheriff's station. By the time we get there, your parents should be waiting."

Four hours later I was in a hospital waiting room, staring sightlessly at a tiny TV as we waited to see if Cody would be all right. They'd whisked him into surgery upon his arrival, which had lasted nearly three hours. He'd made it through but was still in critical condition, and they were slowly bringing him back to consciousness.

Shannon's wound had been bandaged and the remaining bullet fragments removed. The bullet hadn't caused any major problems, though Shannon was already griping about using crutches and the possibility of being forced to take a vacation. He was cranky, unshaven, and badly needed a shower.

"Maybe my captain won't even know," he said. "Who'd tell her? I mean, if I can ditch the crutches."

"Paige," I said.

His partner was here. In fact, at the moment she was hunting for our breakfast. She'd missed all the excitement, though, and she was irritable because of it.

I received a couple of stitches in the back of my head, though I couldn't for the life of me remember injuring that part of my body. Worse, I'd broken my second toe on my left foot in that last fight with Levine, and after my boot was taken off, it had swollen as big as a banana. My brain was fried, jumbled with scenes from the day's imprints, and I felt like falling down and sleeping for a month. In the mirror, I looked even worse, my bruises purple and mottled, raw red patches everywhere. But nothing else was broken or dislocated, and I would recover completely. I felt lucky.

"If you're going stir crazy with not working, you can always help me with the new shelves I want to build," I told Shannon. "You're good with your hands, aren't you?"

He reached for me. "I'm good at a lot of things." His lips touched my undamaged cheek in a light kiss, and then another, as he worked his way to my mouth.

Something on the TV caught my attention and I sat up, destroying the moment.

"What—" Shannon followed my gaze where an early morning news show recapped the previous night's top news.

The camera panned the hospital lobby, showing the girls talking to uniformed officers. The face of the tough-looking girl appeared on the screen. "Yeah, it was scary," she said, twirling a strand of blue hair. "I was always planning to escape, but I worried about leaving the other girls. Some of them are so young."

Something was different about her, but what? I snapped my fingers. "She's wearing Cody's coat. So that's what happened to it."

"Without that woman," the girl was saying now, "I don't know how we would have gotten away. Her and the old guy that was with her—they're good people."

The anchor reappeared on the screen, talking about strength and luck and how some of the girls were being reunited with their families. "As to the identities of the girls' mysterious benefactors, local police and the FBI have declined to comment, saying only that those involved were under law enforcement authority and wish to remain anonymous."

Shannon's fingers closed around mine. "They got that right."

"It all worked out," I said. "The girls are safe, and Levine's going to prison. Unless he gets out on a plea bargain." Kirt's cousin, Millard, had finally awakened and had agreed to testify against both Levine and Kirt.

"I doubt it. Not with what he planned for those girls. The whole country will be watching the trial. Once they find the body of the real Deputy Levine, his fate will be sealed. His only option now is to talk and help us get his so-called partners before they get to him. If he doesn't, not even prison will be safe for him."

I shivered, feeling suddenly cold, though the waiting room was warm. "He was going to force me to be a part of it—the drugs and the girls. They weren't just worried I'd uncover their operation." Human trafficking. It was still hard to get my brain around the horror.

Shannon frowned. "After they jumped us in Portland, I'd begun to suspect as much."

"Wish you'd let me in on that earlier."

He gave me a lopsided smile. "Would it have made a difference?"

"Probably not."

We sat in silence for a long moment, and then I said, "Thanks for coming on this case with me."

"I had fun. Sort of."

I knew what he meant. It had been hard, but it was one more victory for the good guys.

My phone vibrated in the pocket of the jacket Agent Cross had found for me, having confiscated Levine's for evidence. My own was still missing, and I had only one glove, which I used now to hold the phone. I'd have to get a new phone soon, or at least replace the screen and the case, because every time I touched it, I relived my own imprint of the fear I'd experienced after Cody had been shot and I was in the van, hurtling toward Shannon's location. Not fun.

"My sister," I said to Shannon, jabbing at the answer button with a bare finger. Fast, before an imprint could fully play out.

"Hello?" I said, holding it near my ear but not touching it to my face.

"I saw the girls on the news this morning, and I thought no way is this not connected to you. What's going on?"

"I'll tell you, but it's going to take a while."

I hadn't quite finished explaining the night's events, including how her drawings had come to life, when Cody's doctor appeared, a tall, sturdy man with thinning blond hair. He looked as exhausted as I felt.

"Wait a minute," I said to Tawnia. I rose to my feet rigidly, relaxing slightly when Shannon also stood and put his arm around me, balancing on one crutch.

The doctor cleared his throat. "He's awake and asking for you. At least I think it's you from his description. I'm not sure if he's all there, though. He keeps talking about figures in black with guns."

Considering Cody had been shot, I didn't think that was at all strange. "How is he doing?" I asked. "Medically, I mean?"

The doctor smiled. "He's a tough old bird. If he takes it easy, I think he'll be fine."

Relief spread through me in a wash of energy. We followed him to a room, where Cody lay on a bed, looking fragile and gray beneath his tan and in definite need of a shave. One of his pillows lay on his chest, with his bare hands and arms resting on top of it in a rather awkward position.

"So you're okay." Cody glanced at the door where the doctor had vanished. "Stupid man wouldn't tell me anything about what happened. I saw those guys go toward the house, but when I tried to get out of the car . . ." He shook his head. "Must have passed out."

"We're fine," Shannon said. "So is Jenny."

Cody breathed a sigh of relief. "What about her parents?"

"Jenny has been returned to them." I sank into one of the chairs next to the bed. "And from what I heard, the reporters are hailing you and Mrs. Vandyke as heroes for protecting Jenny from human traffickers."

Cody arched a brow. "Didn't expect that. Thought maybe the commander was out there waiting to arrest me."

"All you did was give Gail Vandyke a place to keep Jenny," I said.

Shannon laughed. "Well, he also impeded an investigation,

but I think given everything else that went on, no one cares. But be prepared for a media frenzy."

"I ain't talking to any of them," Cody muttered. "Vultures."

"Might get you some buyers for your artwork," I said.

"Don't need 'em. Can't keep up as it is. Look, can you get me another top sheet? Whoever folded this one was so angry it left an imprint. I must have relived her fight with her boyfriend hundreds of times while I was unconscious."

That explained the pillow. "Sure. Is the rest of the stuff okay?" He nodded, but before I could move, he added, "So you think you'll be sticking around a bit? For the stories, I mean." His face showed absolutely no expression, as though he was asking about the weather or what I'd eaten for dinner. Like he didn't care.

I knew better.

I'd also experienced firsthand his self-hatred, and I knew I had to choose my next words carefully or risk losing any contact with him.

"Autumn! Whoo-hoo, Autumn!" came a tinny voice.

We all stared at the phone in my gloved hand. I'd forgotten my sister and was probably breaking all kinds of hospital rules having the phone on in the ICU.

"Just one more minute," I said into the receiver. I brought my gaze back to Cody, who was still watching me with a guarded expression.

"I want to hear it all," I said. "Especially about your mother. But there's something I need to tell you first. Something you should know."

An edge of despair crept into his mismatched eyes, so I hurried to finish. "It's not just me. I have a twin sister. Her name is Tawnia. She's the one who found you and sent me to Hayesville in the first place. She'll want to hear the stories too."

I'd let Tawnia tell him about the baby—and plan for the future. She was good at planning.

Tucking the phone into a paper towel from the dispenser near the sink, I passed the phone to him.

"Hello?" he said. "This is Cody Beckett." I didn't think I imagined the hint of tears in his gruff voice.

Returning Shannon's grin, I began to search the cupboards for a clean, imprint-free sheet.

TEYLA BRANTON has worked in publishing for over twenty years. She loves writing women's fiction and traveling, and she hopes to write and travel a lot more. As a mother of seven, it's not easy to find time to write, but the semi-ordered chaos gives her a constant source of writing material. She's been known to wear pajamas all day when working on a deadline, and is often distracted enough to burn dinner. (Okay, pretty much 90% of the time.) A sign on her office door reads: Danger. Enter at Your Own Risk. Writer at Work.

Under the name Teyla Branton, she writes urban fantasy, paranormal romance, and science fiction. She also writes romance, romantic suspense, and women's fiction under the name Rachel Branton. Sign up for a free ebook and to hear about new releases on www. TeylaBranton.com.